# Phalanx

Sarpedon struck Scarphinal's head from his shoulders with a single shining arc, the Axe of Mercaeno slicing through the Space Marine's neck so smoothly the blood had not yet begun to flow when Scarphinal's head hit the floor.

Something dark and prideful, a relic of the old Chapter, awakened in Sarpedon. The love of bloodshed, the exultation of battle. Sometimes, those places locked away in his mind could be useful, and it was with a strange sense of relief that he let the bloodlust take him.

Sarpedon roared with formless anger, and dived into the carnage.

A WARHAMMER 40,000 NOVEL

# Phalanx

## Ben Counter

BLACK LIBRARY

### A BLACK LIBRARY PUBLICATION

First published in Great Britain in 2012 by
The Black Library,
Games Workshop Ltd.,
Willow Road, Nottingham,
NG7 2WS, UK.

10 9 8 7 6 5 4 3 2 1

Cover illustration by Hardy Fowler.

A CIP record for this book is available from the British Library.

UK ISBN: 978 1 84970 146 4
US ISBN: 978 1 84970 147 1

See the Black Library on the internet at
**www.blacklibrary.com**

Find out more about Games Workshop
and the world of Warhammer 40,000 at
**www.games-workshop.com**

Printed and bound by CPI Group (UK) Ltd, Croydon, CR0 4YY

It is the 41st millennium. For more than a hundred centuries the Emperor has sat immobile on the Golden Throne of Earth. He is the master of mankind by the will of the gods, and master of a million worlds by the might of his inexhaustible armies. He is a rotting carcass writhing invisibly with power from the Dark Age of Technology. He is the Carrion Lord of the Imperium for whom a thousand souls are sacrificed every day, so that he may never truly die.

Yet even in his deathless state, the Emperor continues his eternal vigilance. Mighty battlefleets cross the daemon-infested miasma of the warp, the only route between distant stars, their way lit by the Astronomican, the psychic manifestation of the Emperor's will. Vast armies give battle in His name on uncounted worlds. Greatest amongst his soldiers are the Adeptus Astartes, the Space Marines, bio-engineered super-warriors. Their comrades in arms are legion: the Imperial Guard and countless Planetary Defence Forces, the ever-vigilant Inquisition and the tech-priests of the Adeptus Mechanicus to name only a few. But for all their multitudes, they are barely enough to hold off the ever-present threat from aliens, heretics, mutants - and worse.

To be a man in such times is to be one amongst untold billions. It is to live in the cruellest and most bloody regime imaginable. These are the tales of those times. Forget the power of technology and science, for so much has been forgotten, never to be re-learned. Forget the promise of progress and understanding, for in the grim dark future there is only war. There is no peace amongst the stars, only an eternity of carnage and slaughter, and the laughter of thirsting gods.

# CHAPTER ONE

ITS LIKE HAD never been built before, and would never be built again. The secrets of its construction dated from before the foundation of the Imperium of Man, its immense golden form crafted by engineers dead long before the Emperor first united Holy Terra.

The hull of the ship was many kilometres long, its upper surface bristling with weapons and sensorium domes, trailing directional vanes like long gilded feathers. Every surface was clad in solid armour plating and every angle was covered by more torpedo tubes and lance batteries than any Imperial battleship could muster. Countless smaller craft, repair craft and unmanned scouts, orbited like supplicants jostling for attention, and the wake of the titanic engines seemed to churn the void itself with the force of its plasma fire.

The fist symbol emblazoned on the prow was taller than the length of most Imperial spacecraft, proudly claiming that the ship belonged to the Imperial Fists Chapter, one of the most storied Space Marine Chapters in the history of the Imperium. The pale light of the star Kravamesh, and the lesser glow of the Veiled Region's boiling nebulae, played across thousands of battle-honours and campaign markings all over the beak-like prow. The ship had carried the Imperial Fists since the Horus Heresy, and its eagle-shaped shadow had fallen across a hundred worlds that had later shuddered under the weight of a massed Fists assault.

This was the *Phalanx*. Bigger than any ship in the Imperial Navy, it was a mobile battle station the size of a city, that dwarfed any Space Marine Chapter's mightiest battle-barge. It might have been the most powerful engine of destruction in the Imperium. It was a symbol of mankind's very right to live in the stars. Its most potent weapon was the sheer awe that the golden eagle inspired when it appeared in the night sky over a rebellious world.

The *Phalanx* at that moment was not at war, but it was there for a conflict just as bitter. It was to be the seat of a trial at which the soul of a Chapter would be weighed, a stain on the Imperial Fists' honour would be cleansed and retribution would fall as sternly as if it had rained down from the *Phalanx's* guns.

There was no doubt among the Imperial Fists that their mission was as vital to the Imperium as any crusade. For it was on the *Phalanx* that the Soul Drinkers would surely die.

'YOU WILL WISH,' said the castellan of the Imperial Fists, 'that you still called us brother.'

The castellan seemed to fill the cell, even though it had been built to accommodate a Space Marine's dimensions. Its walls were plated in gold, studded with diamonds and rubies in the shape of the constellations across which the *Phalanx* had carried its Chapter in countless crusades. The channels cut into the floor formed intricate scrollwork. Even the drain for bodily fluids was in the shape of an open hand, echoing the fist symbol that was everywhere on board.

The castellan nodded to one of the Chapter functionaries through the small slit window. The functionary, a shaven-headed, drab man in a dark yellow uniform, activated a few controls on his side of the wall and the Pain Glove apparatus shuddered as power flowed into it.

Brother Kaiyon hung in the Pain Glove. He had been stripped of his armour, and the input ports set into the black carapace beneath the skin of his chest were hooked up to bundles of cables hanging from the ceiling. The Pain Glove itself resembled some strange mollusc, a lumpy, phlegmy membrane that covered Kaiyon from neck to ankle. It writhed against his skin, as if trying to ascertain the shape of its captive by touch.

'This one,' he said, 'was one of the flock.' The castellan's words were no longer directed at Brother

Kaiyon. 'He was broken-minded even before we brought them here. I think, my lord, that he will either tell all, or be broken to gibberish.'

'You take eagerly to your task, noble castellan,' came a voice in reply from the room's vox-caster. It was an old and experienced voice, almost wearied with knowledge. 'So ready a hand at the tormentor's tools would be a sin in any but one of your responsibilities.'

The castellan smiled. 'That, my lord Chapter Master, is as high a compliment as I could hope to hear.'

The castellan's armour was crenellated like the battlements of a castle around its collar and the edges of its shoulder pads, and the vents around his torso echoed tall, pointed windows or arrow slits. He looked like a walking fortress, even the greaves around his shins resembling the buttresses of two towers on which he walked. His face was branded with a grid pattern – a portcullis, a forbidding entrance to the fortification he represented.

Kaiyon's face was scarred, too. The Space Marine seemed unconscious, but he proclaimed all his allegiances in the chalice symbols he had carved into himself. His scalp was red with raised channels of scar tissue. Though the rest of his body was hidden in the Pain Glove, the castellan knew that the rest of Kaiyon told the same story. Kaiyon was a Soul Drinker. He had written that fact into his flesh.

'I know,' said the castellan to Kaiyon, 'that you are awake. You can hear me, Kaiyon. Know, then, that nothing you do here, no token effort of resistance, will gain you anything whatsoever. Not even the satisfaction of delaying me, or frustrating my intentions to break you. These things mean nothing to me. The mightiest of fortresses will fall, though we can chip away but a grain of sand at a time. The end result is the same. Your Chapter has secrets. The flock of Iktinos has secrets. I will have those secrets. This is a truth as inevitable as your own mortality.'

Kaiyon did not speak. The castellan walked right up to Kaiyon, face to face.

The Soul Drinker's eye was slitted. He was watching the castellan, and even in that tiny sliver of an eye, the castellan could see his hate.

'What,' said the Chapter Master over the vox, 'if this one does not talk?'

'There are others,' replied the castellan. 'More than twenty of the surviving Soul Drinkers are members of this flock. I'll wager you'll have your answers with twenty renegades to break.'

'So long as Chaplain Iktinos himself is not reduced thus,' replied the Chapter Master. 'I wish him in possession of all his faculties for the trial. Justice is a mockery when it is administered on one already forsaken by sanity.'

'Of course, my lord,' said the castellan. 'It will not come to that.'

'Good,' said the Chapter Master. 'Then proceed, brother castellan.'

The vox-link went dead. The Chapter Master, as was traditional, need not witness this least delicate of the castellan's duties. The castellan gestured to the crewman at the controls, and a metal panel slid shut over the slit window.

'You have,' said the castellan, circling Kaiyon, 'one final chance.'

Kaiyon's hate did not falter.

'You understand, I must make this offer. I know as well as you do, between us two Space Marines, that it has no meaning. There are traditional forms that must be followed.'

The castellan flicked a few switches on the control console mounted on the wall, one from which snaked the wired now hooked up to the interfaces in Kaiyon's body. The Pain Glove slithered over him as if agitated.

The Pain Glove was a complex device. Controlling its many variables was akin to directing an orchestra, with great skill required in keeping every variable in harmony. Just a taste of the Pain Glove was enough to break normal men. A Space Marine required far more finesse – the Pain Glove was even used as a conditioning tool for the Chapter's novices in its less intense configurations.

The castellan was a maestro with the device. The membrane excreted chemicals that laid open every nerve ending on every millimetre of skin. The pulses of power humming through the cables stimulated every one of them into extremity.

Brother Kaiyon, in that moment, discovered just how much it took to make a Space Marine scream.

*What will the universe remember of us?* wrote Sarpedon.

*What does it matter our deeds, the principles of our character, if it is the memory of the human race that matters? The future for us, when we are gone, is surely determined not by our deeds but by what is remembered of our deeds, by the lies told about us as much as by the truths of our actions.*

Sarpedon put the quill down. The Imperial Fists had taken his armour and his weapons, and even the bionic which had replaced one of his eight arachnoid legs. But they had left him with the means to write. It was a matter of principle that this cell, even though it was windowless and cramped, and allowed him no communication with his fellow Soul Drinkers, had a quill, a desk and a pot of ink. He was to defend himself before a court of his peers. He was at least entitled to the means to prepare his defence. They had left him his copy of the *Catechisms Martial*, too, the manual of the Soul Drinkers' principles and tactics authored by the legendary philosopher-soldier Daenyathos.

Sarpedon thought for a few long minutes. The pages of parchment in front of him were supposed to hold every argument he might make to justify his actions. Instead, he had poured out every thought into them in the hope that at least he would understand what he thought.

*The galaxy will not think well of us,* he wrote. *We are traitors and heretics. We are mutants. Should truth have any value in itself then it will do us no good, for these things are true. My own mutations are so grotesque that I wonder if there will be anything thought of me at all, for there is little room in any man's recollection for anything but this monstrous form.*

*What does it matter what the galaxy thinks of us when we are gone? It is the only thing that matters at all. For we will surely die here. There is only one sentence that our brethren can lay upon us, and that is death. I must take what solace I can from what we will leave behind, yet there can be no solace in the story the Imperium will tell of the Soul Drinkers. Those who can will forget us. Those who cannot will hate us. Though I seek some victory for myself and my battle-brothers even in this, I can find none.*

*Perhaps one of my brethren can draw something other than defeat from our situation. I cannot. I look deeper into my heart than I have ever done, and I find nothing but failure and desolation.*

Sarpedon looked over what he had written. It disgusted him. He screwed up the parchment and threw it into a corner of the cell. A Space Marine did not succumb to self-pity, no matter how true his failure seemed to him. He would lie to himself if that was what it took.

A gauntleted hand boomed against the cell door. Sarpedon looked round to see a window being drawn back to reveal a face he had last seen on the surface of Selaaca, looming over him as he lost consciousness. It was the face of Captain Darnath Lysander of the Imperial Fists First Company, a legend of the Fists and the man who had bested Sarpedon to take the Soul Drinkers into custody.

'I trust,' said Sarpedon, 'your captive is a wretched as you hoped.'

'Bitterness becomes not a Space Marine,' replied Lysander. 'I take no joy in the fall of another Space Marine. I have come not to gloat, if that is how low you think of me. I have come to give you the chance to confess.'

'Confess?' said Sarpedon. 'With no thumbscrews? With my skin still on my frame?'

'Do not play games,' snapped Lysander. 'We took those you call the flock; those who follow your Chaplain Iktinos. Their minds were broken before we ever took them in. Whatever influence your Chaplain had on them, it changed them. One of them has broken in the Pain Glove, and told us everything. Brother Kaiyon is his name. He thought the Lord castellan was Rogal Dorn himself, and spoke your Chapter's secrets to him as if the primarch had demanded it.'

'I have heard of your Pain Glove,' said Sarpedon.

'Then you know it is a part of the initiations every Imperial Fist has undergone. I myself have been subject to it. It served no more than to shake Brother Kaiyon out of the state the flock have fallen into since their incarceration here. He is insane, Sarpedon. He spoke through madness, not pain, and that madness was not our doing.'

'Then he could have spoken lies in his madness,' retorted Sarpedon.

'He could,' replied Lysander. 'My Chapter is even now ascertaining the truth of his words. This is why I have come here. If you confess, and that confession matches what Kaiyon had told us and can be proven true, then there may be some leniency won for your compliance.'

'Leniency?' Sarpedon rose up on his haunches. He had originally had eight legs, arranged like those of an arachnid, spreading from his waist. He had lost one on an unnamed world, ripped off by a champion of the Dark Gods. Another had been lost on Selaaca, mangled in his fight with the necron overlord of that dead world. He still had six, and when he rose to his full height he towered over even Lysander. 'You talk to me of leniency? There is not one Imperial Fist who will abide anything but our execution! Our death sentence was decided the moment we surrendered!'

'Ours is a Chapter with honour!' shouted Lysander. 'Your trial is more than a mere formality. It is our intention to see every correct procedure and tradition adhered to, so that no man dare say we did not give you every chance to redeem yourselves. You will die, yes; I cannot lie to you about that. But there are many ways to die, and many matters of honour that can accompany your death. If you deserve a good death then you and your battle-brothers shall receive it. You can win a better death if you tell us now what we shall soon discover. Deceit, however, will win you nothing but suffering.'

Sarpedon sank back down to his haunches. He could not think what Kaiyon might have told the Imperial Fists interrogators. The Fists knew the Soul Drinkers were mutants – one glance at Sarpedon was enough to tell them that. The Fists had collected evidence of the Soul Drinkers' deeds, including many that had pitted them against the forces of the Imperium from which the Soul Drinkers had rebelled. He could think of nothing more damaging than any of that.

But what had happened to the flock? They were the Soul Drinkers whose officers had died in the gradual erosion of the Chapter's strength, and who had turned to Chaplain Iktinos for leadership. They had become intense and inspired under Iktinos, but insane? Sarpedon did not know what to make of it.

'I don't know what Kaiyon told you,' he said to Lysander. 'Good luck with confirming his words. I doubt whatever you find can make our fate any worse.'

'So be it, Sarpedon,' said Lysander. 'The trials will begin soon. The fate of your Chapter rests in no little part on what you will have to say to yourself. I suggest you think on it, if you believe your brothers deserve more than a common heretic's death.'

'I have nothing to say,' said Sarpedon. 'Certainly nothing that will change any fate you have in mind for me.'

'I could have executed you on Selaaca,' said Lysander. 'Remember that the next time you bemoan your fate.'

The window slammed shut. Lysander was correct. He had defeated Sarpedon face to face on Selaaca and few servants of the Imperium would have had any compunction about killing him out of hand.

Sarpedon turned back to the desk and took up the quill again.

*I have seen,* he wrote, *that our present and future, the mark we will leave on the galaxy, depends on the insistence of one misguidedly honourable man to execute us in accordance with the word of law.*

*Is this a mockery by the galaxy, to condemn us by the virtues of another? I could decide it is so. I could curse the universe and rail against our lot. But I choose to see the Emperor has given us this – a stay of execution, a few moments to have our say before our peers – as a gift to those who served Him instead of the Imperium.*

*What can we make of this? What victory can we mine from such a thin seam? It is the way of the Space Marines to see victory in the smallest hope. I shall seek it now. My brothers, I wish I could speak with you and bid you do the same, but I am isolated from you. I hope you, too, can see something other than despair, even if it is only a thought turned to hope and duty when the end comes.*

*Seek victory, my brethren. I pray that in your souls, at least, the Soul Drinkers cannot be defeated.*

'THRONE ALIVE,' HISSED Scout Orfos. 'Such death. Such foul xenos work.'

The surface of Selaaca rolled by beneath the Thunderhawk gunship. Through the open rear ramp, the grey landscape rippled through ruined cities and expanses of tarnished metal, obsidian pillars rising from deep valleys choked with pollution and the shores of black, dead seas lapping against shores scattered with collapsed buildings.

The human presence on Selaaca was now no more than scars, the ruined crust of a long-dead organ. The necrons had built over it, vast sheets of metal, pyramids, tomb complexes and patterns of obelisks which had no discernible purpose other than to mark Selaaca as a planet that belonged to them.

'Dwell not on the xenos,' said Scout-Sergeant Borakis. He was old and grizzled where the scouts were young, his voice gravelly thanks to the old wound on his throat, his armour festooned with kill-marks and trophies while the scouts under his command were not yet permitted to mark their armour. Borakis leaned towards the open ramp, gripping the handhold mounted overhead. 'It is not your place to seek to understand the enemy. It is enough to know only that he must be killed!'

'Of course, scout-sergeant,' said Orfos, backing away from the ramp.

The Thunderhawk flew down low over a range of hills studded with obelisks and pylons, as if metallic tendrils had forced their way out of the ground to escape the bleak gravity of Selaaca. Patterns of silver like metal roads spiralled around the peaks and valleys, and sparks of power still spat between a few of the pylons.

'We're closing in on mark one,' came the pilot's voice from the cockpit of the Thunderhawk. The crew were two of the thousands of Chapter staff and crew who inhabited the *Phalanx*, a vast support network for the Imperial Fists' campaigns. Using star maps developed by the Adeptus Mechanicus, the strike cruiser *Mantle of Wrath* had penetrated further into the Veiled Region than any Space Marine craft before it, to follow up the information extracted by the castellan during his interrogation of a captive Soul Drinker.

The ground rippled as the Thunderhawk hovered down low to land. The landing gear touched the blasted earth and Borakis led his squad out. Borakis and his four scouts deployed with the speed and fluidity that years of training had given them, spreading out to cover all angles with bolt pistols. Borakis carried a shotgun as old and scarred as he was, and in his other hand checked the auspex scanner loaded with the coordinates the castellan had given him.

'Laokan! Take the point! Orfos, you're watching our backs. Kalliax, Caius, with me.' Borakis pointed in the direction the auspex indicated, over the dead earth.

Once, these hills had been forested. Stumps and exposed roots remained, shorn down to ground level. Up close the pylons looked like spinal columns worked in steel, blackened by the haze of pollution that hung overhead. The obelisks were fingers of a substance so black it seemed to drink the light. A faint hum ran up through the ground, the echo of machinery far below.

'The xenos have not departed this place,' said Orfos quietly. 'This world is dead, but these xenos never lived.'

'It is an ill-omened world,' agreed Scout Caius. 'I hope our work here is quick.'

'Hope,' said Borakis sternly, 'is a poisoned gift, given by our weaknesses. Do not follow hope. Follow your duty. If your duty is to fight on this world for a thousand years, scout-novice, then you will give thanks to the Emperor for it. Move on.'

The squad moved down the hillside into a narrow valley where mist coiled around their ankles and the valley sides rose like walls of torn earth. The auspex blinked a path towards a formation of rocks that would have been completely uninteresting if it had not corresponded to the location given by Brother Kaiyon under interrogation. On closer inspection the rocks formed two pillars and a lintel, a doorway in the valley wall blocked by a tangle of fallen stone.

'Charges,' said Borakis.

Brother Kalliax crouched by the rocks, setting up a bundle of explosive charges. The cog symbol on his right pauldron signified his acceptance as an apprentice to the Techmarines of the Imperial Fists.

'What do you see, Orfos?' said Borakis.

'No movement, sergeant,' replied Orfos, scanning the crests of the valley ridges for signs of hostiles.

The intelligence on Selaaca's hostiles was sketchy. The Imperial Fists had fought the necrons before, but their inhuman intelligence made the xenos impossible to interrogate and their goals could only be guessed at. Selaaca's necrons were, according to the interrogated Soul Drinkers, a broken and leaderless force, but there were certainly necrons still on the planet and no telling how they might have organised themselves since the Imperial Fists had captured the Soul Drinkers there.

'Ready,' said Kalliax.

The scout squad backed away from the entrance and Kalliax detonated the charge, blowing the blockage apart in a shower of dirt and stone. The blast echoed across the valley, shuddering the valley walls and starting a dozen tiny rockfalls.

'Move in,' said Borakis.

Laokan moved through the falling earth, his bolt pistol trained on the darkness revealed between the lintels. The darkness gave way to dressed stone and carvings inside.

The walls of the passageway were carved with repeating chalices, intertwined with eagles and skulls. The squad shadowed Laokan's movement as he crossed the threshold into the passageway.

The floor shifted under his feet. Laokan dropped instinctively to one knee. A line of green light shimmered over him and a camera lens winked in the ceiling as it focussed on him.

'Bleed,' said an artificial voice.

Laokan backed away slowly. The lens stayed focused on him.

'Bleed,' repeated the voice.

'Stand down, scout,' said Borakis. He walked past Laokan and drew his combat knife. The blade was as long as the sergeant's forearm, serrated and etched with lines of Imperial scripture. Borakis's scout armour, much less bulky than a full suit of power armour, had an armoured wrist guard that Borakis unbuckled from his left arm. He drew the knife along his left wrist and a bright scarlet trail ran down his hand.

Borakis flicked the blood off his hand into the passageway. It spattered across the walls and floor.

'Adeptus Astartes haemotypes detected,' said the voice again, the lens this time roving over the sergeant.

Light flickered on along the passage way, lighting the way deep into the hillside.

'We're in the right place,' said Borakis. 'Follow me.'

Borakis and the scouts entered the hillside, pistols trained on every shadow.

The *Mantle of Wrath* had two missions over Selaaca. The first was to deliver the scout squad to follow up the castellan's intelligence. The other was to begin the destruction of the Soul Drinkers.

The *Mantle* was one of the better-armed ships in the Imperial Fists fleet, but for this mission its torpedo bays had been stripped out and replaced with high-yield charges normally used for orbital demolitions. The *Mantle* did not have long to wait in orbit over Selaaca before its target drifted into view, its massive bulk darkening the glare of Selaaca's sun.

Few Imperial Fists would ever need more proof of the Soul Drinkers' corruption than the *Brokenback*. Many a Fist had fought on a space hulk, one of the cursed ships lost in the warp and regurgitated back into realspace teeming with xenos or worse. The *Brokenback* was as huge and ugly a space hulk as any had seen: hundreds of smaller ships welded into a single lumbering mass by the tides of the warp. Imperial warships ten thousand years old jostled with xenos ships, vast cargo freighters and masses of twisted metal that bore no resemblance to anything that had ever crossed the void.

Thousands of crew on the *Mantle* prepared the torpedo arrays as the strike cruiser manoeuvred into position. Damage control crews were called to battle stations, for while the *Brokenback* was unmanned no one could be sure of what automated defences the hulk might have. As the *Mantle* approached firing position, the Imperial Fists' officers and the unaugmented crewmen waited for the space hulk to leap into life and rain destruction from a dozen warships onto the *Mantle of Wrath*.

The hulk's weapons stayed silent. A spread of torpedoes glittered against the void as they launched from the *Mantle*, leaving ripples of silvery fire in their wake. Defensive turrets, which would normally have shot down every one of the torpedoes, stayed silent as the first spread impacted into the space hulk amidships.

Bright explosions blossomed against the void; flashes of energy robbed of power an instant later by the vacuum. Shattered chunks of hulls floated outwards in clouds of debris, leaving open wounds of torn metal in the side of the *Brokenback*.

The space hulk was too big to be destroyed with a single volley, even of the high-yield demolition charges. The *Mantle of Wrath* pumped out wave after wave of torpedoes. One volley blew an Imperial warship free of the space hulk's mass and the ship span away from its parent, trailing coils of burning plasma and revealing the twisted steel honeycomb inside. Ruined orbital yachts and xenos fighter craft tumbled out of the rents opened up in the hull.

Moment by moment, the whole *Brokenback* came apart. Selaaca's gravity drew the fragments down and the whole hulk rotated. The volley had opened up a weak point in the depths of the hulk's mass and an enormous section of the stern bent away from it, dragged down towards the greyish disc of Selaaca.

The *Brokenback* could not resist orbital decay any longer. Its idling engines, which did the bare minimum of work to keep it in orbit, failed as plasma reactors collapsed and power systems were severed. Over the course of the next few hours the stern of the hulk was scoured by the upper atmosphere and broke away entirely, followed by millions of chunks of debris raining down onto the planet. Like a dying

whale the rest of the *Brokenback* lolled over and fell
into the gravity well of Selaaca, gathering speed as it
fell, its lower edges glowing cherry-red, then white,
with friction.

The *Brokenback* disappeared into Selaaca's cloudy
sky. Most of it, the *Mantle's* augurs divined, would
come down in one of Selaaca's stagnant oceans, the
rest scattered over a coastline.

The *Mantle of Wrath* had fulfilled one of its duties.
The space hulk *Brokenback* was gone, and no renegade would ever use it to resurrect the Soul Drinkers'
heresies.

The only duty keeping the ship over Selaaca was the
scout squad currently deployed on their service. Soon
they would return, and the *Mantle* would leave this
forsaken place behind forever.

BROTHER CAIUS DIED first.

The walls folded in on themselves, revealing rows of
teeth lining the inside of a vast bristling throat. Caius
had been the slowest to react. The rest of the squad
threw themselves into the alcoves along the tunnel,
which each contained statues of Space Marines with
their armour covered in the ornate chalice of the Soul
Drinkers. Caius's leg had snagged on the spikes and
he had been dragged down the throat as it rippled
and constricted; the sound of grinding stone competing with the tearing muscle and bone.

Caius did not scream. Perhaps he did not want to
show weakness in his final moments. Perhaps he did
not have time. When the corridor reformed, Caius's
vermilion blood ran down the carvings and no other

trace of his body remained.

Borakis hissed with frustration as Caius's lifesigns winked out on his retinal display.

'Caius!' shouted Orfos. 'Brother! Speak to us!'

'He is gone, scout,' said Borakis.

Kalliax held his bolt pistol close to his face, his lips almost touching the top of the weapon's housing. He crouched in the alcove opposite Borakis. 'Repaid in blood shall every drop be,' he said, face set.

'First, your duty,' said Borakis. 'Then let your thoughts turn to revenge.'

'This place was a trap!' replied Kalliax. 'I should have seen it. By the hands of Dorn, why did I not see it? Some mechanism, something that should not be here, it should have been obvious to me!'

'If you think you killed our brother,' said Borakis sternly, 'then take that pistol and administer your vengeance to yourself. If not, focus on your duty. This place was a trap, but it was not placed here in isolation. It protects something. That is what we have come here to find.'

The sound of breaking stone came from the alcove in which Brother Laokan had taken cover. The remnants of the alcove's statue toppled into the tunnel and smashed on the floor.

'Speak, novice!' ordered Borakis.

'Through here,' said Laokan. 'This is a false tunnel. Behind this wall is another way.'

Borakis braced his arms against the alcove walls and kicked hard against the statue. The wall behind gave way and the statue fell into the void beyond, revealing a long, low space lit by yellowish muted glow-globes set into the walls.

'Follow, brothers!' said Borakis.

Kalliax and Orfos kicked their way through the false wall and followed the sergeant into the hidden space. They had not yet completed their transition into full Space Marines but their strength was already far beyond that of normal men.

Up ahead of Borakis was a chapel with an altar, at the far end of the long room. The ceiling loomed down low, hung with stalactites that had formed from water dripping down. The altar was a solid block of grey stone topped with a gilded triptych depicting Rogal Dorn standing in the centre of a battle scene.

Borakis took the point himself this time. Now he knew there was danger here, he had a duty to place himself in its way, for part of his duty was to see his young charges safely back to the Chapter.

On the altar stood a chalice cut from black stone, studded with emeralds. Borakis kept his shotgun levelled on the altar as he approached it. The scouts spread out behind him.

The altarpiece's rendition of Rogal Dorn was in gold with diamond eyes. Dorn was twice as tall as the gilded warrior battling alongside him. The enemy were aliens, or perhaps mutants, humanoid but with gills and talons. Dorn was crushing them beneath his feet. It was a passable work. Dozens of higher quality could be found in the chapels and shrines of the *Phalanx*.

'Sergeant?' said Orfos. 'Anything?'

Borakis leant closer to the altar. The chalice was not empty. Something shimmered darkly inside it. In the dim light it was impossible to tell, but it looked like blood.

Blood could not remain liquid down here for the length of time the chapel had evidently been sealed. Borakis knew the smell of blood well enough. He put his face close to the chalice and sniffed, knowing his genhanced senses would confirm what the liquid was.

Borakis's breath misted against the polished stone. He noticed for the first time the thin silvery wires covering the chalice in a network of circuitry.

The warmth and moistness of a human breath made the filaments move. Expanding, they completed a circuit, wired through the base of the chalice to the mechanism behind the triptych.

Rogal Dorn's diamond eyes flashed red. A pencil-thin beam glittered across the chamber.

Sergeant Borakis fell, twin holes bored through his skull by the pulse of laser.

'Back!' shouted Laokan. 'Fall back!'

Kalliax darted forwards to grab Borakis's body by the collar of his armour and drag him away from the altar. The panels of the triptych slid aside, each revealing the veiny flesh of a gun-servitor supporting double-barrelled autoguns. Green and red lights flashed over Kalliax as he tried to scramble away, hauling Borakis's corpse with him.

The autoguns opened up, the gunfire filling the chamber to bursting. Kalliax almost made it to the hole leading to the tunnel. His armour almost held for the extra second he needed. Bursts of torn ceramite, then blood and meat, spattered from his back as bullets hit home. Kalliax fell to the floor as a shot blew his thigh open, revealing a wet red mess tangled around his shattered femur. Kalliax dropped Borakis's body and returned fire with his bolt pistol. His face and upper chest disappeared in a cloud of red.

Laokan and Orfos broke back into the tunnel, its walls still wet with Caius's blood. Orfos saw Kalliax die, and he felt that same instinct that must have seized Kalliax – grab the body of his fallen battle-brother, carry him back to the Chapter, see him interred with honour alongside the rest of the Chapter's venerated dead. But Orfos choked down the thought. That was what had killed Kalliax. Orfos would leave him to be entombed in this place. That was the way it had to be.

The back wall was falling in, showering the altar with rubble. The gun-servitors, one with a gun arm hanging limp thanks to Kalliax's bolter fire, lumbered out of their hiding place towards the surviving scouts.

'Don't look back!' shouted Laokan above the gun-fire, and pushed Orfos into the carved corridor.

The walls shifted again. Orfos made a decision with the quickness of mind that years of hypno-doctrination and battle training had given him. He could go for the entrance of the tunnel, to escape back into the valley. But Caius had died in that stretch of tunnel – Orfos knew that way was certainly trapped. That certainty did not exist for the other direction, deeper into the structure built into the hillside. It was not particularly compelling logic, but it was all he had.

Orfos broke into a sprint towards the darkness at the far end of the tunnel. Laokan was on his heels, and the racket of the gunfire was joined by the grinding of stone on stone. The tunnel was closing up again, the ripple of shifting panels accelerating towards them from the tunnel entrance. Chunks of Caius's body were revealed, tumbling around the vortex of stone. A severed hand, a battered and featureless head, Caius's bolt pistol warped out of shape.

Orfos was fast. In the tests after each surgical procedure, he had always been. The sergeants of the Tenth Company had suggested his aptitude was for the Doctrines of Assault due to his speed and decisiveness of action.

Laokan was not so fast. He was a marksman. A trailing arm was caught between spiked panels and Laokan was yanked back off his feet. Orfos heard Laokan yell in shock and pain, and turned long enough to grab Laokan's boot, pulling his fellow scout free of the chewing throat.

Laokan's arm came off, bone and sinew chewed through. Laokan collapsed onto Orfos and tried to propel himself forwards, buying time for them both. Orfos grabbed Laokan's remaining arm and dragged him behind him as he carried on running.

Laokan snagged on something. Orfos hauled harder and dragged Laokan along with him, every nerve straining to keep his battle-brother free of the fate that had claimed Caius.

There was no light now. Even the scout's augmented vision, almost the equal of a full Space Marine's, could make out nothing but dense shadow.

The floor gave way beneath Orfos's feet. The lip of a stone pit slammed into the side of his head as he fell, and teeth cracked in his jaw. He was aware, on the edge of consciousness, of his body battering against the carved sides of the pit as he and Laokan fell.

ORFOS WOKE, AND realised that he had been knocked out. He cursed himself. Even if only for a moment, he should fight for awareness at all times. He had no bolt pistol in his hand, either. He had dropped his weapon. Borakis would assign him field punishment for such a failing. But Borakis, recalled Orfos with a lurch, was dead.

Orfos could still see nothing. He fumbled with the tactical light mounted on the shoulder of his breastplate. The light winked on and fell on the face of another stone Space Marine, far larger than in the alcoves above – twice life-size. Orfos read the inscription on the storm shield carried in the statue's left hand, a counterpart to the chainsword in its right. It read APOLLONIOS. Orfos recognised the trappings of a Chaplain among the weapons and armour of an assault-captain. Beside the statue was another of a Chaplain, this one inscribed with the name ACIAR.

'Brother,' said Orfos. 'Brother, what of this place? What have we found?'

Laokan did not reply. Orfos looked for his brother, who must have also been knocked out in the fall.

Laokan lay a short distance from Orfos, next to Orfos's bolt pistol. Laokan's body was gone from the mid-torso down, and trails of organs lay behind him in bloody loops. Laokan was face down, nose in the dust.

Orfos knelt beside Laokan's corpse. 'Forgive me,

brother,' he said, but the words seemed meaningless as they fell dead against the chamber walls. 'I can pray for you later. I will, brother. I promise I will.'

Orfos picked up his bolt pistol and let the light play around the chamber. A third statue was mounted high up, above the lintel of a doorway framing a pair of steel blast doors. This statue, again of a Space Marine Chaplain, bore the name THEMISKON. Orfos recognised the chalice symbol on the statue's shoulder pad, echoing the statues in the alcoves above. It was the symbol of the Soul Drinkers.

Another crime laid at the feet of the Soul Drinkers – this death trap, laid out to claim the lives of good Imperial Fists. Orfos spat on the floor. Whatever holiness this place might have had for the Soul Drinkers, Orfos wanted to defile it. Whatever it meant to them, he wanted it made meaningless.

Orfos looked up. The walls of a shaft rose above him. The carvings were probably deep enough to climb, but it would not be easy, and another fall might break a leg or an arm and render him unable to escape that way. He turned his attention to the door.

The metal was cold, drinking the warmth from Orfos's hands and face from a good distance away. A control panel was set into the stone. Orfos was not in enough of a hurry to press any of the buttons. He put a hand to the metal – it was freezing, and this close Orfos's breath misted in the air.

The doors slid open. Orfos jumped back, bolt pistol held level. Beyond the doors was darkness – the light on Orfos's armour glinted off ice and played through freezing mist that rolled from between the doors.

Orfos stepped slowly away from the doors. 'Whoever you may be,' he called, 'whatsoever fate you may have decided for me, know that I will fight it! I am an Imperial Fist! Die here I may, but it is as a Fist I shall die!'

The doors were open. The lump of ice inside, hooked up to the walls by thick cables hung with icicles, shuddered. An inner heat sent cracks blinking through its mass. Chunks of ice fell away. Orfos glimpsed ceramite within, painted dark purple under the frost.

The ice crumbled to reveal a shape familiar to Orfos. A massive square body on a bipedal chassis, squat cylindrical legs supported by spayed feet of articulated metal. The blocky shoulder mounts each carried a weapon – one a missile launcher, the other a barrel-shaped power fist ringed with flat steel fingers.

It was a Dreadnought – a walking war machine. All the Dreadnoughts of the Imperial Fists were piloted by Space Marines who had been crippled in battle, who were kept alive by the Dreadnought's life-support systems and permitted to carry on their duties as soldiers of the Emperor even after their bodies were ruined and useless. The Dreadnought's sarcophagus was covered in purity seals and the symbol of a gilded chalice was emblazoned across the front.

Orfos's bolt pistol would do nothing to the Dreadnought's armoured body. The power fist could crush Orfos with such ease that the pilot, if there was one, would barely register the resistance provided by Orfos's body before his armour and skeleton gave way.

It would be quick. A Space Marine did not fear pain, but Orfos did not see the need to pursue it as some Imperial Fists did. He had made his stand. He had not run; he had done his best to keep his battle-brothers alive. His conscience was clear. He told himself he could die. He tried to force himself to believe it.

The Dreadnought shifted on its powerful legs and the fingers of the power fist flexed. Flakes of ice fell off it. The cables unhooked and fell loose, showering the chamber floor with more chunks of ice. Lights flickered as the Dreadnought's power plant turned over and the chamber was filled with the rhythmic thrum of it.

'All this talk of death,' came the Dreadnought's voice, a synthesised bass rumble issuing from the vox-units mounted on the hull. 'Such morbidity. I have no wish to disappoint you, novice, but you will not die here.'

Orfos swallowed. 'What are you?' he said. 'Why lie you here, in a place designed to kill?'

'Your obtuseness has not yet been trained out of you,' said the voice again. Orfos looked for some vision slit so he might glimpse the pilot inside, but he could find none. 'My tomb was built to ensure that none but a Space Marine could make it this far. So sad the Imperial Fists chose to send scouts to do the work of a full battle-brother. But you have made it, and I have no intention to see you go the way of that unfortunate brother who lies behind you.'

'That is an answer to only one question,' said Orfos. 'I asked you two.'

'Then I shall introduce myself,' said the Dreadnought. 'I am Daenyathos of the Soul Drinkers.'

# CHAPTER TWO

'GREETINGS, GREAT ONE,' said the lead pilgrim, his head bowed. Behind him snaked a chain of fellow pilgrims, decked out in sackcloth and, symbolic restraints around their wrists.

'I am Lord Castellan Leucrontas of the *Phalanx*,' replied the castellan. The cavernous docking bays of the *Phalanx* were Leucrontas's domain, just as the brig decks and Pain Glove chambers were his, and in spite of the high ceilings and enormous expanse of the docking chamber his stature still seemed to fill the place. 'Wherefore have you come to this place? You have not been asked, nor has your arrival been announced beforehand. I must warn you that accommodating your ship was a courtesy extended only in the light of it not being armed, and such a courtesy is mine to withdraw.'

The pilgrim's head seemed to bow even lower, as if his spine were permanently bent in an attitude of prayer. 'I would ask forgiveness, great one,' he said, in a rasping voice shredded by years of thunderous sermons, 'but it is not mine to offer apologies in the Emperor's name. For it is to do His work that we have come to this place.'

Castellan Leucrontas regarded the pilgrims emerging from the airlocks. Their ship, a converted merchantman, was a sturdy and ancient vessel, essential qualities for a craft that had evidently made it to the *Phalanx's* isolated location at short notice. Nevertheless, there had been great risk in taking them so close to the Veiled Region, with its pirates and xenos, in an unarmed ship. The pilgrims had clearly been willing to court death to make this journey, and still more to risk the chance that the Imperial Fists would refuse them a berth and leave them to drift.

'Then you represent the Church of the Imperial Creed?' said Leucrontas. 'That august congregation has no authority here. This ship is sovereign to the Imperial Fists Chapter.'

The lead pilgrim pulled back his hood. The face inside was barely recognisable as a face – not because it was inhuman or mutilated, but because the familiarity of its features was almost entirely hidden by the tattooed image of a pair of scales that covered it. The image was an electoo, edged in lines of light, and the two pans of the scales flickered with intricately rendered flames.

'We come not to usurp your rule, good lord

castellan,' said the pilgrim. 'Rather, we are here to observe. The standards, my brothers, if you please.'

Several other pilgrims jangled to the front of the crowd. Altogether there must have been three hundred of them, all hooded and chained like penitents. Several of them unfurled banners and held them aloft. They bore symbols of justice – the scales, the blinded eye, the image of a man holding a sword by the blade in a trial by ordeal. Other pilgrims were bent almost double by the loads of books strapped to their backs, each one a walking library. Still others had spools of parchment encased in units on their chests so they could pay out a constant strip of parchment on which to write. Some were writing down the exchange between their leader and the castellan, nimble fingers scribbling in an arcane shorthand with scratching quills.

'Our purpose,' said the pilgrims' leader, 'is to follow the course of justice. The Emperor Himself created the institutions that see justice called down upon His subjects and His enemies. We are the Blind Retribution, and whenever the process of justice is enacted, we are there to observe. It has come to the notice of the Blind that a Chapter of the Adeptus Astartes is to be tried here for several charges of rebellion and heresy. And so we are here to watch over this process and record all the matters of justice therein. This is the will of the Emperor, for His justice is the most perfect of all and it is to His perfection that we aspire.'

The castellan gave this some thought. 'It is true,' he said, 'that the *Phalanx* is to see these renegades put to trial. Your presence here, however, must be at the sufferance of the Chapter Master. I permit you entrance, but only he can permit you to stay, and should he withdraw my decision of welcome then you will be ejected.'

'We understand,' said the leader of the Blind Retribution. 'And we will obey. Might we beg of your crew some place to stay?'

'I shall have the crew find you lodgings,' replied the castellan. 'You can expect no more than an unused cargo bay. The *Phalanx* is large but it has no shortage of population.'

'We would ask nothing more,' said the leader. 'Ours is a way of poverty and denial. Indulgence dulls the sharp edge of justice, and luxury dims the focus. Now we take our leave, lord castellan. There are prayers and devotions to be made before our souls are fit to look upon the business of the Emperor's justice.'

Leucrontas watched as the pilgrims finished filing into the docking bay. They took loops of prayer beads from their robes and spoke droning prayers of thanks and humility.

The pilgrims were a small matter. The crew officers, who maintained the day-to-day workings of the *Phalanx* while the Imperial Fists attended the matters of war, could deal with them. Leucrontas had many more duties he had to see to before he could give the Blind Retribution another thought. Soon the Soul Drinkers would be in the dock, and many more powerful observers than the Blind Retribution would be watching the results closely.

\* \* \*

THE FIRST SIGHT Sarpedon had of this place was of the hands over his face, clamping the mask down.

Even then, barely conscious, the soldier's part of his mind demanded to know how he had been taken. Nerve gas, pumped into his cell? A rapid, merciless assault? Some drug administered by a sly needle or dart? He was angry. He wanted to know. His memory of the last few hours was a dark fog.

He thrashed. The hands clamping the mask to his face snapped away. They were not the gauntlets of Space Marines – Sarpedon was in the custody of Imperial Fists functionaries, unaugmented men and women who served the Fists as spaceship crew and support staff. The *Phalanx* was full of them. Somehow it was a greater insult that it did not take Space Marines to hold Sarpedon down.

Sarpedon struggled. He was held so fast he would have snapped his limbs before he loosened them. Incoherent voices shouted; medical code words barked between the staff of the *Phalanx's* apothecarion. Cold rivers wound through his body as sedatives were pumped into his veins.

Sarpedon was being wheeled on his back through a corridor with a ceiling that looked like the negative cast of a giant spinal column. The walls were webs of bone.

The sedatives took hold. Sarpedon couldn't even flex the muscles that had forced uselessly against his bonds. His eyes still moved – he looked down at his body and saw metal clamps around each of his limbs, holding them fast to the metal slab on which he lay. The *Phalanx's* crew must have had to make the restraints specially to fit his six remaining legs.

Sarpedon was also aware of a constriction around the sides of his head. No doubt it was an inhibiting device to dull his psychic powers. His cell had been fitted out to hold a psyker – the wards and anti-psychic materials built into its construction had rendered him completely blunt, unable to even taste the psychic resonance of his surroundings. The hood holding back his head made him similarly useless psychically. Not that he would have needed his psychic prowess to kill every one of the crewmen dragging him through the apothecarion, if only he could get free.

But they were just ordinary men and women, Sarpedon told himself. They believed as much as he did that their work was the work of the Emperor. Perhaps they were right.

Sarpedon passed through into a hall where the gnarled walls were lined with ceiling-high nutrient tanks, each with cultured organs suspended in viscous fluid. Gilded autosurgeons were mounted on the ceiling.

The next face that loomed over him was that of a Space Marine – close-cropped hair, hollow cheeks and a sharp chin and nose, with a bionic like a miniature microscope mounted over one eye. An eyebrow arched up.

'Behold the enemy,' said the Space Marine. It was an Imperial Fist by the symbol on his shoulder pad, and an Apothecary by the white panels of his armour. 'What manner of creature has the galaxy placed this time upon my slab? Many foul things have I seen, and some of them once human in form. But this! Ah, this shall be a challenge and a privilege. The imager!'

An ornate piece of machinery, like an arch of inscribed panels, was slid over Sarpedon. Sarpedon wanted to speak, if only to tell the Apothecary that he was no enemy, but a Space Marine as the Apothecary himself was. But his tongue was as paralysed as the rest of him. He had only his senses.

Speckles of light played against Sarpedon's retinas as lasers measured every aspect of him. A screen unfolded from one wall, in glowing green lines displaying Sarpedon's skeleton and the complex pattern of a Space Marine's organs.

'The weapons carried by a Space Marine begin with those augmentations within him,' said the Apothecary. 'All are present. Evidence here of extensive wounding and healing internally, as typical of a veteran. Most recent are extensive fractures to the skull and ribs. Note the abnormal shape of the omophagea, typical of this Chapter's gene-seed.'

The crewmen, the orderlies of the *Phalanx's* Apothecarion, were scribbling down the Apothecary's pronouncements with autoquills.

'And he is awake,' continued the Apothecary, noticing the movement of Sarpedon's eyes. 'We have an audience! What think you, Lord Sarpedon, of the hospitality aboard the *Phalanx*?'

The imager moved down over Sarpedon's body. The orderlies had to manoeuvre it past Sarpedon's restrained legs.

'The mutations,' said the Apothecary, 'are implicit throughout. The subject's musculo-skeletal strength is at the top end. I doubt there is any man-mountain of a Space Wolf who can match him. Material mutations begin with the thickened lumbar spine and the pelvis.' Again the Apothecary addressed Sarpedon. 'And what a pelvis! All the scholars of Mars could not machine such a hunk of bone! I have no doubt the strengthening properties of its shape shall make it a classic of its kind. I shall have it preserved and gilded, I think, and keep it here among my most prized samples. Perhaps the Mechanicus shipwrights can use it to develop some new form of docking clamp? Certainly I shall not permit it to be incinerated with the rest of you.'

The imager moved lower. Now on the screen were the muscle-packed exoskeletal segments of Sarpedon's legs.

'The subject's legs number six,' said the Apothecary. 'These are the most significant material mutations. Originally they numbered eight; note the remnants of the bionic joint around the centre left and the recent partially healed damage to the rear right socket. The structure of the legs is roughly arachnoid but has no direct analogue. The uncleanliness of such deformities is profound. I have no interest in these. They can burn after the execution.'

The imager was withdrawn. Now Sarpedon found points of pain all over his body as the orderlies worked over him. They were looping wires and thin tubes around him, fixing them with needles in the gaps around his black carapace and in the muscles of his abdomen. One was slid into a vein in his neck, another on the underside of one wrist.

'Begin,' said the Apothecary.

Sarpedon was bathed in pain. It was a pure, unalloyed pain. It was not like a blade in his skin, or scalding-hot liquid, or any other pain he had suffered. It was completely pure.

Sarpedon's mind shut down. Nothing in his consciousness found purchase in the endless, white landscape of pain. Time meant nothing. He no longer felt his restraints, or his anger at the arrogance of the Apothecary in dissecting him like any other specimen. He no longer felt anything. He was made of pain.

The sensation of tearing ligaments loomed through the pain. It was subsiding, being replaced with the normal input from his senses. His legs had forced against the restraints. His neck muscles had almost torn against the psychic inhibitor holding his head in place and his lungs burned against the breastplate of fused ribs in his chest. He gasped, unable to control his body's reactions to the onslaught.

'Note the reaction to pain,' the Apothecary's voice continued. 'It is within normal tolerances. So we see the core of a Space Marine is present, but much embellished by corruption. I have no doubt that this subject can be considered a Space Marine by most definitions and can be tried as one.'

One of Sarpedon's legs hurt more than the others. It hurt more because it had some freedom of movement in the hip joint. The restraint holding it just above the talon was coming loose.

And he could move. Just a little, but he could do it. The sedatives were wearing off. The dose was too low. He had greater body mass than a normal Space Marine thanks to his mutated legs, and the less obvious mutations inside him had changed his metabolism. He was getting movement back.

Sarpedon fought against it. The Apothecary was describing the results of some blood and tissue sample tests to the orderlies. Sarpedon ignored them. The restraint was working loose. With the greater range of movement afforded to his other limbs, he could gain more leverage against their restraints and they, too, were giving way.

Sarpedon took in a breath. He forced his chest upwards and dug his talons into the slab, trying to level himself off it.

The ping of snapping metal alerted the Apothecary, who broke off his talk mid-word.

Bolts sheared. Metal bands fractured. Sarpedon's lower body ripped itself free. He thrashed one arm free in a matter of seconds – the orderlies starting back at the sight of their captive's lower limbs slashing around him.

Sarpedon reached up to the head restraint and tore it off its moorings. He rolled off the slab and sprawled on the floor. The drugs in his system were still powerful enough to rob him of his coordination and he could not get all his legs moving him in the same direction at once. He yanked the remaining arm free just as the Apothecary drew his plasma pistol.

'What are you?' slurred Sarpedon. He clawed at the inhibitor device still clamped around his temples. 'What can you claim to be that you judge me? I am not some xenos thing on a slide! I am of the Adeptus

Astartes!'

'You are a traitor,' said the Apothecary. He had his plasma pistol levelled at Sarpedon's head. 'The dignity we give you in trying you before true and loyal Space Marines is more than you deserve.'

'But try me for what?' demanded Sarpedon. He lost his footing and crashed into one of the specimen tanks. The glass broke and the thick, cold nutrient fluid washed out over him, lapping around the feet of the orderlies who cowered against the far wall. 'How many enemies of man have fallen to the Soul Drinkers? How many catastrophes have we averted?'

'And how many Space Marines have fallen to you?' retorted the Apothecary. 'Our brethren in the Crimson Fists and the Howling Griffons could attest to that. If you had lost as many of your own to an enemy as mankind has to you, you would not hesitate to seek that enemy's death!'

Sarpedon tried to get to his feet, leaning against the wall behind him to force himself up. He tried to find a weapon among the debris around him, a shard of glass or a medical implement, but his head was swimming and he couldn't focus.

'If you had seen,' he said, 'what we had seen, then you would cross the galaxy to join us, though a legion of your own stand in your way.'

'Had I my mind, traitor,' said the Apothecary, 'I would have had you executed as soon as Lysander had brought you in, as a mercy to the human race so that you would be excised like the cancer you are. But the Chapter Master has said you must stand trial. He has more mercy in him than I, or any battle-brother

I know. You should be sobbing your gratitude to us. Enough of this.'

The Apothecary operated a control on a unit attached to the waist of his armour. A white, dull sensation throbbed through Sarpedon's head, conducted from temple to temple by the inhibitor. Then Sarpedon was falling, his mind ripped free of his body. His sight failed and everything went white as he fell, and he did not stop falling until he could feel nothing at all.

THE FIRST TO arrive to take their part among a jury of the Soul Drinkers' peers were the Crimson Fists. On their strike cruiser *Vengeance Incandescent*, the whole 2nd Company attended their representative to the *Phalanx*. The Crimson Fists, a brother Chapter to the Imperial Fists just as the Soul Drinkers had once been, claimed a special place in the forthcoming trial, for they had suffered more than most at the hands of the renegades.

Chapter Master Vladimir Pugh had left his usual place among the tactical treatises and fortification maps of the Librarium Dorn to welcome Captain Borganor as he boarded the *Phalanx*. Attended by the 2nd Company's honour guard, Borganor descended the embarkation ramp of his shuttle with a slight limp given him by the bionic with which his right leg had been replaced. His dark blue armour was swathed in the deep crimson cloak embroidered with his personal heraldry, an image in gold and black thread of a burning standard and a Crimson Fist with his head bowed in shame and his hands at prayer.

Borganor was as blunt and crude as his gnarled features suggested, and with a clap of his hand against his gilded breastplate he acknowledged Pugh's salute.

'Chapter Master, it is an honour,' said Borganor. 'Would that I stand in your presence on a happier occasion, and without the stain of failure that still lies upon me.'

Vladimir Pugh of the Imperial Fists nodded sagely. He was, above all other things, a master tactician, a man of a solemn and slow manner, with a habit of dissecting a situation as cold-bloodedly as he weighed up potential recruits. The golden yellow of his artificer armour was polished to a mirror finish, and the red closed-fist symbols on his shoulder pads and breastplate shone as if they were cut from rubies. The intelligent face beneath his close-shorn hair suggested something more than a mere soldier. 'Long have I lamented the loss of your standard to the renegades,' he said to Borganor. 'It is an ill that will surely be repaid when justice is pronounced upon the renegades.'

Discomfort broke through Borganor's features for a moment. The standard of the 2nd Company had been lost to the Soul Drinkers under Captain Reinez's command. Reinez had subsequently renounced his captaincy before it could be stripped from him, and had embarked on a quest to achieve some great victory and redeem himself in his Chapter's eyes. Borganor, who had taken over the depleted company, bore no little responsibility for the standard's loss in his own mind.

'No doubt,' said Borganor. 'I wish to request one

favour from you, however, before proceeding on.'

'Name it, brother-captain,' said the Chapter Master.

'That before Sarpedon is executed, I am first given liberty to remove his limbs, and leave him with a single leg, as he left me.' Borganor's eyes flitted to his bionic leg. 'My crippling was Sarpedon's doing, and I would repay him for it as a personal debt.'

'We are not here to execute your petty vengeance, captain,' replied Pugh. 'A far greater vengeance must be satisfied. If it is decided that the traitor Sarpedon is to suffer greatly before death, perhaps you can have a part in deciding the exact manner in which that suffering is to be inflicted. Until that decision is made, make justice your only goal.'

Borganor bowed before Pugh. 'Forgive me,' he said. 'Such hatred burns in my heart for all those that would befoul the name of Rogal Dorn.'

'That such hatred should have its voice,' said Pugh, 'is the reason you have your place at this trial.'

Borganor led the seventy Space Marines of the Crimson Fists 2nd Company onto the *Phalanx's* docking bay. Their numbers were still recovering from their losses at the hands of Sarpedon and the aliens with which he had allied. Three companies of Imperial Fists, numbering more than three hundred Space Marines, were already stationed on the *Phalanx* – the Crimson Fists would be the next biggest contingent on board. But they would not be the only visitors to the *Phalanx* for the trial. Sarpedon and the Soul Drinkers had tangled with many Imperial servants, and every one wanted his voice to be heard.

* * *

IN A GOLDEN orbital yacht launched from the Inquisitorial escort ship *Traitorsgrave*, Lord Inquisitor Kolgo made his entrance into the *Phalanx*. Ahead of him danced a troupe of acrobats and musicians, enacting in elaborate mimes and song the greatest achievements of their master's long career hunting the enemies of the Emperor. Kolgo himself, in jet-black Terminator armour bearing the 'I' of the Inquisition proudly on his chest, was flanked by several battle-sisters of the Adepta Sororitas. They were led by Sister Superior Aescarion, who had requested the duty of accompanying Kolgo so that she, too, could witness at first hand the trial of the renegades whose deeds she had personally witnessed. She had previously been assigned to Inquisitor Thaddeus, and she had no doubt that the Soul Drinkers were responsible for his death since he had disappeared hunting down evidence of their activities.

The Adeptus Mechanicus, who had more cause than most to despise the Soul Drinkers, were present in the form of Archmagos Voar. Voar had been instrumental in the capture of the Soul Drinkers, in doing so helping to set right an age-old debt owed to the Mechanicus by Sarpedon and his renegades. Alongside Voar was a ceremonial guard of gun-servitors, marching precisely in time. Voar's legs had been lost on Selaaca and so he moved towards the engine sections of the *Phalanx*, where he had been given quarters, on a set of simple tracks he had fashioned to use until more suitable replacements could be found. There was none of the hatred in him that the other attendees flaunted, for Voar was an analytical creature for whom emotion was an inconvenience.

The word had spread beyond those who had personally encountered the Soul Drinkers after they had turned renegade. The *Killing Shadow* of the Doom Eagles Chapter and the *Judgement Upon Garadan* of the Iron Knights dropped out of warp near Kravamesh and demanded that they, as loyal Space Marine Chapters, also take part in the trial. Shortly after this they were joined by contingents of Angels Sanguine and Silver Skulls, both Chapters who had heard of the Soul Drinkers' capture and found they had officers stationed close enough to Kravamesh to have a presence at the trial.

Chapter Master Pugh listened to their petitions. It was down to his judgement whether or not these Space Marines would be welcome. He accepted that the existence of renegade Space Marines was an affront to the whole Adeptus Astartes, and that the crime of any one renegade Chapter was a crime against them all, for it blackened the name of Space Marines, their primarchs and even the Emperor Himself. So Pugh gave the order for the Chapter representatives to be welcomed on board the *Phalanx*, and quartered among the monastic cells usually used by Imperial Fists who were on operations elsewhere in the galaxy.

Amid the pageantry of so many Chapters all announcing their presence and bringing their own officers and honour guards on board, the existence of a band of ragged pilgrims in the forward cargo sections was all but forgotten.

\* \* \*

IN THE DUSTY, long-empty cargo hall, Father Gyranar knelt and prayed. Decades before, this place had been crammed with supplies of ammunition, food and spare parts long since used up, and it remained only in the memories of a few crewmen who recalled it when asked if there was somewhere the pilgrims of the Blind Retribution could be quartered. Those pilgrims now knelt on bedrolls or attended to their holy books, preparing their souls for the solemn duty of overseeing the great trial to come. No one had thought to tell them when the trial was expected to begin, but the pilgrims did not care. They would always be ready.

Father Gyranar, who had spoken with Castellan Leucrontas, was the oldest among them, and few of them were young. His own prayers were so familiar to him that he had to stop and think about the words, to stop them slipping through the well-worn channels of his mind. When he murmured that the Emperor's will was his will, he forced himself to pause and consider what that actually meant. That he had no will of his own, that he was the vessel for a higher power, that his own wishes and desires had long since withered away to be replaced with what the Emperor wanted for this particular instrument.

Gyranar carried a prayer book, but he had not opened it in thirty-seven years. He knew it by heart.

His evening prayers complete, Gyranar stood. 'Advance the standards,' he said.

The other pilgrims did not expect this. It was not a part of their normal routine. After a few moments of confusion the standards of the Blind Retribution were unfurled and held aloft.

'This place is now holy ground,' said Gyranar. His voice was brittle and frail, but the other pilgrims listened so attentively that he could have been no clearer with a vox-caster. 'The time for confession has come.'

'Confession, father?' said Brother Akulsan. He was the Blind Retribution's deacon, who oversaw the few permanent places of worship they had established on the worlds where they had settled for a while. On a pilgrimage such as this he became a second leader, a check to Gyranar's authority.

'Indeed,' said Gyranar. 'A confession most vital. There is in us all a sin. The task we undertake here is of such import that I would have it spoken aloud by all of us.'

'Many times have I made confession,' said Akulsan. 'Indeed, the very pride of confessing has itself become as a sin, and required yet more confession. I feel there is little in me that is still dangerous and unspoken, prideful though that thought may be.'

'Sister Solace?' said Gyranar.

'Every night I beg forgiveness for my failures,' replied Sister Solace, in a voice hoarse with endless prayers. Those not familiar with the Blind Retribution sometimes expressed surprise that Solace was a woman, for she had the dusty voice of an old man and it was impossible to tell gender through her robes. Most people never suspected there were women in the Blind Retribution at all. 'I yearn to be free of them. What confession can I make now that I have not in every moment before?'

'You know,' said Gyranar, 'of what I speak.' He had

been kneeling but he now stood. He had never been a big man and now he was bent and drained, but still the pilgrims looked down or shied away a little as if he had the presence of a Space Marine. 'Though the greater part of your soul may deny it. Though you beg the Emperor that it not be true. Though you have forced yourselves to forget all but its shadow, yet all of you know of what I speak.'

The pilgrims were silent. The only sound was the distant hum of the *Phalanx's* engines and the pulsing of the air recyclers overhead.

'Then I shall begin,' said Gyranar. 'O Emperor, I speak unto you the darkness of my deeds, and the poverty of this spirit so unworthy to serve you. My confession is of a time long ago, when first I wore the habit of the Blind. In the night as I lay in cloisters, a shadow came to me, clad in darkness. I am sure he was another brother of this order, though I know not his name. Perhaps it was that same father who counselled me in your ways. He said nothing, and did no more than place a chalice beside the slab on which I slept. Tell me, brethren, is there some confession in you that begs to be released, that has some of the same character as mine? Is there some echo of recognition that tugs at you, though it be gone from your memory?'

The pilgrims said nothing. So rapt were they by Gyranar's words that the Imperial saints could have descended in that moment and not broken their concentration on what the old man had to say.

'Then I shall continue,' he said. 'In this chalice was a liquid dark and cold. The shadow bid me drink with a gesture, and I did so, for I was afraid. And then into my mind there flooded a terrible waterfall of knowledge. I saw destruction and suffering! But I saw also the good that would come of it, the sinners that would be purged and the dead flesh of this bloated Imperium burned away. And I saw this time, when the Angels of Death, the Emperor's own warriors, shall be brought to trial before their peers, and I saw the part we were to play therein. The sin I confess is that I have known since that night that this time would come, and that the Blind Retribution must be there not only to observe that justice be done, but to enact a most crucial and terrible act that is the Emperor's will. I have kept it secret, locked up in my soul. Knowing that the day would come when everything I saw will come true. That is my confession. Who will follow mine with the excision of their own sin? Who?'

For a few moments, there was silence. Then one of the pilgrims raised a hand – Brother Sennon, one of the younger brethren who had been with the Blind Retribution only a few years. 'I drank of the chalice,' he said, his voice wavering. 'I saw... I saw the *Phalanx*. I thought it was a gilded eagle, a symbol of the Emperor's presence but... but when I looked upon this ship, I understood that whatever is to befall us must happen here. And it will be most dreadful. I saw flame, and blood, and torn bodies. Space Marines battling one another. There was a terrible injustice, I am sure, which by this violence might be averted. And... Father Gyranar, I am sure that I must die.'

'Brother Sennon,' said Gyranar, 'your courage is

that of one far beyond your years and wisdom. To have made this confession here, before your brothers, is an act of great bravery. Who else here can show such valour? For he is not the only one with something to confess.'

'I, too,' said Sister Solace, 'have seen what I must do. It is indeed a terrible thing. But it was brought to me while at prayer. There was a searing pain about my temples and when my senses returned my mind was full of visions. I saw the *Phalanx*, and all that you have spoken of. I have hidden this for so long because I was afraid. I thought I was the only one. I thought that if I spoke of it I would be accused of corruption, and so I pushed it down to the depths of my soul. Only now am I able to acknowledge it within myself.'

More voices spoke out. Many had drunk of the chalice offered to them. Others had been struck by sudden visions while ill with a fever or at prayer. Some had been granted prophetic dreams. All of them had hidden what they had seen, and all of them had seen the same thing. The *Phalanx*. Fire and warfare. Destruction. And all had the same absolute certainty that what they saw was the Emperor's will. Every pilgrim cried out his own confession, finally unburdening himself of the dark thoughts that had been inside him since the days of his novicehood in the Blind Retribution.

Gyranar held up a hand to silence them. 'Now our confession is finished,' he said, 'is any one of you in doubt as to what he must do? Does any fail to understand his task in this, our final act of devotion?'

This time, there was silence again.

'Good,' said Gyranar. 'Then the Emperor's will must be done, dreadful though it is. And true, many of you will die, though the fear of death has no hold on you, I see.'

'Rather death,' said Brother Akulsan, 'than to live on with this task undone.'

'Good,' said Gyranar. 'Then we are all of the same mind. And now, let us pray.'

IF ARCHMAGOS VOAR could have truly admired anything, he would have admired the Forge of Ages. The complex angles of its construction, wrought in iron and bronze to form a great segmented dome, were lit from beneath by the molten metal running in channels between the four great forges in which blades and armour segments were being heated by crewmen in heavy protective suits. The sound of steel on steel rang like the falling of metallic rain. The work was overseen by the Techmarines of the 4th, 7th and 8th Companies of the Imperial Fists: those companies present on the *Phalanx* for the trial. The Techmarines checked each piece for flaws after its cooling in the huge vat of water in the centre of the dome, throwing those pieces that failed back into the streams of molten metal.

Voar did not really like anything in the traditional human sense, since he had lost much of his emotional centre over the course of his various augmentations. But as much as he could, he liked this place. It was a place of both industry and wisdom. The exacting standards of the Techmarines were something to admire, as was the devotion the crewmen had to the orders of their Imperial Fists masters. The Forge of Ages could have been lifted straight out of an Adeptus Mechanicus forge world, which was as high a compliment as a magos of the Mechanicus could pay.

Archmagos Voar had been summoned here. Ordinarily one did not summon an archmagos, but he was a guest here on the *Phalanx* and his datamedia still contained enough matters of etiquette to suggest he should accept the request to come to the Forge.

In the centre stood a Space Marine who was not a Techmarine. He wore Terminator armour, its yellow ceramite panels lit red and orange by the molten streams. He was testing the weight and balance of several hammers recently forged and left by the cooling pool. Each hammer was as long as a man was tall, but the Imperial Fist swung them as if they weighed nothing. He swung each in turn a few times, running through a simple weapons drill, then scowled and placed each one back in the pile. None of them seemed to please him very much. None of them, presumably, was the equal of the thunder hammer he carried strapped to the back of his armour.

'Demenos!' shouted the Imperial Fist over the din.

One of the Techmarines turned to him. 'Captain Lysander?'

'What grade of material are you using for your hammer heads? These things feel like they would splinter against a child's hand! And the shafts are about as sturdy as straw!'

Techmarine Demenos bowed his head. 'Many of my forgemen are new, captain,' he said. 'They have yet to understand the artificer's art. These weapons are exemplars of their competence thus far. They shall be used as training weapons, I would imagine.'

'If you wish to train our novices to fear the failing of their wargear, then they will do perfectly,' retorted Lysander. He picked up a sword this time and made a few thrusts and chops with it. 'This is better,' he said. 'This would go through a few skulls.'

'My own work,' said Demenos.

'Then you need to learn how to balance a hilt. Good work, though.' Lysander spotted Voar trundling between the forges towards him. 'Archmagos! I am glad you could come. I think perhaps this place is more suited to your tastes than the rest of the *Phalanx*.'

'I have no tastes,' replied Voar. 'A magos metallurgicus could gain no little pleasure from the specifications of your forges, no doubt, but my specialities lie in the fields of reverse engineering and theoretical mechanics.'

'Well, be that as it may,' said Lysander, 'the Forge of Ages itself is not why I requested your presence. This is.' Lysander took from a compartment in his armour a tube of black metal, as long as a normal man's forearm. Its surface was knurled into a grip and on one end it had a small control surface with indented sensors. 'Perhaps you recognise it?'

Voar walked up to Lysander and took the cylinder. Voar's bionic hand did not fit the grip well – it was sized for a Space Marine's hand.

'This is the Soulspear,' said Voar flatly.

'As seized at the Lakonia Star Fort,' said Lysander.

'The seed of the conflict between the Priesthood of Mars and the Soul Drinkers. We recovered it from the *Brokenback* before it was scuttled. I understand that it is to be considered your property. It was taken from you by the Soul Drinkers, and as heretics they have no right to it. Therefore its possession defaults to the Adeptus Mechanicus. Specifically, you.'

Voar turned the weapon over in his artificial hand. 'I confess that my dealings with emotive matters are long behind me,' he said, 'but still I have the impression, a remnant of some human sense if you will, that you are not happy about this situation.'

'The Soulspear is a relic of our primarch,' replied Lysander. 'Rogal Dorn himself found and re-engineered it. By rights it should belong to one of the successors of Dorn's Legion, the Imperial Fists or one of our brother Chapters. I have no shame in that belief. Any son of Dorn would say the same. But my Chapter Master has no wish to see another rift between the Adeptus Astartes and the Mechanicus, and I must bow to his decision. Here.'

Lysander touched a finger to one of the control surfaces and a tiny laser pulse punched a microscopic hole through the ceramite of his gauntlet's finger joint. Twin blades of pure blackness shot out of each end of the cylinder. The air sighed as it was cut apart by the voids of the blades.

'Vortex blades,' said Lysander. 'A vortex field bound by Throne knows what technology from before the Age of Imperium. Activated by a gene-lock keyed to the genetic signature of Rogal Dorn. This was wielded by Dorn's own hand, archmagos. A man of whom no Fabricator General can claim to be the equal. The saviour of the Emperor Himself at the height of the Heresy. The greatest soldier this galaxy has ever seen, and I say the greatest man, too. Remember that, whatever you choose to do with this relic. Fail to show Dorn's own handiwork the proper respect and the Imperial Fists just might choose to risk a new rift after all.'

'I see,' said Voar. 'Your information has been logged and will be made available to all those given the honour of examining this device.'

'In return for this,' said Lysander with obvious disdain for Voar's manner, 'the Chapter Master expects the Adeptus Mechanicus to conduct their part in the trial with all the honour that your status as a guest here demands. This is no place to settle a feud between the Soul Drinkers and the Mechanicus. No place for vengeance.'

'Your battle-brothers are not all of the same mind,' said Voar. 'Nor, logic suggests, will many of the visiting Chapters agree with such a stance. There is a great deal of vengeance sought on the *Phalanx*, and the better part of it stems not from the Mechanicus.'

'Chapter Master Vladimir Pugh has pronounced on the subject,' said Lysander. 'He has tasked me, among others, with seeing his word made law.'

'Then it shall be abided by,' said Voar with a nod of his head. It seemed the archmagos was not capable of any gesture of greater deference. 'Our interest is in justice.'

'If you cared about justice, archmagos, you would give the Soulspear to us.'

'And if you cared about justice, brother-captain, then Sarpedon would have died on Selaaca.' Archmagos Voar wheeled around and left the forge, the Soulspear clutched in his bionic hand.

# CHAPTER THREE

THE CELL BLOCK had been built for the use of the Imperial Fists' own penitents. When battle-brothers believed themselves guilty of some failure, they came here, to the Atoning Halls. They knelt in the dank, cold cells lining the narrow stone-clad corridors and prayed for their sins to be expunged. They begged for suffering with which to cleanse themselves, a suffering regularly gifted to them by the various implements of self-torture built into the ceilings and floors of each intersection. Nerve-gloves and flensing-racks stood silent there, most of them designed to be operated by the victim, so that through pain he might drive out the weaknesses that had led to some perceived failing.

The cells had not been built with locks, for all those who had spent their time there had done so voluntarily. But the Atoning Halls had locks now. Its current penitents were not there by choice.

'Salk!' hissed Captain Luko. Luko was chained to the wall of his cell, with just enough freedom in his bonds to stand up or sit down. Like the rest of the Soul Drinkers imprisoned in the Atoning Halls, he had been stripped of his armour, with his wargear kept somewhere else on the *Phalanx* to be used as evidence in the trial.

'Captain?' came Sergeant Salk's voice in reply. The Soul Drinkers officers had mostly been locked in cells far apart from one another, but the Atoning Halls had not been built to contain a hundred prisoners and so it was inevitable two would end up in earshot.

'I hear something,' said Luko. 'They are bringing someone else in.'

'There is no one else,' replied Salk. 'They took us all on Selaaca.' Though Luko could not see Salk's face, the despondency, tinged with anger, was obvious in his voice. 'They must be coming to interrogate us. I had wondered how long it would take for them to get to you and me.'

'I think not, brother,' said Luko. 'Listen.'

The sound of footsteps broke through the ever-present grinding of the *Phalanx's* engines. Several Space Marines, and... something else. A vehicle? A servitor? It was large and heavy, with a tread that crunched the flagstones of the corridor.

Luko strained forwards against the chains that held him, to see as much as possible of the corridor beyond the bars of his cell. Two Imperial Fists came into view, walking backwards with their bolters trained on something taller than they were.

'Throne of Terra,' whispered Luko as he got the first sight of what they were guarding.

It was a Dreadnought. It wore the deep purple and bone of the Soul Drinkers, but to Luko's knowledge no Dreadnought had served with the Chapter since he had been a novice. He had thought the Chapter had not possessed any Dreadnought hulls at all.

The Dreadnought's armour plating was pitted with age. Its weapons had been removed, revealing the complex workings of the mountings and ammo feeds in its shoulders. Even so the half-dozen Imperial Fists escorting it kept their guns on it, and one of them carried a missile launcher ready to blast the Dreadnought at close range.

As it stomped in front of Luko's cell, the Dreadnought turned its torso so it could look in. Luko saw that its sarcophagus had been opened partially, and he glimpsed the pallid flesh of the body inside. Large, filmy eyes shone from the shadows inside the war machine, and Luko's own eyes met them for a moment.

'Brother,' said the Soul Drinker inside the Dreadnought, his voice a wet whisper. 'Spread the word. I have returned.'

'Silence!' shouted one of the Imperial Fists in front of the Dreadnought. 'Hold your tongue!' The Space Marine turned to Luko. 'And you! Avert your eyes!'

'If you wish me blinded,' retorted Luko, 'then you will have to put out my eyes.'

Luko had a talent for eliciting a rough soldier's respect from other fighting men. The Imperial Fist scowled, but didn't aim his gun at Luko. 'Maybe later,' he said.

'Daenyathos has returned!' said the Dreadnought.

Luko jumped forwards against his chains. 'Daenyathos!' he echoed. 'Is it true?'

'Daenyathos!' came another voice, then another. Every Soul Drinker's voice was raised in a matter of seconds. The Imperial Fists yelled for silence but their voices were drowned out. Even the bolter shots they fired into the ceiling did not quiet the din.

Luko did not know what to call the emotions searing through him. Joy? There could be no joy here, when they were facing execution and disgrace. It was a raw exultation, a release of emotion. It had been pent up in the Soul Drinkers since they had seen Sarpedon fall in his duel with Lysander, and now it had an excuse to flood out.

Daenyathos was alive! In truth, in the depths of his soul, Luko had always known he was not truly dead. The promise of his return seemed written into everything the legendary philosopher-soldier had passed down to his Chapter, as if the *Catechisms Martial* had woven into it a prophecy that he would walk among them once more. Amazingly, impossibly, it seemed the most natural thing in the galaxy that Daenyathos should be there when the Chapter faced its extinction.

Only one voice was not raised in celebration. It was that of Pallas, the Apothecary.

'What did you do?' shouted Pallas, and Luko just caught his words. They gave him pause, even as his twin hearts hammered with the force of the emotion.

'What did you do, Daenyathos?' shouted Pallas again, and a few of the Soul Drinkers fell silent as they considered his words. 'How have you fallen into their hands, the same as us? Have you come here to face justice? Daenyathos, warrior-philosopher, tell us the truth!'

'Tell us!' shouted another. Those words soon clashed with Daenyathos's name in the din, half the Soul Drinkers demanding answers, the other half proclaiming their hero's return.

Daenyathos did not reply. Perhaps, if he had, he would not have been heard. The Imperial Fists hauled open a set of blast doors leading to a side chamber that had once been used to store the volatile chemicals required by some of the torture devices. Its ceramite-lined walls were strong enough to contain the weaponless Dreadnought. The Imperial Fists marshalled the Dreadnought inside and shut the doors, slamming the thing that called itself Daenyathos into the quiet and darkness.

Outside it took a long time for the chants of Daenyathos's name to die down in the Atoning Halls.

More than three hundred Space Marines gathered in the Observatory of Dornian Majesty. Most Imperial battlezones never saw such a concentration of might, but these were not there to fight. They were there to see justice done.

The Observatory was one of the *Phalanx's* many follies, a viewing dome built as a throne room for past Chapter Masters, where the transparent dome might afford a dramatic enough view of space to intimidate the Chapter's guests who came there to petition the lords of the Imperial Fists. Pugh had little need for such shows of intimidation and had closed off the Observatory for years.

It was one of the few places large enough to serve as the courtroom for the Soul Drinkers' trial. The ship's crew had built the seating galleries and the dock in the centre of the floor, an armoured pulpit into which restraints had been built strong enough to hold an accused Space Marine. The Justice Lord's position was on a throne the same height as the dock, facing it from the part of the gallery reserved for the Imperial Fists themselves.

The whole court was bathed in the light from the transparent dome. The Veiled Region was a mass of nebulae that boiled in the space outside the ship, nestling stars in its glowing clouds and swamping a vast swathe of space in the currents of half-formed star matter. Kravamesh hung, violet and hot, edging the courtroom in hard starlight.

The first in had been Lord Inquisitor Kolgo's retinue of Battle Sisters, ten Sororitas led by Sister Aescarion. They knelt and prayed to consecrate the place, Aescarion calling upon the Emperor to turn His eyes upon the *Phalanx* and see that His justice was done.

The Imperial Fists 4th Company took up their positions, a hundred Imperial Fists gathering to serve as honour guard to their Chapter Master. Next the Howling Griffons filed in, Borganor scowling at the Observatory as if its tenuous connection with the Soul Drinkers made it hateful.

The other captains were next. Commander Gethsemar of the Angels Sanguine was accompanied by a dozen Sanguinary Guards, their jump packs framed by stabiliser fins shaped like white angels' wings and their helmets fronted with golden masks fashioned to echo the death mask of their primarch, Sanguinius. Gethsemar himself wore several more masks hanging from the waist of his armour, each sculpted into a different expression. The one he wore had the mouth turned down in grim sorrow, teardrop-shaped emeralds fixed beneath one eye. Siege-Captain Daviks of the Silver Skulls wore the reinforced armour of a Devastator, built to accommodate the extra weight and heft of a heavy weapon, and his retinue counted among them his Company Champion carrying an obsidian sword and a shield faced with a mirror to deflect laser fire in combat.

The Iron Knights were represented by Captain N'Kalo, an assault captain who wore a proud pano-ply of honours, from a crown of laurels to the many honoriae hanging from the brocade across his chest and the Crux Terminatus on one shoulder pad. He led three squads, his Iron Knights resplendent in the personal heraldry each wore on his breastplate and the crests on their helms. The Doom Eagles came in at the same time, represented by a single squad of Space Marines and Librarian Varnica. Where Var-nica stepped, the stone beneath his feet bubbled and warped, his psychic abilities so pronounced that the real world strained to reject him, even with his power contained and channelled through the high collar of his Aegis armour.

Finally, Captain Lysander led in Chapter Master Vladimir Pugh. Pugh took his place on the throne – as the Justice Lord of this court he was the highest authority, and it was at his sufferance that any defendants, witnesses or petitioners might speak. Lysander did not stand in the gallery, for he was to serve as the Hand of the Court, the bailiff who enforced his Chapter Master's decisions among those present. Lysander looked quite at home patrolling the floor of the dome around the dock, and his fearsome reputation both as a disciplinarian and a warrior made for a powerful deterrent. A Space Marine's temper might move him to leave the gallery and attempt to disrupt the court's proceedings, even with violence – Lysander was one of the few men who could make such a warrior think twice.

The tension was obvious. When Lord Inquisitor Kolgo arrived to join his Battle Sisters, the sideways glances and murmured comments only grew. Space Marines were all soldiers of the Emperor but many Chapters did not have regular contacts with others and some had developed fierce rivalries over the millennia. The Imperial Fists had both retained the livery of their parent Legion and been feted above almost all other Chapters for the service to the Imperium – no little jealousy existed between them and other Chapters who coveted the honours they had been granted, and no one could say that such jealousy was absent from the court.

Fortunately, nothing papered over such schisms like a common enemy.

Sarpedon was led in, restraints binding his mutant

legs, by a gang of crewmen marshalled by Apothecary Asclephin. Asclephin had conducted the investigations into Sarpedon's mutations – indeed, his findings were part of the evidence that would be presented to the court.

Sarpedon was herded into the dock, and his restraints fixed to the mountings inside the pulpit. Sarpedon still had the physical presence to demand a hush from the court in the first moments they saw him. He was bent by his restraints and he lacked the armour that was the badge of a Space Marine, but even without his mutations he would have demanded a form of respect with the scars and bearing of a veteran and the defiance that refused to leave his face. The inhibitor hood clamped to his skull just made him look more dangerous. One of Lysander's primary duties was to watch Sarpedon carefully and subdue or even execute him at the first suggestion that the Soul Drinkers Chapter Master was using his psychic powers.

Sarpedon's eyes passed across the faces of the assembled Space Marines. He recognised Borganor and Lysander, and Pugh he knew by reputation. Kolgo he had never met, but the trappings of an Inquisitor sparked their own kind of recognition. Several times the Soul Drinkers had crossed paths, and swords, with the Inquisition. The Holy Ordos had sent their representative here to take their pound of flesh.

Then Sarpedon's eyes met Reinez's.

Brother Reinez of the Crimson Fists was alone. He had no retinue with him. His armour was pitted and stained, the dark blue of the Crimson Fists and their red hand symbol tarnished with ill maintenance. Reinez wore a hood of sackcloth and his face was filthy, smeared with ash. Strips of parchment covered in prayers fluttered from every piece of his armour.

There was silence for a moment. Their eyes had all been on Sarpedon, and none had seen Reinez enter.

'You,' said Reinez, pointing at Sarpedon. His voice was a ruined growl. 'You took my standard.'

Reinez had been the captain of the Crimson Fists 2nd Company during the battles with the xenos eldar on Entymion IV. The Soul Drinkers had taken the company standard in combat. Reinez was not a captain any more, and his trappings were those of a penitent, one who wandered seeking redemption outside his Chapter.

'The court,' said Pugh, 'recognises the presence of the Crimson Fists. Let the scribes enter it in the archives that–'

'You,' said Reinez, pointing at Sarpedon. 'You took my standard. You allied with the xenos. You left my brothers dead in the streets of Gravenhold.'

'I fought the xenos,' replied Sarpedon levelly. 'My conflict with you was sparked by your own hatred, not my brothers' wish to kill yours.'

'You lie!' bellowed Reinez. 'The life of the xenos leader was taken by my hand! But it was not enough. None of it was enough. The standard of the 2nd was taken by heretics. I travelled the galaxy looking for an enemy worthy of killing me, so I could die for my failings on Entymion IV. I could not find it. I turned my back on my Chapter and sought death for my sins, but the galaxy would not give it to me. And then I heard that the Soul Drinkers had been captured, and were to be tried on the *Phalanx*. And I realised that I did not have to die. I could have revenge.'

'Brother Reinez,' said Pugh, 'has been appointed the prosecuting counsel for the trial of the Soul Drinkers. The role of the Imperial Fists is to observe and administer justice, not to condemn. That task belongs to Brother Reinez.'

Sarpedon could only look at Reinez. He could scarcely imagine that any human being in the Imperium had ever hated another as much as Reinez obviously hated Sarpedon in that moment. Reinez had been shattered by the events on Entymion IV, Sarpedon could see that. He had been defeated and humiliated by warriors the Crimson Fists believed to be heretics. But now this broken man had been given a chance at a revenge he thought was impossible, and if there was anything that could bring a Space Marine back from the brink, it was the promise of revenge.

'The charges I bring,' said Reinez, 'are the treacherous slaying of the servants of the Emperor, rebellion from the Emperor's light, and heresy by aiding the enemies of the Imperium of Man.' The Crimson Fist was forcing down harsher words to conform to the mores of the court. 'The punishment I demand is death, and for the accused to know that they are dying. By the Emperor and Dorn, I swear that the charges I bring are true and deserving of vengeance.'

'This court,' replied Pugh formally, 'accepts the validity of these charges and this court's right to try the accused upon them.'

'Chapter Master,' said Sarpedon. 'This man is motivated by hate and revenge. There can be no justice when–'

'You will be silent!' yelled Reinez. 'Your heretic's words will not pollute this place!' He drew the power hammer he wore on his back and every Space Marine in the court tensed as the power field crackled around it.

'The accused will have his turn to speak,' said Pugh sternly.

'I see no accused!' retorted Reinez. He jumped over the row of seating in front of him, heading towards the courtroom floor and Sarpedon's pulpit. 'I see vermin! I see a foul stain on the honour of every Space Marine! I would take the head of this subhuman thing! I would spill its blood and let the Emperor not wait upon His justice!'

Lysander stepped between Reinez and the courtroom floor, his own hammer in his hands. 'Will you spill this one's blood too, brother?' said Lysander.

Reinez and Lysander were face to face, Reinez's breath heavy between his teeth. 'The day I saw a son of Dorn stand between a Crimson Fist and the enemy,' he growled, 'is a day I am ashamed to have seen.'

'Brother Reinez!' shouted Pugh, rising to his feet. 'Your role is to accuse, not to execute. It is to prosecute alone that you have been permitted to board the *Phalanx,* in spite of the deep shame in with which your own Chapter beholds you. Petitions will be heard and a verdict will be reached. This shall be the form your vengeance shall take. Blood will not be shed in my court save by my own order. Captain Lysander is the instrument of my will. Defy it and you defy him, and few will mourn your loss if that is the manner of death you choose.'

The moment for which Reinez was eye to eye with Lysander was far too long for the liking of anyone in the court. Reinez took the first step back and holstered his hammer.

'The Emperor's word shall be the last,' he said. 'He will speak for my dead brothers.'

'Then now the court will hear petitioners from those present,' said Pugh. 'In the Emperor's name, let justice be done.'

THE ARCHIVISTS OF the *Phalanx* were a curious breed even by the standards of the voidborn. Most had been born on the ship – the few who had not had been purchased in childhood to serve as apprentices to the aged Chapter functionaries. An archivist's purpose was to maintain the enormous parchment rolls on which the deeds and histories of the Imperial Fists were recorded. Those massive rolls, three times the height of a man and twice as broad, hung on their rollers from the walls of the cylindrical archive shaft, giving it the appearance of the inside of an insect hive bulging with pale cells.

An archivist therefore lived to record the deeds of those greater than him. An archivist was not really a person at all, but a human-shaped shadow tolerated to exist only as far as his duties required. They did not have names, being referred to by function. They were essentially interchangeable. They schooled their apprentices in the art of abandoning one's own personality.

Several of these archivists were writing on the fresh surfaces of recently installed parchment rolls, their nimble fingers noting down the transmissions from the courtroom in delicate longhand. Others were illuminating the borders and capital letters. Gyranar cast his eye over these strange, dusty, dried-out people, their eyes preserved by goggles and their fingers thin, bony spindles. Every breath he took in there hurt, but to a pilgrim of the Blinded Eye pain was just more proof that the Emperor still had tests for them to endure.

'Follow,' said the archivist who had been detailed to lead Gyranar through the cavernous rooms. This creature represented the dried husk of a human. It creaked when it walked and its goggles, the lenses filled with fluid, magnified its eyes to fat, whitish blobs. Gyranar could not tell if the archivist was male or female, and doubted the difference meant anything to the archivist itself.

The archivist led Gyranar through an archway into another section of the archives. Here, on armour stands, were displayed a hundred suits of power armour, each lit by a spotlight lancing from high overhead. The armour was painted purple and bone, with a few suits trimmed with an officer's gold. Each was displayed with its other wargear: boltguns and chainswords, a pair of lightning claws, a magnificent force axe with a blade inlaid with the delicate patterns of its psychic circuitry. The armour was still stained and scored from battle, and the smell of oil and gunsmoke mixed with the atmosphere of decaying parchment.

'This is the evidence chamber,' said the archivist. 'Here are kept the items to be presented to the court.'

'The arms of the Soul Drinkers,' said Gyranar. He pulled his hood back, and the electoo on his face reflected the pale light. The scales tipped a little, as if they represented the processes of Gyranar's mind, first weighing down on one side then the other.

'Quite so. Those who wish to inspect them can claim leave to do so from the Justice Lord. Our task is to make them available for scrutiny.'

'And afterwards?'

The archivist tilted its head, a faint curiosity coming over its sunken features. 'They will be disposed of,' it said. 'Ejected into space or used as raw material for the forges. The decision has yet to be made.'

'If the Soul Drinkers are found innocent,' said Gyranar, 'presumably these arms and armour will be returned to them.'

'Innocent?' replied the archivist. The faint mixture of mystification and baffled amusement was perhaps the most extreme emotion it had ever displayed. 'What do you mean, innocent?'

'Forgive me,' said Gyranar, bowing his head. 'A wayward thought. Might I be given leave to inspect this evidence for myself?'

'Leave is granted,' said the archivist. It turned away and left to take up its regular duties again.

Father Gyranar ran a finger along the blade of the force axe. This was the Axe of Mercaeno, the weapon of the Howling Griffons Librarian killed by Sarpedon.

Sarpedon had taken the axe to replace his own force weapon lost in the battle. Such had been the information given by the Howling Griffons' deposition to the court. Its use suggested a certain admiration held by Sarpedon for Mercaeno. It was probable that a replacement weapon could have been found in the Soul Drinkers' own armouries on the *Brokenback*, but Sarpedon had chosen to bear the weapon so closely associated with the Space Marine he had killed.

It was a good weapon. It had killed the daemon prince, Periclitor. Gyranar withdrew his thumb and regarded the thin red line on its tip. The Axe of Mercaeno was also very sharp.

Across the hall from the axe was a pair of oversized weapons, too big to be wielded by any Space Marine, and with mountings to fix them onto the side of a vehicle. Gyranar knew they were the weapons of a Space Marine Dreadnought – a missile launcher and a power fist. They, too, were in the livery of the Soul Drinkers. Their presence told Gyranar that everything the Blinded Eye had foretold was coming to pass. He was a cog in a machine that had been in motion for thousands of years, and that its function was about to be completed was an honour beyond any deserving.

Gyranar knelt in prayer. His words, well-worn in his mind, called for the fiery and bloodstained justice of the Emperor to be visited on sinners and traitors. But his thoughts as they raced were very different.

The archives. The dome being used as the courtroom. The Atoning Halls. The map being drawn in the pilgrim's mind was beginning to join up. Soon, he would hold his final sermon, and the contents of that pronouncement were finally taking shape.

'EVERYTHING,' SAID LORD Inquisitor Kolgo, 'is about power.'

The Inquisitor Lord paced as he spoke, making a half-circuit around the gallery seating, watched by the Battle Sisters who accompanied him. His Terminator armour was bulky, but it was ancient, the secrets of its construction giving him enough freedom of movement to point and slam one fist into the other palm, stride and gesticulate as well as any orator. And he was good. He had done this before.

'Think upon it,' he said. 'In this room are several hundred warriors of the Adeptus Astartes. Though I am a capable fighter for an unaugmented human, yet still the majority of you would have a very good chance of besting me. And I am unarmed. My weapons lie back on my shuttle, while many of you here carry the bolters or chainswords that you use so well in battle. I see you, the brothers of the Angels Sanguine, carrying the power glaives that mark you out as your Chapter's elite. And you, Librarian Varnica, that force claw about your fist is more than a mere ornamentation. It is an implement of killing. So if you wished to kill me, there would be little I could do to stop it.'

Kolgo paused. The Space Marines he had mentioned looked like they did not appreciate being singled out. Kolgo spread out his arms to take in the whole courtroom. 'And how many would like to kill me? Many of you have experienced unpleasant episodes at the hands of the Holy Ordos. I am a symbol of the Inquisition, and casting me down would be to strike a blow against every inquisitor who ever claimed his jurisdiction included the Adeptus Astartes. I have, personally, gained something of a reputation for meddling in your affairs, and am no doubt the subject of more than a few blood oaths. Perhaps one of you here has knelt before the image of your primarch and sworn to see me dead. You would not be the first.' Kolgo held up a finger, as if to silence anyone who might think to interrupt. 'And yet, I live.'

Kolgo looked around the courtroom. The expression of Chapter Master Pugh was impossible to read. Other Space Marines looked angry or uncomfortable, not knowing what Kolgo was trying to say but certain that they would not like it.

'And why?' said Kolgo. 'Why am I not dead? I am satisfied that it is not through fear that you refrain from killing me. A Space Marine knows no fear, and in any case, the fulfilling of a blood oath takes far higher priority than the possibility of being lynched or prosecuted by your fellows. And as I have said, I myself am scarcely capable of defending myself against any one of you. So what is it that keeps me alive? What strange gravity stays your hands? The answer is power. I have power, and it is a force so irresistible, so immovable, that even Space Marines must make way for it sometimes. I say this not to tempt you into action, I hasten to say, but to show you that it is matters of power that determine so much of the decisions we make whether we understand that or not.

'This trial is about power. It is about who holds it, to which power one bows, and the natural order of the Imperium as it is created by the power its members wield. I say to you that the principal crime of the Soul Drinkers is the flouting of that natural order of power. You have refrained from violence against me because of the place I hold in that order. Sarpedon and his brothers would not. They act outside that order. Their actions denigrate and damage it. But it is this order that holds the Imperium together, that maintains the existence of the Imperium and the species of man. Without it, all is Chaos. This is the crime for which I condemn the Soul Drinkers, and thus do I demand to fall upon them a punishment that not only removes them from this universe, but proclaims the horror of their deaths as the consequence for railing against the order the Emperor Himself put in place.'

Kolgo punctuated his final words by banging his armoured fist on the backs of the seats in front of him. He turned, faced the Justice Lord, and inclined his head in as much of a bow as an Inquisitor Lord would give.

'Are you finished?' asked Pugh.

'This statement is concluded,' said Kolgo.

'Pah,' came a voice from the galleries. 'One of a thousand he would give if he had leave. The Lord Inquisitor's desire to hear his own voice borders on the scandalous!' The speaker was Siege-Captain Daviks of the Silver Skulls. The Silver Skulls beside him nodded and murmured their assent.

'You wish to make a counter-statement, siege-captain?' said Pugh.

'I wish for the statements to end!' snapped Daviks. 'This creature in the dock before us is not deserving of a trial. This thing is a mutant! In what Imperium of Man is a mutant afforded the right to be bedded down in this nest of pointless words? Reinez was right. I have never known a trial granted to such a thing. I have known only execution!'

Several warriors shouted agreements. Pugh held up a hand for silence but the din only grew.

'Kill this thing, kill all the creatures you hold in your brigs, and let this be done with!' shouted Daviks.

'I will have order!' bellowed Pugh. He was not a man who raised his voice often, and as he rose to his feet the calls for violence died. 'Apothecary Asclephin has borne witness that Sarpedon is to be tried as a Space Marine. There the matter ends. You will get your execution, Captain Daviks, but in return you must have patience. I will see justice done here.'

'A better illustration of power I could not have created myself,' added Kolgo.

'Your statement is concluded,' said Pugh. 'Who will speak?'

'We have not yet heard from the accused in the dock,' replied Captain N'Kalo of the Iron Knights. 'If we are to have a trial, the accused must speak in his defence.'

Pugh's recent interjections kept the retorts to N'Kalo's words to a minimum.

'I would speak in my defence,' said Sarpedon. 'I would have you all hear me. I did not turn from the authority of the Imperium at some perverse whim.

For everything I have done, I have had a reason. Lord Kolgo's words have done nothing but to convince me further that my every action was justified.'

'You will speak,' said Pugh, 'whether those observing like it or not. But you cannot speak as yet, for further charges are to be levelled against you.'

'Name them,' said Sarpedon.

'That by the machinations of your authority,' said Reinez, 'four Imperial Fists died on the planet of Selaaca, three scouts and one sergeant of the Tenth Company. To the Emperor's protection have their souls been commended, and to the example of Dorn have they measured themselves with honour. Their deaths have been added to the list of crimes of which you are accused.' Reinez spoke as if reading from a statement, and the real anger behind his words was far more eloquent. He enjoyed pouring further accusations on Sarpedon, especially one that hit so home to the Imperial Fists on whose forced neutrality Sarpedon depended.

The Imperial Fists around Pugh made gestures of prayer. The other Space Marines gathered had evidently not heard of these charges, and a few quiet questions passed between them.

'I know nothing of this!' retorted Sarpedon. 'No Imperial Fist died by a Soul Drinker's hand on Selaaca. My battle-brothers surrendered to Lysander without a fight. The captain himself can attest to this!'

'These crimes were not committed during your capture,' said Pugh. 'Scout Orfos?'

The Imperial Fists parted to allow a scout through their ranks. In most Chapters, the Imperial Fists among them, a recruit served a term as a scout before his training and augmentation was completed. Since he was not yet a Space Marine, and since power armour was ill-suited to anything requiring stealth, these recruits served as infiltrators and reconnaissance troops. Scout Orfos still wore the carapace armour, light by the standards of the Adeptus Astartes, and cameleoline cloak of a scout. He was relatively youthful and unscarred compared to the Imperial Fists around him, but he had a sharp face with observant eyes and he moved with the assurance of a confident soldier.

'Scout,' said Pugh, 'describe to the court what you witnessed on Selaaca.'

'My squad under Sergeant Borakis was deployed to investigate a location that the castellan's command had provided to us,' began Orfos. 'In a tomb beneath the ground we found a place that the Soul Drinkers had built there.'

Sarpedon listened, but his mind wanted to rebel. He had never heard of any Soul Drinker travelling to Selaaca before he had gone there to face the necrons. The planet was not mentioned in the Chapter archives. It could not be a coincidence that of all the millions of planets in the Imperium, he should stumble upon one where some forgotten brothers had built a tomb thousands of years ago. A tomb which, as Orfos's evidence continued, had been built to keep all but the most determined infiltrator out.

Sarpedon felt a wrenching inside him as Orfos described the deaths of the other scouts. Orfos was well-disciplined and little emotion showed in his words, but his face and intonation suggested the effort he was making in bottling it up. Orfos had been trained to hate, hypno-doctrination and battlefield experience teaching him the value of despising his enemy. That hate was turned on Sarpedon now. Sarpedon felt, for the first time in that courtroom, truly accused. He felt guilt at the Imperial Fists' deaths, though this, of all his supposed crimes, was the only one that he had not committed.

'It was a Dreadnought,' Orfos was saying. 'The tomb had been built to house it. It had been kept frozen to preserve its occupant...'

'Justice Lord,' said Sarpedon. 'My Chapter has no Dreadnoughts. The last was lost with the destruction of the *Scintillating Death* six thousand years ago. It is made clear in the archives of–'

'The accused will be silent!' snapped Pugh. 'Or he will be made silent.' A glance from Pugh towards Lysander suggested how Pugh would go about shutting Sarpedon up. 'Scout Orfos. Continue.'

'The Dreadnought awoke,' said Orfos, 'and I voxed for reinforcements. A team of servitors and Techmarines made the tomb safe and disarmed the Dreadnought.'

'Did it speak to you?' asked Pugh.

'It did,' said Orfos. 'It placed itself in my custody, and told me its name.'

'Which was?'

'Daenyathos.'

Sarpedon slumped against the pulpit.

Daenyathos was dead. The heretic Croivas Ascenian had killed him six thousand years ago.

His mind raced. The impossibility of it stunned him.

Of all the names he might have heard listed as a traitor, Daenyathos was the last he would have expected. Daenyathos had written down the Soul Drinkers' way of war, and even after casting aside the ways of the old Chapter, Sarpedon had still found infinite wisdom in Daenyathos's works. Every Soul Drinker had read the *Catechisms Martial*. Sarpedon had fought his wars by its words. It had given him strength. Daenyathos was a symbol of what the Imperium could be – wise and strong, tempered with discipline but beloved of knowledge. Now the philosopher-soldier's name had been dragged into this sordid business.

And if he was alive... if Daenyathos truly lived still, as only a Space Marine in a Dreadnought could...

'I swear...' said Sarpedon. 'If he lives... I swear I did not know...'

'And by what do you swear?' snarled Captain Borganor from the gallery. 'On your traitor's honour? On the tombs of my brothers you have slain? I say this proves the Soul Drinkers are not mere renegades! I say they have been corrupt for millennia, under the guidance of Daenyathos, sworn to the powers of the Enemy and primed to bring about some plot of the warp's foul making!'

Voices rose in agreement. Sarpedon's mind whirled too quickly for him to pay attention to them. If Daenyathos was alive, then what did that mean? The Soul Drinkers had gone to Selaaca to stave off the necron invasion of an innocent world, and yet Daenyathos had been there all along. Sarpedon traced back the events of the last weeks, his capture, the assault on the necron overlord's tomb, the battles on Raevenia and the clash with the Mechanicus fleet, and before that...

Iktinos. It had been Iktinos who had suggested the *Brokenback* flee into the Veiled Region. The Chaplain's arguments had made sense – the Veiled Region was a good place to hide. And yet he had led the Soul Drinkers straight to the tomb of Daenyathos. Iktinos must have known Daenyathos was there. And yet Iktinos had been one of Sarpedon's most trusted friends, the spiritual heart of the Chapter...

'Is he here?' said Sarpedon, hoping to be heard over the shouting. 'Daenyathos. Is he here, on the *Phalanx*?'

'He shall be brought to the dock in time,' replied Pugh.

'I must speak with him!'

'You shall do no such thing,' retorted Pugh. 'There will be no provision made for you to plot further! When your trial is complete, Daenyathos's shall begin. That is all you shall know!' Pugh banged a gauntlet. 'I will have order under the eyes of Dorn! Lysander, bring me order!'

'Silence!' yelled Lysander, striding across the courtroom. 'The Justice Lord will have silence! There is no Space Marine here too lofty of station to be spared the face of my shield! Silence!'

'This farce must end!' shouted Borganor. 'So deep the corruption lies! So foul a thing the Soul Drinkers are, and now we see, they have always been! Burn them, crush them, hurl them into space, and excise this infection!'

Lysander vaulted the gallery rail and powered his way up to Borganor. The Howling Griffons were not quick enough to hold him back, and it was by no means certain they could have done so at all. Lysander bore down on Borganor, face to face, storm shield pressing against Borganor's chest and pinning him in place. Lysander had his hammer in his other hand, held out as a signal for the other Howling Griffons to stay back.

'I said silence,' growled Lysander.

'My thanks, captain,' said Pugh. 'You may stand down.'

Lysander backed away from Borganor. The two Space Marines held each other's gaze as Lysander returned to the courtroom floor.

'There will be no further need for calls to order,' said Pugh. 'You are here at my sufferance. When my patience runs out with you, you return to your ships and leave. Captain Lysander is authorised to escort you. Scout Orfos, you are dismissed.'

Orfos saluted and left the gallery, the Imperial Fists bowing their heads in respect to him and his lost brothers as he went.

Reinez had watched the tumult with a smile on his face. Nothing could have pleased him more than seeing Sarpedon's distress, except perhaps Sarpedon's severed head.

'Who will speak next?' said Pugh. 'Who can bring further illumination to the crimes of the accused?'

Varnica of the Doom Eagles stood. 'I would speak,'

he said. 'The court must hear what I have to say, for it bears directly on the nature of the Soul Drinkers' crimes. I bring not rhetoric or bile. I bring the truth, as witnessed by my own eyes.'

'Then speak, Librarian,' said Pugh.

The courtroom hushed, and Varnica began.

# CHAPTER FOUR

THE BEAUTY OF Berenika Altis was a strange thing, like a work of art not understood. It had been built in the shape of an enormous star, two of its five points extending out to sea on spurs of artificial land. Each point of the star was devoted to a different trade, the five legendary guilds that had built and financed this city. The shape was a reminder of its original purpose as an exclusive retreat for those who deserved better than the other bleak, stagnant cities of the planet Tethlan's Holt. At the centre of the star was the Sanctum Nova Pecuniae, once a palace existing purely for the beautification of Berenika Altis, and one that now served as the seat of government of Tethlan's Holt.

Fifteen days ago all communication had ceased

with Berenika Altis. Eight million people had vanished. The planetary authorities, those who had not disappeared with the rest of the government, reacted as any good Imperial citizen would when confronted with the unknown. They had sealed off the city, quarantined it, and resolved to pretend that it had never existed.

The Doom Eagles were not satisfied with such solutions.

'A BRITTLE BEAUTY,' said Librarian Varnica as the Thunderhawk droned in low over the north seaward spur of Berenika Altis. The rear ramp was down and Varnica had disengaged his grav-couch restraints, holding onto the rail overhead to lean forwards and get a better look at his target from the air.

'I see only stupidity,' replied Sergeant Novas. His voice did not sound over the gunship's engines, but the vox-link carried it straight into Varnica's inner ear. 'A shift in the sea floor and two-fifths of that city would sink into the ocean.'

'Perhaps,' said Varnica, 'that's the point. Nothing speaks of wealth like spending a great deal of it on something that might be gone any moment.'

'Looks like they got their wish,' said Novas. 'Eventually. It wasn't the sea that got them, but something did.'

'Quite the conundrum,' said Varnica. 'What a puzzle box they built for us.'

As the Thunderhawk swooped lower, the streets were revealed. Each spur of the city had been dedicated to a different guild and though centuries of rebuilding and repurposing had followed, the original imprint remained. The Embalmers' Quarter was arranged in neat rows, the buildings resembling elegant tombs. The Jewelcutters' Quarter was all angular patterns, triangular sections of streets and many-sided intersections echoing the complex facings of a cut diamond. The Victuallers' District was a gloomy, sheer-sided area of warehouses and long, low halls. The industrial feel of the Steelwrights' Cordon was entirely an affectation, with rust-streaked metal chimneys and crumbling brickwork concealing the salons and feasting halls where the great and good of Berenika Altis had celebrated their superiority. The Flagellants' Quarter, founded with the money taken from those who paid to have their sins scourged from them, echoed the flagellants' frenzy with twisted, winding streets and asymmetrical buildings that seemed poised to topple over or slide into rubble. The Sanctum Nova Pecuniae held the disparate regions together, as if it pinned them to the surface of Tethlan's Holt to keep them from crawling off to their own devices.

The streets were visible now, the buildings separating into distinct blocks. The streets seemed paved with a haphazard mosaic of blacks and reds, the same pattern covering every avenue and alley.

It was a mosaic of corpses.

The smell of it confirmed the few reports that had reached the Doom Eagles. The smell of rotting bodies. It was familiar to every Space Marine, to every Emperor's servant whose business was death.

Varnica looked on, fascinated. He had seen many

disasters. When not called upon to attend some critical battlezone, it was disasters that attracted the Doom Eagles. Some Chapters sought out ancient secrets, others lost comrades, others the most dangerous sectors of the galaxy to test their martial prowess. The Doom Eagles sought out catastrophe. It was less a policy of the Chapter's command, and more a compulsion, a dark fascination as powerful as the pronouncements of the Chapter Master.

This was a true disaster. Not the side effect of a war, or a revolt that had turned bloody. It was a catastrophe from outside, beyond the context of anything that had happened on Tethlan's Holt. The scale of death was appalling. Millions lay decomposing in the streets. And yet a part of Varnica's mind relished it. Here was not only a mystery, but a scale of horror that made it worth solving.

The Thunderhawk approached its landing zone, a circular plaza in the Embalmers' Quarter. Like every other possible landing site, it was strewn with bodies. Fat flies whipped around the Thunderhawk's passenger compartment as it passed through a cloud of them, spattering against Varnica's armour and the eyepieces of his power armour's helmet. He took it off as the Thunderhawk came down to land.

The grisly cracking sound Varnica heard was the cracking of bones beneath the Thunderhawk's landing gear. More crunched below the lower lip of the embarkation ramp as it opened up all the way. Varnica walked off the gunship onto the ground of Berenika Altis, pushing aside the bodies with his feet so he did not have to stand on them.

'Perimeter!' shouted Sergeant Novas. His squad jumped down after him and spread out around the plaza. Within moments the foul blackish flesh of the bodies was clinging to the armour of their feet and shins, shining wetly in the afternoon sun. The filters built into Varnica's lungs took care of the toxins and diseases in the air, but anyone without those augmentations would have vomited or choked on the stench

Techmarine Hamilca was last out, accompanied by the quartet of servitors that followed him everywhere like loyal pets.

'What do you think, Techmarine?' asked Varnica.

Hamilca looked around him. The tombs of the Embalmers' Quarter showed no sign of gunfire or destruction, and the sun was shining down from a blue sky. If one cast his gaze up far enough, there was nothing to see but a handsome city and fine weather. The bodies seemed incongruous, as if they did not belong here, even though they were undoubtedly the remains of this city's population.

'It is a beautiful day,' said Hamilca, and turned to adjust the sensors of his servitors.

'One day,' said Novas, 'they'll put your brain back in, tin man.'

Hamilca did not answer that. Varnica knelt to examine the bodies at his feet.

What remained of their clothing ranged from the boiler suits of menials to the silks and furs of the city's old money elite. The wounds were from fingers and teeth, or from whatever had been at hand. Tools and wrenches. Walking canes. A few kitchen knives, chunks of masonry, hatpins. One burly man's throat had a woman's silken scarf tied around it as a garrotte. Its previous owner might well have been the slender woman whose corpse lay, broken-necked, beside him. They had killed with anything at hand, which meant the time between normality and killing had been measured in minutes.

'It was the Red Night,' said Varnica.

'Can you be sure?' asked Hamilca.

'I admire your desire to gather evidence,' said Varnica, 'but I need see no more than this. It is my soul that tells me. So many places like this we have seen, and I hear their echo off the walls of this city. The Red Night came here. I know it.'

'Then why are we here?' said Novas. His squad was by now in a loose perimeter formation, bolters trained down the avenues of tombs radiating out from the plaza. Novas's Space Marines were well drilled, and Novas himself possessed a desire to be seen doing his duty, combined with a blessed lack of imagination. These qualities made his squad Varnica's escort of choice. They could be trusted to do their job and leave the thinking to the Librarian. 'The last time we came to a place touched by the Red Night, there was nought to find though we turned that place inside out. Why will Berenika Altis be any different?'

'Just smell,' said Varnica.

Novas snarled with a lack of amusement.

'Do not scorn such advice, sergeant!' Varnica breathed in deeply, theatrically. 'Ah, what a bouquet! Ruptured entrails! Liquefying muscle! They are fresh! Compared to the last places we visited, these bodies are ripe! We have got here earlier than before, Novas. These bodies still have flesh on them. We are not picking over a skeletonised heap but sloshing through the very swamp of their decay. Whatever brought the Red Night here, there is a good chance it still remains in Berenika Altis.'

'We shall not find it here,' said Hamilca. He was consulting readings from the screen built into the chest of one servitor. Another was taking pict-grabs using the lens that replaced both its eyes, roving across the corpse-choked streets. 'Not in these streets.'

Varnica held up the burly man's corpse. It was sagging and foul, the joints giving way so the limbs hung unnaturally loose. The head lolled on its fractured neck. 'He will not tell us anything more, that is for certain.' He looked towards the skyline at the centre of Berenika Altis. The Sanctum Nova Pecuniae rose above the necropoli of the Embalmers' Quarter, its spires scything towards the sky in golden arcs. 'Let's ask the people who count.'

THE RED NIGHT.

It was a wave of madness. Or, it was a disease that caused violent hallucinations. Or, it was a mental attack perpetrated by cunning xenos. Or, it was the natural consequence of Imperial society's repression of human nature. Or, it was the influence of the warp seeping into real space.

The Red Night caused everyone in the afflicted city to tear one another apart. The urge to do so came over them instantly. Most such disturbances led to an exodus of refugees fleeing the carnage, as the madness spread along some social vector. The Red Night, however, worked instantly. No word escaped the city, and so no one could intervene until the lack of communication forced an investigation and the first horrified reports came back of the scale of the death.

It had happened five times that the Doom Eagles knew of. Four times Doom Eagles Space Marines had reached the afflicted city to find nothing but a multitude of well-rotted bodies, their flesh turned to black slurry caking the gutters, and bones already starting to bleach. The fourth time, Varnica perceived a spiralling route that connected the instances of the Red Night and, more through intuition than calculation, plotted a route for his taskforce that took it within two weeks' travel of Tethlan's Holt. When the whispers of the Red Night had been intercepted by the astropath on the *Killing Shadow*, the strike cruiser commanded by Varnica, the ship had dropped out of the warp long enough to point its prow towards Tethlan's Holt.

In time, the Red Night would evolve completely into legend. Every voidborn shiphand would know someone who knew someone who had lost a friend to it. Collected tales of the Red Night would fill half-throne chapbooks. Melodramas and tragedies would be written about it. Street-corner madmen would rave about the Red Night coming the next day, or the next week, or the next year, to take up all the sinners in its bloody embrace.

Varnica would not let that happen. The truth about the Red Night would be uncovered before all hope of its discovery disappeared among the legends. Too often the Imperium caused the truth to atrophy, replaced by fear and madness. It was Varnica's duty, among the many a Space Marine had to the Emperor, to scrape back as much of the truth as he could from the hungry maw of history. Each time the Red Night had struck, he had got a little closer to that truth, something he felt rather than understood, as if the screams of the dying got more intense in his imagination each time he saw those dreadful dead streets from the sky.

The truth was in Berenika Altis. Varnica knew this as only a Librarian could. Only a psyker's inner eye could perceive something so absolutely. Varnica would discover the truth behind the Red Night, or he would not leave this city. He had never been so certain of anything.

THE BODIES SUITED the Sanctum Nova Pecuniae. It resembled a scene from a tragic play, painted by a master who placed it on a fanciful stage of soaring columns and marble, the dead contorted, their faces anguished, every clutching hand and sunken eye socket the telling of another story amid the drama.

The ground floor of the palace was a single vast space, punctuated with columns and shrines. It was possible to walk, and indeed see, from one side of the palace to the other from outside through the vast archways, without encountering a wall. To a new visitor the place would at first seem hollow, as if forming some metaphor for transparency or absence of government. The complex architecture of the roof, however, formed of overlapping vaults and petals, hid the spaces where the government actually met and did business. This was a metaphor, too, thought Varnica as he cast his senses around him, half as a soldier and half as an appreciator of the palace's art. The really important people in Berenika Altis existed on a higher plane, like a heaven sealed off among the friezes and inscriptions of the shadowy ceiling.

The Doom Eagles had entered through an archway, above which were carved words in High Gothic proclaiming that portion of the Sanctum Nova Pecuniae to have been built by the Guild of Steelwrights. Notable past masters of that guild were remembered in the statues that stood in alcoves, forming shrines to the exemplars of the guild's values. They held formidable-looking tools, multiwrenches and pneumohammers, and had faces that looked like they had been beaten out of steel themselves.

'These dead were not mere citizens,' said Hamilca, whose medical servitor was playing its sensors over a knot of corpses at the base of the nearest pillar. 'They wear the marks of nobility. Here, the badge of the Flagellants' Guild. This one wears cloth of gold and ermine.'

'The government must have been in session,' said Varnica. 'Perhaps the timing was deliberate?'

Novas spat on the floor. He was a superstitious type, and the horror of this place was more spiritual than the mundanity of the bodies outside. Showing his contempt with a wad of phlegm scared away the dark things mustering on the other side of the Veil, so the superstitions went.

A pillar a short distance away had a particularly

dense heap of bodies around it. They were three deep, as if they had been clambering over one another to get at the pillar. Bloody smudges from fingers and hands painted the flutes of the pillar. Varnica walked over to them, picking his way past the master artisans and councillors who lay in his way. 'Here,' he said. 'There is a way up.' He hauled on one of the blade-like stone flutes and it swung open, to reveal a tight spiral staircase corkscrewing up through the pillar.

A body fell out. Its face had been torn so much it was impossible to tell the back of the head from the front. Two severed arms tumbled behind it, neither of them belonging to the first body. Varnica looked up the staircase and saw bodies wedged into the pillar, clogging it up before the first twist.

The leaders of Berenika Altis had thought the day-to-day business of government vulgar enough to hide it in the grand architecture of the Sanctum. Men and women had died trying to get at the concealed working of government, even as they were rending each other apart. Was it some bestial remnant of memory that caused them to flee to the only place a nobleman might feel safe? Or had there been something in the madness itself that compelled them to seek something above?

Varnica said nothing. He simple forced his armoured form into the tight space of the staircase and began dragging down the bodies that stood in his way.

HAMILCA'S SERVITORS AIDED the removal of corpses greatly. Thirty more of them lay beside the pillar, all horribly mauled as if chewed up and spat out, before Varnica reached the top. Novas's battle-brothers followed him up, crouch-walking in the cramped space.

Varnica emerged in a chamber of maps and portraits, a sort of antechamber before the government debating chambers and offices. The lower portraits, more stern steelwright masters along with well-heeled embalmers and jewelcutters in their leather aprons, were spattered with blood. Framed maps depicted early layouts of Berenika Altis and the changing political divisions of Tethlan's Holt. Various landmasses were drawn in differing sizes from map to map, reflecting their relative importance. Varnica remembered that every planet in the Imperium had a history like this, shifting, waxing and waning for thousands of years, while the Imperium beyond did not care unless something happened to end that history entirely.

The bodies here were clustered around one door. Hamilca moved to examine them while Novas's squad covered all the entrances.

Varnica took a better look at one portrait, mounted just high enough to have avoided the worst of the spraying blood. It was of a member of the Flagellants' Guild. It was a large woman, well-fed rather than naturally bulky, whose ample bosom was encased ridiculously in an embroidered version of a penitent's sackcloth robe. Spots of red makeup simulated self-inflicted wounds and her hair was piled up in a magnificent structure held in place by the kinds of serrated needles more properly used for extracting

confessions. In one hand she held, like a royal scep-
tre, a scourge with three spiked chains, the implement
of her guild's craft.

In the lower corner was a handprint in blood. It
was made too surely and deliberately to have been
accidental, from a flailing fist. Someone had used this
wall to steady themselves. Someone wounded.

Varnica followed the tracks through the gory mess
of the floor. 'They were following someone,' he said
as he paced carefully towards the body-choked door.
'He was wounded and limping but he wasn't scrabbling along like an animal, as the rest of the souls
were. They were after him. The Red Night sent them
after one man in particular.'

The tracks led to the door where Hamilca's servitors
were making a survey of the various wounds. 'They
dashed themselves to death against the door,' said
Hamilca. 'Few wounds from hands or teeth. They
broke themselves here trying to get through.'

The door had been panelled with wood to make
it in keeping with the rest of the government office,
but that façade had splintered with the assault to
reveal the solid metal beneath. It was a security door
to keep out just the kind of frenzied assault that had
broken against it.

Varnica sighed. He did not like having to use the
full range of his talents. He had always felt that a
psyker should properly be something subtle, an intelligence weapon, reading or remaking minds, perhaps
astrally projecting to make the perfect spy. His own
talents had taken a form that he found ugly in the
extreme. Still, duties were duties, and he had the best

way of getting through the door that would not risk destroying evidence beyond.

He clenched his right fist and thought of anger. The lines of the room seemed to warp around his fist, as if it were encased in a lens that distorted anything seen through it. Reality did not like it when he did this, and he had to fight it.

Black and purple rippled around the gauntlet. Sparks crackled across the segments of armour around his fingers. The region of deviant gravity Varnica willed into being bowed and seethed as he drew back the fist that now disobeyed the laws of force and energy.

Varnica punched the door clean off its mountings. The whole room seemed to shudder, its dimensions flickering slightly out of balance as Varnica's psychic power discharged in a thrust of force. The metal door clanged into the room beyond.

The Librarium of the Doom Eagles liked to classify its members' psychic powers according to categories and strength. Varnica's was referred to as the Hammerhand, a crude but effective power that typically augmented the Librarian's capacity for hand-to-hand combat. Varnica disliked the Librarium's testing of its intensity, but he conceded that it was powerful, and that it would get more powerful the more he exercised the mental muscles that powered it.

Varnica shook out his hand as the power around it dissipated.

Novas smiled. 'No door is locked when one wields the Emperor's key,' he said.

'Quite,' replied Varnica. *The Emperor's key*. It sounded

rather more elegant than 'Hammerhand'.

The room he had opened was an archive. Ceiling-high banks of index cards, yellowing ledger books and scroll racks exuded a smell of old paper that almost overpowered the stink of decay.

On a reading table was sprawled the single body this room contained. It wore grand robes that suggested high office in the planet's government. The dead man still had a dagger in his hand, probably worn more for ceremony than self-defence. The point of the dagger pinned a handful of papers to the tabletop. Several opened drawers and scattered papers suggested he had rooted around and found them in a hurry, and in his last moments made sure that whoever found him would also find those specific documents.

The man had torn his own throat out with his other hand. He lay in the black stain of his blood. His body sagged with decay beneath the robes now filthy with old blood and the seepage of rot.

Varnica pulled out the dagger and looked at the documents this man had fought to call attention to, even while the Red Night was taking control of him.

They were receipts and blueprints for work done on the sewers beneath the Jewelcutters' Quarter, between seventy and forty years before. Varnica leafed through them rapidly. They were nothing more than the detritus of a civil service that loved to remember its own deeds.

'What was he trying to tell us?' asked Hamilca.

'He was telling us,' said Varnica, 'to look down'.

* * *

THE FIRST OF them had a face like a knot of knuckles, deep red flesh that oozed hissing molten metal, sinewy arms that wielded a smouldering blade of black steel. It congealed up from the black mass of old blood pooling in the sewer; that drizzle of gore from the bloodshed above. Its face split open, tearing skin, and it screamed. A whip-like tongue lashed out.

More of them were emerging. Dozens of them.

The sewers. Berenika Altis's greatest achievement, some said. Hidden from the world above, each section of sewer was like a cathedral nave, a monument to glory for its own sake, lit by faded glow-globes and faced with marble and plaster murals. Most cities of the Imperium would have gathered here to worship. On Berenika Altis the combined efforts of the flagellants and the jewelcutters had created instead such a place to accommodate the filth of the city.

It was here the blood had flowed. It was here the Doom Eagles had come, following the signs left them by that unnamed nobleman who had died in the Sanctum. It was here they realised they were getting close to the secret of the Red Night.

'Daemons!' yelled Novas. 'Close formation. Rapid fire!'

More daemons were congealing from the blood that slaked the floor of the sewer section. They rushed at the Doom Eagles, hate in their eyes and their swords held high.

Novas's squad drew in close around Varnica and Hamilca. The ten Adeptus Astartes hammered out a volley of bolter fire. Three or four daemons were shredded at once, gobbets of their molten metal blood hissing against the marble walls. But Varnica counted more than twenty more daemons now charging to attack. Bolter fire would thin them out, but this was a task that had to be finished by hand.

Varnica thrust his right hand into the complex holster he wore on one hip. The sections of his force claw closed around his hand. When he withdrew it, it was encased in a pair of sharp blades in a pincer, each blade swirling with psychoactive circuitry.

Varnica let his psychic power fill his fists. Distasteful as it was, it was for encounters like this that he had trained his mental muscles. The air warped around his hands and the force claw glowed blue-white with its power.

The daemons rushed closer. Novas shot another down, blowing its yowling head from its shoulders. Varnica pushed his way between the two Doom Eagles in front of him and dived into the fray.

His force claw closed on one and sheared it in two. A fountain of red-hot blood sprayed over his armour, hissing where it touched the ceramite. His other fist slammed down, just missing the next daemon in his way and ripping a crater out of the flagstone floor. He span, driving his right elbow into the daemon and backhanding another hard enough to rip its whole jaw off.

He imagined his fists were meteors, smouldering masses of rock, attached to him by chains, and wherever he swung them anything in the way would be destroyed. That was the secret of many a psychic weapon – imagination, the ability to mould them in a psyker's mind's eye into whatever he needed them to be. Varnica needed them to be wrecking balls smashing through the hideous things that reared up around him. Their bodies were walls to be battered down. They were doorways to be opened with the Emperor's Key.

Rapid gunfire sprayed around him. Hamilca's servitors were not just scientific instruments – one had opened up, its torso becoming an archway of metal and skin within which were mounted a pair of rotator cannon. They blazed away at Hamilca's direction, even as Hamilca himself took aim with his plasma pistol and blew the arm off another daemon before it could fully congeal into existence.

Varnica's shoulder guard turned away one daemon's blade and he ducked under another. He rose, claw first, lifting a daemon above his head and letting the pincers snap open so the daemon was sheared in two. He stamped down on the blade of the first daemon and, as it fought to wrench its weapon up to strike again, Varnica drove an elbow into its face and punched it in the chest as it reeled. Purple-black light shimmered around the gravity well of his fist as it ripped through the thing's ribs and burst out through its back.

Hands grabbed Varnica by the collar and backpack of his armour, wrenching him down. He fought to straighten up but the strength and suddenness of the attack had caught him off-guard.

He saw the face of Novas, whose hands were pulling him down. Another Doom Eagle fired past Varnica, bolter shells blasting ragged holes in the daemon who had been about to decapitate Varnica with its blade.

'Must I nursemaid you through every fight?' growled Novas.

The Doom Eagles now formed an execution line to bring their bolters to bear on the remaining daemons. Varnica had scattered their charge and now they were trying to regroup, or to attack in ones and twos easily shot down. A final few volleys of bolter fire brought down the remaining daemons, blasting off limbs and shredding torsos. The remnants dissolved into the mass of blood and filth that covered the sewer floor.

Novas helped Varnica to his feet.

Varnica clapped the sergeant on the shoulder. 'You see, brother?' he said. 'We are close. Blessed is the enemy that announces himself to us so!'

'Blessed is your brother that keeps you alive,' said Novas.

'We know,' said Hamilca, adjusting the programming of his gun-servitor, 'that the enemy fears our closing in on him. Therefore, we approach some place of significance to him. The documents from the Sanctum suggested the importance of a major intersection three hundred metres to our west.'

'It's the blood,' said Varnica. 'The bloodshed in the city finds its way down here, to the sewers. The enemy places himself some place where the blood gathers, and then... uses it? Fuels something with it?'

'Bathes in it, for all we know,' said Novas.

Varnica checked his wargear. The daemons' blood had burned pockmarks into his armour. Nothing important was damaged. One of Novas's squad had suffered a deep sword wound to one arm, and the helmet of another's power armour had been smashed. Varnica recognised the pugnacious features of Brother Solicus, a veteran of Novas's command. Solicus would make a point of ignoring the minor wound on the forehead and the blood that trickled down his face.

No great harm done, thought Varnica.

'Move on,' he said, and led the way westwards.

WHEN HE LOOKED back on the Red Night of Berenika Altis, it would always be the face of Gunther Kephilaes that Varnica would remember first. That look of surprise when he saw the Doom Eagles entering his realm, to be replaced with an awful smile, as if they were guests he had been waiting for all this time.

The second memory would be of the writing on the walls. Kephilaes, later identified as an arch-heretic who had escaped repeated attempts to execute him on a dozen worlds, had chosen for his base of operations a cistern in the sewers of Berenika Altis. This place, an enormous tank built to accommodate overflow from the sewers, had been drained of water so that when the Red Night occurred, it had filled up with blood. The roof was an enormous dome carved with images of jewelcutters on one side, flaunting their elaborate arrays of jewellery and gems, and on the other a parade of flagellants lashing supplicants with their scourges. This dome, and every visible surface of wall and pillar, was covered in writing. At first it appeared black, but it was in fact a dark reddish brown. Every word had been written in blood.

Varnica, like every Space Marine, had been taught that speed of decision was essential in the opening seconds of battle. Even before Gunther Kephilaes's face had broken into that mad grin, Varnica had decided that Novas would pin the heretic down with gunfire while Varnica himself would close across the duckboards and jerry-built rafts that had been lashed together over the surface of the blood. Kephilaes sat on an island made of toppled pillars in the centre of the blood, hundreds of books and tattered papers lying on the broken stone or floating on the surface around his makeshift pulpit. Varnica could reach him, scale the drums of the broken pillars and get to grips with this heretic in a handful of seconds. He just needed those seconds, and the job would be done.

A few hand signals passed the orders on to Novas's squad, who immediately began to fan out around the ledge running around the cistern to get multiple angles of fire on the enemy.

Varnica knew by now why Kephilaes was happy to see them. These intruders meant fresh blood in which to dip the quill he held in one gnarled hand, the white feather stained with old blood. As Varnica ran forwards he noted the scholarly robes Kephilaes wore, the straggly white hair and hooked axe-like face, the way the substance of his large white eyes seemed to liquefy and run in greyish tears down his cheeks.

Kephilaes raised his quill and sketched a symbol in the air. The same symbol appeared scored into the chest of Brother Kouras of Novas's squad, the channel

cut deep down through the armour in the flesh of
the Adeptus Astartes's chest and abdomen. Kouras
slumped to one knee and toppled forwards into the
blood. Another of the squad ran to grab him and haul
him onto the ledge. With a flourish, Kephilaes drew
another symbol into the second Adeptus Astartes's
face, the faceplate of his helmet sliced into pieces and
revealing the red wetness of the scored meat inside.
The second Space Marine was dead before he fell into
the blood behind the first.

The gunfire began. Bolter shells erupted against
the fallen pillars. Kephilaes drew a letter that hung
in the air in lines of burning red, a complex sigil that
formed a shield against which the bolter fire burst
harmlessly.

Varnica leapt from one platform to another. This
one nearly gave way beneath him. He jumped the
last few metres, scrabbling for a handhold on the pillar drum he hit chest-first. A few more seconds. He
needed a few more seconds, and then it would be
over, and he would know what the Red Night meant
at last.

He made his own handholds, the stone warping
against his fingers as the psychic field around them
leapt into life.

Kephilaes laughed and whooped as he scrawled in
the air with abandon. Squad Novas dived for what
little cover they could find as deep burning letters
appeared sunk into the blood-spattered stone behind
them. The letters were in an unfamiliar alphabet
but somehow they made an appalling sense as
Varnica glanced behind him. They were exultations,

celebrations of some vast power that had reached down from the warp and torn out what little sanity this heretic had possessed. The white-haired lunatic above Varnica had done all this to extol the virtues of heresy.

Novas fell just as Varnica closed on the heretic. A message in that profane alphabet appeared across his face, chest and left shoulder. It said that this vile thing was no longer an enemy, but was a gift to the Dark Gods, with a message of thanks scrawled upon it, to serve as an offering. Varnica could see the wet masses of Novas's lungs pumping and the glistening loops of his entrails.

Varnica roared. The hate turned white around his hands and the fire blazing around them was almost too much for him to control. He scrambled up the last of the pillars and was face to face with the madman.

The man Varnica would later identify as Gunther Kephilaes seemed happy to see him. He held out his arms, and Varnica saw the letters he had carved into his own chest beneath his scholar's robes.

'Welcome,' he said.

Varnica punched the heretic in the face with enough force to topple a wall. Kephilaes did not come apart under the blow as honest human flesh would. Dozens of sigils burned pain fully bright around him, channelling the power away from him. Enough force got through to knock Kephilaes to his knees. He held up a hand to beg.

'No,' the heretic gasped. 'You do not understand. Look around you! You do not understand.'

Varnica bent down and wrapped his arms around a section of pillar. The psychic warp around his hands made it light. He hauled it up over its head, and felt a thrill of satisfaction as its shadow passed over the heretic.

Varnica slammed the stone down. The heretic was completely crushed, the last of his witchcraft protection bled away by Varnica's first assault.

Varnica felt the crunching of bones and the wet slurp of the flesh torn flat. Just to be sure, he lifted the stone again and hammered it down once more.

Something about the deadness suddenly in the air told him this heretic had breathed his last.

Their gods always abandon them, thought Varnica. In the end.

THE RED NIGHT had been created by Gunther Kephilaes to provide the vast amounts of angrily-shed blood he needed to write down what his gods dictated to him. This was the conclusion made by the Doom Eagles' Librarium after all the evidence, including the script transcribed from the walls by Hamilca's servitors, was presented to the Chapter.

Varnica had buried Sergeant Novas that morning. Novas and the three Doom Eagles who had died at Kephilaes's hands were laid on stone slabs, anointed with medical incense to seal up the wounds where their gene-seeds had been removed, and lowered into the funerary pits where the Chapter interred their dead. Novas was buried with his bolter, his copy of *Principles of Squad-Level Purgation of the Emperor's Foes*, and the shell of a bullet that had wounded him early in his career and which he had saved as a memento mori. Varnica had prayed at the graveside, and wondered how it was that an Adeptus Astartes, with his soul steeled against the worst the galaxy could throw at him, could still feel such a human thing as grief.

Now Varnica sat among the archives of the Chapter Librarium, surrounded by freshly inked tomes filled with the profane writings of Gunther Kephilaes. Some Chapters would have destroyed the writing on the walls, and compelled any Space Marine who had seen them to cleanse himself with fire or denial until their corruption was gone. But the Doom Eagles were not like those other Chapters. They wanted to *understand*.

The Librarium's scribe-servitors were still transcribing the complex code-language into High Gothic, and filling ledger after ledger with the ramblings that resulted. Varnica had one such book in front of him, leafing through the parade of obscenity. Kephilaes had been a prophet, in part at least, and the endless train of prodigies and omens filled Varnica's mind with images of stars boiling away and the galaxy burning from core to rim.

'Librarian,' came a familiar voice.

Varnica looked up to see Techmarine Hamilca walking among the small forest of servitors that chittered away as they wrote. 'I had heard tell I would find you here.'

'Where else would one find a Librarian,' replied Varnica, 'but in a library?'

Hamilca smiled. 'Your levity need be a shield no longer, Librarian. Not while you and I are the only ones to see it. The loss of Novas has affected you more deeply than an Adeptus Astartes is apt to admit.'

'One more trial on the path, brother. One more trial.'

'What did Kephilaes have to say for himself?'

Varnica closed the tome he had finished scanning through. 'At the last count, Techmarine, seventeen million people died so he could tell us that a great feathered serpent was going to swallow the sun. And that a plague of cockroaches would devour a great empire. No details on which sun or which empire.'

'Perhaps,' said Hamilca, 'this is a task that could be shared?'

'One mind, I fear, is better than two when it comes to such things. I consider reading Kephilaes's drivel a penance for losing good Doom Eagles under my command.'

'So be it, Librarian. I and my servitors shall be ready to assist you.' Hamilca finished making a few adjustments to the scribe-servitors, and the hum of their scribbling autoquills changed pitch slightly. 'And so, brother I leave you.'

'Wait,' said Varnica. Hamilca stopped just as he was turning away. Varnica had opened another volume of the heretic's writings. 'Here. And here. The same name. A daemon prince. This is a record of its deeds.'

'Kephilaes's patron?' asked Hamilca.

'Perhaps. It was one of the most powerful of its kind, one of the brood of the Change God. Throne alive, I fear I shall need the services of the Flagellants' Guild to purify myself after reading this. It was... it was a plotter without compare. A manipulator. "There was not one living soul without a flaw that he could not widen to a chasm into which that soul would fall. A saint would be prey to this great cunning."'

'This daemon prince,' said Hamilca, sitting opposite Varnica and taking a book for himself. 'It is active now? The Red Night was some form of sacrifice to it?'

'It is possible. There is more. Here – a record of its deeds. It polluted the gene pool of a triad of worlds, so they became barbarians and warred with one another. An obscene tale about Saint Voynara, who before she died gave in to despair and called upon this prince to deliver her. And its masterpiece, the crowning glory... by Terra, what foulness I see before my eyes!'

Hamilca leaned forwards. 'Librarian? What is it? What have you seen?'

'It took a Chapter of Adeptus Astartes,' read Varnica, 'and it found in them a fatal flaw. It was their pride. That same sin we all commit, brother. Our pride, our weakness. And it turned this Chapter into an instrument of its will, through trickery compelling them to do its bidding while they thought they were doing the Emperor's work.'

'What Chapter was this?' asked Hamilca. 'Many have fallen from grace or disappeared. Is this the truth behind the fall of the Brazen Claws or the Thunder Barons?'

'No,' replied Varnica. 'This daemon prince, when its name was spoken, was called Abraxes. The Chapter it commanded was the Soul Drinkers.'

# CHAPTER FIVE

'IT WILL NOT hurt, brother,' said Sister Solace to Brother Sennon. In the cramped cell, once the living space of an engineer among the cavernous workings of the *Phalanx*, a few candles guttered, giving a struggling yellowish light. In Solace's hands was a wide-gauge needle hooked up to a pump and an intravenous bag.

'I do not fear pain,' replied Sennon, who lay bare-chested on a mattress. Sweat beaded on his face in spite of his words, and his voice came from a dry throat. He had never looked younger. In the shadows he seemed a child, defying the cowardice that his youth should have brought him.

'We need not make ourselves suffer now,' replied Solace. 'The time for such things is over. Let the

121

Emperor's kindness soothe you, and I shall make you as comfortable as possible.'

Sennon swallowed, and winced as the tip of the needle touched the vein Solace had located on the inside of his elbow. The needle slid under his skin, the pump began to work and the intravenous bag filled up. Solace hooked up a second bag, this one filled with a clear bluish liquid.

'Speak to me, my brother,' she said as Sennon's eyes drifted out of focus. 'What can you see?'

'I see you, my sister,' said Sennon. His throat constricted and he grimaced as he fought to breathe. Solace took his hand and squeezed. 'I see… this place is gone. There are no walls. The *Phalanx* is gone.'

'What is it? What do you see?'

'I see… a battlefield.' Sennon's body relaxed and his eyes seemed to focus on a point far off, past the ceiling of the cell with its rag-tag collection of mementos from a life among the engines of the *Phalanx*. Cogs and valves were piled up on a shelf beneath a metal icon painted with the symbol of the Imperial Fists. A few ragged sets of protective clothing were hung up above an alcove containing three pairs of battered steel-toed boots. A paltry collection of religious verses and children's stories filled a small cupboard beside the mattress on which Sennon lay, and on the ceiling a previous occupier had drawn images of stars and crescent moons. Sennon saw none of it. Solace thought for a moment that she could see an endless landscape of rolling plains and mountains reflected in the youth's eyes as his pupils expanded to black pools.

'It goes on forever,' said Sennon, his breath hushed. 'They are all there, all those who have died in the Emperor's name. They are there to join him in the battle at the end of time.'

'Tell me,' said Sister Solace. She adjusted the pump, which hummed louder as the liquid coursed faster through Sennon's veins. Gauges on the side of the pump read various pressures and she tried to keep them aligned. Too fast or too slow and the youth would die.

'I see billions of them, the uniforms of the Imperial Guard,' said Sennon. A million regiments, bayonets fixed, stretching across a world. And others too, ordinary men and women in a great throng. All the pious souls that have ever died. And at the forefront are the Adeptus Astartes, the Angels of Death!'

Solace looked up. A trickle of blood ran from Sennon's nose. 'As Gyranar told us?' she asked.

'Yes! Oh, sister, they are beautiful! Their armour gleams, and they have wings of gold on which to fly!' Sennon's face spread into a rapturous smile, even as blood collected in the corner of his mouth. 'Their eyes are aflame! Mighty blades shine in their hands. But… but the Enemy is here also. The Adversary. All the foul tongues of the warp have spoken into existence an army even greater!'

Sennon's body began to shudder. Solace took the youth's pulse from his wrist: his heart was hammering, his face now showing an awestruck fear.

'Speak to me of them, brother,' said Solace. 'There is nothing to fear in them. They cannot harm you. Speak to me.'

'Monsters without form. Flesh turned liquid, bathed in fire. Legions of the hateful warp-spawned, like regiments on the parade ground. Things of living corruption, smothered under a blanket of flies, seething masses of filth! Mountains of rot that vomit torrents of their progeny onto the field! And worse… sister, worse things, so sinful and lascivious in form that I cannot look away! Tear my eyes from them, sister, before they infect my soul!'

'Do not fear, brother. I am with you. The Emperor is with you. No harm can befall you, for you are under His protection. Believe in Him, believe, brother!'

'And still more,' continued Sennon, his voice speeding up into a near-gabble. 'The generals and the overlords of the Adversary. They tower! Their shadows cast whole continents into darkness! Mighty horned things, wielding blades wreathed in flame! I see a beast with a hundred heads, crowned with laurels of entwined bodies. I see… I see a creature red-skinned and immense, its wings blocking out the sun, the axe in its hand oozing blood! I can see all the galaxy's hatred in its twisted face. But it cannot harm me. Though its eyes fall on me, it cannot harm me!'

'No,' said Solace. 'It cannot.' She lacked the equipment to read Sennon's vital signs properly, so she had to do it by eye, reading the youth's pulse and the dilation of his pupils, the spasming of his fingers and toes, the alternating rigidity and weakness of his limbs. The *Phalanx* had some of the finest medicae facilities in the Imperium within its apothecarion and the sickbays used by the crew, but Solace had to do this work away from the eyes of the Imperial Fists and the *Phalanx's* crewmen. It had to be done this way.

And if Sennon died, there were others. She would go through the whole Blinded Eye if she had to. If it came to it, she would do this to herself.

'I see the gods of the warp!' gasped Sennon. 'Saints take my eyes! Faithful hands strip me of my senses! I see such things that creation cannot contain! Talon and hateful eye, wing and feather, an ocean of rotting flesh and the awful knotted limbs of the eternal dancer! And yet… and yet they are in shadow, cast by a far greater light…'

Solace checked the gauges. Most of Sennon's blood was gone. The fluid that replaced it was pumping through him, but it might not be fast enough. This was the most dangerous point, where the body hovered between bleeding to death and being suffused with its replacement blood.

'The Primarchs stand ready to command the host. Sanguinius the Angel paints his face with a million tears, one for every blood-brother who stands by his side. Russ and the Lion are side by side, their hatred for one another gone, the Wolves of Fenris and the Dark Angels standing proud. Guilliman and his host, vaster than any other army ever assembled. The Khan, the Iron-Handed One, and Vulkan, all gathered, exhorting their brothers to war! And Dorn, holy Dorn, sacred Dorn, the greatest of them, I see the banner in his hands spun from the starlight of every sun within the Emperor's domain! He is the Champion of the Emperor, the first to fight, the tip of His spear and the lightning that shall be cast down among the enemy! He shines like gold, such a blaze of fire that the enemy are blinded and they howl in anguish at the presence of such holiness!'

Sennon gasped and his eyes rolled back. Solace grabbed his hand and squeezed it tighter. 'Brother! Keep talking, brother! Tell me what you see! Sennon, tell me what you see!'

Sennon just gasped in response, spraying flecks of blood down his chin.

Solace scrabbled in the meagre selection of medical gear that lay on the floor around her. She found a syringe and tore its wrapping open. The syringe was pre-loaded with a fat needle as long as a finger and a steel cylinder of a body. Solace held the syringe point-down over Sennon's chest, muttered a prayer, and stabbed down.

The needle punched between Sennon's ribs. The liquid inside flooded into his heart and his whole body juddered as if hit with an electric shock. Solace had to lean over him and put her body weight on him to keep the needle from breaking off or tearing too big a hole in the youth's heart. Sennon gasped, sputtering more blood. A mist of it spattered against the side of Solace's face. His body tensed and arched, joints creaking.

Sennon slumped down again. He let out a long rattling breath from a painfully dry throat.

'I see the Emperor,' he murmured. 'He tells me not to be afraid. He tells me to fight.'

Solace looked down at the gauges and readouts again. They had stabilised. The exchange was complete.

She withdrew the needle from Sennon's arm and

placed a dressing on the wound. She wiped the blood from his face with a wet cloth.

'You will fight, my brother,' she whispered. 'I promise.'

IN THE TUMULT following Librarian Varnica's evidence, Chapter Master Pugh had called an adjournment to the trial. Sarpedon had been led back to his cell, the Imperial Fists refusing any answer to his requests to speak with Daenyathos. The alleged presence of the Philosopher-Soldier still had his mind in a whirl. The dismay that he had felt to have Abraxes's existence revealed to the trial was a new counterpart to that confusion. Piece by piece, everything he had been sure of was falling apart.

He was grateful for the cell, though he had never thought he could think so. Its cramped walls and deadening psychic wards, smothering though they were, were preferable to the hatred that surrounded him in the courtroom. He crouched against one wall, and stared for a few minutes at the heap of crumpled papers, all that remained of his attempts to pen final words to his battle-brothers.

What could he say? What would make any difference? He had thought he would face this trial with dignity and courage, perhaps even to make his execution, when it came, a reluctant act on the part of the executioners. Now even that small victory felt very far away.

'I will not kneel,' he said to himself. 'I will not despair. I am Adeptus Astartes. I will not despair.'

'I fear for your sake, Chapter Master, that whether

to despair is not your decision to make.'

Sarpedon's eyes snapped to the opening in the cell door. It was not the voice of a Space Marine – it was a woman. This one had a note of familiarity to it, though.

Sarpedon scuttled up to the door. Beyond it, flanked by a pair of Imperial Fists with bolters at the ready, was Sister Aescarion of the Adepta Sororitas. She, like the Space Marines, wore her full armour to the trial and still had it on now, a suit of polished black ceramite emblazoned with the iconography of the Imperial Church. Her own weapon was the power axe but it was strapped to the jump pack of her armour now and she did not have it to hand. She was a full head shorter than a Space Marine for she was not augmented like them, and had a stern, angular yet handsome face with red-brown hair tied back in a ponytail.

'I recall you from Stratix Luminae,' said Sarpedon.

'An encounter I would sooner forget,' replied Aescarion.

'None of us wish to remember the sight of an adversary who departs the battlefield alive.'

'And you are still my adversary,' said the Battle Sister. 'Nothing has changed on that score. You are a traitor.'

'And yet,' said Sarpedon, 'you willingly exchange words with me. It seems women are as a strange a breed of creature as men say.'

'Not as strange as a condemned prisoner who makes light of his situation,' said Aescarion with a withering look that had no doubt been the scourge of the Sororitas novices she had trained.

'I trust you have not come here to swap insults, Sister,' said Sarpedon.

Aescarion glanced at the Imperial Fists flanking her. 'If you please,' she said to them. 'A few minutes are all I ask.'

'Stay in sight,' replied one of the Imperial Fists. The two Adeptus Astartes parted and walked several paces down the corridor outside Sarpedon's cell, out of earshot.

'They run a tight ship, these sons of Dorn,' said Sarpedon. 'As strait-laced as they come. It must be a comfort to be in the presence of Space Marines who jump when Terra demands it.'

'I find no comfort while enemies yet live,' replied Aescarion sharply. 'But I have nothing but admiration for the Imperial Fists, it is true. I find a little of my faith in humanity restored.'

'I have faith in humanity as well, Sister. It is not the people of the Imperium I have ever had a problem with. It is the structures by which the Imperium maintains itself, clinging to existence through blood and cruelty. I have seen them over and over. And you have too, Sister Aescarion. Worlds condemned to misery or death. Freedom and rebellion given the same names and crushed beneath the mass of the shiploads of captives sent to Terra to–'

'Enough! Do not speak of such things.'

'And pretend, instead, that they never existed?' Sarpedon reared up and put his face close to the window in the cell door.

'No! Accept them as necessary for the survival of

the human race, and turn our minds instead to the glory of our survival! That is how the Sororitas are taught.'

'You think this is survival?' Sarpedon held his arms wide, indicating not just his cell but everything beyond. 'The human race is in its death throes! It inflicts miseries upon its people to protect them from its enemies, and yet it is those miseries that bring such enemies into being! Why do so many desperate people turn from the Emperor's light and make pacts with the Dark Powers? Why do they cry out to be delivered and so walk right into xenos hands? The Imperium inflicts these wounds upon itself. It is nothing more than the slow death of mankind.'

'You will need to find a far better orator than yourself, Sarpedon, to sway the mind of a Sister of Battle,' retorted Aescarion sourly. 'I did not come here to let you practice your closing arguments on me. I am here about my late master, Inquisitor Thaddeus. You know of him?'

Sarpedon sat back down on his haunches. 'Yes. I knew him.'

'Personally?'

'A little.'

'Thaddeus had the chance to take you down on Stratix Luminae. Perhaps kill you. But he did not take that chance. I was with him at the time and I did not understand his decision. I still do not. I want to know why Inquisitor Thaddeus, a servant of the Emperor and sworn enemy of all that hates mankind, chose to let you go.'

Sarpedon's memories of Inquisitor Thaddeus were

of a man who, at first sight, was completely out of his depth. He had looked like a functionary of the Administratum, some middle-ranking nobody. Some inquisitors proclaimed their office with the most obvious and terrifying battlegear they could find, huge retinues of warriors and experts, even fleets and armies of their own. But Thaddeus walked softly in his duties.

'After Stratix Luminae he tried to keep track of us, even after the Inquisition ordered us deleted from Imperial history,' said Sarpedon. 'When he found us on Vanqualis he had been hunting down every rumour of us. He had found... there were legends of us in places I was sure the Chapter had never been. One was of the Black Chalice. Another was the Ashen Grail. I did not give much thought to them at the time but now I fear there is some web that has been spun out there, in which the Soul Drinkers have their part but of which they are ignorant. Thaddeus was trying to unravel it.'

'But he did not succeed,' said Aescarion.

'No. I imagine he is dead. The Howling Griffons crossed our path there, perhaps Captain Borganor can tell you more after he stops complaining about me cutting off his leg.'

'But Thaddeus knew none of this on Stratix Luminae. Why not kill you then when he could?' insisted Aescarion.

'Perhaps,' replied Sarpedon, 'he knew we were right?'

Aescarion lost her cool for a second. She slammed the palm of her hand into the cell door. 'You dare!'

she hissed. 'He would never have thrown in his lot with your kind. Thaddeus was a good man. The best of men.'

'But you want me to tell you that he was not corrupted. That hardly suggests you have great confidence in the man.'

'You are just toying with me, Sarpedon. I will not provide you with any more amusement. You don't know Thaddeus's motives and I will content myself with that.' Aescarion turned, about to rejoin her Imperial Fists minders and leave.

'He tried to warn us,' Sarpedon said. 'The Ashen Grail and the Black Chalice, and everything else he found, it all pointed to something he was trying to warn us about. I don't think even he knew what he had found, but his misgivings were deep enough for him to defy the deletion order and seek us out.'

'Then he was leading you into a trap,' said Aescarion.

'And you have misgivings too. Otherwise you would not have sought me out here. How many lashes would a Sororitas receive for conversing with a known heretic? And yet you come to my cell looking for answers. You see it too, just like Thaddeus did. Something about this trial is wrong and you know it. Daenyathos's return, here of all places, is no coincidence.'

'There is no coincidence. You came to the Veiled Region to seek him out. You and he both are puppets of that thing Abraxes that Varnica spoke of.'

'Well, sister, if you have made up your mind about everything already there hardly seems a need to question me at all.'

Aescarion shook her head. 'Part of me wishes

to know what must have to happen to an Adeptus Astartes before he can turn from the Emperor's light. But I fear that such knowledge itself has the power to corrupt. I should have let you keep your silence, traitor. I hope this trial ends before you can do any more damage.'

'Then I doubt you and I have anything more to say to one another.'

Aescarion didn't bother to reply. She turned smartly on an armoured heel and walked out of sight down the brig corridor. One of the Imperial Fists slammed the window shut, and Sarpedon was alone again.

WHEN VISITORS SOUGHT an audience with Chapter Master Pugh on the *Phalanx*, he often chose to receive them in the Sigismarch Forest. This artificial woodland occupied an area amidships on one of the uppermost decks, its greenery illuminated by an artificial sun that made a circuit once every twenty-four hours. A river ran though it, fresh water diverted from the crew's drinking supply to create the illusion that the forest was just part of a far greater lush and peaceful land where, even on board a vast weapon of war, a place of contemplation might be found.

'So,' said Pugh, taking his place sat on a tree stump by the river bank where he was accustomed to receive his petitioners. 'Speak.'

In the clearing before Pugh stood Reinez. Behind him were the officers of the Adeptus Astartes who had come to the *Phalanx* for the trial. They included Varnica, whose evidence had prompted this re-evaluation of the whole trial. None of the captains and Librarians had brought their retinues with them, for this was not the place for a competitive show of arms.

'I put it to the Justice Lord,' began Reinez, 'that the accused Sarpedon must be considered a moral threat. Librarian Varnica's evidence proves the accused's complicity with powers of the warp. This trial must cease and the executions be administered immediately.' Reinez spoke with a snarling bluntness that made it clear he had thought this from the very start.

'I see,' said Pugh. 'Indeed, Varnica's statements have changed the complexion of this trial. And yet I must see to it that justice is not only done, but that no man can find any reason to suggest that the course of justice has not been followed. For evidence of warpcraft, I have but the evidence of one Adeptus Astartes. As high as the esteem in which I hold you, Librarian Varnica, you are but one.'

'That I cannot deny, my lord,' replied Varnica. 'But I know what I saw. The stink of the warp hangs over this whole affair.'

'And when was suspicion ever insufficient evidence in matters of a moral threat?' added Reinez.

'I know that you long to see Sarpedon dead, Reinez,' replied Pugh, pointedly omitting any rank when he addressed the Crimson Fist, for since Reinez had become a penitent he had abandoned all rank within his own Chapter. 'But this trial is not held to give you your vengeance. If you are to remain in the position of prosecutor you must be patient.'

'Patient? Must I have the patience to endure that heretic speaking in his own defence? And from whence shall I gather the patience, Justice Lord, to sit unmoved through all the lies of the Soul Drinkers? Is Daenyathos to speak, too? Luko, and Salk, and all the Soul Drinkers, are they to have their chance to utter corruption as well?'

'If that is what it takes for me to be satisfied that justice is done,' said Pugh, 'then yes.'

'The Soul Drinkers are not the only ones who will have their time to speak,' said another voice, one who had not joined in the discussion as yet. It was that of Captain N'Kalo of the Iron Knights. The Iron Knights were, like the Soul Drinkers, a successor Chapter of the Imperial Fists, and the stain on Dorn's honour had seemed enough to bring a delegation from the Iron Knights to the *Phalanx*. Suddenly, the other Adeptus Astartes present were not so sure that N'Kalo was here just as a matter of course.

'You have seen the Soul Drinkers for a moral threat?' asked Reinez.

'No,' replied N'Kalo levelly. 'I will speak in their defence.' N'Kalo's expression was impossible to guess at since his face was covered. He wore, even in the presence of the Chapter Master, a helm with an eye slit reminiscent of plate armour from some feudal world. Everywhere on him were hung campaign medallions, laurels and purity seals, the steel of his armour only just showing through the brocade of his many honours.

'Their defence?' snarled Reinez.

'N'Kalo, brother, what are you saying?' demanded Siege-Captain Daviks.

'I say just what I say,' replied N'Kalo. 'I wish to

speak in defence of Sarpedon and the Soul Drinkers. Will you deny me that right?'

'I shall!' barked Reinez. 'As the prosecutor in the Emperor's name I deny you any right to interfere in the punishment of that heretic!' Reinez jabbed a finger in N'Kalo's face, but the Iron Knight did not flinch.

'Reinez!' shouted Pugh. 'This is not your decision to make.'

'By the Throne, I say it is! Upon my honour as an Adeptus Astartes, you will have to go through me before you utter one word that does not condemn the traitors!'

'If I may,' interjected Commander Gethsemar of the Angels Sanguine, 'I believe that the precedent exists for him to do just that.' Gethsemar, like N'Kalo, had spoken little, and his voice was a smooth, honeyed sound quite at odds with the warrior heritage of his Chapter.

'Is that what you desire, Reinez?' said Pugh. 'An honour-duel with Captain N'Kalo?'

'If that is what it takes,' replied Reinez, still face to face with N'Kalo. 'If the Emperor lends strength to my arm, N'Kalo stays silent and the Soul Drinkers are condemned no matter what he wishes.'

'And if I best you,' said N'Kalo, 'I say my piece.'

'It does not matter what you will do,' said Reinez. 'I have torn the throats from warp-beasts a million miles from any battle-brother. I stood on worlds as they died and fought through armies of the damned to survive. You are a child compared to me. You cannot win. Drop to one knee now, acknowledge me your superior, and there need be no duel. I will accept your surrender without your having to suffer at my hand.'

'I would not deny you the pleasure of breaking my bones,' said N'Kalo, voice still calm.

'Where is this duel to be held?' said Gethesemar.

'Here,' replied Reinez. 'This is the place where Sigismund, the first Templar, came to contemplate his duty, is it not?'

'It is,' replied Pugh.

'Then perhaps Captain N'Kalo will have the chance to contemplate his own duties as he lies on this ground beneath my boot.'

'Enough talk, Reinez!' said Pugh. 'Gethsemar, since you proposed it, you shall oversee the duel. Brothers, gather your Adeptus Astartes so that all will witness the result. N'Kalo, Reinez, select your weapons and make yourselves ready. Then we shall have no more discussion of this matter. The honour-duel shall be final. This is the Emperor's justice, and all aboard will hold to it as His word.'

'Amen,' said Reinez with a smile.

GETHSEMAR REVELLED IN his role as master of ceremonies. He changed his mask for one with a stern brown and downturned mouth, ruby eyes and a stylised scar on one cheek. His Sanguinary Guard stood watch alongside him, glaives drawn, framed by the wing-like stabilising fins on their jump packs. Their gilded armour gleamed almost painfully bright as the forest's artificial sun came overhead and bathed the riverside glade in light. Lysander waited behind them, knowing that although he was here to enforce Pugh's will just as much as the Angels Sanguine, there was no need to impede Gethsemar's sense of showmanship.

Around the edge of the clearing were stood the Space Marines attending the trial. There had not been enough room for all the Howling Griffons so Borganor looked on flanked only by his honour guard. A single squad of Imperial Fists attended Pugh. Kolgo was there too, with his Sisters of Battle in attendance. The Iron Knights who had accompanied N'Kalo stood a little apart, perhaps aware that if their commander lost this duel they would be leaving the *Phalanx* very quickly.

Reinez had chosen his thunder hammer to fight with. It was a well-used weapon, its adamantium head well-scored in hundreds of battles. Reinez made a few warm-up swings, loosening his arms and shoulders, and the weapon thrummed through the air as if it were purring with pleasure at the impending combat.

N'Kalo had chosen a double-handed sword from the armoury of the *Phalanx*, a weapon normally wielded by the Imperial Fist chosen to serve as the Emperor's Champion while on campaign. As an Iron Knight who called Rogal Dorn his Primarch like the Imperial Fists, N'Kalo had the right to wield such a weapon. It was a compromise – his own power sword, now held by one of his Iron Knights, was one-handed, and might have been shattered or knocked from his hand trying to parry Reinez's thunder hammer. The champion's blade would not break, but it would be slower.

'In the sight of Rogal Dorn,' intoned Gethsemar, 'beneath the aegis of blessed Sanguinius and of the Emperor of Mankind, our battle-brothers here seek justice through the clash of holy arms. May the Emperor lend strength to the arm of the righteous! Begin!'

For a long moment, neither Space Marine moved as they gauged each other's stance, deciding which way to go. Reinez crouched low, hammer held behind him ready to strike. N'Kalo's sword was up in a guard, the point hovering level with Reinez's eyeline.

Reinez moved first. N'Kalo barely reacted in time, bringing the blade down to block the blow that Reinez aimed at his legs. N'Kalo pivoted and caught Reinez with an elbow, but it clanged harmlessly into the Crimson Fist's breastplate. Reinez hooked N'Kalo's leg with his hammer and threw him head over heels backwards, to sprawl on the grass.

Reinez's hammer arced down. N'Kalo rolled aside as it slammed into the ground, throwing up a great shower of earth and leaving a crater in the dark soil. N'Kalo swung wildly, a vast steel crescent that Reinez sidestepped with ease before landing a kick so hard in N'Kalo's side that the Iron Knight was thrown to the ground again.

'I'll hear your surrender any time,' gasped Reinez. 'There is no shame in it. Any time.'

N'Kalo responded with a reverse strike from the ground, the sword's point arrowing up behind him towards Reinez's throat. Reinez batted it aside with the haft of his hammer and cracked the butt of the weapon into the side of N'Kalo's head. N'Kalo reeled and Reinez closed, driving his shoulder into N'Kalo's midriff and hauling the Space Marine off the ground.

Reinez hefted N'Kalo into the air and threw him. N'Kalo tumbled over the bank of the river and into the water, the powerful stream foaming around him. Reinez jumped in after him, dragging N'Kalo to his feet. The water came up to each Space Marine's chest. Reinez slammed a headbutt into the face of N'Kalo's helm, denting the ceramite faceplate.

N'Kalo drove a knee into the inside of Reinez's thigh. Reinez stumbled back a step, feet slipping on the stones and mud of the artificial riverbed. N'Kalo crunched an elbow into the back of Reinez's head and pulled his sword from the water again, slicing left and right. Reinez deflected each blow with his hammer or they glanced off his shoulder pads.

N'Kalo paused, having created the space he needed between the two combatants. He shifted his footing to plant himself more firmly on the bed of mud and rocks. Behind him, rapids rushed around several large boulders, plunging down a low waterfall. The branches of overhanging willows almost brushed the river's surface. If it were not for the two Adeptus Astartes struggling to shed one another's blood, it would have been a tranquil and beautiful place.

N'Kalo's breath was heaving. Reinez looked like he had barely broken a sweat. N'Kalo had not yet managed to draw blood from the Crimson Fist.

'Do you think this will be over?' said Reinez as he forged through the waters, trying to force N'Kalo back towards the rapids. 'If the galaxy turns upside-down and you beat me, how long do you think your victory will last? You think you will have any brothers here? They will turn their backs on you.'

'They are not so consumed with bitterness as you, Reinez,' replied N'Kalo. 'They have not let failure make them less of an Adeptus Astartes.'

Reinez's face darkened. He spat a wordless syllable of anger and charged – not at N'Kalo, but at the closest tree that clung to the riverbank. Reinez wrenched the tree free of its roots, showering dirt and loose stones across the water.

Reinez's anger gave him strength. N'Kalo had barely the time to get his sword up before Reinez slammed the shattered tree trunk into him, throwing him backwards into the water. The impact was enough to knock him senseless and his heavy armoured body thudded onto the riverbed, waters rushing around him.

Reinez pounced from the bank into the water, one knee pounding square into N'Kalo's solar plexus. Reinez hauled the Iron Knight over his head, out of the water, and slammed him down into one of the massive boulders making up the rapids. The boulder shattered under the impact and N'Kalo sprawled against it, water foaming white around him, unable to move.

Reinez planted a foot on N'Kalo's midriff. Both hands free now, his hammer holstered, he grabbed the lower edge of N'Kalo's helmet and wrenched it halfway around, forcing it off N'Kalo's head.

The helmet came free with a shower of sparks. Reinez was looking into a face severely burned, every blister and scour looking like it had just been inflicted, red and weeping. N'Kalo's lips were pale streaks in the blackened skin, his eyes kept open only by artificial surfaces of milky glass that made them look blind. His jaw and back teeth showed through the tears in his cheeks, and segments of cranium glinted as if polished between the stringy remnants of his scalp.

'When I am finished with you,' spat Reinez, 'you will look back and remember how handsome you were.'

Reinez shouldered N'Kalo over the rapids down the falls. The Iron Knight was barely sensible as he plunged into the pool formed by the waterfall. Reinez stood on the rapids, hauling another rock up from the riverbed. He hurled it down at N'Kalo, who got an arm up to ward off the worst of the impact but who was crushed down into the pool, trapped by its weight.

Reinez jumped down onto the rock that pinned N'Kalo in place. N'Kalo was not quite beneath the surface but little more than his ruined face could be seen above the water. Reinez stood and took his hammer off his back, holding it with both hands, the well-worn head of the weapon aiming down at N'Kalo's face.

Reinez drove the hammer down at N'Kalo. N'Kalo forced his sword out from below the rock and slashed the hammer aside. Expecting an impact and off balance, Reinez fell forwards, landing face to face with N'Kalo.

The other Adeptus Astartes had by now gathered on the bank of the river and they watched as the two

Space Marine wrestled in the water, Reinez trying to force N'Kalo's head below the surface, N'Kalo trying to wriggle from under the rock and bring his sword to bear. The thunder hammer lay in the water, abandoned, as Reinez went at N'Kalo with his bare hands.

The watching Space Marines parted as Pugh joined them. He stood on one of the flat rocks that made up the rapids, no expression on his face.

N'Kalo hurled the rock away. Reinez had to jump back to keep his own legs from being trapped under it. N'Kalo slammed the pommel of his sword into Reinez's side and kicked out at him, trying to drive him against the stone wall carved by the waterfall. Reinez spun, locked N'Kalo's sword arm in the crook of his elbow and ripped the sword from N'Kalo's hand. Reinez threw the sword aside and it disappeared under the foaming water.

Both Space Marines were bleeding now. N'Kalo's armour was dented from the impacts, to the extent that it was as much a hindrance to his movement as protection. Reinez's nose might have been broken, judging by the blood spilling down his chest, black against the dark blue of his breastplate.

When the two closed in and locked up in a wrestler's clinch, every Space Marine watching knew it was for the last time. N'Kalo was a fine combatant, but his wounds, more severe on the inside than the outside, drained the strength from his limbs. Reinez had been fighting for the last few years without any battle-brothers at his side, learning to survive by his wits alone, with fists and teeth if need be. Reinez pushed N'Kalo down onto one knee, wrenched one of the Iron Knight's shoulders out of its socket, and dropped into a shoulder charge that smashed N'Kalo into the riverbank.

N'Kalo could not raise his free arm into a guard. Reinez slammed his fist into N'Kalo's face.

'They will cast you out!' roared Reinez, his fist hitting home again. 'They will banish you! You will know my pain!'

Reinez punched over and over. Ultra-dense Adeptus Astartes bone fractured. N'Kalo's cheekbone caved in, then his jaw. One eye socket was stove inwards, half-shutting his eye. Bloody skin clung to Reinez's knuckles.

'Outcast! Pariah! You shall be no man's brother!'

'Stop,' said Pugh.

Reinez did not stop. Another half-dozen blows rained down. Broken teeth clotted the blood that oozed from N'Kalo's shattered mouth.

The boot that cracked into Reinez's face belonged to Captain Lysander, who had stepped out of the watching crowd at a signal from Pugh. The blow caught Reinez by surprise and he fell backwards off N'Kalo, sprawling in the water.

'I said stop,' said Pugh.

Reinez scrabbled to his feet, wiping the back of one gauntlet across his face to remove the worst of N'Kalo's blood. 'You see?' he gasped. 'The Emperor lent me strength. Dorn has spoken. The duel is over.'

'It is,' said Pugh. 'My brothers, the apothecaries among you attend to Captain N'Kalo while the *Phalanx's* own medicae staff are summoned. I must have him conscious to present his evidence.'

'Lord Pugh!' protested Reinez. 'He was defeated! The duel was won! I demand N'Kalo's silence as is my right by victory!'

'The duel is won, Reinez,' replied Pugh, 'but you may claim no victory. We are not at war, and Captain N'Kalo is not your enemy. In showing such brutality to him, even at the moment you became the victor, you abandon all semblance of honour. In an honour-duel, that is as good as a physical defeat. You have forfeited the duel, and Captain N'Kalo is the winner.'

Reinez stood speechless in the rushing river as the Space Marines on the bank picked up the winner and carried him off to the apothecarion.

THE FIRST THING Sarpedon noticed as he was led to the dock again was the Iron Knight without his helm. He had encountered the Chapter once before but there had been no way of telling, beneath the feudal helm, if the Iron Knights' commander was the same Adeptus Astartes he had spoken with on Molikor. Now, there could be no mistake. It was the same man.

Half of N'Kalo's face was still hidden, this time by medical dressings covering fresh wounds. The rest, however, was that familiar mask of burn tissue, and the one visible eye was the same glassy prosthetic.

Sarpedon tried to hold N'Kalo's gaze, but he was shoved into the accused's pulpit by the Imperial Fists who had escorted him from his cell, and found himself looking at Lord Pugh.

'Justice Lord,' said Sarpedon before anyone else could speak. 'I would know of my brothers.'

'They are safe and well,' said Pugh.

'And Daenyathos?'

'He is captive, like them. And like them, he has not been harmed.'

'I know that I am to die here, Lord Pugh. I wish to speak with my battle-brothers before that happens. And I must have leave to speak with Daenyathos, even if only to ascertain that the Dreadnought you hold indeed contains him. My Chapter thought him dead for thousands of years. I must at least see for myself that he lives.'

'What you ask is a luxury that cannot be afforded to the condemned,' replied Pugh. 'The nature of your crimes means that you cannot be given the chance to conspire further with your fellow accused. Such requests are denied.'

Sarpedon did not argue. It was a motion he had to go through. He had to show that he had not given up, not completely. It was a feeble gesture among so many warriors, but it was made.

'Brethren,' began Pugh. 'During the last adjournment the matter of the Soul Drinkers' defence was decided. Commander N'Kalo?'

Sarpedon realised that among the assembled Space Marines, he could not see Reinez.

N'Kalo stepped forwards. 'Brothers,' he said, and Sarpedon recognised the grating voice of an improvised vox-unit. It was hooked up to N'Kalo's dented breastplate, amplifying the voice that struggled to get past his shattered jaw. 'I must speak to you of a world called Molikor.'

# CHAPTER SIX

MOLIKOR'S ENDLESS EXPANSES of broken delta, islands of swampy grasses and gorse separated by the sludgy children of the planet's great rivers, were a good place to hide. An entire nation hid there among the rotten trees and root cages, the odd chunk of rock eroded clean by the passage of the shifting waters. They had their strongholds among the mangrove swamps closer to the shore, where the biting insects swarmed so thick they could pick a man up off the ground, and the waters were infested with a thousand different forms of sharp-toothed creature. That nation, which called itself the Eshkeen, was as much a part of the landscape as the dour grey-streaked clouds overhead and the way the soft ground threatened to swallow up a power-armoured foot. That nation had risen up in defiance. That nation had to die.

Commander N'Kalo took the magnoculars from the eyeslit of his armour. His augmented vision was enough to tell him that the foe had no intention of making itself seen, and a closer look had confirmed it. Behind him the strikeforce of nearly forty Iron Knights Space Marines was forming a perimeter lest the enemy close in from an unexpected angle, the bolters of Squads Salik, K'Jinn and Tchwayo scanning the indistinct horizon for targets. Sergeant Borasi's Devastator Squad had left its anti-tank weapons behind and sported a complement of heavy bolters, perfect for chewing through forested cover and ill-armoured enemies. Though the delta could have been deserted for all the Iron Knights could see, the Devastators were still ready to deploy, weapons loaded and shouldered.

'They give us good sport,' said Sergeant Borasi, standing just behind N'Kalo. 'It disappoints me so when the enemy show themselves too early.'

'Would that this weremere sport,' replied N'Kalo. 'The Eshkeen revolt against the rule of the Imperium. Books of atrocities have already been written about their campaigns of violence against the Imperial cities of this world, and if Molikor falls the whole of this frontier could follow.'

'Nevertheless, captain, I am reminded of the best hunting grounds of Seheris. Below the equator, where the great rivers of the Zambenar meet the oceans. I lose count of how many reapermaw tusks my bolter has won for me down there.'

'Then the hunting will be good, brother,' said N'Kalo, stowing the magnoculars in a belt pouch. 'If it is a hunt you see unfolding here.'

On Seheris, the home world of the Iron Knights Chapter, the unforgiving deserts and plains bred a thousand hardy peoples divided into tribes that treated the land as an adversary to be conquered. The Iron Knights were drawn from such people, and their wish to test themselves against an environment, as much as against a foe, never left them. They took pride in the fact that they fought in warzones which would have been deadly whether any enemy waited there or not – radioactive rock deserts, carnivorous jungles, archipelagos scattered across an ocean that seethed with sea monsters, and every other Emperor-forsaken place that a man could imagine. When the Parliaments of Molikor had requested help against a foe bent on exterminating the Emperor's presence on their world, the Iron Knights had seen not only a task to be achieved to keep the Ghoul Stars Frontier intact, but the chance to test themselves against Molikor's own dangers.

Too often, thought N'Kalo, his brother Space Marines treated war as a sport. The fact that he could see beyond that had marked him out as commander material. That was why he had been sent here to Molikor, to oversee his eager battle-brothers as they killed every Eshkeen on the planet.

MILE AFTER MILE, the Eshkeen drew the Iron Knights in.

It was clearly their tactic. Even as he walked the paths laid out for him through the winding delta paths, N'Kalo knew that the enemy had laid on

Molikor a trap to cut off, surround and butcher any-one the Imperium sent to fight them. He read the landscape like a book, like any Iron Knight would, and he saw the thinking behind every dammed stream and felled copse.

The easiest path into the delta forests and swamps, where the Eshkeen surely waited, passed through two towering forests separated by a stretch of swamp where the shallow waters rushed over the sodden grassland. The soft-edged shadows, cast by a sun hidden behind the overcast sky, rendered this gap dark and its footing uncertain. The ways on either side were deep and difficult to traverse, and N'Kalo's magnoculars had picked out the log dams on the distant highlands that had helped flood those regions to force any attackers to take the path between the forests.

N'Kalo's strikeforce reached the first shadows cast by the tallest trees. The forest was dense and tangled, an unmanaged mass of broken branches and diseased trunks, clustered around rocky hills that broke the surface of the marshes and trapped enough soil for the trees to grow. N'Kalo could see no sign of the Eshkeen, but knew they were there as surely as if they were standing there in front of him.

'You cannot trap a Space Marine,' said Sergeant Borasi over the strikeforce's vox-net. 'You can shut yourself in a room with him, but it is not he who is trapped.'

N'Kalo halted the strikeforce at the head of the forest gap. On the other side was a stretch of open marsh, tempting for any force making for the coastal strongholds with nowhere for the enemy to use as an ambush. N'Kalo imagined the Parliamentarian commanders who had fallen for such a trick, before Molikor had requested the assistance of Imperial forces, and how they must have decided that it was acceptable to risk this one ambush spot to ensure they had a clear run at the enemy. How many of them had the Eshkeen killed, moulding the landscape into their ally? How many cavalry forces had wheeled in panic on just such a path, stuck with thousands of arrows and, later, riddled with bullets from captured guns, fired from an enemy so well hidden it seemed the forest itself wanted them dead?

'Salik, Tchwayo, take the fore,' voxed N'Kalo. 'K'Jinn, cover the rear. Borasi, up front with me.'

The strikeforce took up position in the mouth of the trap. Borasi's Devastators knelt, heavy bolters covering their front arc.

To an observer unfamiliar with the Space Marines, it would seem the Iron Knights were pausing in trepidation, making up their minds whether to continue down the narrow path laid out for them.

'Open fire!' ordered N'Kalo.

The heavy bolters hammered out a dreadful cacophony as their fire shredded the edge of the right-hand forest, splintering tree trunks and sending clouds of spinning shards through the air.

'Advance!' shouted N'Kalo, his voice just audible over the din. 'Advance and engage!'

As the Devastators reloaded, the three Tactical squads ran for the forest, bolters spitting fire as they headed onwards. N'Kalo had his power sword in one hand and his plasma pistol in the other, and as the last splinters of tree trunk fell he caught the first sight of the enemy.

The Eshkeen were heavily scarified, and wore strips of coloured cloth and leather wrapped tight around them to ward off the spines and stingers of the forests. The ridges of scar tissue that ran across their faces and bodies were high enough to be pierced with bones and thorns, and spikes were implanted under the shorn skin of their scalps. They resembled the figures from some primitive world's visions of Hell. Perhaps they modelled themselves after Molikor's own myths, delving into their images of damnation to put fear into Parliamentarian hearts.

The Eshkeen returned fire as best they could as they dragged the wounded and dead from what remained of the treeline. Autogun and lasgun fire spattered down at the Iron Knights, hissing in the damp ground or ringing off ceramite. The Space Marines did not slow and headed straight for the enemy.

The ambush plan relied on the Space Marines staying in the open, thinking themselves unable to make any headway through the forest. Unfortunately for the Eshkeen, that plan, which would work horrendously well against the armies of the Parliamentarians, fell apart when confronted with an armoured Space Marine whose weight and strength could force him through the forest as fast as he moved in the open. Squad Salik reached the trees first and they did not slow down, shouldering their way between the tree trunks, rotten wood crumbling under their weight. The Eshkeen screamed war-cries as the Iron Knights were among them, streams of bolter fire criss-crossing through the forest and slicing Eshkeen in half.

N'Kalo felt, in spite of himself, a faint disappointment. None of the Eshkeen would get close enough for him to use his power sword. Already Squad Tchwayo were into the rapidly thinning forest. Men were dying among the twisted roots and falling tree trunks. N'Kalo would not take any heads today.

N'Kalo himself had reached the trees. Bodies lay twisted and broken among the fallen branches. One was still alive, moaning as he tried to force himself to his feet, apparently ignorant of the fact he had lost one of his arms at the elbow. Others had huge ragged holes in their torsos, cut down by bolter fire aimed at the central mass. Another had the side of his head crushed by a bolter stock. N'Kalo stepped over them, glancing around for targets as Borasi and K'Jinn advanced behind him.

Suddenly, N'Kalo could not hear the heavy footsteps and bolter fire of the battle-brothers behind him. He looked back, not wanting to slow his own advance, but he could not see them.

'Squads report!' said N'Kalo into the vox. Blank static was the only reply. 'Report!' he repeated, but got nothing.

The forest was seething. It was alive. The Eshkeen were barely recognisable as humans now, slipping in and out of tree trunks, their flesh merging with the mossy wood. They slithered along the ground like snakes, limbs as flexible as liquid, and slid into the ground before N'Kalo could take aim. They flitted overhead, birds on the wing.

'What witchcraft is this?' demanded N'Kalo. His power sword hummed into life and he slashed about him, felling the trees on either side as he pushed on. 'A Space Marine fears not such devilry! He knows no fear!'

The forest warped around him. Trees bowed in and hands reached out of the earth to snare his ankles. N'Kalo fired at movement, his plasma pistol boring a glowing orange channel through the foliage, but he could not tell if he had hit anything. Everywhere he cut left and right, forging on through the path he hacked. He called for his battle-brothers, but there was no reply. Faces were leering from the trees now, blood welling up from the ground. The sky, where he glimpsed it through the writhing branches overhead, seemed blistered and burned, as if some malignant energy was forcing its way down towards him.

N'Kalo slammed into an obstacle that did not give way to his weight. He stumbled back a pace and saw another horror. A Space Marine from the waist up, a mutated monstrosity below, insectoid legs tipped with vicious talons, reared up to spear N'Kalo's torso. The Space Marine was no Iron Knight – his armour was painted purple, with a gilded chalice on one shoulder pad, and the high aegis collar of a Librarian.

N'Kalo slashed at the apparition with his sword. The mutant brought up the haft of an ornate axe to turn the blow aside. Without seeming to move the mutant was upon N'Kalo, its weight bearing down on him, legs forcing him back onto one knee. One insect leg snared his sword arm and the other batted his plasma pistol aside.

The forest was shifting again, this time back to normal. N'Kalo could hear his battle-brothers' voices filling the vox-net.

'Fall back!' came K'Jinn's voice. 'Regroup at the far side!'

'I have brothers down!' shouted Salik. 'Forming defensive!' Bolter fire hammered away over the vox-net, volley and counter-volley shearing through the trees.

The mutant kicked N'Kalo's sword aside.

'What are you?' gasped N'Kalo. He struggled to get free, but the mutant was stronger even than a Space Marine.

'I am the truth,' replied Sarpedon.

THE FORTRESSES OF the Eshkeen were cunningly wrought so as to be invisible from the air. The finest siege-wrights of the Imperium could not have strung out fortifications of wooden stakes and pit traps with such subtlety, seeding the approaches to the dense coastal forests so that attackers on foot would find their numbers thinned out well before they came within bowshot of the fortress walls. The fortresses themselves were built on two levels, the first hidden trenches and murder-holes on the ground, the second walkways and battlements in the trees overhead. The canopy was thick enough to hide them, and the short distances between them were made deadly with tangles of cured razorvine, layers of dried earth concealing stretches of sucking mud, and even nests of forest predators herded into position by the Eshkeen. Two Parliamentarian forces had driven this far

into Eshkeen territory and none of them had been
seen again, save for a couple of messengers permitted
to live so they could explain that the Eshkeen were
not impressed by the glittering cavalry regiments and
sumptuous banners of the Parliamentarian armies.

The fortresses backed against the sea, although it
was difficult to tell where the sea began. Mangroves
formed layers of root canopy over the murky waters,
infested with Eshkeen fishermen who found their
harpoons were as adept at picking off soldiers wading out of landing boats as they were at spearing fish.
The shallow waters and hidden reefs were enough to
dissuade all but the most glory-hungry admiral from
attempting a landing there. Unfortunately for the
Parliamentarians they had once possessed such an
admiral, whose ships now lay a few hundred metres
from the shore where they had foundered, their men
trapped there for months before starvation and Eshkeen snipers had seen to the last of them.

These defences, as formidable as they were, would
not have stopped a force of Space Marines determined
to enact justice on the Eshkeen. The Iron Knights,
however, had not been given that chance.

The first N'Kalo saw of the Eshkeen stronghold was a
ceiling of wooden planks and plaited vines. He struggled to move and found that he was not bound. He
was high up in the air, the structure around him built
into the thick, gnarled trunks of the mangroves. The
humid air had a faint tang of decay, the smell of fallen
plant matter turning to watery sludge, mixed in with
the salt breeze off the sea. Eshkeen were everywhere at
watch, eerily still as they scanned the approaches with

their bows or guns to hand. N'Kalo saw, for the first time, their women and children. Some of the sentries were women, and a gaggle of children crouched in a doorway watching N'Kalo with a mix of fascination and fear. They were scrawny in a way that only growing up outside civilisation could explain, tough and sinewy, with painted skin echoing the scarring of their elders.

N'Kalo sat up. The children squealed and scattered. He was in a barracks or communal living space, full of empty beds. He could not see his weapons, but his armour had been left on.

He touched a gauntlet to his face as he realised his helmet had been removed. No wonder the children had fled. The burns he had suffered long ago, which he had chosen to hide under the knightly helm of his Chapter's commanders, must have made him look even more of a monster than any other Space Marine.

'Commander N'Kalo,' said a too-familiar voice. N'Kalo jumped to his feet as the mutant from the forest entered.

'Where am I? What of my brothers?' demanded N'Kalo.

'They are safe. I cannot permit them their liberty yet. They will go free soon, as will you.'

The mutant Space Marine was armed with his power axe and a bolt pistol, and N'Kalo had not been a match for him when he had his power sword. Unarmed, he did not fancy his chances against the mutant. Better to talk and wait for the right time than to throw his life away trying to fight here, when he was bound to fail. 'And you did not answer my question. What are you?'

The mutant shrugged. It was seemingly too human a gesture for such a grotesque creature. 'I am a Space Marine, like you. Well, not exactly like you.'

'You are a witch.'

'I am, if you prefer that term. I am Librarian and Chapter Master Sarpedon of the Soul Drinkers. And we are similar in more than just bearing the arms of the Adeptus Astartes. We are both, Commander N'Kalo, students of justice as much as of war.'

'Justice? My brothers have fallen at your hand!'

'Fallen, but not dead. My Apothecary is seeing to them. Two have bolter wounds and another was felled by a chainsword. Though they will not fight for a while, the three will survive. They are being held at ground level, below us, watched over by my battle-brothers. Sergeant Borasi gave us a great deal of trouble. He should be commended for his spirit, misplaced though it is. He owes us several broken bones.'

N'Kalo had heard of the Soul Drinkers. Like the Iron Knights, they were successors to the Imperial Fists, with Rogal Dorn as their Primarch. N'Kalo had never met any of the Soul Drinkers but he recalled they were famed for their prowess in boarding actions and that they had won laurels during the battle for the Ecclesiarchal Palace during the Wars of Apostasy. N'Kalo and Sarpedon should have been brothers, not just as Space Marines but as sons of Dorn.

'Why do you oppose us?' said N'Kalo. 'We are here doing the Emperor's will!'

'The Imperium's will,' replied Sarpedon. 'Not the Emperor's.'

'And I suppose you, a mutant, one who has raised

arms against my brethren, is the one doing the Emperor's will?'

'Looking at it that way,' said Sarpedon, 'I can understand your doubts. I do not believe, however, that you know the full story of what is happening on Molikor.'

'And you are going to tell me?' spat N'Kalo.

'No. I am going to show you.'

N'KALO SAW HIS brothers guarded by a ring of Soul Drinkers. The Iron Knights had been disarmed but, as Sarpedon had said, few of them were hurt. A Soul Drinkers Apothecary was operating on the wounded leg of one sedated Iron Knight – all the rest were conscious and, led by Borasi, started up a chorus of plaudits for their commander and insults hurled at Sarpedon as soon as they saw N'Kalo. A couple of the other Soul Drinkers were mutants, although not as dramatically malformed as Sarpedon. One had an enormous mutated hand, and N'Kalo wondered what other mutations were hidden beneath their armour.

It was a strange feeling to be led, not quite a captive and not quite an equal, through the Eshkeen forest by Sarpedon. N'Kalo's soldierly mind sized up every chance to attack Sarpedon, drag him down to the ground or stab him in the back with a fortuitous weapon snatched from a nearby Eshkeen, but Sarpedon had his own warrior instinct and every opportunity was gone before it began. If he had a weapon, N'Kalo thought, he could kill Sarpedon and, if not complete his mission, at least rid the Imperium of this enemy – but even with a bolter or a power sword in his hands, could he beat Sarpedon when he had been defeated before?

The Eshkeen watched curiously as N'Kalo moved through their domain. They walked paths almost hidden in the forest, avoiding traps and dead ends sown liberally throughout the forest. In places N'Kalo could see the waters of the ocean between the roots underfoot, and glimpse Eshkeen walking there, too, wading through the waters to fish or keep watch over the coastal approaches. In other places the ground underfoot was solid, with tunnels and bunkers dug into it. The Eshkeen themselves wore patchworks of body armour and scraps of captured uniform, the most colourful belonging to those who looked the most experienced and deadly. The right to sport the captured garb of the enemy was evidently a privilege that had to be earned.

In the heart of the stronghold was a fortification of stone instead of wood, concentric circles of jagged battlements forming a huge granite maw around a pit in the centre. Sarpedon followed a complex path through the fortifications, leading N'Kalo through them even though he could probably have scrambled over them with ease thanks to his arachnid limbs. The trees did not grow here, so an artificial canopy had been stretched out overhead, a lattice of vines and ropes woven with leaves to keep it hidden. There were no Eshkeen keeping watch among the fortifications, but many of them had gathered in the trees around the clearing to watch the two Space Marines descending to the pit.

'Like you,' said Sarpedon, 'we heeded the distress

call from the Parliaments of Molikor. But we have
learned to be circumspect. A little more suspicious,
perhaps, of our own Emperor-fearing citizens. We
arrived here without informing the Parliaments of
our presence, and spoke instead to the Eshkeen.
When we hear only one side of the story, I find we
inevitably miss out on the more interesting half.'

The pit was a shaft lined with carved stones, forming a spiral frieze winding down into the darkness.
The frieze depicted an endless tangle of human bodies, contorted and wounded, missing limbs or eyes,
faces drawn in pain. The Eshkeen who had sculpted
it, countless generations ago, had used a stylised
technique that removed the subtleties of the human
form and left only the pain. Winding wooden stairs
provided a way down into the shaft.

'When Imperial settlers were brought to Molikor,'
explained Sarpedon as he and N'Kalo descended the
shaft, 'they sent out explorers to tame the marshland
and forge a path to the ocean. They hoped to build
a port on this coast and spread to the planet's other
continents. They never managed it, mainly because
the land was too marshy and the Eshkeen rather
unfriendly. But one of them did find this.'

N'Kalo made note of Sarpedon's words with one
half of his mind. The other half was trying to work
out how he could turn on Sarpedon. They were alone
now, and Sarpedon's fellow Soul Drinkers could not
come to his aid. If N'Kalo got behind Sarpedon, and
if he was quick enough, he could throw Sarpedon
off the staircase down the shaft. But the fall would
not be guaranteed to kill him – indeed, N'Kalo could

now see the bottom of the shaft strewn with leaves
and broken branches, and a Space Marine would
barely be inconvenienced by the distance. He could
grab Sarpedon's neck in a choke, but his aegis collar would make that difficult and besides, a Space
Marine could go a long time before his three lungs
gave out. By then Sarpedon could have climbed up
the shaft and brought N'Kalo to the Soul Drinkers to
face retribution.

And perhaps most importantly, N'Kalo felt a truth
in Sarpedon's words. N'Kalo wanted to know what
was hidden down here, what could cause a Space
Marine, even a renegade one, to fight his brothers. So
he held back and followed as Sarpedon reached the
bottom of the shaft and headed down a tunnel that
led away to one side.

This tunnel was also carved with images. Eyes and
hands covered the walls, symbols of watching and
warding. N'Kalo could hear, on the hot, damp breeze
washing over him from the far end of the tunnel,
the reedy strains of voices. They were screaming,
hundreds of them, the sounds overlapping like the
threads of a tapestry.

A cavern opened up ahead, wet stone lit from
beneath by a blood-red glow. The screaming got
louder. N'Kalo tensed, unsure of what was ahead,
one part of his brain still watching for a drop in
Sarpedon's guard.

'Molikor,' said Sarpedon, 'has a curious relation-
ship with its dead.'

The tunnel reached the threshold of a sudden drop.
Beyond it was a cavern, as vast as an ocean, filled

almost to the level of the tunnel entrance by a sea of writhing bodies.

N'Kalo was all but stunned by his first sight of it. The awfulness of it, the impossibility, seemed intent on prying his mind from his senses. The bodies were naked, men and women, all ages, the whole spectrum of shapes, sizes and skin tones. The glow was coming from their eyes, and from the wounds that wept bloody and fresh in their bodies. Many bore the scarring of the Eshkeen but there were countless others, from dozens of cultures.

'Who are they?' said N'Kalo.

'Everyone who has ever died on Molikor,' replied Sarpedon. 'No one knows how far down it goes. When you die on Molikor, your body decays and is absorbed by the earth. Then it reforms here, vomited back up by the planet. Here they are, everyone this world has claimed since the Age of Strife.'

'Why… why are you showing me this?' said N'Kalo.

Sarpedon unholstered his bolt pistol. For a moment N'Kalo thought the Soul Drinker would turn on him, but instead Sarpedon held it handle-first towards N'Kalo. 'Because I could not expect you to just take my word for it,' said Sarpedon. 'And besides, I haven't shown you anything yet.'

The bodies heaved up, like a breaking wave. N'Kalo barely had time to close his hand around the bolt pistol before they were surging around him, a terrible flood of gasping limbs. N'Kalo saw they were not corpses, nor alive, but something else, reborn as they had been at the moment of death and filled with the same emotions – fear, anger, abandonment.

Their screams were wordless torrents of pain. One wrapped its arms around N'Kalo, trying to force his head down – N'Kalo blasted it apart with a shot to the upper chest and it flowed past him, reforming in a burst of blood-coloured light.

Sarpedon grabbed N'Kalo's free wrist. 'Follow,' he shouted above the screaming, and hauled N'Kalo off the edge of the drop and into the cavern.

It took a long time for the two Space Marines to forge their way through the dead of Molikor. Sarpedon's arachnid limbs proved adept at opening up a tunnel through the writhing bodies, and their path was lit by the red glow of whatever energy animated these echoes of the dead. The screaming was muffled now, like the crashing of a distant ocean, with the occasional shriek reaching through. N'Kalo followed as Sarpedon burrowed on, winding a path downwards. N'Kalo contemplated shooting him with his own bolt pistol, but then he would be trapped in this ocean of bodies and he did not know if he would be able to climb out of it. And besides, he wanted to know what Sarpedon had to show him. That curiosity was a human emotion, not that of a Space Marine, but nevertheless it gripped N'Kalo now.

Sarpedon pulled back a final veil of bodies and revealed an opening, like an abscess, in the mass. It had formed around a spike of stone, a stalagmite, to which was chained another body.

This body was that of a male Imperial citizen, N'Kalo could tell that at first glance. He had a glowing, raw hole over one eye where a bionic had once been implanted, and the Imperial aquila had been tattooed on one shoulder. He was the only one of Molikor's dead that N'Kalo had seen who was restrained in this way.

'This,' said Sarpedon, 'is Manter Thyll. He was sent by the Parliaments of Molikor to explore the delta marshlands. He found the Eshkeen and bargained his way into the pit, to see what they were so intent on protecting. They thought when he saw this place, he would treat its protection as a sacred undertaking just like they did. But they were wrong.'

Sarpedon took a data-slate from the belt of his armour. N'Kalo hadn't noticed it before, since his attention had been focussed on Sarpedon's abhorrent mutations to the exclusion of such a detail.

'This is the report he sent back to the Parliaments,' said Sarpedon.

The image was of poor quality, only just recognisable as the face of the man chained to the rock. In life, Manter Thyll had combined an explorer's ruggedness with a gentlemanly façade, his well-weathered face surmounted by a powdered periwig.

'*–the Eshkeen had guarded it for generations, my lords. And though at first appearance it was a horrible sight, yet upon closer examination and the questioning of my Eshkeen hosts I came to understand it is the greatest treasure this world possesses. They are not living beings, you see, but they are not dead. They do not age, they do not tire. They simply exist. Think, my lords! Think what a resource they could be! An endless source of brute labour! If they can be trained then all is well, if not then a simple system of electronics and interfaces would suffice to make* *them useful. I believe that the dead of Molikor are the most potent natural resource on this entire–'*

Sarpedon paused the recording. N'Kalo stared dumbly for a few seconds at Thyll's image, then at the man's face.

'He came back to bargain with the Eshkeen for access to the pit,' said Sarpedon. 'They knew what he wanted by then. They killed him.'

'Did they chain his body here?' said N'Kalo.

'No. I did, so that I could show it to someone like you. What Thyll and the Parliamentarians did not realise, but what the Eshkeen have known for thousands of years, is that power like this cannot be tapped without consequences. The veil between realspace and the warp is thin here. The emotions of the dying find form in the warp and are cast back out into this pit. The ancestors of Molikor's tribes knew it, and they sent their best warriors to guard the pit. They grew to be the Eshkeen. When the Imperium settled Molikor, the Parliamentarians learned of the pit and they decided they wanted it for themselves, without having any idea what it truly was.'

Sarpedon began to tear at the mass again, opening a path back up towards the surface. N'Kalo could only follow, conflicting emotions coursing through him. The immensity of what Sarpedon was saying, the concept of a world that regurgitated its dead as these mindless things, the claim that the Parliamentarians were the aggressors and that the Eshkeen were the only thing standing between Molikor and damnation – it weighed on him, and would not sit straight in his mind. Everything N'Kalo had believed about Molikor, everything he had assumed, was wrong.

THE FIRST PARLIAMENT of Molikor, the Father of Power, the Imperial Seat, the Font of Majesty, towered over the assembled councillors like a second set of heavens. The dome of the First Parliament was painted to resemble a sky: dramatic clouds backlit by golden sunlight echoing fanciful images of Terra's own glories. The members of the First Parliament, drawn from the lesser parliaments of Molikor's cities, were resplendent in the uniforms of the planet's many militaries or the finery of their mercantile houses, wearing the symbol of the aquila to proclaim their loyalty to the Imperium.

Three thousand men and women were gathered beneath the First Parliament's dome, the centremost place taken by Lord Speaker Vannarian Wrann. Wrann, as the mouthpiece of the First Parliament, was recognised as Molikor's Imperial Governor. He was a sturdy and squat man, ermine-trimmed robes hanging off wide shoulders. He wore the massive gilded chain of his office around where his neck would have been had one existed between his barrel chest and shaven, glowering lump of a head. On the chain hung a silver aquila studded with diamonds and rubies, to match the fat gemstones on the rings he wore on his stubby fingers.

'Men and women of the First Parliament!' shouted Wrann. 'You sons and daughters of the Imperial Will! We hereby recognise Commander N'Kalo of the Iron Knights!'

N'Kalo made his way down the aisle towards the centre of the dome. Every eye followed him. Jaded as they were by every honour and beautification Molikor could place before them, the sight of a Space Marine was something new to them. Those closest shuddered in fear as N'Kalo walked past, for even in his knightly armour with its crests and laurels there was no mistaking that he was fundamentally a killing machine.

'Honoured councillors of Molikor,' began N'Kalo as he approached Wrann. 'Many thanks for receiving me to the heart of your government. The Iron Knights, as you do, claim the will of the Emperor as their warrant to arms, and in this we are brethren beneath His sight.'

'You are welcomed, Commander N'Kalo, and your brother Space Marines are granted all honours it is the First Parliament's right to bestow. Truly you stand before us as saviours of our people, as deliverers of our citizens from the threats that have so gravely beset us.' Wrann's words were met with polite applause from the First Parliament's members. 'Do you come here to tell us that the rebellion has been quashed?' he continued. 'That the hateful Eshkeen will no longer plague our lands with their savagery, and that the Emperor's rule shall continue on Molikor?'

N'Kalo removed his helm. In spite of the need to keep up appearances, many councillors could not help grimacing or even turning away at the sight of N'Kalo's burned face, its skin here blackened, there deformed like wax that had melted and recooled, and elsewhere missing entirely.

'No, Lord Speaker,' he said. 'I have not.'

His words were met with silence. Those councillors who did not stare in grim fascination at N'Kalo's face glanced uneasily between their neighbours.

'Commander?' said Wrann. 'Pray, explain yourself.'

'I have seen the pit,' said N'Kalo. 'I have heard the words of Manter Thyll. When my Iron Knights answered the call for intervention from this Parliament, they did so without critical thought, without exploring first the history of this world and the true nature of its conflicts. Ours is the way of action, not contemplation. But we were forced into examining Molikor by allies of the Eshkeen, who also responded to your pleas for assistance, but to find out the truth, not merely destroy the Eshkeen as you desired.'

'Of what pit do you speak?' demanded Wrann. 'And this Manter Thyll? We know nothing of–'

'Do not lie to me!' shouted N'Kalo. The councillors sitting closest to him tried to scramble away, ending up on one another's laps to put some distance between them and the angry Space Marine. 'I sought to understand for myself. I went to the historical archives in Molik Tertiam. Yes, to that place you thought hidden from the eyes of outsiders! My battle-brothers stormed the estate of Horse Marshal Konigen, that hero of your history, and demanded of him the truth of why he first led his armies into the delta lands! We know the truth, my brothers and I. The war on Molikor is not about an uprising by the Eshkeen. It is about your desire to exploit Molikor's dead as labour for your mines and shipyards! It is about the wealth they can bring you! It is about your willingness to exploit the powers bleeding from the warp, and the Eshkeen's determination to prevent you from committing such a sin!'

'Then what would you have us do?' shouted Wrann. 'This frontier hangs by a thread! Without the war materiel that such labour could produce, we will never hold the Ghoul Stars! Humanity can barely survive out here as it is! Would you have us enslave our own? Would you have us grind our own hands to bone?'

'No,' replied N'Kalo calmly. 'I would have you leave.'

The *Judgement upon Garadan* made little concession to the embellishment and glorification that endowed many other Adeptus Astartes strike cruisers. It was every inch a warship, all riveted iron and hard, brutal lines, and as it hung in orbit over Molikor it seemed to glower down at the clouded planet. The lion-head crest, mounted above the prow like heraldry on a feudal knight's helm, was the sole concession to appearances.

Inside, the *Judgement* was much the same, with little to suggest the glorious history the Iron Knights brought with them. N'Kalo conducted most of his ship's business from the monastic cell in which he trained and meditated when his flag-captain did not require him on the bridge. The pict screen mounted on one wall showed a close-up of the space above Molikor's main spaceport. N'Kalo watched as a flock of merchant and cargo ships drifted up from the cloud cover, a shower of silvery sparks. On those ships was the Imperial population of Molikor, among them the Parliamentarian leaders. Those leaders had, less than three days ago, received an ivory scroll case containing orders to evacuate their planet on pain of destruction. Those orders were signed with a single 'I', which gave them an authority within the Imperium second only to the word of the God-Emperor Himself.

Inside the scroll case had also been a string of rosarius beads. It was a traditional message. If you defy these orders, they implied, then use these beads to pray, for prayer is your only hope of deliverance.

Events moved slowly in space, given the vast distances involved. The pict screen flicked between the views of the fleeing Parliamentarian ships, and the single vessel, its livery gold and black, that drifted in from its concealed observation position behind one of Molikor's moons. This ship, of which N'Kalo did not know the name, had arrived at Molikor so quickly it must have possessed archeotech or even xenos drives to have made so rapid a journey through the warp.

It was a vessel of the Inquisition. N'Kalo needed no communications with the craft to know that. His flag-captain had hailed it anyway and, as expected, there had been no reply. The Adeptus Astartes had done their job on Molikor. Now the Inquisition took over, and they answered to no one.

N'Kalo had seen quarantine orders enforced before. He hoped that everyone had got off Molikor safely. Though he had little love for the Parliamentarians, once the lead conspirators had been weeded out those who remained would be largely blameless

Imperial citizens. The Inquisition would quarantine the world, destroy the spaceport and let it be known that it was forbidden thanks to the bizarre warp disturbance beneath its crust that caused it to spew its dead out as mindless facsimiles. The Parliamentarians who had sought to exploit the pit would be tried, questioned and probably executed for dabbling so willingly in matters of the warp. N'Kalo did not think much about their fates. Worse things happened to better people with every moment in the Imperium. He would not waste his thoughts on them. This was a grim business, but he had faith that this was the way it had to be.

The Soul Drinkers did not have faith, not in the Imperium. Perhaps that was understandable, thought N'Kalo. He had seen the same things they had, the same brutality and the spiteful randomness of how the fortunes of the Imperium were parcelled out. He had not strayed beyond the Imperial line – he had informed the Inquisition of the threat on Molikor, after all – but he was forced to wonder, considering the recent events there in his cell, whether he would have to have seen many more injustices to end up renegades like the Soul Drinkers.

'Commander N'Kalo,' came a vox from the flag-captain. 'We are receiving a communication, tagged for you by name.'

'Send it,' said N'Kalo.

'Greetings, commander,' said a voice that, until a short time ago, had been an unfamiliar one reaching N'Kalo's ears through the gunfire and crunching branches of the forest gap.

'Sarpedon,' said N'Kalo. 'I had not expected you to still be around. You should be warned that the Inquisition would dearly love to listen in.'

'My ship has communications even the Inquisition cannot intercept in a hurry,' replied Sarpedon. His voice was transmitted in real time, meaning the Soul Drinkers and their ship had to be close by. 'I wanted to thank you for doing the right thing by Molikor and the Eshkeen. You could have followed the Imperial line, but you did not. That takes something beyond mere bravery.'

'I did not turn in the Parliaments of Molikor to garner thanks,' replied N'Kalo. 'I did it because it had to be done. The moral threat on that world could not have been left unchecked. But I am glad that I was not the instrument of injustice and so I should pay thanks to you, for showing me all the paths I might take.'

'And yet I suspect that your gratitude will not prevent you from turning in a renegade and a mutant like myself,' said Sarpedon, 'and so I must leave here.'

'I concur, Sarpedon. That would be wise. I have one question before you go.'

'Speak it.'

'What happened to the Eshkeen?'

N'Kalo thought he heard a small chuckle. 'Do not fear for them,' said Sarpedon. 'My Chapter possesses the means to transport them somewhere they can start anew, and where the Imperium will not rediscover them for a very long time.'

'I see. For my sake it is best I leave it at that. Fare well, Sarpedon, and I shall pray that our paths do not cross, for I feel if they do I must fight to bring you in.'

'I shall pray for that too, Commander N'Kalo. Emperor's speed to you.'

The comm-channel went dead.

In the hours to follow, the scanners of the *Judgement upon Garadan* detected the possible signature of a ship making a warp jump near the outlying worlds of the Molikor System. The signature suggested a ship far bigger than any Imperial craft, however, and one that seemed dark and shadowy as if cloaked by some stealth system beyond Imperial technology. N'Kalo did not challenge his flag-captain when the event was logged and dismissed as a sensor error, and the Soul Drinkers vanished from the Chapter history of the Iron Knights.

# CHAPTER SEVEN

'AND WHAT,' SAID Captain Borganor of the Howling Griffons, 'does this excuse?'

The court was not as vocal as it had been after Varnica's evidence. Instead, it simmered. The Howling Griffons murmured oaths and spat on the ground. The Imperial Fists tried to stay impartial but they could not keep the disdain from their faces as N'Kalo's testimony had come to an end. Reinez had fought to remain silent, eyes closed, face downturned and grim.

'How many of my battle-brothers does this return from their tombs?' continued Borganor. 'The Soul Drinkers intervened in some backwater spat. What does this say about them? They still fought the Imperial divine right. All they have achieved to tickle Commander N'Kalo's sense of righteousness is the deliverance of one band of savages to Throne knows what fate. Are we to absolve Sarpedon of my own brethren's fall? Will someone speak for the Howling Griffons?'

'Or for the Crimson Fists?' interjected Reinez. 'What have the Eshkeen done to earn a voice in this court? Every one of my fallen brothers is worth a thousand times the heathens the Soul Drinkers saved!'

'If I may,' interrupted Gethsemar of the Angels Sanguine, 'I feel I can shed a little more light on the matters pertinent to the fate of the Soul Drinkers.'

'What could you say, you gilded peacock?' spat Reinez.

'Reinez, you will yield the floor!' demanded Chapter Master Pugh.

'What has his kind suffered at Sarpedon's hand?' retorted Reinez. 'He comes here for nothing more than the spectacle of this mutant! This is entertainment for him! He treats the sacred ground of the *Phalanx* like a sideshow!'

'Your objections,' said Pugh coldly, 'are noted. Commander Gethsemar, say your piece.'

Gethsemar waited a moment, as if to ensure that all the attention of the court was on him. The mask he wore now had no tears, and the forehead and cheeks were inscribed with High Gothic text. 'Indeed, my piece is more relevant than any of the protestations Captain Reinez has yet made,' he said. 'And I feel that few will recall words more incandescent in this matter than those I have to say now.'

'Get on with it, you popinjay,' muttered Reinez.

'The Sanguinary Priests of my order,' continued

Gethsemar, 'have long conducted studies into the link between the gene-seed every Space Marine carries within him and the blessed flesh of our primarchs, after whose characteristics the gene-seed of the original eighteen Legions was modelled. Indeed, much had been revealed to us of holy Sanguinius, the father of our own Chapter, and thus we gain revelations of him that steel our souls on the eve of battle. It so happened that the Angels Sanguine came into possession of a sample of gene-seed originating from the Soul Drinkers Chapter, delivered unto us in the hope that we could ascertain if their rebellion was founded in a corruption of such gene-seed.'

'Where did you get it from?' said Sarpedon. 'Which brother of mine supplied it?'

'No brother of yours, I fear,' said Gethsemar. 'It was given to us by the Soul Drinker to whom it belonged, one who had defied your usurping of the Chapter's command and sought, through Inquisitorial means, a way to exact his revenge.'

'Michairas,' said Sarpedon bleakly. 'I thought I had killed him. I did so at the second time of asking, on Stratix Luminae. I underestimated my old novice. He still tries for revenge, even after death.'

'And he has it,' continued Gethsemar. 'Space Marines of the court, Lord Justice, the Sanguinary Priests went about their research in the expectation that they would find the blueprint of Rogal Dorn's own flesh as the starting point for the Soul Drinkers' gene-seed. But they did not.'

'What are you saying?' asked Sarpedon.

'I am saying that Rogal Dorn is not your primarch,'

said Gethsemar simply. 'I cannot say who is. The Sanguinary Priests have yet to complete their discourses on the matter. But Dorn's gene-seed is among the most stable and recognisable of all those among the Adeptus Astartes, and there can be no doubt that the Soul Drinkers do not possess it. This is the news I came to the *Phalanx* to deliver. That is why the Angels Sanguine sought a place at this court.'

Sarpedon pushed against his restraints, half-clambering out of the accused's pulpit. 'No!' he yelled. 'You have taken everything from us! Our freedom! Our war! You will not take away Rogal Dorn!'

'The defendant will be silent!' yelled Pugh, above the sound of dozens of bolt pistols being drawn. Every weapon in the dome was being aimed then at Sarpedon, in case he burst through his restraints to do violence to Gethsemar. Lysander stood between Sarpedon and Gethsemar, ready to slam Sarpedon into the ground if he showed any signs of breaking free.

Reinez did not move. He had seen all the damage done to Sarpedon that could be done. For the first time since he had come to the *Phalanx*, there was a smirk on his face.

BROTHER SENNON LIMPED through the Atoning Halls, barely drawing a glance from the Soul Drinkers who sat in its cells, chained to the walls waiting for a decision to be made in the Observatory of Dornian Majesty. The news of Daenyathos's survival had left them as confused as elated. The Philosopher-Soldier's presence there had been brief, a few seconds, before the Dreadnought had been sealed away, and now none of the Soul Drinkers could be completely sure they had seen him at all. Their minds were occupied as the single pilgrim walked down the corridor.

Two Imperial Fists walked behind him as guards, but Sennon looked in more danger from his own health than from the Soul Drinkers. His skin was bluish and sweating, his eyes rimmed with red, his shoulders slumped as if he could barely hold up his own weight. His breath was a painful wheeze.

He passed the cell where Sergeant Salk was held. The sergeant was exhausted, his arms bruised from forcing against his restraints long past the point where it was obvious he would not break free. Other Soul Drinkers were at prayer or simply at rest, half their minds shut off while the other half watched, a Space Marine's habit made possible by the catalepsean node each had implanted between the hemispheres of his brain. The Soul Drinkers had been fed by regular servitor rounds, but that was the sole concession made to their comfort. Since Daenyathos had been sealed away they had been silent, every one contemplating his situation in his own way, eager for news of Sarpedon and the trial but unwilling to beg their Imperial Fists captors for it.

One cell held Chaplain Iktinos. This cell had been sealed so no other Soul Drinker could see or hear the Chaplain. Iktinos's rhetoric was considered one of the biggest threats to keeping the Soul Drinkers captive, and so a steel plate had been welded over the bars of his cell. The Soul Drinkers who had made up his flock, those who had lost their officers and gone to Iktinos for leadership, had been spread out through the Atoning Halls to minimise their ability to conspire. Sennon passed the sealed cell and touched it with two fingers, murmuring a prayer for Iktinos's soul.

Sennon halted at Captain Luko's cell, and knelt on the floor.

'Take care,' said Luko. 'You don't look like you could get up again.'

'I have come to pray for you,' said Sennon.

'Pray for yourself,' replied Luko. 'All the prayers that might help us were used up on Selaaca.'

'You are not beyond hope,' said Sennon, apparently unconcerned with the mix of pity and scorn with which Luko looked at him. Luko, compared to Sennon, was a chained giant, and the power held within every Space Marine was not lessened by the manacles that held him against the back wall of the cell or the bars that stood between the two of them. 'There is none so close to the precipice that the Emperor's grace cannot bring him back.'

'And what of those who have gone over the precipice? What about them? To pray for them is a sin, is it not?'

'I do not believe you are among them, Captain Luko.'

'You know my name,' said Luko.

'I have read of the Soul Drinkers,' said Sennon. 'The Imperial Fists made available much of their information so that my sect might better observe the process of justice. The Blinded Eye we may be, but we do not do our duty by remaining blind when knowledge is available.'

'The Inquisition passed a deletion order on us, you

know,' said Luko. 'They could probably hang you for knowing we exist.'

'It is the Imperial Fists who hold sway here,' replied Sennon. 'The Inquisition may have its due from us once we leave the *Phalanx*, but that is an acceptable price to pay to see justice done in so grave a case as this.'

'It must be such a relief to see such a simple galaxy around you,' said Luko, but the scorn was drying out from his voice. 'Imagine knowing what is right and wrong. Imagine believing, completely believing, that one way was good and another was bad, and never having to think for yourself about it. I have such envy for you, pilgrim.'

'Then you doubt that you have taken the right path? Doubt is a sin, Captain Luko.'

Luko smiled without humour. 'Thanks. I'll add it to the list.'

'I shall pray for you.'

'No, you will not. I will not be prayed for.'

'You are in chains. You have no say in whether you are prayed for or not.'

That, at least, was something Luko had no stomach to argue. Sennon knelt before Luko's cell, eyes closed and head bowed. His breathing became quieter, and for all Luko knew the young pilgrim might have died there before his cell.

'I have such envy for you,' said Luko, too quiet for anyone but himself to hear.

SARPEDON BARELY REGISTERED the journey back to his cell as the Imperial Fists marched him out of the

Observatory of Dornian Majesty once again. The first couple of times he had sized up his guards and the route they took for the best time to attempt escape. His hands were manacled but he still had the use of his legs – the six he had remaining, at least – and he was faster and stronger than any of the four Imperial Fists flanking him.

But he could not take them all down. They were armed and armoured; Sarpedon was not. The inhibitor collar prevented his use of the Hell, which might have sown enough confusion for him to flee. From what he had gathered about the layout of the *Phalanx*, it would be difficult to put any distance between himself and the dome, crammed with hostile Space Marines, before the alarm was raised. The idea of escape was now all but forgotten, filed away in that part of an Space Marine's mind where rejected battle plans lay waiting to be dusted off again.

Captain Borganor was ahead of Sarpedon and his Imperial Fist minders, at a junction of corridors where the science labs and map rooms surrounding the Observatory met the stone-lined corridors of the Atoning Halls.

'Halt, brethren,' said Borganor. 'I would speak with the prisoner.'

'On what authority?' said the lead Imperial Fist.

'On that of brotherhood,' said Borganor. 'I have no dispensation from Lord Pugh, if that is what you ask. I merely wish to put the question to the defendant that every Space Marine on this ship has longed to ask. I shall not hold you long. As a brother, I ask this of you.'

'We have all heard the outrages visited upon the Howling Griffons by the Soul Drinkers,' said the Imperial Fist. 'Ask if you will, but you shall not hold us long.'

'My thanks,' said Borganor. The Imperial Fists backed away from Sarpedon a little to give Borganor a semblance of privacy as he approached Sarpedon.

Sarpedon thought again of escape. Or, at least, of fighting. He had beaten Borganor before, as evidenced by the bionic leg Borganor sported. But attacking the Howling Griffon would not get him free. More to the point, it would not achieve anything. Sarpedon had no particular hate for Borganor. The Howling Griffon was a victim of the viciousness of the Imperium, in his own way. Sarpedon backed down mentally, and decided that he would not fight here.

'What do you wish to know?' said Sarpedon.

Borganor was close to him now. He had been as bellicose as anyone in the courtroom, but Borganor seemed to have calmed down a little since then. Perhaps the certainty that the end was close, that Pugh and the other Space Marines were even now deciding how Sarpedon was to be executed, had cooled some of the fire in him.

'What do you think?' said Borganor. 'I want to know why.'

'Why?'

'Why you turned on the Imperium. In all the debating and argument, no one has yet understood why you turned the Soul Drinkers renegade. Was it Abraxes? Did your rebellion start with corruption? Speak the truth, Sarpedon, for there is no use for lies now.'

'We saw,' said Sarpedon, 'what the Imperium really was. I believe we had already known it, but that the weight of history and tradition muted that understanding in us. The Imperium is a wicked place, captain. How many citizens live free of fear and misery? I doubt you could name a single one. It is built on cruelty and malice. And in punishing its people and committing the evils it says are necessary, it gives a breeding ground to those enemies it claims to be fighting. The armies of Chaos do not materialise from thin air. They are made up of those who were once citizens of that same Imperium, but who were corrupted first by its horrors. That is what leaves them susceptible to the whispers of the Dark Gods. Were the Emperor able to walk among us still, He would look on what mankind has created in horror and seek to tear it down. The Imperium is not the last bastion against the enemy. It *is* the enemy.'

'Then you claim what Varnica said is untrue? That Abraxes never led you down his own path?'

'Abraxes used us, that is true,' replied Sarpedon. 'He took our anger at the Imperium and used it to manipulate us into destroying his enemies. But that anger was there before he got his claws into us, and we killed Abraxes for what he did. I am not proud of how blind he once made us. It was his touch that gave me these mutations, and I was ignorant of what they truly meant until Abraxes was gone. But he did not teach us to despise the Imperium. We managed that on our own.'

Borganor shook his head. 'So deep your delusions cut that you see them only as truth,' he said.

'I am minded to say the same about you, captain.'

'I begged of Pugh the right to kill you myself,' continued Borganor. 'To pay you back for all my battle-brothers you killed. For Librarian Mercaeno, a man far better than any of your brethren.'

'And did he grant you that right?'

'He did not.'

'You could do it now,' said Sarpedon calmly. 'These Imperial Fists would not turn their guns on you. You would finish me off before they could stop you, I have little doubt about that.'

'No, Sarpedon. I wanted to do it slowly.' Borganor was almost face to face with Sarpedon now. 'To pull your legs off like a child does to a fly.'

'Because I took your leg?'

'Because you took my leg. But I wanted to understand what could drive a Space Marine as far as you have gone, before I did it.'

'And do you understand?'

Borganor took a step back. 'I understand that Abraxes warped your minds and implanted in you the belief that your rebellion was your own idea. There must have been something dark and heretical in your souls to begin with, to let his influence in. You were the weakest of all your Chapter, which is why it chose you as its instrument. You are damned, and death is too merciful for you however it is administered. That is what I believe.'

'What a comfort it must be, Captain Borganor, to have the Dark Gods to blame for anything you are too afraid to understand.'

'Brothers!' came a cry from down the corridor.

An Imperial Fists scout was running towards them. He paused to salute Borganor. 'Captain! Lord Pugh requests your return to the Observatory. A verdict has been reached.'

'Already?' said Sarpedon.

'There can have been little debate,' said Borganor with a grim smile. 'Good.'

'Then follow,' said the scout. 'The accused must be present. Any sentence will be carried out immediately.'

'Oh, I do not think anything will be immediate,' said Borganor. 'Remember, Sarpedon? As a child does to a fly?'

The Imperial Fists closed in around Sarpedon, shepherding him back towards the Observatory of Dornian Majesty. Sarpedon glanced back at Borganor, who followed. There was nothing in the Howling Griffon's demeanour to suggest he had any intention but to pull Sarpedon apart piece by piece, regardless of what Pugh decreed.

But he would decree execution, whatever form it was to take. There had been no doubt about that from the moment Sarpedon had squared up to Lysander on Selaaca. He had come to the *Phalanx* to die. He had taken comfort that his Chapter would be executed under the eye of Rogal Dorn, who at least would know that the Soul Drinkers were not the traitors the Imperium perceived them to be... But now, with Gethsemar's revelation, even that was in doubt.

Sarpedon would die alone. The galaxy was too cruel, he supposed, to have expected anything else.

*  *  *

'IT IS DONE,' said Brother Sennon. He clambered to his feet, unsteady, his knees having locked up during his long prayer.

'What did you ask Him for?' said Luko. There was sarcasm in his voice, but Sennon didn't seem to have picked it up.

'I asked Him for what He promises everyone. He grants us, if there is any piety in our hearts, a second chance. In our final moments we can be redeemed, if we are pure of heart when our souls come to be weighed against His example.'

'We must leave,' said one of the Imperial Fists escorting Sennon. 'Time in the heretics' presence is rationed. They are a moral threat.'

'My soul is steeled against such things,' replied Sennon. 'I am frail on the outside, but there is none stronger within than a follower of the Blinded Eye.'

'Be that as it may,' said the Imperial Fist, 'we all have our orders.'

'Of course.' Brother Sennon looked up and down the corridor of the Atoning Halls. At one end was a complicated rack, where Imperial Fists in the past had mortified their flesh to atone for some slight against the honour of their Chapter. At the other was a pair of blast doors, sealed. 'Is this where the Dreadnought is held?' asked Sennon, walking towards the doors.

'It is,' replied the Imperial Fist. 'We have no business there. Daenyathos, if it truly is he, will be dealt with separately when the judgement has been pronounced.'

'To think of it,' said Sennon. 'He must be six thousand years old. He fought at Terra, you know, during the Wars of Apostasy. To us a time of legends, to him, living memory.'

'Past deeds mean nothing when corruption rules the present,' said the Imperial Fist. 'Brother Sennon, we must leave.'

Sennon was right in front of the blast doors now. He placed a hand against them, as if feeling for a heart-beat. 'Just a moment more,' he said. 'Just a moment.'

Sennon turned back towards the Imperial Fists, a smile on his face like that of a saint rendered in stained glass. He seemed about to speak again, and then Brother Sennon exploded.

THE COURT WAS full, all the Space Marines in attend-ance to witness the condemnation of Sarpedon. After him the rest of the Soul Drinkers would be filed through here to receive their death sentences, but it was Sarpedon's that really counted. In the eyes of those who wanted vengeance against them, Sarpedon *was* the Soul Drinkers, and his fate fell on them all.

Reinez stood, arms folded, waiting for the sen-tence as if he were in attendance as executioner. It was more likely that Captain Lysander would do the deed, standing as he was beside the pulpit with his hammer in his hand. Commander Gethsemar wore his weeping mask again, perhaps to remember the Space Marines who had died at Soul Drinker hands. N'Kalo wore his helmet again – presumably it had been hammered back into shape in the forges of the *Phalanx*, and N'Kalo's twice-ruined face was hidden once more. Chapter Master Pugh stood among the

Imperial Fists, ready to pronounce his findings.

'The accused will take to the pulpit,' said Pugh.

Sarpedon did as he was told. If there had been a time to fight back, save for the ill-fated lashing out in the apothecarion, then it had long since passed. It would serve no purpose, either. He had no particular hate for the Space Marines who had gathered here to see him killed. He had been like them once, except perhaps a little more prideful, a little more arrogant. He did not even hate Reinez. A moment of pity, perhaps, but not hate.

'Sarpedon of the Soul Drinkers,' began Pugh. 'Words have been said for and against your conduct. The evidence gathered has been examined with criticism as well as zeal. I am confident that honour and tradition have been served in every action of this court, and that the conclusions we draw are true and just before the sight of Rogal Dorn and the Emperor Most High.'

'May I speak?' said Sarpedon.

'Speak if you will,' said Pugh, 'but our conclusions have been arrived at, and need only pronouncement. Your words will mean nothing.'

'My gratitude, Lord Justice,' said Sarpedon. 'Space Marines, I call you brothers, though I know you think yourselves no brothers of mine. When I turned on Chapter Master Gorgoleon and took command of my Chapter, I did it because I saw in us a terrible corruption. Not the corruption of the warp, nor some darkness of the xenos, but a very human corruption of the soul. We believed ourselves to be superior, to be the shepherds of the human race, for we were ordained within the priesthood of Terra with the role of watchdogs and executioners. Yet that priesthood, and the Imperium it ruled, were the true enemy. For every human killed or made to suffer by the predations of the warp or the alien, a billion more are dealt the same fate by the Imperium. The Emperor is just a hollow figurehead now, an excuse for the cruelty the Imperium inflicts, yet when He walked among us He strove for the safety and glory of every man and woman. Would you have me grovel and beg for forgiveness, for leading my Chapter to do the will of the Emperor when it conflicted with the malice of the Imperium? The death of every Space Marine weighs on me. The Howling Griffons and Crimson Fists who died in our conflicts I feel as sharply as the deaths of my own brothers. But I will not say that I am sorry. I have done nothing wrong. And if the story of the Soul Drinkers causes any one of you to doubt the right of the Imperium to oppress and murder the Emperor's faithful, then our deaths will not have been in vain.'

Reinez met Sarpedon's words with sarcastic applause, slow hand claps that echoed in the Observatory of Dornian Majesty. Everyone else was silent.

'Then I pronounce on you the sentence of death,' said Pugh, 'to be administered by the Imperial Fists swiftly, as befits the death of another Space Marine, and the striking of the name Sarpedon and those of all the Soul Drinkers from any bonds of oath or honour. To carry out this sentence I appoint Captain Lysander as executioner and Apothecary Asclephin as overseer. Sarpedon, you will be taken from this place to the Chapel of Martyrs where you will be killed, your body incinerated and any remains jettisoned into space. Your battle-brothers will follow. That is the pronouncement of this court.'

Sarpedon bowed his head. It was as good as he could have expected.

A stirring in the assembled Space Marines broke his train of thought. Several of them were looking upwards, through the dome. The smeared lights of the Veiled Region silhouetted a form approaching rapidly – a spaceship, smaller by magnitudes than the *Phalanx*, its engines burning full thrust as it hurtled right towards the dome.

Fire spat towards it. The automated turrets of the *Phalanx* had activated in time and the shape exploded in the brief burst of flame that was sucked away by the vacuum a split second later. But the ship was not vaporised, merely blown apart, and a chunk of its hull still spun on its original course towards the dome.

'The pilgrim ship,' said Lysander. 'Close the dome!'

The dome was protected by armour plates that began to close like the lids of a huge circular eye, but every Space Marine could see it would not close fast enough.

'Everyone out!' yelled Pugh. 'We are betrayed! Enemies abound! Brothers, flee this place!'

'The condemned seeks vengeance!' shouted Reinez over the growing commotion as the Space Marines left their seats and headed for the exits, the burning mass of the pilgrim ship's hull looming larger through the dome. 'His allies want to take us with him! I will not flee while this traitor yet lives!'

'Damnation, Reinez!' yelled Lysander. 'Get–'

The hull segment crashed into the dome. The armoured shutters were halfway closed when it hit. The dome shattered, shards of thick armoured glass falling like knives. The air boomed out and a terrible half-silence fell, the shrieking of metal and the howling of flame muffled as if coming from beneath the earth.

Sarpedon's augmented lungs closed his windpipes to preserve what air he had in his body. The disaster unfolded around him in slow motion. Space Marines were diving for cover from the chunks of burning metal raining down. In surreal slow motion, one Imperial Fist lost his leg at the knee, sheared off by a shard of the dome. Another, along with a Howling Griffon, disappeared under a torrent of twisted steel and fire. Space Marines were thrown aside as Pugh's honour guard fought to force him through the doors. Gethsemar's Angels Sanguine leapt from the seats out through the entrances on the exhaust plumes of their jump packs.

All was Chaos. The bulk of the pilgrim ship's hull was wedged in the blinded eye socket of the dome, but it had split open along the lines of its hull plates and was spewing torrents of burning wreckage into the dome. Sarpedon couldn't see Reinez or Lysander, the two Space Marines who had been closest to him, and his body instinctively fought against his restraints.

One part of him was screaming that he had no air, and that even a Space Marine's three lungs could not hold out for long in hard vacuum. The other part fought to escape. Sarpedon had never tested his bonds in the pulpit properly, for there had never been any chance of him escaping beneath the sight of so many Space Marines. Now he pulled against the manacles and shackles with strength he was not sure he still had.

The structure of the pulpit gave way. Hardwood and steel broke under the force. Sarpedon ripped his manacles off and grabbed the struts of the shackles that held his six remaining legs in place. They broke away, too, and Sarpedon, though still dragging his restraints behind him, was free.

He ran for the nearest exit. A sheet of steel, a section of the pilgrim ship's deck, fell like a giant guillotine blade, and he skidded to a halt just before it sliced him in two. He scrambled up it, almost as nimble over a vertical surface as a horizontal one, and saw ahead of him the blast doors closing. A klaxon was blaring, the sound transmitted through the floor and his talons, explosions like dull thuds all around, the whole chamber vibrating as metal tore. He saw a dying Howling Griffon, one side of his torso opened up, organs trailing from his torn armour. His eyes were rolled back and he was convulsing. Sarpedon could not help him.

Sarpedon jumped and skidded through the blast doors. A tangle of wreckage was blocking them from closing completely. He hauled the twisted metal free and the doors boomed close, air howling around him and screaming in his ears as the corridor beyond repressurised.

Sarpedon took a breath. It felt like the first in a lifetime. His throat was raw as he gulped down air. His

mind, tight and dull in his head, seemed to flow back
to full capacity with the return of oxygen.

Sarpedon looked around him. He was in a tech
lab, with benches heavy with verispex equipment
and banks of datamedium racked on the walls. It
was where Techmarines and their assistant crewmen
would conduct experiments on captured tech, or craft
the delicate mechanisms of bespoke weapons and
armour. The walls were inlaid with bronze geometric
designs and a cogitator stood against one wall like an
altar, its brass case covered in candles that had half-
burned away. The floor was scattered with broken
equipment and the detritus of their work, thrown
about by the gale of escaping air.

Sarpedon paused. He did not know the layout of
the *Phalanx*. He remembered the way back to his cell
well enough, but he doubted there was any point in
returning there.

What point was there in doing anything? He could
not escape the *Phalanx*, surely. The Imperial Fists
would be hunting him down as soon as they had
counted their own dead. He was free, but what did
it matter?

It had to count for something. He fought the fatal-
ism that had weighed him down since his capture.
While he still lived, he could still fight, he could still
make his life mean something...

'Sarpedon!' yelled a voice that he recognised with
a lurch.

Reinez, his pilgrim's tatters even more ragged and
his face scorched, limped from a doorway into the
lab. He had been caught in the flames and the edges

of his armour were singed, but he had not lost his grip on the thunder hammer that served him like an extension of his own body.

'Captain Reinez,' said Sarpedon. 'I see that neither of us is easy to kill.'

'You are not free, traitor!' barked Reinez. 'There is no freedom under my watch! I sought your execution, and it will happen this day!'

Sarpedon was unarmed and unarmoured. He had not fought for what was, by his standards, a long time, and his lungs and muscles still burned. But he was still a Space Marine, and the moment did not exist when a Space Marine was unprepared to fight.

Reinez charged, yelling as he held his hammer high. It was a move of pure anger, reckless, unthinking. Wrong. Sarpedon scuttled up one wall, talons finding purchase in the raised designs, and Reinez's hammer slammed into the wall behind him. The hammer ripped a deep dent in the wall, wires and coolant pipes spilling out as he wrenched it free.

Sarpedon clung to the web of lumen-strips and wires that covered the ceiling. Reinez yelled in frustration and swung up at Sarpedon, but he dropped down onto a lab bench in front of him and kicked a complex microscope array into Reinez's unprotected face. Dozens of lenses and sharp brass struts shattered and Reinez stumbled back, blinded for a moment.

Sarpedon pounced on him, front limbs striking down, back limbs wrapping around. Reinez fell back with Sarpedon on top of him, fighting for the hammer which was the only weapon between them. Sarpedon tore it from Reinez's hands and threw it aside, the power field discharging like caged lightning as the weapon tumbled across the room.

Reinez punched up at Sarpedon. Sarpedon batted Reinez's fist aside and followed up with a punch of his own, his knuckles cracking against Reinez's jaw. With his armour on, a gauntleted fist would have broken the jaw – as it was Reinez was merely stunned for a moment, long enough for Sarpedon to roll him over, lift him up off the floor and drive him head-first into the cogitator against the room's back wall.

Power flashed. Components pinged out of the ruined machine, valves popping, cogs firing out like bullets. Reinez pulled himself free, blood running down his face and the pitted surface of his tarnished breastplate.

'You are no executioner!' yelled Sarpedon. 'You failed! You have become this unthinking, hating creature, because you cannot accept that you failed! If you killed me your failure would still stand and your life would mean nothing! You should be grateful I never gave you the chance!'

Reinez coughed up a gobbet of blood. He was still standing, but he wavered as if his legs wanted to give way. 'Heretic,' he slurred. 'Vermin. You were never any brother of mine. The warp took you long ago. Your whole Chapter. Stained… tainted… down to your gene-seed… Even Dorn's blood rejects you!'

Reinez's hand flashed down to his waist and a bolt pistol was in his palm. He raised it in a flash.

Reinez was a fast draw, butarpedon moved faster. He crouched down onto his haunches, behind one of the lab benches. The bolt pistol barked and hit the lab bench, blasting sprays of hardwood and bronze shrapnel. Another few shots and it would come apart.

Sarpedon dropped his shoulder and barged into the bench. It came off its moorings and he powered it towards Reinez. The bench crunched into Reinez, pinning him against the wall and trapping the wrist of his gun arm.

Sarpedon reached over the bench and tore the pistol out of Reinez's hand. As quickly as Reinez had drawn it, Sarpedon had it against Reinez's temple.

'I let you live,' said Sarpedon. 'Remember that, brother.'

Sarpedon smacked the butt of the pistol into the bridge of Reinez's nose, crunching through cartilage and stunning Reinez again. The Crimson Fist's head lolled, insensible. Sarpedon let go of the bench and Reinez clattered to the floor. Sarpedon left him there, scuttling from the tech lab into whatever paths the *Phalanx* had laid out for him next.

THE LIQUID EXPLOSIVE with which Brother Sennon had replaced his blood ignited, and incinerated him in an instant. The door to Daenyathos's cell was ripped off its mountings. The Imperial Fists accompanying Sennon were blown off their feet and hurled down the corridor of the Atoning Halls, their armoured weight crushing the rack that stood at the intersection.

Luko was knocked senseless by the shockwave. When his senses returned, his vision shuddered and his ears were full of white noise. He did not hear the footsteps of the Dreadnought emerging from the smouldering hole, but he saw the rubble-strewn ground shaking. Soul Drinkers stumbled from their cells, for the walls of the Atoning Halls had been forced out of shape and cell doors had sprung open. One or two of them had used shrapnel to lever their restraints open, and helped their fellows in neighbouring cells do the same. Two of them were on the Imperial Fists, who were still stunned and could not fight back as the Soul Drinkers grabbed their boltguns, combat knives and grenades.

Luko kicked against his own cell door. It was still held fast. A shadow fell over him, and silhouetted in the hazy light was Daenyathos. The Dreadnought body, even disarmed, was a powerful and terrible thing. Luko, still deafened, did not speak. The Dreadnought looked at him, the dead eyes of its mechanical head focussing, and then it walked on, disappearing into the swirl of dust and smoke.

Sergeant Salk appeared in the Dreadnought's wake. He had a pair of shears for cutting through chain or bone, likely taken from one of the cases of torture implements with which past generations of Imperial Fists had purified themselves. Salk shouted something that Luko could not make out, then worked on the hinges of the cell door until Salk could wrench it free.

Salk then cut the manacles holding Luko to the back wall, and helped him to his feet. Salk's words were getting through to him now, dulled by the ringing inside Luko's head.

'… have to go now! The Fists will be here in moments!'

'Who… who is dead?' said Luko. His own voice sounded like it was coming from somewhere else.

'Four or five of us, I think. Maybe dead, maybe hurt. There is no time to be sure. There is a way out through the far end, towards the archives.'

Luko saw Apothecary Pallas emerging from the dust and rubble, together with several other Soul Drinkers. Two more were forcing the door off another cell and Luko saw it contained Librarian Tyrendian, the inhibitor collar still clamped around his neck to quell his psychic powers.

'What of Daenyathos?' said Luko.

'He is not in his cell.'

'I saw that. Where did he go?'

'I do not know, brother. I have not seen Chaplain Iktinos, either. We must gather and find somewhere we can defend, brother. We are free, but not for long if we cannot make a stand.'

'Yes. Yes, brother, I agree. We must move.'

'What of justice?' said Pallas. The Apothecary was standing just outside the cell, Soul Drinkers gathering around him. His hands were slick with blood – he must have tried to save Soul Drinkers who had been wounded in the blast.

'Justice?' said Luko.

'We are renegades. We were brought here to face justice. Is it right to flee from it? And what will we do after we have fled? Fight all the Space Marines on the *Phalanx*? We have less than a company's worth. There are three companies of Imperial Fists on this spaceship, and Throne knows how many from other Chapters. What does one more battle mean to us when the outcome will be the same? None of us is getting off this ship, captain. You know that.'

'Then stay, Apothecary,' said Luko. 'While there is freedom left for us, I for one will grasp it. There may not be much left for us, but to die free is worth a fight, I think. Come, brothers! We need to leave this place. Follow!'

Luko and Salk left the cell. Luko saw what remained of the Soul Drinkers Chapter – unarmed, bloodied, they were still marked by the manacles and shackles. But they were his brothers, and for one final time they would fight side by side. The Emperor only knew why Sennon had killed himself to buy this freedom for them – this was not the time to ask such questions. It was enough that they had the chance.

Luko was a man who seized his chances. He took the bolter offered to him by one of the other Soul Drinkers, and led the way through the Atoning Halls towards his final moments of freedom.

# CHAPTER EIGHT

LUKO KICKED IN the door of the archive. Musty air swept out, mixing with the cordite and rubble dust that rolled off the Soul Drinkers. The archive was a high-ceilinged, dim and age-sodden room with rolls of parchment mounted on the walls for several storeys up, and huge wooden reading tables over which bent the archivists, who looked up in surprise as almost sixty Space Marines stormed into their domain.

'Not too bad to defend,' said Salk, taking in the sight of the archives. 'Lots of cover, not many entrances.'

'At least we'll have something to read while we're waiting,' replied Luko.

The archivists fled. None of the Soul Drinkers had any heart to pursue them. They would tell the Imperial Fists where the escapees had holed up, but

the Imperial Fists would learn that anyway, and too
many people had died already.

'Spread out!' ordered Luko to the other Soul Drinkers. With Sarpedon and Iktinos elsewhere, it had
seemed a natural fit for him to take command. 'Find
something we can use! Weapons, transport! It's too
much to hope to find a shuttle that can get us off this
can, but that doesn't mean we shouldn't look.'

'And get me something to take this damned thing
off!' Librarian Tyrendian was still wrestling with the
inhibitor collar around his neck. 'Until then I have to
think down to your level.'

Luko caught sight of movement and his eyes
flickered to the dim interior of the archive. From
the shadows shuffled an old, bent figure, wearing
the same robes and symbols as the youth who had
blown himself up to free the Soul Drinkers from the
Atoning Halls. The archivists had all fled, but this
man, who seemed more decrepit than any of them,
showed no fear.

'Hail!' said the old man. Luko saw the rosarius
beads and aquila icons of a pilgrim, and the symbol
of the blinded eye embroidered on his robes. 'Brethren of the Chalice! How my heart grows to see you
at liberty!'

'Who are you?' demanded Luko. 'One of your pilgrims died to free us, though we didn't ask for it.
What does your kind want from us?'

'I want only for the path of fate to be walked
true,' replied the pilgrim. 'Time has sought fit to
grant me the title Father Gyranar. My brothers and
I are the Blind Retribution, the seekers of justice, the

instruments of fate, the Blinded Eye. For longer than I have been alive, fate has taught us of the part we are to play in the fulfilment of the Soul Drinkers' destiny.' Gyranar limped forwards and took Luko's huge paw in his tiny, dry hands. 'I rejoice that I have lived to see that time! When I drank from the grail, I dared not to beg of the fates that I witness the day the chalice shall overflow!'

'Explain yourself,' said Luko.

'We are a long line of those who have been tasked with making this day happen,' continued Gyranar. 'The Black Chalice, the Silver Grail, and countless others, have all followed the same path, one that would ensure they crossed paths with the Soul Drinkers so they could help destiny become reality. You must go free, Captain Luko, you and all your battle-brothers! You must fight here, and see that whichmust be, shall be! I have broken your shackles, but only you can strike the blows!'

'What fate?' demanded Luko. 'If we are here to do something, then it is news to me. We were brought to the *Phalanx* against our will, and at the risk of sounding ungrateful, our freedom was something equally unsought.'

'But now you fight one last battle!' said Gyranar. The old man's eyes were alight, as if he was looking beyond Luko to some religious revelation. 'Instead of a dismal execution, you die fighting, and in doing so your sacrifice will change the Imperium for the better! All human history hinges on this point, captain!'

Luko pulled Gyranar close. The old man barely came up to Luko's solar plexus. 'He who longs for one last battle,' Luko said darkly, 'has never truly fought a battle at all.'

'Fate cares not that its instruments are ignorant of their importance,' said Gyranar. 'I have been given the blessing of knowing what is to come. You, captain, are no less blessed for having it revealed to you at the moment of your glory.'

Luko let Gyranar go. The pilgrim had no fear. A Space Marine knew no fear because he mastered it, broke it down and discarded it as irrelevant. Gyranar had no fear to begin with, as if even an angry Space Marine bearing down on him was a scene from a play which he had seen many times.

'You remind me of someone I once knew,' said Luko. 'He was Yser, and much like you, a believer. He was the pawn of a power greater and darker than he could have imagined, and it killed him. You will find few friends among the Soul Drinkers, Father Gyranar.'

'As I said,' replied Gyranar, 'there were others. I am merely the most fortunate.'

'Captain!' yelled Tyrendian from deeper within the archive, among the shadows that clung around the many archways leading out from the main chamber. 'I've found something. You want to see it.'

Luko followed Tyrendian's voice. The Librarian stood in an archway leading into another chamber, this one lit sparingly by a few spotglobes that shone their shafts of light onto hundreds of exhibits, like the inside of a museum.

Almost a hundred suits of power armour stood there, on racks that made it look as if their owners were standing there in ranks. The armour of the

Soul Drinkers, still spattered with the mud and ash of Selaaca, still with the scars of necron weapons and the claws of the wraiths that had nearly killed so many of them. Sarpedon's armour was there, battered by his struggle with the necron overlord. Luko's own armour, too, with the haphazard heraldry of his career as a renegade painted over the dark purple of the Chapter's livery.

Beside the armour were the weapons. Boltguns racked up as if in an armoury. The Axe of Mercaeno, Sarpedon's own weapon. Sergeant Graevus's power axe and Luko's lightning claws, the huge armoured gloves with their paint scorched and peeling by the constant discharging of the claws' power fields.

'The evidence chamber,' said Tyrendian with a smile.

'Arm up!' yelled Luko. 'Tyrendian, check around and find ammunition and power packs.'

'Perhaps we can make a stand after all,' said Salk as he saw the arms displayed before him. Several Soul Drinkers were already going for their armour, while Sergeant Graevus had gone straight for his power axe. With the axe in the sergeant's mutated hand he suddenly looked more like a Soul Drinker, more like a warrior, and less like anyone who could have been held captive.

Luko slid a hand into one of his lightning claw gauntlets. Its weight felt tremendous, and not just because Luko hadn't yet donned the power armour that would help compensate for its size.

'I used to dream,' he said to Salk, 'of all this ending peacefully. At least, I told myself, an execution is not a battle. But there is one last battle now. You would have thought I'd have learned by now that there is always one last battle.'

'Captain?' said Salk.

'I hate it,' said Luko. 'Fighting. Bloodshed. I have come to hate it. I have lied about this for a long time, Sergeant Salk, but there hardly seems much point now.'

'I can barely believe you are saying these things, captain.'

'I know. I disgust myself too, sometimes.'

'No, captain,' said Salk. 'You don't understand. You hate war, but you fight it because you know you must. There is nothing to disgust in that. Sometimes I take pride, or even pleasure, in it, and I take that and carry it with me to bring me through the worst of it. But without that, I do not know how I could fight. You are braver than I, Captain Luko.'

'Well,' said Luko, 'that's one way of looking at it.'

'Let's make our execution a little more interesting, brother,' said Salk.

Luko clamped one of his greaves around his left leg. 'Amen to that, brother.'

THE COMMANDERS GATHERED in the Forge of Ages, safe from the decompression zones around the Observatory. In the ruddy glow of the forges they first counted off their surviving battle-brothers, appointed officers to take note of the dead, and then turned to the task of recapturing the Soul Drinkers.

There was no doubt that the Soul Drinkers had engineered their escape, with the use of accomplices among the pilgrims who had been allowed onto the *Phalanx* to observe the trial. Castellan Leucrontas had been silent as the commanders discussed their losses and the state of the *Phalanx*, for it was only a matter of time before his decision to allow the pilgrims onto the ship was examined.

No Angels Sanguine had been lost, added to which Commander Gethsemar and his Sanguinary Guard seemed completely unblemished by the carnage. Howling Griffons had died. Imperial Fists, present in the greatest numbers, had lost correspondingly the most. One Silver Skull and two Doom Eagles were missing, presumed dead and cast into the void by the explosive decompression. Crewmen in void suits were already taking their first steps into the Observatory dome, to hunt for the fallen among the torrents of scorched wreckage, but hopes were not high that survivors would be found.

'Brothers!' came a shout from the entrance to the Forge of Ages. Reinez, severely battered and bloodied, walked in, dragging an unarmoured Space Marine behind him. Reinez's armour, which had been in poor repair when he had arrived on the *Phalanx*, was now so filthy with blood and scorch marks that the colours of the Howling Griffons were barely discernible. 'Are you looking for answers? Perhaps a few explanations? I have done what you cannot do by bickering among yourselves, and found you some!'

Reinez shoved the Space Marine into the centre of the Forge. The captive showed no resistance, and fell to his knees.

'It is good that you are alive, Reinez,' said Chapter

Master Pugh. Siege-Captain Daviks stepped forwards and lifted the bowed head of the Space Marine.

'He's a Soul Drinker,' said Daviks, pointing to the chalice symbol that marked the centre of the surgical scars on the Space Marine's chest. 'What is your name?'

'Apothecary Pallas,' said the Soul Drinker.

'One of the accused,' said Pugh. 'You were to be executed. Why did you not flee with the rest of the condemned?'

'Because we are not free,' said Pallas. 'I do not know why we were released, or who is responsible, but we did not seek it. I have been manipulated before, by Abraxes when our Chapter first turned from the Imperium, and I will not be used like that again. If I am to be executed here then so be it. I do not care about that any more. But I will not be a pawn in the scheme of another.'

'Then who?' demanded Daviks. 'Who committed this outrage? My battle-brothers died because someone set the Soul Drinkers loose. Answer me!'

'I don't know!' retorted Pallas. 'Someone who benefits from a battle on the *Phalanx*. Someone who wants a last laugh from the Soul Drinkers before we are gone. Your guesses are as good as mine.'

'They have left this one behind to sow confusion,' said Daviks to the other Space Marines. 'Recall the strategies of cowardice, as recounted in the Codex Astartes!'

'There has been dissent in the ranks of the Soul Drinkers before,' said Pugh. 'They turned on one another at Nevermourn. Reinez, you witnessed that, I believe. That this Apothecary chose not to follow his brothers in evading justice is not impossible.'

'Dissenter or not,' said Reinez, 'we should get everything he knows out of him.' Reinez took a tool from the closest forge – its metal prongs glowed from the heat. 'I suggest we not delay.'

'There will be no need for that,' said Pugh. 'If he is here to misinform us then he will be prepared to spread lies under duress. If he is not, then there is no need for the infliction of suffering.'

'Then what are we to do with him?' sneered Reinez. 'Give him a commission?'

'He is an Apothecary. He can help tend to the wounded,' replied Pugh. 'Apothecary Asclephin, you will oversee his work once he has answered one question.'

'Name it,' said Pallas.

'Where is Sarpedon?'

Pallas looked up at Pugh. 'The last I knew of it, he was in the courtroom. You are in a better position to know his whereabouts than I.'

'Space Marines died in his escape' said Pugh. 'You understand that justice will fall on him sooner or later, and that your own manner of death will depend on how satisfied we are with your part in that justice.'

'I barely care for life or death any more, Chapter Master,' said Pallas. 'I do not know where he is. Decide among yourselves if I speak the truth, but I know that I do.'

'Another question, with which our Soul Drinker friend may not be able to help us,' said Gethsemar smoothly, 'is the location of Captain N'Kalo.'

Instinctively, the Space Marine officers looked around. They were all there save for N'Kalo. His Iron Knights were present, but not their commander.

'He made it out of the dome,' said Daviks. 'I saw him.'

'But he did not make it here,' answered Gethsemar.

'Then locating him is a priority,' said Pugh, 'but not one as high as locating Sarpedon and the Soul Drinkers who broke out of the cell block. If they have a plan then it most likely involves them staying together. If we are to break them with a minimum of losses, we must do so quickly, before they dig in. Lysander!'

'Chapter Master?' said Lysander with a salute.

'You will lead the hunt. You have our three companies at your disposal. Officers, I ask that you cede command to Lysander in my name, and that he send your battle-brothers as he sees fit. I need no reminding of the protocols it breaks to request you place yourselves under the command of another Chapter, but this is not the time to dally over such things.'

'I will kill Sarpedon,' said Reinez.

'You will not put the lives of my battle-brothers at risk,' said Pugh. 'If it is expedient, another will eliminate Sarpedon, not wait for your permission.'

'My oath of revenge is more important than life.' Reinez shoved Pallas aside as he took a few steps closer to Pugh. 'Even the life of a brother.'

'And delivering Dorn's justice upon the Soul Drinker is more important than either,' said Lysander, putting a hand on Reinez's shoulder pad. Reinez shrugged it off angrily.

'For one who despises time wasted in talking,'

said Gethsemar, 'Brother Reinez does enjoy his little speeches.'

Reinez gave Gethsemar a look that could have killed a star, as the officers rallied their Space Marines for the hunt.

CAPTAIN N'KALO FORCED off the slab of wreckage that pinned him down. His ears rang and the world was painted in blotchy blacks and reds. He was somewhere in one of the *Phalanx's* tribute galleries, the deck divided into displays of art, standards and captured arms evoking the history of the Imperial Fists.

The ceiling had collapsed on him as he fled the dome. The galleries had sealed behind him before they were decompressed, but the shockwaves of the pilgrim ship's suicide attack had caused enough damage of their own. N'Kalo saw he had been trapped beneath a spiderlike carapace, complete and preserved in a transparent layer of resin, which had been mounted on the ceiling to give the impression it was about to ambush visitors to the galleries from above. The carapace was that of a creature with ten legs and a span of four or five metres across, and still bore the charred bolter scars that had felled it. It was the relic of a battle millions of miles and probably thousands of years distant.

On one side of N'Kalo was a mural of Imperial Fists dragging the enemy dead from sucking tar pits on a primeval world of volcanoes and jungle. The enemy had the blue-grey skins and flat features of the tau, xenos who had tried to expand into Imperial space and been fought to a stalemate at the Damocles Gulf.

On the other side were armour plates torn from a greenskin vehicle, a strange, brutal majesty in the savage simplicity of their skull and bullet designs and the blood that still stained the lower edges of a tank's dozer blade.

N'Kalo tried to get his bearings. He did not know if he was alone. He looked and listened around him, trying to find crewmen or Space Marines through the displays and sculptures.

The hiss of a nerve-fibre bundle reached his ears. The clicking of one ceramite plate on another.

'Brother?' called N'Kalo. 'Are you hurt? Speak to me!'

There was no reply.

N'Kalo tensed. Perhaps Sarpedon had survived the attack, and was free. Perhaps the other captive Soul Drinkers were free, too. He could not afford to think of the *Phalanx* as safe ground any more. For all he knew, this was enemy territory.

N'Kalo drew his bolt pistol. He wished he had his power sword with him, but he had stowed it in his squad's cell-quarters when he had exchanged it for the executioner's blade in the duel.

On the wall next to the vehicle armour plates hung a bladed weapon shaped like a massively oversized meat cleaver, with teeth and jagged shards soldered to its cutting edge. A greenskin weapon. N'Kalo felt distaste as he lifted it from its mountings and tested its weight. A xenos weapon, and one that no Iron Knight should ever use, but circumstances were extreme.

A shadow upon a shadow, through arches between the trophies and memorials, coalesced into the shape of a power-armoured figure. N'Kalo ducked out of sight, behind the mural of the Imperial Fists' victory over the tau.

'I spoke for you,' said N'Kalo. 'No one else would. I spoke up for your Chapter! Do what the court did not and listen to me.'

Something metal clattered to the floor. Ceramite boots sounded on the tiles.

'Give yourself up, brother,' continued N'Kalo. 'If you will not, if you fight us here, your fate will only be worse.'

'It is not my fate,' came the reply, 'with which you should concern yourself.'

N'Kalo did not recognise the voice. It had an edge of learning and confidence, a calmness quite at odds with its potential for violence.

'Name yourself,' said N'Kalo.

'You will know my name soon enough,' came the reply.

N'Kalo risked a glance past the mural. The muzzle of a bolt pistol met him. He ducked back as the gun fired, blasting a shower of wooden shards from the edge of the wall.

N'Kalo dived past the other side of the mural, head down, barrelling forwards. He crashed through a display of captured standards, leaping the plinth to close with his enemy.

The bolt pistol fired again. N'Kalo took the shot on his chest, feeling blades of ceramite driven into his ribs. Not too deep. Not too bad. He would make it face to face.

N'Kalo led with his shoulder and slammed into

his assailant. He saw not the purple armour of a Soul Drinker, but the skull-encrusted black of a Chaplain. The chalice on one shoulder pad confirmed the Chapter, however.

Iktinos. The Chaplain of the Soul Drinkers, and the man considered the most likely moral threat among the captives until Daenyathos had been dug up. The second man slated for execution after Sarpedon. Armed and armoured, and free.

N'Kalo drove the greenskin blade up under Iktinos's arm. Iktinos wrenched his own weapon around quickly enough to lever the blade away from him, throwing N'Kalo onto the back foot. N'Kalo realised with a lurch that Iktinos carried the crozius arcanum, the mace-like power weapon that served as a Chaplain's badge of office.

Iktinos smacked his bolt pistol against the side of N'Kalo's head. N'Kalo reeled, one side of his battered helmet caved in again along the cracks opened up by Reinez.

'Kneel,' said Iktinos, bolt pistol levelled at N'Kalo's face. 'Kneel and it will be quick. Is that not what the Soul Drinkers were offered? Submission for a quick death? Then that is what I offer you, Captain N'Kalo of the Iron Knights.'

N'Kalo dropped to one knee and grabbed one of the standards he had knocked onto the floor. It was an iron spear with a ragged banner hanging from it, the standard of some rebellious Imperial Guard regiment.

Another shot caught N'Kalo in the head. His helmet was torn open and one eye went black. N'Kalo thrust the standard pole forwards with everything he had, catching Iktinos in the hand and throwing the bolt pistol off into the shadows.

N'Kalo fell back onto one knee. He wrenched the ruined helmet off his head. He felt hot blood flowing down his face and his fingers brushed wet, pulpy mass where one eye had been. His head rang, and it felt like his skull was suddenly a few sizes too small.

A fractured skull, then. He had suffered that before. Not the worst. He could fight on.

Iktinos strode forwards, crozius in his good hand. He swung it down at N'Kalo, who deflected it away with the greenskin blade he had snatched off the floor at the last second. The blade shattered like glass and N'Kalo was driven onto his back by the force of the blow. He reeled, his good eye unable to focus, Iktinos just a black blur over him.

'Iktinos!' yelled Sarpedon. For a moment Iktinos thought that Sarpedon was the man attacking him, that he was back in the Eshkeen forests with his battle-brothers. Everything since then had been a dream and he had never left that stretch of marshland.

But no. Iktinos was the enemy. Sarpedon was somewhere nearby. Iktinos dragged N'Kalo to his feet and wrapped an arm around his throat, hauled him into a corner and grabbed his bolt pistol off the floor. The muzzle of the pistol was against the side of N'Kalo's head.

Sarpedon stood in the middle of the gallery, unarmoured as he had been in the courtroom.

\* \* \*

'IKTINOS!' YELLED SARPEDON. He could barely believe that the first Soul Drinker he had come across since his escape was engaged in fighting the one Space Marine who had stood up for the Chapter at the trial. Still stranger was that it was Iktinos, and that he had already found his armour and weapons.

N'Kalo looked nearly dead. His face was barely recognisable as belonging to a human. One eye socket was a gory ruin. Iktinos had disarmed him, and now had him up as a human shield with a gun to his head.

'Chaplain,' called Sarpedon. 'What are you doing?'

'I am surviving,' said Iktinos.

'N'Kalo is my friend. Let him go.'

'The Soul Drinkers have no friends. N'Kalo is coming with me.'

'Hostages will do us no good, Iktinos! You know that!'

'Then it is for the best that I have him, not you. Do not seek to follow, Sarpedon. There is only sorrow this way. Go to your brothers. They are re-arming in the archives.'

'What are you speaking of, Chaplain? Whatever fate waits for us here, are you not a part of it?'

Iktinos dragged N'Kalo towards a pair of double doors at the far end of the hall. 'Fight, Sarpedon! Fight on! That is what fate demands of you. Stand by your brothers and die a good death!'

'I know that someone has guided us here without my realising. Someone has used me just as surely as Abraxes did. Is it you, Iktinos?'

'Goodbye, Sarpedon. A good death to you, my brother!'

'Is it Daenyathos?'

Iktinos hauled N'Kalo through the doors. They boomed shut behind him. Sarpedon rushed forwards, trying to cover the ground to the doors before Iktinos could turn a corner and get out of sight.

Sarpedon heard the tiny sound of the grenade hitting the floor. He threw his arms up in front of him, supernatural reflexes giving him the warning a split second before the grenade went off in his face. The doors were ripped off their mountings and slammed into him, throwing him back across the display room, crashing through captured arms and victory monuments.

Sarpedon skidded along the floor on his back. When he came to a halt he brushed the debris from his eyes and saw the doorway was full of smoke and rubble. Sarpedon had no way of following Iktinos.

Daenyathos. Rogal Dorn. The pilgrim ship's suicide attack. Now Iktinos, with an agenda of his own. Everything Sarpedon had believed about the galaxy was falling apart, and he did not know how it could end but with his death and the deaths of every one of his battle-brothers.

One thing that Iktinos had said made sense. Sarpedon had to fight. He had to win a good death, and help his brothers do the same. He owed himself that much. It was not much to fight for, but at that moment it was all he had.

Sarpedon snatched up a sword from a fallen display behind him, and struck out for the archives.

* * *

SOMETIMES A COLD wind blew through the *Phalanx*. It was a trick of the ship's atmospheric systems, or perhaps a random current created by the coolant pipes and superheated reactor cores of the engine sectors. It howled now through the science labs and triumphant galleries around the Observatory dome, strewn with wreckage. It picked up shards of debris and flapped the Imperial Fist banners that lined the way Chapter Master Pugh had used to enter the now-ruined Observatory of Dornian Majesty.

It stirred the dust in the Atoning Halls, whistling between the frames of the wrecked torture racks and the bars of the empty cells. A few Space Marines lay there: Soul Drinkers who had been caught in the worst of the explosion and killed. Their battle-brothers had taken a few bodies with them but some still lay where they had fallen, their torn bodies still chained in their cells.

It turned the pages that lay on the reading tables in the archives. The reading hall was held by only a handful of Soul Drinkers, among them Librarian Scamander, the pyrokine who had not so long ago served as a scout. He crouched in the shadows cast by the dim light and the enormous parchment rolls, waiting with the Soul Drinkers chosen to stand watch with him. When the enemy came – for they had to be called the enemy now, no matter what they had once been – they would come through here, and in force.

The enemy was now gathering in the crew mess hall, which Captain Lysander had designated as the staging post for the assault on the Soul Drinkers. The Imperial Fists and Howling Griffons made up the bulk of the force and Lysander had already had to deal with the competing demands to be the first in against the Soul Drinkers. The *Phalanx* was Imperial Fists ground and they had the say on who should have the moments of greatest honour in the fight to come, but Captain Borganor had demanded that his Howling Griffons be given the task of charging into the archives and letting the first Soul Drinkers blood. Lysander had agreed, for the Soul Drinkers were enemy enough and he did not need vengeful Howling Griffons facing up to him as well.

Commander Gethsemar picked up a handful of rubble dust from a collapsed wall, felled by the shockwave from the Atoning Halls' explosion. He let the dust drift on the wind, as if it were a form of divination and from the eddies of the wind he could read the pattern of bloodshed unfolding into the immediate future. His war-mask was a death mask of Sanguinius, cast from the features of the divine primarch as he lay dying, felled by the Arch-Traitor Horus ten thousand years before. Sanguinius was unspeakably beautiful, and even stylised in gold and gemstones the death mask cast an aura of supernatural majesty that the Sanguinary Guard used as one of their deadliest weapons.

'What do you see?' asked Librarian Varnica of the Doom Eagles.

Gethsemar turned to Varnica but his eyes were hidden behind ruby panes set into the mask's eye sockets and his expression could not be read. 'Such fates that intertwine here, my brother, are beyond any of us,' replied Gethsemar. 'Long have our sages tried to unravel them. Long have they failed. They strive even now, knowing that the future will be forever hidden from them, but that to endeavour in such an impossible task is its own reward. Our immediate task here is far from impossible, but I fear a greater undertaking is revealed that will never end.'

'Explain,' said Varnica. 'As you would to a layman.'

'Think upon it, brother,' said Gethsemar. 'Here Space Marine fights Space Marine. There is nothing new about that. But will it be the final time?'

'I think not,' replied Varnica.

'Then you begin to see our point. What is a Space Marine? He is a man, yes, but he is something far more. He is told that he is far more from the moment he is accepted into his Chapter, when he is little more than a child. His earlier memories may not even survive his training. He may conceive in his own mind of no time but one where he was superior to any human being. What might result from a mind so forged?'

'He has no doubt and no fear,' replied Varnica. 'Such alteration of a man's mind is necessary to create the warriors the Imperium needs. I see it as a sacrifice we make. We give up the men we might have become to instead serve as Adeptus Astartes. If you believe this is a mistake, commander, then I would be compelled to differ with you.'

'Ah, but there it is! Do you see, Librarian Varnica? It is true that what we do to our minds to make us Space Marines is as necessary as teaching us to shoot. But what sin is locked into us through such treatment?'

'Brutality?' said Varnica. 'Many times Space Marines

have gone too far in punishing the Emperor's enemies, and ordinary men and woman have suffered
as a result.'

'Brutality is a necessity,' said Gethsemar. 'A few thousand dead here and there mean nothing compared to
the millions spared through the intimidation of our
foes that our potential for brutality allows. No, it is a
far deeper sin of which I speak, something not so far
removed from corruption.'

'Corruption is a strong word,' said Varnica, folding
his arms and straightening up. The threat was clear.
'Then what is it?'

'It is pride,' replied Gethsemar. 'A Space Marine does
not just think he is superior to the ordinary citizens
of the Imperium. He thinks, whether his conscious
mind accepts it or not, that he is superior to other
Space Marines, too. We all have our way of doing
things, do we not? Would we all resist any attempt
to change us, though violence may be the only route
doing so can take? So prideful we are that Space
Marines will never stop killing Space Marines. For
every Horus Heresy or Badab War, there are a thousand blood duels and trials of honour brought about
by our inability to back down. That is the real enemy
we face here. The Soul Drinkers were turned from the
Imperium by pride. It is pride that motivates us in
destroying them, for all we talk of justice. Pride is the
enemy. Pride will kill us.'

Varnica thought about this. 'Throne knows we all
have our moments,' he said. 'But the mind of a Space
Marine is a complicated thing. Can such a simple
thing as pride really be its key? And from the way

you speak, commander, I would imagine you have a solution?'

'Oh, no,' protested Gethsemar. 'The Sons of Sanguinius all accept that we are doomed. A Space Marine's destructive pride is the only thing keeping us all fighting, and we are the only thing keeping the Imperium from the brink. No, it is our way to observe our in-fighting for the death throes they are, to understand what we truly are before the end comes.'

Varnica smiled grimly. 'For all your gilt and finery, Angel Sanguine, you are a pessimist. The Doom Eagles seek out the worst atrocities the galaxy commits because we want to put things right. It will not happen in any of our lifetimes, but it will happen, and it is the Space Marines who will do it whether we are too prideful for our own good or not. Why fight, if you believe all is lost no matter what you do?'

Gethsemar shook out his hand, and the dust drifted away on the thin wind. 'Because it is our duty,' he replied.

Lysander stomped past, hammer in hand. 'Daviks and the castellan are in position,' he said. 'Make ready. Two minutes.'

Gethsemar and Varnica broke away to join their own squads. The main assault force, gathered in the mess halls, consisted of the 9th and 7th Imperial Fist companies and the Howling Griffons' 2nd. Varnica and Gethsemar's squads were to follow the Griffons in and, if Borganor was to be believed, clean up the mangled remnants of the Soul Drinkers the Howling Griffons were sure to leave in their wake. Lysander was walking the lines, inspecting the Imperial Fists ranked up along the width of the crew mess hall. The rooms had been built for the normally proportioned crew of the *Phalanx* and the Space Marines could barely stand upright in it.

Whole planets had been broken by fewer than the two hundred Space Marines that the Imperial Fists fielded for this battle. The Howling Griffons were impatient, broken up by squads to be spoken to in turn by Borganor. Lord Inquisitor Kolgo was there, too, at the back of the hall with his Battle Sisters bodyguard, looking more like a battle observer than a combatant in spite of his Terminator armour.

Varnica returned to his squad. Sergeant Beyrengar, who had been elevated to squad command after Novas's death, had gone through the pre-battle wargear rites and prayers already. There was little for Varnica left to do.

'This is where the solution to that puzzle box lies,' he said. 'We have pursued the Soul Drinkers, though we did not know it, from the moment the heretic Kephilaes made the mistake of drawing our attention. What we began then, we finish here. We know what the Soul Drinkers are, and more importantly, we know what they are not. They are not our brothers. When you face one of them through a haze of gunsmoke, do not see a brother. See one more symptom of corruption, and excise him as you would any cancer of the human race.'

'Borganor!' came Lysander's yell from the Imperial Fists lines. 'The honour is yours!'

'Gladly taken!' cried out Borganor in reply. 'Howling Griffons! Roboute Guilliman looks on! Let us show him a fight he will not forget!'

The deck of the *Phalanx* shuddered as the Howling Griffons advanced.

SCAMANDER ALMOST RAISED the alarm, but he realised that the silhouette entering the reading room was multi-legged. He stood and saluted. 'Commander!' he said. 'We did not know if you were still alive.'

'I had plenty of opportunities to die,' replied Sarpedon. 'I failed to grasp any of them.' He shook Scamander's hand. 'How long do we have?'

'Not long,' said Scamander. 'The Imperial Fists are gathering to attack us even now. They know we are here.'

'And the plan?'

'Hold the library stacks. Don't die. Circumstances demand our tactics be simple.'

'I see.'

'We have your armour, and the Axe of Mercaeno.'

'Then at least I will not die here unclothed! That would be too humiliating a way to go.'

Scamander smiled. For all the battles he had fought and the dangers his psychic powers posed, he was still a youth. By the standards of the Soul Drinkers, he was just a boy.

Sarpedon headed through the reading room to the archway Scamander had indicated. It led to a maze of bookcases and tables, shelves of volumes stacked high to the ceiling, a thin layer of dust covering everything disturbed by the armoured footprints of the Soul Drinkers. Sarpedon glanced at the books – histories of Imperial Fists actions, battle-philosophy, stories of individual Imperial Fists and their deeds. Sarpedon was reminded of the chansons the Soul Drinkers had once written, epic poems to glorify themselves. Sarpedon had abandoned his own chanson when he had thrown Michairas, his chronicler, out of an airlock during the first Chapter war. The thought gave him an unpleasant taste in his mouth.

Soul Drinkers saluted as he passed. He saw battle-brothers he had fought alongside for years. Some had argued against him, some had sided with him in everything, but they had all followed him into the Veiled Region. They had all accepted capture by Captain Lysander and the Imperial Fists without a fight, because he had ordered it. And they would die here ultimately, because he had ordered it.

'Commander,' said Sergeant Graevus as Sarpedon walked past. Sarpedon returned his salute and noted the Assault Squad that Graevus had assembled from the Chapter's survivors. He had picked veterans: bloody-minded Space Marines who could be trusted to give each centimetre of the stacks in return for buckets of blood shed by their chainblades. Sergeant Salk was instructing his squad, and paused to nod his own salute to Sarpedon. Sarpedon scuttled over makeshift barricades of upturned tables, and squeezed through the bottlenecks formed by the chaotic layout of the stacks. In the centre of the book-lined labyrinth, he found Captain Luko standing at a reading table.

Luko grabbed Sarpedon around the shoulders. 'Good to see you, brother,' he said. 'I thought the festivities would begin without you.'

'I would not miss it for the galaxy,' replied Sarpedon.

'How many of our brothers do we have here for the celebration?'

'A little under sixty,' said Luko. 'A few were lost in the escape. Pallas stayed behind. And others have gone missing. It is to be expected, I suppose, but it is strange…'

'Iktinos's flock,' said Sarpedon.

Luko took a step back. 'How did you know?'

'Iktinos is not with us,' said Sarpedon. 'His flock must have joined him.'

'Not with us? What do you mean?'

'Iktinos brought us here. He has been doing it for years now, manipulating us towards this place and time. Why, I do not know. Probably it is at the behest of Daenyathos. Whatever the reason, he has his goals and we have ours, and they do not coincide.'

'The Chaplain has betrayed us.'

'Yes,' said Sarpedon. 'He has.'

Luko's customary joviality was gone. 'I will kill him.'

'There will be a queue,' said Sarpedon. 'Focus for now on your survival. You have picked a good place to make our stand, brother. I would think twice before attacking such a place.'

'We have your armour, and your axe,' said Luko. 'They are stored behind that bookcase. We could not find the Soulspear among the evidence, though.'

'Then I shall do without. The Axe of Mercaeno is weapon enough for me.'

'You know, the Howling Griffons would want that back.'

'Then Borganor can take it from my dead hand,'

replied Sarpedon. 'I have no doubt he will be seeking just that chance. Many stories will end here, captain. Borganor and I is just one of them. If we can give those stories endings worthy of these histories, then we will have won our victory.'

Scamander's voice reached them over Luko's vox. 'Captain! The Howling Griffons are advancing! I'm falling back towards Graevus's position!' The deep spatter of gunfire sounded over his words, and Sarpedon could hear the thuds of bolter impacts through the walls of the library.

'Then it is done,' said Sarpedon. 'I shall arm. To the end, Captain Luko.'

'To the end, Chapter Master,' replied Luko. 'Cold and fast.'

Sarpedon saluted. 'Cold and fast, Soul Drinker.'

# CHAPTER NINE

THE DAYS FOLLOWING the Horus Heresy formed the forgotten apocalypse of the Imperium. The Heresy itself was the subject of legends known throughout the realm of mankind – the traitor Horus, waxing great in his jealousy of the Emperor, his treason against the human race and his death at the hand of the Emperor himself. The Scouring, the period of reformation that followed Horus's death and the Emperor's ascension to the Golden Throne, was an afterthought, a footnote in the approved histories preached by the Imperial Church. But the truth, appreciated only by a few historians who skirted with heresy in their studies, was that the Imperium was born in the Scouring, and it was born in a terrible tide of blood.

It was a time of vengeance. All those tainted by the deeds of Horus and the many who had sided with them, even worlds who had bowed to Horus under threat of destruction, were destined to suffer. The remaining loyal primarchs led a campaign of bloody reconquest in which collaborators were hanged in their billions. Planets full of refugees were purged lest their number contain the wrong type of war criminals. A thousand civil wars sprang up in the Heresy's wake, the combatants left by the Imperial Army to fight among themselves until the survivors were weak enough to be conquered, subjugated and re-educated.

It was a time of reform. The Space Marine Legions were split up into Chapters, a process which sparked its own share of shadow wars and near-catastrophes as Space Marines fought in all but open warfare for the right to the heraldries of their parent Legions. The Imperial Army broke up into millions of fragments, miniature fiefdoms with no central command. The Imperial Creed was born among the religious catastrophes that tore at humanity in the wake of the Emperor's ascension and the Adepta of the Imperium were formed to hold the shattered mass of humanity together. Born in desperation, the Priesthood of Terra and its component Adepta founded the principles of fear and suspicion that would determine their every action in the ten millennia that followed. Whatever image the Emperor had cherished for the future of humanity, its broken remnants were formed by the Scouring into something flawed, something half-born, something fearful when the Emperor had sought to form it from hope.

It was a time of Chaos. The powers of the warp had made their play for power over the human race and though the Emperor's sacrifice had thwarted them, they had sunk a thousand tendrils of influence into realspace and clung on jealously. The daemonic legions unleashed in the Battle of Terra took decades to hunt down and exterminate; the Blood Angels and their newly-formed successor Chapters seeking them out to exact vengeance for Sanguinius's death. Horus's acolytes had opened portals to the warp in the Heresy's dying days, seeking to seed the fledgling Imperium with secrets waiting to be uncovered and suffered by generations to come.

No one knew how many such portals had been built by the sorcerers and madmen under Horus's command. Some were vast gateways on forgotten worlds, ready for explorers or refugees to speak the wrong words or cross the wrong threshold. Some were built into the foundations of cities rebuilt in the Heresy's wake, runes worked into the streets or dread temples far beneath the sewers and catacombs. Others took stranger forms – prophecies woven into a tainted bloodline, the words of a story that opened the way a little more with every telling, a song sung by desert spirits which would become a gateway to the warp as soon as it was written down.

One gateway was an eye, ripped from some titanic predator that glided through the warp. Acolytes of the Dark Powers, gathered on a spacecraft in orbit around a star, brought the eye into realspace. Like another – living – planet, it settled into its own orbit.

It looked out upon the void and wherever its gaze fell, daemons danced. The acolytes who had summoned it were shredded by the daemons that sprung up around them, their last thoughts of thanks towards the Dark Gods who had permitted them to be a part of such a glorious endeavour.

The Predator's Eye was seen in divinations and séances across the Imperium. It was Rogal Dorn who stood up and swore to close it. The Chapters that venerated him all sent their own champions to assist, and in orbit around the blighted star were fought many of the most terrible and costly battles of the Scouring. Rogal Dorn himself set foot on the Predator's Eye, evading the biological horrors that budded out of its gelatinous surface as well as the daemons that scrabbled to intercept him. But even as battle-brothers fell around him, Rogal Dorn did not falter. He was a primarch, and in him flowed the blood of the Emperor. He plunged a fist into the pupil of the Predator's Eye, and the eye, blinded, closed in agony.

Rogal Dorn's surviving battle-brothers included a number of Space Marine Librarians, and for three days without rest they enacted a ritual to seal the eye shut. Dorn led their chanting and finally a sigil of power, born of his own valorous spirit, was branded against the shut eye to keep it closed.

Dorn did not possess enough battle-brothers to destroy the Predator's Eye permanently. His Librarians were exhausted and many had not survived the ritual. He knew that one day he would have to return to finish the job. The Predator's Eye would have to be opened before it was destroyed, and so Dorn placed a condition on the ward that sealed it so that only his own blood could open it. He buried the Eye's location in myths and legends, such that no single Chapter would know the full story of its location and purpose, and swore that one day, when the countless other threats had subsided and he had found another corps of Librarians and champions to face down the terrible gaze of the Predator's Eye, the warp portal would finally be destroyed.

But the Imperium was beset on all sides by threats that did not let up. For every daemonic foe that was despatched, rebellion or the predations of the xenos would spring up, every new danger threatening a new form of oblivion for the Imperium. For centuries the Predator's Eye lay hidden just below the level of mortal sight, blinded yet possessing a bestial sense of anger and frustration born of the warp's own hatred. And eventually, Rogal Dorn died, to join the Emperor at the battle at the end of time.

The Predator's Eye remained orbiting its star, forgotten.

The name of that star was Kravamesh.

SCAMANDER BRAVED THE first volley of bolter fire that streaked across the archive. The walls exploded in torrents of burned and shredded parchment around him as bolter rounds from the Howling Griffons flew wide. One caught Scamander in the chest and blew him back a pace. Another tore through the reading table in front of him and exploded against his thigh. A storm of shrapnel crackled against him.

'You will never see us kneel!' yelled Scamander and

he looked up to the ceiling, his bared throat glowing scarlet. Flames licked up from his hands, over his shoulder guards and face. Ice crusted around the table and the floor around him as the heat energy bled into him to be concentrated and forced out by the psychic reactor that churned in his mind.

Scamander looked down at the Howling Griffons, face wreathed in flame. They were charging heedless towards him, competing for the honour of first blood. Captain Borganor was among them, ripping out volleys of bolter fire.

Scamander breathed out a tremendous gout of flame that washed over and through the first Howling Griffons. Some were thrown off their feet by the wall of superheated air that slammed into them. Others were caught in the blast, ceramite melting in the supernaturally intense heat, armour plates exploding. Three or four fell as the nerve-fibre bundles in their armour were incinerated, robbing them of movement as the joints melted and fused.

Borganor leapt through the fire, crashing through a reading table already collapsing to ash under the force of Scamander's assault. He took aim without breaking stride and put a bolter round square into Scamander's abdomen, throwing the Soul Drinker back onto one knee.

Other Soul Drinkers returned fire in the wake of Scamander's attack, and the Howling Griffons struggled through the flame to get into cover and drive them out. Borganor ignored the rest of the fight and dived under the table Scamander was using for cover, his bionic leg powering him forwards.

Borganor came up face to face with Scamander. Scamander's bolt pistol was in his hand and the two wrestled over their guns. Scamander was half-glowing with heat, half-slippery with ice, but Borganor kept the muzzle of Scamander's pistol away from him. His own bolter was too unwieldy for this close-quarters murder – he let it drop from his hand and took his combat knife from its sheath.

Scamander immolated himself in a cocoon of fire. Borganor yelled and fell away. Scamander got to his feet and blasted at Borganor as he stumbled away, holding the wound in his abdomen with his free hand.

Borganor rolled through the flames, bolter fire impacting on his shoulder guards and backpack. Chains of bolter fire hammered across the archive room and shredded parchment fell in a burning rain, filaments of ash rising on the hot air and flames licking up the walls. The huge rolls of parchment were ablaze, falling in spooling masses like waterfalls of fire and silhouetting the shapes of the Howling Griffons as they ran from cover to cover, firing all the time.

Scamander raised his free hand, black with charred blood from his wound. Flame sprayed from his fingers and Borganor grabbed hold of a table leg to keep the burst of fire from carrying him off his feet. He trusted in his ceramite, in the rites with which he had blessed his wargear and the spirit of Roboute Guilliman he had beseeched to enter his heart and make him more than a man, more than a Space Marine. He trusted in the force of his vengeance, the shield of contempt which could spread out from his iron soul and keep him alive long enough to execute the traitor he faced.

Borganor forced himself forwards a pace, knife held out in front. Scamander raised his pistol again but Borganor swatted it away.

'Traitor,' hissed Borganor. 'Witch.'

Scamander replied with a breath of fire, a narrow tongue of flame as concentrated as a las-cutter's beam. Borganor ducked it and rammed the knife up into Scamander's face. The blade passed up into Scamander's jaw, ripping through teeth and tongue. The flame sputtered as a clot of blood sprayed from Scamander's mouth.

Borganor leapt forwards, a knee on Scamander's wounded stomach. Scamander fell against the back wall of the archive room, where he was bathed in the burning remnants of centuries of parchment records. Borganor grabbed the back of Scamander's head and wrenched it up, exposing the Soul Drinker's throat.

Scamander's eyes were full of hate. Borganor grinned as he saw the tiniest glimmer of fear there, a twitch at the corner of the eye.

'Everything you die for is a lie,' said Borganor, and slit Scamander's throat.

The Howling Griffon had to push the Soul Drinker's body up against the wall so the gout of fire that ripped from his torn throat shot upwards instead of into his face. The fountain hit the ceiling and spread, flame like liquid pooling outwards. Then it sputtered as if whatever fuelled it was running out and Scamander fell limp. Fire licked from the corners of his eyes, his mouth, his ears, and smoke coiled from the joints in his armour.

Borganor threw the body aside. He looked around him. The burning room was in Chaos, half held by the Howling Griffons, half by the Soul Drinkers. Many Howling Griffons had died to the Soul Drinkers Librarian, but now Soul Drinkers were dying to the numbers and firepower of the Howling Griffons.

Borganor's fight with Scamander had brought him out of cover. Only smoke and flames concealed him from Soul Drinkers guns.

'Brothers! The trickster is dead! Let bolter fire be your truth!' Borganor yelled over the gunfire, standing proud of the fight even as bolter shots fell around him. He snatched his bolter up off the floor and got into the battle proper, hammering volley after volley into the hazy purple-armoured shaped that loomed through the smoke.

'Onwards! Onwards! This is but a welcome, my brothers! The celebration is yet to come!'

SARPEDON HEARD THE gunfire, and smelled the smoke rolling in from the reading room. In the heart of the library labyrinth, alongside Captain Luko, he waited for the wave to break against the Soul Drinkers defences.

'Scamander is lost,' said Luko.

'Then we have something to avenge,' replied Sarpedon calmly.

'I promised myself that no more Space Marines would die by my hand,' said Luko. 'I have made many such promises to myself, but I have a problem keeping them.'

'You promised yourself peace, captain,' said Sarpedon. 'You will have it. But not just yet. Hold on for a few more moments, for your battle-brothers.'

The first volleys of bolter fire, sharp and crisp, cackled from the interior of the library. The Howling Griffons were in, past Scamander's forlorn hope and into the death-trap the Soul Drinkers had created for them.

'At last it will end,' said Luko. 'I don't have to lie any more. Thank the Emperor it ends here.'

'And we decide how it ends,' added Sarpedon. 'How many men can ever say that?'

Luko did not reply. The power field around his lightning claws flared into life, and loose papers on the shelves scattered in the electric charge.

The gunfire rose towards a crescendo as the vox channels filled with bedlam.

'SIDE BY SIDE with me, brothers!' yelled Graevus, charging shoulder-first down the narrow corridors of the library. Burning books rained down around him, thousands of words flitting by as pages turned to ash.

Graevus crashed around a corner straight into a Howling Griffon wielding a two-handed chainsword like an executioner's axe. The blade screeched down and Graevus turned it aside with his power axe, his mutated strength redirecting the blow into one of the bookcases beside him. The chainsword tore into the ancient wood and the Howling Griffon paused for a moment to wrench it free. That was all the time

Graevus needed to bring his axe up into the Howling Griffon's chest, carving through ceramite, ribs and organs as his opponent's chest was cleaved in two. The Howling Griffon was still alive as he fell but his death was held off only by his fury. His lungs were laid open, a well of blood flooding his bisected rib-cage and pouring like an overflowing fountain across the dusty floor.

More charged in behind him. This was the position of honour for the Howling Griffons – the head of the charge, the first men in, who suffered the greatest chance of death but would bring out of the battle the greatest acclaim whether they fell or survived.

GRAEVUS WAS SUPPOSED to have Scamander alongside him. Scamander was dead. Graevus would have to do the killing for both of them.

More Howling Griffons were forcing their way through the narrow library corridors. A burning, armoured form crashed through the bookcase ahead of Graevus – a Howling Griffon, blazing from head to toe, the shape of a flamer-wielding Soul Drinker just visible through the curtain of smoke and flame that surrounded him. Graevus hacked off the Howling Griffon's head with one slice of his power axe, whirled with the force of the blow and followed up with a lateral strike that shattered the chainblade in the hand of the Howling Griffon who charged around the bend just ahead of him.

Soul Drinkers behind Graevus vaulted over the body of the dead Howling Griffons to get to grips with the enemy. In the confines of the library there was no room for numbers to tell. The battle was a series of duels, vicious face-to-face struggles without enough room even to feint or manoeuvre. It was war without skill: strength and fury the sole factors in victory. Graevus had plenty of both.

A Soul Drinker fell beside him, a plasma pistol wound bored right through him in a charred tunnel. Graevus dived into his killer, slamming him against the bookcase and smashing the butt of his hammer into his face. The stunned Howling Griffon fell to one knee and Graevus cut off one of his arms, the backswing shearing the top half of his head off.

Another Soul Drinker died, shattered body riddled with bolter fire. A long corridor up ahead was swept with volleys of fire from a Howling Griffon with a heavy bolter at the far end. The bookcases were disintegrating and Graevus could see the tally the Howling Griffon had already reaped through rents in the wall. Burning books gathered in drifts around his feet, gutted spines falling while their pages flitted up towards the ceiling on a scalding breath of hot air.

Graevus charged on through the bookcase. It splintered underneath him. Heavy bolter shots erupted around him, filling their air with a thousand explosions. Graevus relied on his momentum to take him through the weight of fire and he slammed into the Howling Griffons warrior, hacking and wrestling as the two fell into the flames.

Graevus let the battle-lust in him take over. It was a rare that he permitted himself to completely let go, to abandon everything that made a Space Marine a disciplined weapon of war and allow the born warrior, the celebrant of carnage, to take control.

Graevus's mutated hand clamped around the Howling Griffon's head and dropped his axe among the burning debris. He twisted the Howling Griffon's head around until a seal gave on his helmet, and the helmet came away.

The Howling Griffon was the image of Graevus himself, a gnarled and relentless veteran, the kind of man that could be trusted to hold any line and execute any order when the fire came down.

These are our brothers, thought Graevus.

They are the same as us.

The thought broke through Graevus's battle-lust. He tried to force it down but it would not be quieted.

Graevus took a step back from the Howling Griffon. The Griffon, disarmed with his heavy bolter lying down in the wreckage, scrabbled away from Graevus. Graevus picked up his axe, not taking his eyes from his opponent.

'Fall back!' shouted Graevus. 'Fall back! To your lines! Fall back!'

An instant after Graevus gave the order, the library in front of him erupted in flame and ash. Heavy weapons hammered through the bedlam. The Howling Griffons had brought their big guns up.

Their first attack was to drag the Soul Drinkers into the fight, to bog them down in melee. The second was to shatter the cover of the library and fill the Soul Drinkers positions with burning ruin, to open up enough space for the Howling Griffons to use their numbers to their fullest.

Ordinary soldiers could not have done it. The men

of the first line would have been at fatal risk from the
heavy guns of the men behind them. But the Howling Griffons were not ordinary soldiers; the first Space
Marines in trusted in the aim of their battle-brothers.

The library was torn apart. Graevus forged through
the flames, kicking shattered wooden bookcases out
of his way and shielding his face from the thousands of burning books falling as thick as a blizzard.
Lascannon blasts lanced through the Chaos, glittering crimson and shearing through everything they
touched. Fat white-hot bursts of plasma fire ripped
out of the smoke.

Graevus saw the form of a fallen Soul Drinker at his
feet. He grabbed the downed brother by the shoulder
guard and dragged him after himself as he ran. The
Soul Drinkers had fortified choke points and firebases
further in and Graevus saw one of them up ahead,
guarding a wide corridor with toppled bookcases and
heaps of broken furniture as a barricade. The Soul
Drinkers behind it – Graevus recognised Sergeant Salk
among them – waved Graevus over and he vaulted the
barricade.

The battle-brother he had brought with him had
been shot in the thigh, hit by a lascannon blast. The
leg was hanging on solely through the tangled strips of
torn ceramite that remained of his leg armour. Graevus could not tell if the Soul Drinker was alive. Other
Space Marines dragged him down out of danger.

'They're burning us out!' shouted Graevus to Salk.
'Big guns and flamers!'

'Then we are the gun line!' shouted Salk. 'We're
ready!' He handed Graevus a bolter, no doubt taken

from a wounded or dead Soul Drinker who had no more need for it. Graevus nodded, checked the movement of the bolter, and took his position kneeling at the barricade. His left hand was his trigger hand, because his mutated right was too large to fit a finger into the trigger guard.

Howling Griffons stalked through the smoke. It was impossible, with the smoke rolling thick and dense, to tell now where the remnants of the library stood, where they burned, and where they had been completely shattered. The air was too thick and toxic for a man to breathe; only the lung augmentations of the Space Marines kept both sides from choking. Visibility was well below bolter range.

Graevus could see the red and yellow livery of the Griffons, smudged and filthy through the haze and soot, reduced to a contrast between light and dark forming the quartered design the Griffons wore on their armour. Half a dozen approached down the fire point's field of view.

'Fire!' yelled Salk. The Soul Drinkers at the barricade, six or seven of them, including Graevus, opened fire. They rattled through half a magazine of bolter rounds each, pumping shells into the armoured shapes advancing on them.

Some fell, cut down. Others stumbled, alive but wounded. All who still lived returned fire and the barricade shuddered as the thick wooden slabs were chewed through, a layer of cover getting thinner with each half-second. Explosive shells threw handfuls of splinters into the haze and Graevus gritted his teeth against the stinging rain that fell against his face.

Salk swapped out a magazine. A Soul Drinker had slipped down to the floor beside him.

'It's not bad,' said the Soul Drinker. Salk clapped a hand to the wounded Space Marine's shoulder, then turned to fire another volley.

Graevus strained to see through the smoke. The wounded were being dragged away. A bookcase had been toppled for cover and the Howling Griffons were regrouping. Soul Drinkers up and down the line were sniping at movement but the Howling Griffons would not attack in ones and twos. They would advance again, coordinated to move as one.

'This is no battle,' said Graevus. 'This is not warfare. This is just…'

'Attrition,' said Salk. 'We killed Mercaeno. They all made an oath to avenge him. They're willing to spend a few of their lives if that means they are the ones who get to kill us. They have more bodies than we do. That's what it comes down to.'

'It's no way for a Space Marine to fight,' snarled Graevus. 'By the Throne, they could starve us out if they wanted. They don't have to die.'

Salk looked at Graevus, uncertain.

'They don't have to die!' repeated Graevus. 'Our Chapters are brothers! On Nevermourn it was different, but here there is no need to fight! What does it matter to them how we are killed? None of us are leaving the *Phalanx* alive, this battle is needless murder!'

'They made an oath,' said Salk. 'Mere logic cannot compete with that.'

* * *

'LET NONE MOURN the losses,' said Gethsemar. 'Let no sorrow cloud the celebrations of our victory. Bring joy, my brothers, as you bring death.'

In the shadowy confines of choristry chamber, the Angels Sanguine had gathered to pray. The chamber was lined with servitor choirs, the corpses of gifted singers transformed into machines that could sing for days on end without need for maintenance. On the *Phalanx* they were used in rituals of contemplation, when the deeds of Rogal Dorn were matched against every Imperial Fist's qualities and achievements. Now they were silent, their hairless heads bowed on their metal shoulders, the lungs stilled.

Gethsemar's war-mask glanced between his Sanguinary Guard, as if he were speaking a silent prayer that only each of his brothers could hear. Then Gethsemar drew his glaive, a two-handed power weapon with a blade of polished blue stone.

'We are ready,' he said.

'Thank Guilliman for that,' said Siege-Captain Daviks.

Daviks's Silver Skulls and the Angels Sanguine had gathered in the choristry chamber because it adjoined the library. Daviks's warriors, skilled siege engineers, had already set up the demolition charges on one wall. The sound of gunfire came from beyond it as the Howling Griffons alternately advanced through the burning ruin of the library and swept the Chaos with heavy weapons fire.

'You see no art in war,' said Gethsemar. 'And if a Space Marine's life must consist of nothing but war and the preparations for it, that means there is no place in your lives for art at all. So sad, my brother. So sad.'

'We live with it,' replied Daviks.

'This is Borganor!' came a voice over the vox-channel. 'We have them engaged! Now is the time!'

'Very well,' replied Daviks. 'We're going in.'

Daviks gave a hand signal to the Silver Skull holding the detonator. The Space Marines backed off and knelt, turning away from the wall, and the charges went off. They were shaped to direct the full force into the wall and it disintegrated, leaving a huge black hole from floor to ceiling. The shockwave and debris toppled many of the servitor choir, once-human components spilling out.

Gethsemar's Angels Sanguine charged in before the debris had finished pattering onto the floor. Smoke boiled out past them and the gunfire was louder, the yells of orders overlapping with the cries of pain as Space Marines fell.

Daviks followed Gethsemar. His squad was a siege engineer unit, armed with bolters and demolition charges, while Gethsemar's was an all-out assault unit. Gethsemar soared forwards, his jump pack hurling him horizontally down the narrow alley of bookcases that confronted him. His Sanguinary Guard were equally nimble with their jump packs, jinking around the tight corners with bursts of exhaust, their feet barely touching the ground. A Soul Drinker watching the rear of the library was cut down as Gethsemar roared past him, his power glaive slicing the sentry's arm off before another Sanguinary Guard finished the job with a downward cut that nearly bisected him.

The first Soul Drinkers were reacting to the sudden second front opening up in the library. Daviks swapped bolter fire with Soul Drinkers who ran around the corner in front of him, scattering books in the volley of bolter fire his squad kicked out in reply. Two Soul Drinkers fell and Daviks paused in his advance for long enough to put a bolter round through the head of each. A Silver Skull did not take death for granted. It was his way to be sure.

Gethsemar fell back past a corner up ahead. His golden armoured body crashed against the bookcase behind him.

'Gethsemar!' yelled Daviks into the vox. 'What is it?'

The thing that lumbered around the corner after Gethsemar was an abhorrence that Daviks's senses could barely contain. Composed of screaming heads gathered in a roughly humanoid shape, its lumpen shoulders brushed the ceiling of the library. The terrible cacophony that keened from it was enough to all but stun Daviks, filling his mind with the awful sound of pain and grief distilled. The thing's hands were bunches of withered and broken human arms, arranged like fingers, and its head was a yawning maw ringed with bleeding jawbones. In its throat, thousands of eyes clustered. The thing stamped a pace closer to Gethsemar, trailing masses of entrails and tangled limbs in its wake.

Daviks's squad opened fire, covering Gethsemar as he scrambled out of the beast's way. Bolter fire thudded into its hundreds of heads but it did not falter. It turned to Daviks, mouth yawning wide as it roared, and a gale of utter foulness shrieked around the Silver Skulls.

Bloodied hands reached from the bookcases. Mouths filled with gnashing teeth opened up in the floor to snare their feet. The Angels Sanguine were stumbling through the confusion, laying about them with their glaives at every shape that loomed through the smoky gloom.

'Stand fast!' yelled Daviks. 'Onwards, brethren, for the honour is ours! Though the Griffons reap the tally, it is we who shall take the head of the arch-traitor! Sarpedon is here! Onwards and take his head!'

Daviks felt a flare of pride. It was unbecoming for him to lust after an honour in battle, but it came unbidden, and he let it push him forwards through the horrors unfolding around him.

He knew that Sarpedon was here.

He knew it, because he had walked right into Hell.

'Do you know where you are?' said the grating metallic voice of Daenyathos.

N'Kalo struggled. He was chained. His consciousness barely surfaced over the thudding of pain, but the feeling of his restraints sang clearly. He forced against them, but they held.

He had been battered senseless. He remembered Iktinos, the skull-helm of the Soul Drinkers Chaplain emotionless as the crozius hammered again and again into the side of his head. Where and how still escaped him. He was a captive, he was sure, and over him stood a purple-armoured Dreadnought that could only be the legendary Daenyathos.

N'Kalo did not answer.

'You are somewhere you will never leave,' said Daenyathos.

N'Kalo was aware of a room of immense size. His vision swam back beyond the dreadnought and he saw that he was in a cargo hold, a vast space that could hold legions of tanks and Rhino APCs. It was empty now save for the area set up in the centre, at the heart of which N'Kalo was chained. He was surrounded by a complicated circular pattern scorched into the deck, scattered with bones and flower petals, gemstones and bundles of herbs, pages torn from books, human teeth, bullets and chunks of rock torn from alien worlds. Around this sigil knelt the pilgrims who had arrived on the *Phalanx*, they had claimed, to oversee the trial of the Soul Drinkers, and they held their standards of the blinded eye aloft. They were hooded and robed and issued a low chant, dark syllables repeated in a terrible drone.

N'Kalo was aware that he still wore his armour and his battered helm was back on his head. It made no sense for his captor to leave him armoured. He might not have a weapon in his hand, but a Space Marine in armour was still more dangerous than one without. It could help him when he broke out, and there was no doubt in his mind that he would. Whatever agenda Daenyathos had, and whether the Soul Drinkers were heretics or blameless, Daenyathos and Iktinos had revealed themselves to constitute a moral threat and N'Kalo had a duty to escape and bring them to justice.

'You wear your thoughts on you as if they were

written on your armour,' said Daenyathos. 'You desire escape. That is natural. A Space Marine is not created to be caged. And you desire revenge. You would call it duty or justice, but it is ultimately death you wish on me for orchestrating your defeat and capture. This, again, is natural. A Space Marine is a vengeful creature. But do you see now, helpless as you are, what a pitiful animal you truly are? Freedom and vengeance – what do these things mean, when compared to the matters that shape the galaxy? How much does your existence mean?'

N'Kalo struggled again. His chains were set into the deck of the cargo hold. They were probably chains built into the deck to keep tanks from sliding around when the *Phalanx* was in flight. One Space Marine could not break them.

'My duty is within myself,' said N'Kalo. He knew he should have stayed silent, but something in Daenyathos's words, in the way he seemed genuinely passionate in spite of the artificiality of his voice, compelled him to reply. 'Though the galaxy may burn and humanity collapse, I must fulfil my duty regardless. And so I call myself a Space Marine.'

'That is the response of a weak mind,' said Daenyathos. The Dreadnought's body turned away to something off to the side, outside N'Kalo's frame of vision. 'You choose to ignore the matters that affect the galaxy, and shrink your mind down to one battle after another, one petty victory over some xenos or renegade, and tell yourself that such is the totality of your potential. I chose instead to abandon the duties that restrict me, and rise to become one of those very factors that mould the galaxy at their whim. It is a choice I made. Yours is a mind too small to make it. The Soul Drinkers were like you, and I had to make that choice for them. Were they wise enough to understand, they would have thanked me.'

Daenyathos's massive tank-like torso swivelled back to face N'Kalo. One of his arms was a missile launcher, while the other ended in a huge power fist. That fist was now encased in a gauntlet from which protruded several smaller implements – manipulator limbs, blades, needles, an assortment of attachments for finer control than the Dreadnought's power fist afforded.

'What is this?' said N'Kalo. 'Why have you brought me here?'

'That is a question I am willing to answer,' said Daenyathos. 'But not through words.'

A circular saw emerged from among the implements. N'Kalo tensed, forcing against his bonds with every muscle he had. He felt joints parting and bones cracking, shots of pain running through him as his muscular power pushed beyond the limits of his skeleton.

The chains did not move. Perhaps N'Kalo could break and twist his limbs until they could be slipped out of their bonds. Perhaps he could crawl away, steal a weapon from one of the cultists.

The circular blade cut through N'Kalo's breastplate. Sparks flew, and bright reflections glinted in the lenses set into Daenyathos's armoured head.

Daenyathos worked quickly, and with great precision. Soon the breastplate was lifted off in sections, smaller manipulator limbs picking apart the layers of ceramite until N'Kalo felt the recycled air of the *Phalanx* cold on his chest.

The chanting changed to a terrible falling cadence, a piece of music about to end. N'Kalo felt the power charging in the air and saw a glow overhead, as if from a great heat against the ceiling of the cargo hold. Crackles of energy ran down the walls, earthing off the massive feet of Daenyathos's Dreadnought body.

N'Kalo felt pain. He gasped in spite of himself, the impossibly cold touch of the saw blade running in a red line along his sternum.

The ceiling of the cargo hold was lifting off, metallic sections peeling apart and fluttering into the void like dead leaves on the wind. The hull parted and the air gushed out. The pilgrims looked up at the rent in the side of the *Phalanx*, calm and joy on their faces even as the sudden pressure change made their eye sockets well up red with burst vessels. Hoods were blown back by the swirling gale and, in spite of the pain, N'Kalo's mind registered the face of a woman ecstatic as foaming blood ran from her lips. Another one of the pilgrims was their leader, impossibly ancient, and his dry and dusty body seemed to wither away as he raised his wizened head to the origin of the light that fell on him.

The light was coming from Kravamesh, the star around which the *Phalanx* orbited. A burning orange glow filtered down through the debris swirling around the hull breach. The hull parted further, like an opening eye, and the last tides of air boomed out.

The pilgrims were dying, each moment robbing

another of consciousness. N'Kalo realised his armour had been left on so that he could still breathe while the cargo hold fell apart.

The saw was withdrawn. Without air, the only sound was now vibrations through the floor. The faint whir of servos as a manipulator arm unfolded. The rattling breath N'Kalo drew through the systems of his armour as the cold hit the open wound in his chest.

'Do you know,' said Daenyathos, the sound of his voice transmitted as vibrations through his feet, 'what you are to become?'

N'Kalo gritted his teeth. He could see Kravamesh above him, its boiling fires, and though its fires looked down on him its light was appallingly cold.

'The key,' continued Daenyathos. The manipulators extended and hooked around N'Kalo's ribs. N'Kalo yelled, the cry not making it past the insides of his own armour. 'Dorn's own blood is the only key that will fit the lock he built around Kravamesh. The Soul Drinkers do not have it, though it suited me for them to continue believing they did. You have it, Iron Knight. The blood of Dorn flows in your veins.'

The manipulators forced at the edges of N'Kalo's fused rib breastplate. The bones creaked. N'Kalo strained every muscle in his body, forcing against the pain as well as his restraints.

He saw Rogal Dorn, his golden-armoured body kneeling at the Emperor's fallen form. He saw the Eye of Terror open, and the battlements of Earth burning. Some ancient memory, written into the genetic material on which his augmentations were based, bled in the final moments into his mind.

N'Kalo felt the impossible pride and fury of Rogal Dorn. They filled him to bursting, too much emotion for a man, even a Space Marine, to contain. The Primarch was an impossible creature, in every aspect superior to a man, in every dimension vaster by far.

N'Kalo could see Rogal Dorn at the Iron Cage, the vast fortifications manned by the soldiers of Chaos, the shadow of the entire Imperial Fists Chapter falling on it as Dorn orchestrated the assault.

The last images were ghosted over the monstrous eye of Kravamesh opening wide, vast and unholy shapes emerging from its fires.

Daenyathos punched the mass of his power fist into N'Kalo's chest, splintering through the ribs. Daenyathos ripped the fist free and N'Kalo's organs were sprayed across the cargo bay deck in the shape of bloody wings. The gore iced over in the cold of the void.

Daenyathos's massive form leaned back from N'Kalo. The pattern scorched into the deck glowed red as if it were drinking N'Kalo's spilled blood. The glow was met by the burning orange light from above. The head of Daenyathos's chassis looked up towards the tear in the hull as the fires of Kravamesh billowed suddenly close.

From space it looked as if a bridge of fire were being built, reaching from the mass of Kravamesh towards the speck of the *Phalanx*. Shapes rippled along the bridge, tortured faces and twisted limbs, howling ghosts that split and reformed like liquid fire.

The observation crews on the *Phalanx* saw it right away. Every sensor on the Imperial Fists fortress-ship screamed in response. But the *Phalanx* was embroiled in open warfare, its crew managing the Chaos unfolding from its archives, and without the whole crew at their stations the huge and complex ship could not react in time.

The tendril of fire touched the hull of the *Phalanx*. Daenyathos stood in the swirling mass of flame that incinerated the remains of N'Kalo and the pilgrims. From the flame emerged shapes – leaping, gibbering things, limbs and eyes that turned in on one another in an endless mockery of evolution. They danced madly around Daenyathos as if he were the master of their revel. Reality shuddered and tore as the insanity formed a huge circular gate in the centre of the cargo bay, the fire rippling around a glassy black pit that plunged through the substance of the universe and into a place far darker.

Daenyathos stood before the warp portal. The fires of the warp washed around the feet of his Dreadnought chassis, and the daemons slavered as they slunk through the flame. But Daenyathos did not falter. He had seen this moment a million times before. He had dreamed it over thousands of years in half-sleep under Selaaca.

Vast mountains of filth and hatred shifted in the darkness beyond the portal. Tendrils of their sheer malice rippled through the substance of the cargo hold, blistering up the metal of the deck with spiny tentacled limbs. Blood-weeping eyes opened up in the walls. The daemon cavalcade shrieked higher and higher as one of the forms in the portal detached itself and drifted, half-formed, towards the opening.

It coalesced as it approached, taking the shape of something at once beautiful and appalling. A vast and idealised human figure, glistening pale skin clad in flowing white silk, surrounded by a halo of raw magic. Torn minds flowed in its wake, ruptured spirits shredded into madness by the warp. A taloned hand grasped the flaming edge of the portal, hauling its vastness towards reality.

The perfect, maddening shape of the head emerged. Its features looked like they were carved from pure marble, its eyes orbs of jade. The music of the warp accompanied it, a thousand choirs shorn of their bodies.

'It is time,' said Daenyathos. 'The threads of the destiny meet here.'

'Free!' bellowed the daemon prince in its thousand voices. 'Banishment, agony, all over! A vengeance… vengeance flows like blood from a wound! The wound I shall leave in the universe… the hatred that shall rise in a flood. Oh unriven souls, oh undreaming minds, you shall be laid to waste! Abraxes has returned!'

# CHAPTER TEN

ARCHMAGOS VOAR WAS surrounded by a cordon of servitors as he hurried through the guest quarters towards the saviour pod array. Beyond the lavish guest rooms, he knew a shuttle could be found, normally used for diplomatic purposes but perfectly suitable for taking him off the *Phalanx* and onto one of the nearby ships – the *Traitorsgrave*, perhaps, on which Lord Inquisitor Kolgo had arrived, or a Space Marine ship like the *Judgement upon Garadan*.

Voar had betrayed the Soul Drinkers on Selaaca. None of his logic circuits entertained the concept that it might have been the wrong thing to do, either logically or morally. But that did not change the fact that the Soul Drinkers were loose and they might well want Voar, in particular, dead. The *Pha-lanx* was not safe for him.

Voar's motivator units, damaged on Selaaca, had been repaired well enough for him to make good speed through the nests of anterooms and state suites, winding around antique furnishings and art-works whose uselessness accentuated their sense of the lavish. The Imperial Fists were pragmatic in their dealings with the wider Imperium, willing to receive diplomats from the various Adepta in a fashion acceptable to the Imperium's social elite. The servi-tors Voar had taken from the *Phalanx's* stores wound around the resulting tables, chairs and light sculp-tures with rather more difficulty than Voar himself.

Voar paused at the infra-red signature that flared against his vision. His sight, like most of the rest of him, had been significantly augmented to bring him away from corruptible flesh and closer to the machine-ideal. He had seen a heat trace, just past one of the archways leading into an audience chamber. Reclining couches and tables with gilt decorations, imported from some far-off world of craftsmen, stood before an ornate throne painted with enam-elled scenes of plenty and wealth. Beneath the room's chandeliers and incense-servitor perches, something had moved, something interested in keeping itself hidden for as long as possible.

Voar drew the inferno pistol, another item liber-ated from the *Phalanx's* armouries. The servitors, responding to the mind-impulse unit built into Voar's cranium, formed a tighter cordon around him. Their weapons, autoguns linked to the targeting units that filled their eye sockets, tracked as Voar's vision switched through spectrums. He saw warm traces of footprints on the floor, residual electrical energy dissipating.

Chaplain Iktinos knew he had been seen. There was no use in trying to stay hidden when he was over two-and-a-half metres tall and in full armour. He walked out from behind the dignitary's throne, crozius arcanum in hand.

'You have failed, Soul Drinker,' said Voar. There was no trace of fear in his voice, and not just because of its artificial nature. His emotional repressive surgery had chased such petty concerns like fear from his biological brain. 'Your escape from the *Phalanx* is a logical impossibility. You gain nothing from exacting revenge against me.'

'Logic is a lie,' came the reply. 'A prison for small minds. I am here for a purpose beyond revenge.'

Voar waited no longer. Negotiations would not suffice. He dropped back behind an enormous four-poster bed of black hardwood as he gave the impulse for the servitors to open fire.

Eight autoguns hammered out a curtain of fire. Iktinos ran into the storm, faceplate of his helmet tucked behind one shoulder guard as he charged. The armour was chewed away as if by accelerated decay, the skull-faced shoulder guard stripped down through ceramite layers, then down to the bundles of cables and nerve fibres that controlled it.

Iktinos slammed into the servitors. One was crushed under his weight, its reinforced spine snapping and its gun wrenched out of position to spray

bullets uselessly into the frescoed ceiling. The crozius slashed through another two, their unarmoured
forms coming apart under the shock of the power
field, mechanical and once-human parts showering
against the walls in a wet steel rain.

Voar ducked out of cover as Iktinos beheaded the
last servitor with his free hand. Voar took aim and
fired, a lance of superheated energy lashing out and
slicing a chunk out of the Chaplain's crozius arm.

Voar's mind slowed down, logic circuits engaging to
examine the tactical possibilities faster than unaugmented thought. He had to keep his distance since,
up close, Iktinos was lethal, while Voar's inferno pistol
was the only weapon he had that could hope to fell
a Space Marine. The targeting systems built into his
eyes would make sure that his second shot would not
miss. As long as he saw Iktinos before the fallen Chaplain could kill him, Voar would get one good shot off.
The plan fell into place, paths and vectors illuminating in blue-white lines layered over his vision.

Voar jumped out of cover, his motivator units
sending him drifting rapidly backwards towards an
archway leading into an elaborate stone-lined bath
house, with a deep caldarium, a cold-plunge pool
and a Space Marine-scaled massage table. Mosaics
of Imperial heroes lined the walls and valet-servitors
stood ready. Voar's inferno pistol was out in front of
him, ready to fire.

Iktinos was not within his frame of vision. The
archmagos's logic circuits fought to create new tactical scenarios. He should have been feeling panic,
but instead his altered mind was generating a burst

of useless information, a confused tangle of targeting solutions for a target that suddenly wasn't there.

Iktinos's armoured mass slid out from under the enormous massage table, crashing into the lower half of Voar's body. Voar was thrown against the archway. He fired, but Iktinos was moving too rapidly and the shot grazed him again, carving a molten channel along the side of his helmet. Iktinos slashed at Voar with his heavy powered mace. The archmagos cut his motivator units and dropped to the floor, and the crozius sliced through the stonework of the arch.

Iktinos's other arm grabbed Voar's gun wrist, spun the archmagos around and slammed him against the wall, his forearm pinning Voar's back.

'I am not here to kill you,' said Iktinos. 'Your life means nothing to me. Give me the Soulspear.'

'Take it,' said Voar. A small manipulator limb emerged from the collar of his hood. It carried the haft of the Soulspear, a cylinder of metal with a knurled handgrip.

Iktinos took the Soulspear and turned it over in his hand, keeping Voar up against the wall.

'To think,' he said. 'Such a small thing. Even now I wonder if it was this that set us on our path. Many of your tech-priests died over this, archmagos. Many of my brothers, too. It is right that it be delivered into the hands of Daenyathos.'

'You have what you came for,' said Voar. 'Let me go.'

'I made no promises that you would live,' said Iktinos.

Emotions that had not been felt for decades clouded Voar's face. 'Omnissiah take your soul!' he snapped.

'May it burn in His forges! May it be hammered on His anvil!'

Iktinos lifted Voar into the air and slammed the tech-priest down over his knee. Metal vertebrae shattered and components rained out of Voar's robes. Iktinos plunged the crozius arcanum into Voar's chest, the power field ripping through layers of metal and bone.

Senior tech-priests could be extremely difficult to kill. Many of them could survive anything up to and including decapitation, trusting in their augmentations to keep their semi-organic brains alive until their remains could be recovered. A few of the most senior, the archmagi ultima who might rule whole clusters of forge worlds, even had archeotech backup brains where their personalities and memories could be recorded in case of physical destruction. Voar did not have that level of augmentation, but Iktinos had to be thorough nevertheless.

Iktinos tore open Voar's torso completely and scattered the contents, smashing each organ and component in case Voar's brain was located there. He finished destroying the spine and finally turned to Voar's head. He crushed the cranium under his boot, grinding logic circuits and ocular bionics into the floor with his heel. Quite probably, Voar died in that moment, the last sensory inputs gone dark, the final thoughts flashing through sundered circuitry.

Iktinos finished destroying Voar's body, then took up the Soulspear. It was a relic of the Great Crusade, found by Rogal Dorn himself during the Emperor's reconquest of the galaxy in the name of humanity.

He had given it to the Soul Drinkers at their founding, to symbolise that they were sons of Dorn as surely as the Imperial Fists themselves.

That was the story, of course. In truth, the origin of the Soulspear, like the rest of the Soul Drinkers history, was as murky as anything else in Imperial annals. The Soulspear was gene-activated and would only respond to someone with a Soul Drinker's genetic code, so whoever had created or found the artefact, it had not been Rogal Dorn. The Soulspear, like the rest of the universe, was a lie.

That did not mean it did not have its uses. Daenyathos understood that. Just like the Imperium, the Soulspear might be founded on lies, but it could still become a part of the plan.

Daenyathos's transformation of the Imperium would not be a pleasant process. Nothing worth doing ever was. But in spite of the blood, in spite of the suffering and the death, the universe would thank Daenyathos when it was done.

Iktinos left Voar's remains scattered on the floor of the diplomatic quarters, and headed towards the Predator's Eye to witness the Imperium's future unfold.

GETHSEMAR AND DAVIKS charged into the heart of the library labyrinth at the same time, charging in from two directions to catch Sarpedon off-guard.

Sarpedon was never off-guard. Silhouetted in the flames that ran across the bookcases behind him, he turned to face the Angels Sanguine and Silver Skulls warriors as if he had been expecting them.

Daviks opened fire. Sarpedon's reactions were so fast that the bolter shots burst against the blade of the Axe of Mercaeno as the mutant flicked it up to defend himself.

Gethsemar erupted towards Sarpedon on a column of fire from his jump pack. Sarpedon's left-side legs flipped the reading table behind him into Gethsemar's path and the heavy hardwood slammed into Gethsemar, throwing the Angel Sanguine into a bookcase, which buried him in a drift of burning books.

In the middle of the fire and slaughter, it was almost poetry that unfolded as the fight continued. Daviks parried the Axe of Mercaeno with the body of his bolter, only to be thrown to the floor by Sarpedon's lashing legs. Gethsemar jumped to his feet and lunged with his glaive, Sarpedon ducking the blow with impossible grace and barging the butt of the axe into Gethsemar's abdomen to throw him off-balance.

Captain Luko vaulted through the flame to crash into Daviks before the siege-captain could join the assault again. The two warriors of the Adeptus Astartes traded blows as fast as a man could see, Luko's lightning claws lashing in great arcs of blue-white power, batting aside Daviks's bolter before Daviks could get a shot.

Gethsemar launched himself into the air and dived down out of the flames overhead. Sarpedon reached up and grabbed Gethsemar, hauling him in close where the Angel Sanguine's blade could not be brought to bear. Gethsemar and Sarpedon wrestled, Sarpedon using his mutated physiology to grapple from unexpected angles and drag Gethsemar to the floor. He forced the Axe of Mercaeno down, the edge of the blade pressing against Gethsemar's throat. Gethsemar fired his jump pack but Sarpedon was stronger, and his taloned legs dug into the floor to keep himself upright.

'Fall back!' came an order over the Imperial Fists vox-channel. It was Lysander's voice, transmitted to the Howling Griffons, Silver Skulls and Angels Sanguine. 'All troops, fall back to rally points! Disengage immediately!'

The moment's confusion this caused was enough for Sarpedon to drive a fist into Gethsemar's face-plate. The death mask of Sanguinius dented and blood spurted from the carved mouth. Gemstones pinged out of the gilded surface and Gethsemar juddered as the impact ran through his whole body.

Daviks saw that Gethsemar was going to die. He ducked Luko's swinging claw swipe and charged into the Soul Drinker's legs, hauling Luko off his feet and ramming him right through the bookcase behind. He threw Luko and, using the moment of distance he had opened up, brought his bolter around and sprayed a volley in Luko's direction. The Soul Drinker rolled out of the way, putting hardwood shelving and millions of burning pages between him and Daviks's gunfire, but that was what Daviks needed.

Daviks sprinted to where Gethsemar lay, the shadow of Sarpedon's axe cast over him by the light of the flames. Daviks grabbed Gethsemar's wrist and dragged him out of the way as Sarpedon's axe came down, ripping a deep gash in the deck.

'We leave, brother!' gasped Daviks. 'Lysander has ordered us back!'

'The fight is not done,' replied Gethsemar, his voice thick with blood. 'The enemy still stands.'

'Lysander has command! We fall back! Muster your brothers and get back to the choristers' chamber! We will cover you!'

The two Space Marines dropped back through the smoke and wreckage. Sarpedon watched them go, not eager to pursue them when their battle-brothers must surely be just behind them.

Luko emerged smouldering from the wreck of the bookcase he had been thrown through. 'Damnation, I will have your hide!' he yelled after Daviks.

Sarpedon put a hand on Luko's shoulder. 'Stay, brother,' he said. 'Something is wrong.'

GRAEVUS DARED A glance over the barricade. The last volley of bolter fire the Soul Drinkers had kicked out had not been replied. He saw the shapes of the Howling Griffons receding through the smoke, a few kneeling to fire while the majority fell back.

Graevus stood and took aim, firing off a few shots snapped into the half-seen shapes through the smoke. Salk was beside him now, echoing Graevus's own fire.

'They're retreating,' said Salk as he paused to swap magazines.

'We haven't hit them that hard,' said Graevus. 'I thought they would be on us.'

'Then something else has happened,' said Salk.

'Don't be too thankful. They could be mustering for another push.'

'No,' replied Salk. 'Not when they had us pinned in place. Not the Howling Griffons, not here. They would have pushed on until either they or we were all dead. This… this is no plan of theirs.'

'Maybe logic prevailed,' said Graevus.

With the gunfire reduced to sporadic shots, the roar of the flames and the clattering of armour became like another form of silence, as if the library were in the eye of a storm that had just passed over and now everything was still. Behind the barricade lay two fallen Soul Drinkers, brought down by bolter fire and shrapnel – one was dead, both Graevus and Salk could see that, his torso split open and blood already congealing in a crystalline mass around the enormous spine-deep wound. The other was still but the wound to his leg, severe though it was, should not kill him.

'We need Pallas,' said Graevus.

'We do not have him,' replied Salk. 'Soul Drinkers! Bring the fallen and retreat to Sarpedon's position! Brother Markis, Thessalon! Cover us!'

Other Soul Drinkers, the survivors of a dozen Howling Griffons assaults, were moving through the smoke. They looked like the ghosts of some long-distant battle hovering just on this side of reality, clinging on as they enacted the same bloodshed night after night. Most had survived with bearable wounds, but there had been no doubt that the numbers and fury of the Howling Griffons would have soon prevailed. But now the Griffons had fallen back, and in their place was surely an unknown enemy no more inclined to give the Soul Drinkers any respite.

'No,' said Graevus. 'On second thoughts, there is no reason here.'

'BRING ME EVERYTHING you know,' said Chapter Master Pugh.

'Of course,' replied Castellan Leucrontas. 'We know little, but I can confirm that the starboard dorsal cargo section has been lost.'

Leucrontas had been summoned to the Forge of Ages, which had become Pugh's command post. Pict-feeds from the battle site showed little more than screens full of smoke and the vox-channel was full of barked orders and the confusion that the sudden order to retreat had brought about. In spite of that, the Howling Griffons were falling back in good order and even now mustering around the crew mess. That was not the issue.

'Lost?' said Pugh. He leaned forwards on the steel throne from which the Imperial Fists Techmarines usually oversaw the work of the forge-crews.

'It is gone. Full breach and depressurisation. Any crew in the area are dead, no doubt.'

'Any Adeptus Astartes casualties?'

'I do not believe so.'

'What caused it?'

'The psychic wards built around the librarium contemplative chambers reacted,' replied Leucrontas. 'And the readings so far obtained are esoteric.'

'A psychic attack?' said Pugh.

'If so, my lord, it is a vast and destructive one, well beyond the capacity of an Adeptus Astartes psyker.'

'Then,' said Pugh, his chin on his fist, 'a moral

threat? An assault from the warp?'

'Librarian Varnica's testimony did suggest the Soul Drinkers had daemonic allies,' said Leucrontas. 'And there is... something... happening to Kravamesh.'

'Kravamesh? The star? What has the star around which we orbit to do with the Soul Drinkers?' Pugh held up his hand before Leucrontas replied. 'No, castellan, I ask not for an answer. I merely muse upon it. We must see to the security of the *Phalanx* before we seek the origin of this new threat. Once the assault on the archives has been withdrawn, we must redeploy our strength around the dorsal cargo bays to keep them contained. A smaller force can maintain the cordon around the archives. Draw up the battle stations and see that Lysander has access to them. Nothing must get in or out of either area without running a gauntlet of bolter fire.'

'Yes, my lord. And the crew?'

'Order them to arms. Protect the critical areas of the ship. I had hoped that even after the escape this would be limited to Space Marine versus Space Marine. It seems events have compelled us to think beyond that.'

'It will be done.'

'Keep me apprised of everything, and...'

Pugh's voice was interrupted by the bleating of an alarm. From the armrest of the throne slid a pictscreen that shuddered into life.

'The tech-adepts must have got dorsal security back online,' said Leucrontas.

The screen showed a view of a corridor, bulkhead doors standing open along its length. Mist clung to the floor and rolled through the doorways.

Shapes were coalescing. Tentacles, eyes, mouths, malformed limbs, writhing masses of entrails that moved with an impossible impression of intelligence and malice. Teeth, blades of bone, tides of filth, all wrapped into dimensions that refused to fit into reality. Like a stain the madness was spreading out, a tide of filth and insanity that warped the fabric of the *Phalanx* as it advanced.

'Daemons,' snarled Pugh. He looked up at Leucrontas. 'Bring me the Fangs of Dorn.'

IN THE SMOULDERING ruins of the archive, Sarpedon and his officers convened. The smoke that still clung to everything made it look as if they were wanderers in dense mist who had come across one another by accident. They gathered around one of the few intact reading tables, where the ground was knee-deep in charred pages and gutted spines.

Graevus and Salk joined Luko, Tyrendian and Sarpedon where they waited. 'The dead have been counted,' said Graevus.

'What is the tally?' said Sarpedon.

Salk stepped forwards. 'Fifteen,' he said. 'Those who remain number forty-seven.'

'Was it ever true that there were once a thousand of us?' said Sarpedon.

'No,' replied Tyrendian. 'The old Chapter boasted a thousand warriors. We are not that Chapter.'

'Then they died,' said Sarpedon, 'as we surely shall. Now is not the time to bar that truth from our souls. Many times a Space Marine facing death refuses to allow it into his mind, for by defying the inevitable we can sometimes rob it of victory. But not here. I think I accepted our deaths here when the Imperial Fists first faced us on Selaaca, but if any of you still rage against our fate then I ask you to abandon it. Take the certainty of death into yourselves, welcome it, and make peace with it. It is not an easy task, but now, it is the right path to take.'

'If we fight not to survive,' said Luko, 'then why? Why not simply present ourselves to the Howling Griffons so they might put a bullet in the back of our heads and be done with it?'

'Because there are matters unfinished amongst us that our enemy's retreat has permitted to us to address,' replied Sarpedon.

'You mean Daenyathos,' said Salk, 'and Iktinos.'

'We still have no understanding of what they intend here,' said Tyrendian. Somehow he, as always seemed the case, had come through the battle in the archive with barely any scar or blemish on him. Perhaps his psychic talent was not limited to throwing lightning bolts in battle, but also gave him some kind of inviolability, some ward against the ugliness of war. 'Presuming it was Iktinos, under Daenyathos's direction, who brought us to this juncture, there is no indication of what he actually wants to achieve here.'

'Then we shall find out,' said Sarpedon. 'The Howling Griffons will attack again soon, or a cordon will be set up to contain us. Either way, if any of us are to begin the hunt for Iktinos and Daenyathos then we must do so soon. I do not believe our whole force can move through the *Phalanx* quickly enough. The whole of the Imperial Fists and Howling Griffons will mobilise to stand in our way. But if a smaller force does so while the main force must also be dealt with, we will have a greater chance of breaking through any opposition and finding Daenyathos.'

'Then who will go?' said Tyrendian.

'Sergeant Salk,' said Sarpedon. 'I ask that you select a squad and accompany me. I cannot do this alone. Captain Luko, you shall take command of the rest of the Chapter.'

'You are our Chapter Master,' replied Luko. 'It is to your leadership that our battle-brothers look. Would you deny them that in their final battle? Let one of us go.'

'No, captain,' retorted Sarpedon. 'I am faster than any Space Marine. Foul as they are, my mutations serve me well in that regard. Not to mention, I would send no man to face Iktinos or Daenyathos save myself. And I may be their leader by right, but ask any Soul Drinker what man he would prefer to fight alongside and those who are honest will name Captain Luko.'

Luko did not reply for a long moment. 'If I was asked that question,' said Luko levelly, 'then I would say Chapter Master Sarpedon. Is it my fate that I will be denied that in these, our last moments?'

'It is,' said Sarpedon. 'I promised you peace, captain. It will come soon. I did not promise I would be there when it arrived. Forgive me, but these are my orders.'

Luko said nothing, but saluted by way of reply.

'Our objectives?' asked Tyrendian.

'Draw in our enemies, keep them busy. The fiercer the fight here, the shorter odds you buy for Salk and myself.'

'I shall round up a squad,' said Salk. 'I know who to choose. It will not take long.'

'Then we must part,' said Sarpedon. 'Remember, regardless of whose blood flows in us, we are still sons of Dorn. If there was ever a man who did not know when to give up, it was Rogal Dorn. We are blessed with a battle in which we cannot fail. Think on Dorn, and forget how to lose.'

The assembled Soul Drinkers saluted their commander. Then, to a man, they bowed their heads to pray.

LIKE A POISONED barb in flesh, like an infection, the warp portal had caused to grow around it a corrupted cyst that ran with blood and pain. From the steel of the *Phalanx* it had chewed out a great cathedral of gore, its arching ceiling ribbed with clotted veins of filth and its walls of vivid, oozing torn flesh. Blood washed in tides born of Kravamesh's gravity, like wine swirled in a bowl, and through it slithered all the foul things of the warp.

Every power of the warp wanted its hand played on the *Phalanx*. So many of their servants had been banished or destroyed by the Imperial Fists and the other Chapters represented there that even their aeons-old hatreds could not stop them from sending their minions to join Abraxes's own. Brass-skinned soldiers of the Blood God marched from the blood onto the shore of torn metal, their black iron swords at attention and their muscular bodies moving in time as if they were on a parade ground. Flitting snakelike things with long lashing tongues darted here and there, quick as hovering insects, snapping at the morsels of flesh that scudded on the surface of the blood. And a horde of decaying forms hauled on rusted chains as they dragged an enormous thing of rotting flesh out of the mire, a contented smile on its bloated face as it plucked a tiny squealing daemon from the rents in its skin and swallowed it down. It seemed that every shape of the warp's hatred was emerging from the blood-gate, beyond which vast intelligences gathered to watch this invasion of the Imperial Fists sanctum.

On an island of corroded metal, all that remained of the docking bay deck, stood Daenyathos. He seemed the only solid thing in an arena of flesh that mutated at the whim of the Dark Gods, as if the Dreadnought's chassis anchored the whole scene in realspace and without him it would all collapse into the warp under the weight of its own madness.

'I brought you here,' he yelled, voice amplified to maximum. 'It is at my sufferance that you walk again in the realms of the real. Abraxes the Fair, Abraxes the Magnificent, I call upon you to hear me.'

Abraxes rose from his throne of bodies, twisted and fused together from crewmen whose minds had shattered under the psychic assault of the gate's opening. The daemon prince's beauty was not marred by the blood that soaked his garments and ran down his perfect alabaster skin. 'Abraxes is not summoned,' he said in a voice like song. 'He arrives not at the whim of another.'

'And yet,' replied Daenyathos, 'you are here. For who else would I bring forth to have his revenge on Sarpedon of the Soul Drinkers?'

Abraxes leaned forward. 'Sarpedon? And yet here I thought that Imperial Fists, as delicious as they would be, were the sole morsels I might find here to soothe my hunger. Yet Sarpedon is here… where is he? The gate is opened fully and the daemon army is ready to march. I would march upon him first, and destroy what remains in celebration of my revenge!'

'I imagine,' said Daenyathos, 'that he will come to you. But mere slaughter is too small an objective for one such as Abraxes, is it not? To butcher a starship full of Space Marines is a worthy endeavour for any petty prince or aspiring daemon, but for Abraxes? Surely your dreams are grander than that?'

'Explain yourself!' demanded Abraxes. 'I grow impatient. See! The horrors of Tzeentch march to my tune. A thousand of them emerge from the warp at my whim! I shall lead them forth without delay unless your words are profound indeed.'

'This is a spaceship,' said Daenyathos. 'A spaceship as huge and deadly as any the Imperium has ever fielded. And now it is a spaceship with a warp portal. I have stolen the Predator's Eye from the star Kravamesh and embedded it in the *Phalanx*. What could the great Abraxes desire more than a doorway into the warp from which spills all the legions under his command, and that he can take between the stars as he wishes?'

Abraxes clenched a fist, and his thoughts could almost be read on his face. They were not human thoughts – they would not fit in a human mind. 'I shall extinguish stars,' he said. 'I shall weave a pattern across the galaxy, even unto Terra!'

'I can lead you there,' continued Daenyathos. 'For a lifetime I studied the path that will take you beyond the reach of the Imperium's cumbersome armies and into the orbits of its most populous worlds. It is a path that leads to Terra, I assure you. But it leads also through the very soul of humanity! Imagine world after world falling, drowned in madness, their last sane vision that of the *Phalanx* appearing like a dread star above them! A thousand times a thousand worlds shall share this fate, so that by the time you reach Terra it shall be to deal the death blow to a species cringing on its knees before you!'

'And for what reason would a Space Marine lead me on such a dance?' said Abraxes. 'You who were born of the Emperor's will. You who have sworn so many oaths to destroy all such as me. Why do you wish your species to undergo such a tortuous death?'

'I need no reason,' said Daenyathos. 'Hatred is its own justification.'

'Ah, hatred!' said Abraxes, jumping to his cloven feet. The blood washed around his ankles, mindless predators slithering from the foam. 'The human gift to the universe. The greatest work of man. Even your Emperor himself was in thrall to it. There has been no creation to rival it. It builds worlds and brings them down. Aloud it is war, and in silence it is peace. The human race is nothing but a trillion manifestations of hatred! When humanity is gone, I think I shall preserve alone its hatred. From it I shall mould whatever I see fit to succeed them. Hatred alone shall rule among the stars.'

'And so it shall be,' said Daenyathos. 'But first, the *Phalanx* must become your own.'

'That,' replied Abraxes with scorn, 'is a task worthy of my notice only because Sarpedon's death shall be a part of it. Sarpedon is the last of the universe I once knew, one in which Abraxes could fail. When he is gone, only victory shall be left. I can see the fates twining out towards destruction. There is no thread that humanity can follow to safety. Sarpedon dies. They all die. Then your universe shall follow!'

With the atonal braying of a hundred pipes, Abraxes's army gathered on the blood shore. Greater daemons, hateful lumps of the warp's own will given form, were the generals of a thousands-strong army. Bloodletters of Khorne chanted in their own dark tongue, bodies smouldering as their lust for slaughter grew. Abraxes's own horrors were a shuddering tide of formless flesh, shifting in and out of solid forms at the speed of thought. Plaguebearers, emissaries of the plague god Nurgle who had once been Abraxes's sworn enemy, fawned around the enormous drooling avatar of rot that was their leader.

Abraxes strode to the head of his army. In response, the walls of the cyst opened into vast orifices, leading towards the interior of the *Phalanx*. Lesser daemons scrambled forwards, shrieking and gibbering with the joy of approaching battle. The lords of the daemonic host howled a terrible cacophony of bellowed orders and the army advanced, horrors of Tzeentch following Abraxes like the wake of a battleship.

Daenyathos could see in the army's advance another thread of fate winding its way towards a conclusion. Even Chaos had to observe the inevitability of fate. Abraxes, a being that had perfected its use of unwitting pawns such as the Soul Drinkers, had been drawn by that same fate to serve Daenyathos's design. Through Abraxes, Daenyathos's own will would be done.

It had taken so long and so much to reach this point, but that was merely a prelude. The bloodshed on the Phalanx was the true beginning of Daenyathos's remaking of the galaxy.

SARPEDON HAD NOTHING but raw instinct to go on. He knew a little of Daenyathos and rather more of Iktinos's ways, but even so it was barely more than guesswork that took him through the cordon of Imperial Fists and into the vast training section of the *Phalanx*, where sparring circles and shooting galleries were equipped with hundreds of target-servitors and racks of exotic weapons from cultures across the galaxy.

The industrialised sections of the *Phalanx*, the cargo bays and engineering sections towards the rear of the ship, were the best place for a single Space Marine to hide. Even a Dreadnought would find places to hole up there. That was where Sarpedon resolved to look, but first he would have to cross the training sections.

'We should take the mock battlefield,' said Sergeant Salk. His squad, picked from the survivors of the battle in the archive, was advancing in a wide formation to give them the widest angles of vision. Ahead, a jumble of deck sections formed a series of slopes, hills and valleys, each section on hydraulics which could move them into a new topography to create a constantly changing battlefield. It was here that Imperial Fists recruits were put through days-long battle simulations, waves of target-servitors and the shifting landscape combining to create a test that was as much mental as it was physical.

'Agreed,' said Sarpedon. 'We must make good time.'

'If we find Iktinos, commander, what will we do?'

Sarpedon raised an eyebrow. 'Kill him,' he said. 'What do you think?'

The atmosphere of real battlefields clung thickly to the recreation. It was not just the bullet scars from live-fire exercises on the forests, ruined villages, jungles and alien environments wrought from flak-board and steel. It was the echo of all the imaginary wars that had been fought there, battles which had their own echo in the real bloodshed the Imperial Fists trained there later encountered. The skills they learned there served them well, or failed them, in the depths of war on Emperor-forsaken alien worlds, and the traces of those desperate times clung to the mock fortifications like a freezing mist.

'Contact!' came a vox from up ahead.

'Close in!' ordered Salk. 'Cover and report targets!'

Ahead was the recreation of a village ruined by shellfire, craters moulded into the floor sections and the blank, broken walls featureless save for the empty eyes of windows and doorways. A building in the shape of a chapel, its walls devoid of sculpture, dominated the centre of the village with its bell tower tailor-made for snipers. Sarpedon scuttled into the shell of a mock house, crouching down on his haunches by a doorway. Sarpedon couldn't see most of Salk's squad, spread out and in cover as they were, but he knew they were there.

At the far end of the mock village, Reinez walked into plain view. The Crimson Fist's armour still had the filth and scorching of battle, and in the quiet he jangled with the many icons and seals hanging from him. He looked just as Sarpedon had left him in the lab, battered and bruised, but with none of his fires dimmed.

'Sarpedon!' called Reinez. 'I know you are here, you and your traitors. I think we left some business undone when last we met!'

'Orders, commander?' voxed Salk quietly.

'Hold,' replied Sarpedon.

'We could take him down.'

'You have my orders. Hold fire.'

Reinez walked forwards to the town square in the shadow of the church. 'Well?' he shouted. He had his hammer in his hand, and scowled at the ruins as he searched out the purple of Soul Drinkers armour. 'Do not tell me you care nothing for the fate of Reinez! You took my standard, you humiliated me, you cast me out from my own Chapter with your treachery! How can you do all this and yet let me live?'

Sarpedon stood up from his cover and walked into the open, his talons clicking on the hard deck sections. Reinez watched him coldly, wordlessly.

Sarpedon took the Axe of Mercaeno in one hand. 'This need not happen,' said Sarpedon. 'We are both Space Marines. For one to shed another's blood is heresy.'

'You speak of heresy?' barked Reinez. 'You, who have already slain so many of my brothers? There has not been enough Adeptus Astartes blood spilled yet for my liking. A few drops more and then it will be done.'

'Reinez, I have no quarrel with you here. I seek one of my own, the one who has orchestrated all that you have railed against. It is he who deserves all your hate, just as he deserves mine. If you truly want revenge for what happened to your brothers then let me pass or join me, but please, do not stand in my way.'

'You knew it would not end any way but the two of us to the death,' said Reinez. 'You knew that from the moment a Crimson Fist fell to a Soul Drinker's hand. Fate will not let us go and it will kill one of us before either walks away.'

Sarpedon let out a long breath. 'Then that is the way it must be,' he said. 'You have argued for a reckoning since you arrived on the *Phalanx*. You will have it, if that is what you truly want.'

Reinez crouched down into a guard, hammer haft held across his body. He flexed and bounced on his calves, judging distance and winding up for the strike.

Sarpedon knew that Salk's squad had all their guns trained on Reinez. They would not fire. Perhaps they would if Reinez killed Sarpedon, but by then it would not matter.

Reinez darted forwards, faster than Sarpedon remembered him moving. Sarpedon whirled and swung the

Axe of Mercaeno around, slamming the head into Reinez's side. He discharged a blast of psychic power through the force blade and though Reinez caught the worst of the blow on the haft of his hammer, the explosive force was enough to throw him from his feet and into the flakboard side of the fake church. The wall buckled under his weight, but Reinez rolled to his feet and swung his hammer at ankle height as Sarpedon charged to follow up.

Sarpedon leapt up. He scuttled along the wall, talons clinging to the flakboard.

Reinez tried to get his bearings, unused to fighting an enemy who could climb walls like a spider.

'Now!' yelled Reinez. 'Now! Fire! Fire!'

From every direction, bolters hammered. Muzzle flashes betrayed hidden firing positions around the far side of the mock village. Bullet fire ripped into the flakboard around Sarpedon, and a flash of pain burst through one of his back legs. Sarpedon ran up the wall and onto the roof of the church, volleys of fire chewing through the church all around him. In the lee of the church tower he found a semblance of cover, the flakboard tearing apart and the tower sagging above him.

'Contacts everywhere,' voxed Salk. 'It was a trap. Engage!'

'Who are they?' demanded Sarpedon.

'It's us,' came Salk's shocked reply. 'It's Soul Drinkers!'

Sarpedon could glimpse purple armour among the debris and gunsmoke of the firefight erupting across the village. Iktinos's flock, the Soul Drinkers who were loyal to the Chaplain first and Sarpedon a distant second, whose allegiance Sarpedon had been too blind to question.

'You are too honourable, Soul Drinker!' yelled Reinez from somewhere below. 'Too quick to give a sworn enemy a fair fight! Now it will be the death of you all!'

Reinez clambered up the wall and vaulted onto the roof. Sarpedon lunged and the two fought, axe and hammer flashing, blows parried and driven aside as bolter fire shrieked around them. Sarpedon hacked a chunk out of Reinez's shoulder armour. In response, Reinez stamped down on Sarpedon's wounded leg to pin him in place and crunched the head of his hammer into Sarpedon's chest. Sarpedon was faster than Reinez but the Crimson Fist had prepared for this fight for many years and this time he had the advantage of numbers. Iktinos's flock comprised many more warriors than Salk's squad and among the flock were those with good enough aim to pick out Sarpedon from the melee. Bolter fire slammed into the tower behind Sarpedon or sparked from his armour, knocking him back a pace or throwing him off-balance.

Sarpedon powered forwards, a desperate move more suited to a rude brawl than a duel to the death. Forelegs and arms wrapped around Reinez, forcing him down under Sarpedon's greater weight.

'What have you done, Reinez?' growled Sarpedon.

'Iktinos promised me a chance to kill you,' replied Reinez, voice strained as he fought to burst Sarpedon's hold on him. 'There was nothing else anyone could offer me.'

'Iktinos is the enemy! He is the source of all this suffering.'

'Then I will kill him next,' snarled Reinez.

Sarpedon picked up Reinez and threw him down, putting all his strength into hurling the Crimson Fist off the roof. Reinez landed badly and Salk's return fire drove him into the cover of a ruined building adjoining the church.

The flock were moving across the village. More than twenty of them had survived the breakout from the Atoning Halls, double Salk's numbers. Sarpedon recognised Soul Drinkers he had called brothers, who had been stranded when their officers were killed. Iktinos had taken them in and Sarpedon had been grateful that the Chaplain was willing to give them spiritual leadership. But Iktinos had been warping them, finding their sense of loss and turning it into something else, a devotion to the Chaplain alone that meant they followed him instead of Sarpedon. The Chapter Master had been confronted with many results of his failures as a leader, but none of them had struck him as sharply as the sight of the flock did then, moving with murderous intent across the town square to batter Salk's squad into oblivion.

Salk's Soul Drinkers were falling. They were surrounded and outgunned. Salk himself leaned out from cover to fell one of the flock, and in response a cluster of shots knocked him out of sight in a shower of blood. Sarpedon's twin hearts felt like they were tightening in his chest, all the heat squeezed out of his body to be replaced with cold and dust.

Sarpedon leapt down from the church into the

centre of the village. He landed in the heart of the advancing flock. Faces he had known for years, since before the first Chapter war, turned on him and saw nothing but an enemy. Sarpedon saw nothing in them any more, no brotherhood, no hope, none of the principles that had made them turn on the old Chapter's ways. He was their enemy, and they were his. Suddenly, it seemed simple.

Sarpedon knew the closest Soul Drinker to him was Brother Scarphinal, one of Givrillian's squad. Givrillian had been Sarpedon's closest confidant and best friend, and he had died on a nameless planet to the daemon prince Ve'Meth. There was nothing left of Givrillian's command in Scarphinal now. His eyes were blank and his bolter turned towards Sarpedon without hesitation.

Sarpedon struck Scarphinal's head from his shoulders with a single shining arc, the Axe of Mercaeno slicing through the Space Marine's neck so smoothly the blood had not yet begun to flow when Scarphinal's head hit the floor.

Something dark and prideful, a relic of the old Chapter, awakened in Sarpedon. The love of bloodshed, the exultation of battle. Sometimes, those places locked away in his mind could be useful, and it was with a strange sense of relief that he let the bloodlust take him.

Sarpedon roared with formless anger, and dived into the carnage.

# CHAPTER ELEVEN

The *Phalanx* had been designed – whenever it had been designed, before the Age of Imperium – to survive. Any hostiles who boarded the immense ship might find themselves trapped in the tight, winding corridors of the engineering and maintenance areas just beneath the hull's skin, separated from the ship's more vulnerable areas by hundreds of automated bulkhead doors and whole sections of outer deck that could be vented into hard vacuum with the press of a control stud.

The hostiles currently on the *Phalanx* had bypassed every design feature intended to contain them. They had been disgorged directly into the ship's interior, spilling through cavernous shuttle bays and swarming into crew quarters, riding torrents of blood through automated cargo motivator systems. The *Phalanx* had no way to stop the daemonic invaders.

So it was up to the Adeptus Astartes instead.

CHAPTER MASTER PUGH stood at the threshold of the Sigismunda Tactica, and looked out across the battlefield. It spanned the barracks deck and was a kilometre and a half wide. This was the vulnerable heart of the *Phalanx*, the ground across which an invader could charge with impunity from the lost starboard docking bays towards the engines and reactors. The Forge of Ages anchored one end, beyond which was a tangle of engineering areas and power and coolant conduits. The other flank terminated in the Rynn's World memorial, an amphitheatre of granite inscribed with the names of the Crimson Fists lost in the infamous near-destruction of their fortress-monastery. Beyond this memorial were the steel catacombs, tight nests of cramped candlelit chambers where generations of crew members were laid to rest in niches scattered with bones. The conduit decks and catacombs would slow down the invaders' advance, funnelling them through the open areas of the barracks, chapels and hero-shrines rolling out in front of Pugh.

'I can smell them,' said Captain Lysander, emerging from the Sigismunda Tactica behind Pugh. 'The enemy are close.'

'Of course you can smell them,' said Pugh. 'I wonder if we will ever get the stink of the warp off my ship.'

'Borganor is in position at the Forge of Ages,' continued Lysander. 'Leucrontas and the 9th will hold the memorial.'

'And everyone else will take the centre,' finished Pugh. 'Can it be held?'

'Our 3rd and 5th are enough to hold anything,' said Lysander.

'You realise you will stake your life on that belief?'

'We all will, Chapter Master. If this line breaks, everyone on the *Phalanx* will die.'

'Tell me, captain. Is it wrong that I have dreamed of a day like this?' Pugh drew the Fangs of Dorn from the scabbards on either side of his waist – twin power swords, their blades broad for stabbing, their hilts semicircles of glinting black stone. 'That I have knelt at the altars of Dorn and prayed that one day I would face the enemy like this, in a battle that will decide whether my Chapter lives in glory or is banished to a penitents' crusade in disgrace? I have begged the Emperor to give me such a battle, toe to toe, no retreat, everything at stake. Is it wrong that I feel some joy in me that it is here?'

'We all see something else in battle,' replied Lysander. 'Perhaps it is a mirror in which we see a reflection of ourselves. I see a grim task to be completed, something ugly and crude, but an evil necessary for the survival of our species. You see something different.'

'Most Imperial Fists would simply have said "No", captain.'

'Well, that's why you made me a captain.'

Among the complexes of barracks cells and the shrines to long-dead heroes, the 3rd and 5th Companies of the Imperial Fists were taking up their battle positions. Low buildings formed the anchoring points beneath the grey sky of the ceiling. Battle-brothers knelt to icons of past captains and Chapter Masters, their home suddenly transformed into a battleground.

The Tactica itself was one of the most defensible buildings on the deck. It was a circular building of black stone, its arched entrances leading to dozens of map tables on which famous past battles of the Imperial Fists had been recreated. The buildings over which Imperial Fists had fought and died were scrim-shawed from alien ivories and laid out on miniature battlegrounds of polished obsidian. In the Tactica, named after Sigismund, one of Dorn's greatest generals and the founder of the Black Templars Chapter, Imperial Fists officers could contemplate victories of the past, dissecting the battle plans the Chapter's leaders had enacted and the follies of the enemies who tried to stand against them. If the Imperial Fists and the other Adeptus Astartes on the *Phalanx* could prevail, perhaps the Tactica itself would be recreated on one of those ornate maps.

Lord Inquisitor Kolgo was walking among the map tables, casting his eye over the Imperial Fists history. He wore black Terminator armour embellished with silver symbols of the Inquisition, making him even bulkier than a Space Marine in power armour. His Battle Sisters retinue kept a respectful distance, Sister Aescarion waiting patiently with power axe in hand.

'I take it,' said Pugh, 'that you know rather more about the forces of the warp than can be entrusted to lesser minds like ours.'

Kolgo looked up, as if he had not expected to be interrupted, to see Pugh walking through one of the Tactica's lofty archways. 'It is a burden we inquisitors must carry, Chapter Master,' he said.

'If there is anything we could do with knowing, then now is the time to tell us.'

Kolgo took a set of Emperor's Tarot cards from a silver case set into his breastplate. On one of the map tables, one which represented a volcanic battlefield where the Imperial Fists had shattered an assault by the xenos tau, he laid out three of them in a row.

'"The Silver Ocean",' said Kolgo, pointing to the first card. 'One who cannot be grasped or comprehended, as subtle as quicksilver. An unknowable foe. The second is "The Altar", a symbol of majesty and glory. But it is inverted, and followed by "The Plague". The enemy is inscrutable and majestic, but that majesty is false and conceals an ocean of foulness beneath its beauty. It is a vessel of corruption in the form of something wonderful. I see the hand of the Lord of Change in the enemy we face, but the foe is its own creature, driven by its own desires.'

'You know what it is?' said Pugh.

'I have my suspicions, which I will not share until they become certainties, especially where the God of Lies is concerned.' Kolgo gathered up the cards and put them away. 'This is more than a battle over your vessel, Chapter Master. That is all I am willing to say.'

'Then keep your own counsel, Lord Inquisitor, as long as you fight alongside us.'

Kolgo smiled. 'Have no fear on that score.'

'Chapter Master,' came a voice over the vox-net. The rune signifying Castellan Leucrontas pulsed against Pugh's retina. 'The enemy is sighted.'

'What is their strength, castellan?' demanded Pugh.

'Hundreds,' came Leucrontas's voice. 'They are advancing on two sides. Holding position.'

Pugh strode out of the Tactica. His own Imperial Fists were in position among the shrines and barracks, and he spotted the colours of the Silver Skulls and Angels Sanguine among them. 'Lysander,' he ordered. 'Be ready to counter-advance on the castellan's flank. Keep the memorial from being surrounded.'

'Yes, Chapter Master,' said Lysander. 'Other orders?'

Pugh did not reply. Instead, he was looking past the Imperial Fists positions ahead of him, towards the steel horizon broken by the spires of hero-shrines and the fluttering banners of the mustering grounds.

The daemon army was advancing. The horizon seethed, a mass of iridescence bleeding into view like a bank of incandescent gas. The sound of its music washed over the Imperial Fists lines, an awful cacophony of a thousand shrieking voices. Shapes towered over the lines, winged masses surrounded by mountains of daemonic followers tumbling over one another like insects swarming from a hive.

'The Emperor has granted you your battle,' said Lysander. 'Now is the time to give thanks.'

'There will be opportunity for that when the victory is won,' said Pugh. 'Kolgo! Get your Battle Sisters to the lines! We are attacked on all fronts!'

From the daemonic horde emerged another winged monster, this one bathed in light as if Kravamesh's light was falling in a bright shaft onto its pale haloed form. It was framed by feathered wings and its skin was so pale it seemed to burn, like ivory lit from within. Its perfect face projected its beauty and authority even as far as the Tactica. Even Pugh found it difficult to tear his eyes away from it, as if it was a vision that originated inside his head and burned its way outwards.

'Behold, your future!' the monster bellowed, its voice tearing across the battlefield like a razored wind. 'I am the end of Empires! I am the woes of men! I am Abraxes!'

SARPEDON SKIDDED ACROSS the blood-slicked surface, the Axe of Mercaeno smouldering in his hand.

Brother Nephael faced him. Nephael's bolter magazine was empty, his last few shots fired wildly through a storm of his own battle-brothers, and he had no time to change the magazine. He snatched Brother Kalchis's chainsword off the ground and swung it as Sarpedon came crashing towards him.

Sarpedon span on a front leg, out of the reach of the chainblade. He swung in low, axe hacking down at Nephael's leg. Nephael didn't have the speed of Sarpedon, and he didn't have the strength. The axe caught Nephael below the knee and flung him head over heels. Sarpedon charged into Nephael as he fell, slamming the flock member into the ground.

Sarpedon rolled Nephael over so he was face up, Sarpedon's weight on the Soul Drinker's chest. He ripped the chainsword from Nephael's hand and threw it aside.

Sarpedon tore Nephael's helmet off. The face revealed was more youthful than most Soul Drinkers, the hair cropped close and the eyes set into bruised slits.

'Where is Iktinos?' demanded Sarpedon.

'He is the future,' spat back Nephael.

'Where is Iktinos?' shouted Sarpedon, slamming the back of Nephael's head into the ground to punctuate each word.

'Go to Terra,' said Nephael, 'when our work is complete. You will find him kneeling at the foot of the Golden Throne.'

Nephael wrenched an arm free and drew his combat knife. Before he could drive it upwards Sarpedon had slithered off him and buried the Axe of Mercaeno in the Soul Drinker's head, cleaving it in half down to the floor.

Sarpedon got back to his feet. Around him, the mock village was strewn with bodies and blood. He had killed them all.

The members of Iktinos's flock who had ambushed him and Salk had fallen either to Squad Salk's guns or to Sarpedon himself. He had dived among them, these Space Marines who had once sworn to follow him to extinction, and he had cut them to pieces. Cracked skulls spilled red-black pools across the flakboard floor. Limbs torn off lay orphaned from their owners, who in turn lay where Sarpedon had speared them with talons or carved them open with the Axe of Mercaeno. Nephael had been the last of them alive but they had all been men that Sarpedon recognised.

That was not mere blood spattered up against the false chapel and ruins. It was the blood of Space Marine. It was the blood of brothers.

Sarpedon forced his pulse and breathing to slow. It had felt good, he was ashamed to realise, to finally come to grips with the enemy that had manipulated his Chapter towards execution. In the middle of the fight, he had felt a certainty that could only be born of the sure knowledge that the man facing you would kill you if you did not kill him first. Now, he was surrounded by dead brothers, and the doubts came back. He swallowed them down, demanded that he become calm.

Reinez had fled. The Crimson Fist could not be seen among the ruins. Sarpedon could not see any movement among Salk's positions, either. Sarpedon ran to the ruin in which Salk had taken shelter, its flakboard now chewed up and splintered by bolter fire.

Salk lay on his back in a ruin of torn flakboard. Bolter impacts had broken through the ceramite of his chest and abdomen. He turned his head weakly, and Sarpedon saw that one side of his face was a pulpy ruin, shattered bone poking through a mass of blood that had already coagulated to a crystalline rind.

'Brother,' said Sarpedon. 'Speak to me. Tell me that Salk has not fallen.'

'Forgive me,' sputtered Salk. 'Failure is my sin.'

'No, Salk. None has been more steadfast than you. There is no failure.'

'Then this is certainly not victory. I had not thought it would be so bleak. I thought there would be some… heroism.'

Sarpedon leaned down close to Salk, unsure if the sergeant's drifting eyes were able to focus on him at all. 'I will kill Iktinos.'

'I know you will. Not for me, commander. Do what has to be done. For everyone.'

Sarpedon tried to pick up Salk, thinking perhaps he could get the fallen sergeant back to the archives where the other Soul Drinkers could tend to him. But he felt Salk getting lighter in his arms, as if the life were evaporating from him and leaving an empty body behind. Sarpedon saw the light going out in Salk's eyes, something impossible to describe, changing with infinite subtlety as the Soul Drinker, his friend, turned into just another body.

Sarpedon held Salk for a long moment. Some primitive emotion in the back of his head begged the Emperor to breathe life back into Salk. Salk had been as solid a squad leader as Sarpedon had ever commanded, before or after the first Chapter war. He had earned his laurels on Stratix Luminae and thereafter proved an unsung and dependable lynchpin of the Soul Drinkers' most desperate moments.

Now, Salk was gone. That was the calibre of man Iktinos and Daenyathos were running down in their charge towards whatever mad future they had concocted.

Sarpedon placed Salk on the ground, and murmured an old prayer. It called upon the Emperor and anyone who served him to shepherd the fallen towards the End Times, to make sure his wargear was waiting for him when he lined up alongside the Emperor for the battle at the end of existence. The fake battleground was a poor burial place for anyone, let alone a Space Marine, but for Salk and the brethren of his squad it would have to do for now. Perhaps the Imperial Fists would give them a basic funeral, dying as they did fighting a mutual enemy.

Sarpedon looked behind him, to the bodies of the fallen flock. The fact that they had been sent to ambush the Soul Drinkers at all meant Sarpedon was getting close. The flock meant Iktinos, and Iktinos meant some measure of revenge.

Revenge. That was all Sarpedon had left now to fight for. But everything a Space Marine did was for revenge, and for Sarpedon, as he picked up the Axe of Mercaeno and headed towards the far side of the training deck, it was just enough.

CASTELLAN LEUCRONTAS JUMPED from cover and led the counter-charge.

It was an insane move against the insane enemy advancing on the Rynn's World memorial. A mad show of bravado, a hand played against an enemy where such crazed fury was the only way to shock them and drive them back.

Leucrontas was followed by more than fifty Imperial Fists of the 9th Company. They vaulted over the carved stone tableaux of battle scenes from Rynn's World, ducking at a run past the slabs inscribed with the names of the lost. They were framed by the sweeping wings of the stone amphitheatre, as if the battle were a grand stage play and this was the climactic scene.

The daemons surged forwards. A titanic being of rotting flesh, its body a vast bloated sac bulging with torn veins and maggoty slabs of muscle, was hauled forwards by their front ranks. It chortled and moaned as if the whole thing were an enormous joke that only it could understand, a mix of the idiotic and cunning on its wide lolling face. Hundreds of daemons pushed it from behind and a hundred more pulled it forwards on rusted chains embedded in its flesh.

'I will not wait for the enemy to do as he will!' yelled Leucrontas as he ran, his storm bolter out ready to fire. 'If he is eager for our blood, let us drive onwards and drown him in it!'

Leucrontas opened fire. Fifty bolters echoed him, full-auto fire burning through magazines. The front rank of the daemons disappeared in a mass of foul torn flesh, torsos bursting like bags of blood and maggots, broken corpses trampled underfoot. A tide of black corrupted blood washed forwards around the Imperial Fists' feet and flies descended, a black haze of them swirling as if controlled by a single ravenous mind.

The daemons were all about Leucrontas now. His storm bolter rattled in his hand, twin barrels glowing blue-hot, until the hammer fell on an empty chamber. Leucrontas dived into the torn mass of flesh around him, combat knife in one hand, bolt pistol in another, laying about him with chop and thrust even as he picked out leering one-eyed heads and put a bolter round into each he saw.

A rusted chain fell to the ground, dropped by the daemons hit by Leucrontas's assault. The daemons fought to surround the castellan and he resembled nothing so much as a walking fortification standing against a sea of hungry foes, the crenellations of his armour holding off blades of corroded iron and lashing, filthy claws.

The Imperial Fists saved him. Charging on in his

wake, they forced the daemons back. Some, with chainswords and combat shields, fought the ugliest sort of battle imaginable, hacking away at the daemonic mass and trusting in their wargear to protect them. Others formed a cordon to keep the daemons sweeping around and cutting off Leucrontas, kneeling to fire disciplined execution squad volleys into the press of enemies.

The greater daemon loomed overhead. Its bloated shadow fell over Leucrontas. The daemons were no longer hauling it forwards and its faces creased in frustration. It reached futilely towards the Imperial Fists, flabby claws flapping at nothing. It forced a stumpy leg forwards as it began to propel its own enormous bulk towards the enemy.

It thundered forwards a step. It smiled now, eager to get to grips with the yellow-armoured figures embedded in the melee below.

Among the steps of the amphitheatre and the monumental sculptures, the rest of the 9th appeared. Armed with the company's heavy weapons, they picked out their targets under the orders of their sergeants who acted as spotters. They pointed out the slavering beasts being goaded towards the front line, the gibbering daemons bearing icons of the warp on their standards. But most of all they pointed out the greater daemon, the monster shambling one step at a time towards the castellan.

Lascannons and heavy bolters opened fire. The memorial's grey stone was painted crimson by the pulses of las-fire. Massive-calibre fire hammered into corrupted flesh, and liquefied muscle and entrails flowed so thickly they were a viscous tide flooding around the legs of the battling Adeptus Astartes.

The greater daemon was battered by the weight of the fire. Its skin tore and split, and loops of intestines slithered out in a crimson-black mass. Tiny gibbering creatures spilled from its wounds, gambolling through the battle lines in their new-found freedom. Its lips parted and it bellowed, face creasing in pain, tiny red eyes narrowing further. Its vast throat yawed open, a red wet pit lined with teeth and inhabited by a long, thick tongue that lashed as if it were its own ravenous creature.

'Now,' yelled Leucrontas. 'Onwards! Onwards!'

The greater daemon leaned forwards into the fire. Even as the flesh of its face was stripped away by heavy bolter blasts, it smiled at the yellow-armoured figure battling towards it. It reached down with a flabby arm, fingers spread to snatch up Leucrontas.

Leucrontas saw it coming. He rattled off half the magazine of his bolt pistol blasting off the greater daemon's thumb. The hand crashed down onto him and his combat knife sliced through tendons. Another finger, as long as a Space Marine was tall, fell useless.

The remnants of the hand closed around the castellan. Leucrontas fought to push the fingers apart, but the greater daemon was stronger, and it was hungry.

Leucrontas fought on as he was picked up off the ground. Imperial Fists dived in around the greater daemon's feet, hacking at its ankles to bring it down, or carving into its titanic belly to cripple it. The greater daemon seemed not to notice them at all.

'Hello, little one,' the daemon said as it raised Leucrontas to its face. Its voice was a terrible rumble, the gurgling of its corrupted lungs as deep as an earthquake. 'What a blessed day is this, my grandchildren! I have found a new plaything!'

Leucrontas's reply was lost in the hungry howl that roared from the greater daemon as its jaws opened wide. The daemon dropped Leucrontas down its throat and swallowed with an awful wet sucking sound, like something vast being yanked out of a pool of sucking mud. The daemon laughed, a deep, guttural sound that shook the stones of the Rynn's World memorial.

The Imperial Fists line bowed as the daemons surged forwards once more. Chainblades rose and fell, barely breaking the surface of the fleshy tide surrounding them, and the guns hammered an endless stream of shells and las-blasts into an equally unending mass of enemies. The greater daemon reached down and parted the daemonic sea in front of it, revealing a knot of Imperial Fists fighting back to back, covered in gore.

The greater daemon leered down at them, took in a great ragged breath, and regurgitated a torrent of bilious filth onto them. The crushed and dissolved remains of Leucrontas crashed over them, the acidic torrent flooding through the seals of their armour and digesting them even as they scrambled to get out of the foul sticky mass.

'Fall back,' came an order from one of the heavy weapons squads' sergeants, taking up command in the wake of Leucrontas's death. 'We cannot hold.'

In the face of the appalling sight of the greater daemon's assault, even Space Marines could do little but retreat and retain what order they could, forcing the daemon army to pay for the ground they took with volleys of bolter fire.

The message that reached Chapter Master Pugh was fragmented and rushed, but its meaning was clear. The Rynn's World memorial had been lost. The first victory in the Battle of the *Phalanx* had gone to the enemy.

THE ECHOES OF the battle reached through the Phalanx. It was not mere sound, although the explosions of heavy weapons fire and the thunder of the daemons' advance shuddered for many decks around. It was a psychic echo, a cacophony of screaming and cackling that wormed into the back of the skull and rattled around as if trying to find a way out.

*Abraxes*, it cried. *I am Abraxes*.

The echo shuddered through the mess halls near the archive, where a rearguard of Imperial Fists and the surviving Iron Knights formed a cordon to keep the Soul Drinkers penned into the ruined library. Sergeant Prexus of the Imperial Fists had to keep the itch for battle in check, for among the Adeptus Astartes under his command he knew there burned the urge to get into the fight unfolding elsewhere.

'Sergeant,' came a vox from one of the battle-brothers keeping watch over the expanse of the mess hall. 'I hear movement, beyond the doors. I think they are advancing.'

'To arms, brothers,' ordered Prexus. In a moment

the Imperial Fists and Iron Knights were behind barricades of upturned furniture or crouched in the cover of doorways, bolters trained towards the double doors, chained shut, through which the Howling Griffons had advanced into the library just an hour ago.

The doors banged on their hinges, chains shuddering. A second blow wrenched one door away completely and a single Soul Drinker stepped through. He went bare-headed, his hair shaved into a single black strip along his scalp, his hands encased in lightning claws. But the power fields of the claws were not activated and the Soul Drinker was alone.

Prexus held up a hand, belaying any order to open fire.

'I am Captain Luko of the Soul Drinkers,' said the newcomer.

'I know who you are,' replied Prexus. 'Are you here to surrender?'

'No,' said Luko. 'I am here to kill Abraxes.'

Imperial Fists trigger fingers tightened. 'Explain yourself,' said Prexus.

'Abraxes is the leader of the force that assails you. You know it and I know it. I have been in its unclean presence before, at the Battle of the *Brokenback* when Sarpedon banished it to the warp. Now it has returned when we are at our weakest to have its revenge, and kill as many Imperial Fists as it can into the bargain. We have heard your vox-traffic and seen the pict-feeds. We know that Abraxes has brought a daemonic legion onto the *Phalanx* and we want to fight it.'

'I have my orders,' replied Prexus. 'You will go nowhere.'

'Then we will go through you,' said Luko. 'I see you have perhaps forty Space Marines. I have a few more, but you are no doubt better equipped and you have no wounded among you. Do you think you can kill us all here? It would be little more than the cast of a die to decide between us, I think. And we are going to die here whether it be to Abraxes's legion or your bolters, so we have nothing to lose. Will you still stand against us, sergeant?'

'There will be no need for bloodshed here,' came a voice from behind Prexus. It was one of the Iron Knights, who walked out of cover into the open.

'Borasi!' said Luko, his face breaking into a smile.

'Captain.' The two Adeptus Astartes approached and shook hands. 'You will have to trust me that this time we meet, I shall break no bones of yours.'

'I shall hold you to that, sergeant,' said Luko.

'You know this warrior?' demanded Prexus.

'We met on Molikor,' said Borasi. 'We were compelled by circumstance to trade blows before we had our facts straightened out for us.'

'I knew you were a poor choice for the rearguard,' said Prexus. 'You could not be trusted to treat the enemy as an enemy.'

'I think there is another enemy on the *Phalanx* you should concern yourself with rather more,' said Luko.

'Let the Soul Drinkers fight Abraxes if they wish it,' said Borasi. 'I will take responsibility. Let them die facing its daemons. That is execution sure enough for anyone.'

'I am in command here!' barked Prexus. 'You are under my authority, sergeant! You are here only at the sufferance of…'

The sudden burst of chatter over the Imperial Fists vox was loud and rapid enough to grab Prexus's attention.

Chapter Master Pugh's voice cut through the chatter. 'All forces of the 9th, fall back to the centre! All other forces, move up to the front! The Rynn's World memorial is lost and Castellan Leucrontas has fallen. Let them be avenged!'

'You heard, sergeant,' said Borasi. 'You have your orders.'

'The Imperial Fists will shoot you on sight,' said Prexus. 'It doesn't matter if you want to join the fight or not. They will kill you as soon as they see you have left the archives.'

'They can try,' said Luko. 'Although they may decide their ammunition is better spent elsewhere.'

'Fall back!' ordered Prexus. 'Squad Makos, take the fore! Iron Knights, take the centre! Move out, Borasi. Do not follow us, Luko, or we shall see just how that close fight you spoke of turns out.'

Borasi saluted Luko as he returned to join the other Iron Knights. The Imperial Fists kept their guns trained on Luko as Prexus's force withdrew from the mess hall, the chatter over their vox-channels continuing to illustrate the collapse of Leucrontas's force and the approach of the bulk of the daemon army.

When the way was clear, Librarian Tyrendian and Sergeant Graevus emerged from the archives to join Luko.

'It's bad,' said Tyrendian. 'I can feel it. Realspace is screaming in my mind. It is Abraxes, I have no doubt about that, and banishment has given him strength through hate.'

'What now, captain?' asked Graevus.

'We have to avoid the Imperial Fists lines,' replied Luko. 'And the Howling Griffons, for that matter. We head for the memorial.'

'I WONDERED,' SAID Iktinos, 'how long you would take. You disappoint me. I had thought a reckoning would have happened long before Selaaca, that you would have seen through what I and my fellow Chaplains have been doing, and that some other thread of fate would be needed to bring you to Kravamesh. But it is as if you were an automaton, programmed to do as Daenyathos wrote six thousand years ago.' He turned to face his opponent, the scar on his skull-faced helmet still smouldering. 'As if you were following his instructions as precisely as I.'

Sarpedon had found Iktinos in the dorsal fighter bays, three decks up from the training decks. He had followed a Space Marine's instinct, the best escape routes, the avenues of flight that allowed for the most cover and the best firing angles, and he had emerged in this cavernous place with its ranks of deep space fighter craft, to see Iktinos making his way across the seemingly endless concourse.

There were fifty metres between the two Soul Drinkers as they faced one another down a row of fighter craft. Each craft was enormous, bigger than the Thunderhawk Gunships of the Space Marines, with blunt-nosed brutal shapes that made no concession to the aerodynamics irrelevant in the void. When the *Phalanx* went to war, these were the craft that swarmed around the vast ship like hornets, but with the enemy having invaded from within they were silent and ignored.

'I have asked myself many times how we have come to this point,' said Sarpedon. He fought to keep his voice level. 'Now I would like to ask you.'

'You presume that I know,' said Iktinos. 'Daenyathos knows. We follow. That was always enough for us.'

'For you? The Chaplains?'

'Indeed. Ever since Daenyathos fell on the *Talon of Mars*, we have followed the teachings he handed down to us in secret. The rest of the Chapter, meanwhile, has followed the commands he laid out in the Catechisms Martial, encoded in his words so that you acted by them and yet remained ignorant of them.'

'Tell me why we are here!' snapped Sarpedon. 'And I hear the name of Abraxes in my head. I hear his pride and his lust for revenge. What has brought him to the *Phalanx*? You?'

'Daenyathos knew that one would rise from the warp at his behest. That it happens to be Abraxes is a testament to fate. He must have been lurking beneath the surface of the warp, hungry for any taste of the Soul Drinkers who bested him. Abraxes is just another pawn, Sarpedon, like you, like me.'

'There are those who have tried to use my Chapter for their own ends before,' said Sarpedon. His grip tightened on the Axe of Mercaeno. 'Do you recall,

Chaplain Iktinos, what happened to them?'

Iktinos drew the haft of the Soulspear from a holster at his waist. His thumb closed over an aperture in the alien metal, a micro-laser pulsed and drew blood through the ceramite of his gauntlet. The gene-lock activated and twin blades of purest liquid black extended from either end of the haft. 'I recall it very well, Sarpedon. I recall that they were amateurs. Daenyathos factored them in, as well. Nothing has occurred that he did not foresee and plan for in advance.'

'Including your death?' said Sarpedon. He crouched down a little on his haunches, the bundles of muscles in his legs bunching ready to pounce.

'If that is what occurs,' said Iktinos, no emotion in his voice, 'then yes.'

Sarpedon circled to one side, talons clicking on the deck. He passed under the shadow cast by the nose of the closest fighter craft. Iktinos followed suit, no doubt gauging Sarpedon's stance, weighing up everything he knew about the speed and fighting skills of his one-time Chapter Master.

The air hissed as molecules passed over the Soulspear's blades and were sliced in two. The sound of distant battle reached the fighter deck as a faint rumble, a shuddering as if the *Phalanx* itself were tensing up. The blank eyes of the fighter craft cockpits seemed to stare, watching for the first move.

Iktinos moved first.

The Chaplain sprinted forwards, Soulspear held back to strike. Sarpedon ducked to one side as Iktinos covered the ground in impossibly quick time, and swung out a spinning, dizzying strike with the Soulspear. The blades of blackness flickered around Sarpedon as he twisted and dropped to avoid them. A chunk of ceramite, sliced from his shoulder pad, thudded to the deck, and a fist-sized lump of chitin from his remaining back leg was cut away.

Sarpedon kicked out and caught Iktinos's shin, He hooked the Chaplain's leg with a talon and tripped him. Iktinos rolled and came up fighting, one end of the Soulspear arcing up and the other slashing from right to left. Sarpedon, poised to slash down with the Axe of Mercaeno, had to jump back to avoid them.

'What is left, Sarpedon?' said Iktinos, the Soulspear held out in front of him like a barrier. 'What is left when every effort you have made to be free has been at the behest of another? What remains of who you are?'

'I am not a traitor,' said Sarpedon. 'That is more than you can say.'

'Treachery is meaningless,' replied Iktinos. 'There are no sides to betray. There is survival and oblivion. Everything else is a lie.'

Sarpedon leapt up onto the side of the fighter craft behind him, and launched himself from above at Iktinos. Iktinos was not ready to be attacked from above and he fell to one knee, spinning the Soulspear in a figure-eight to ward Sarpedon off. Sarpedon landed heavily, let the momentum crouch him down to the deck, and cut beneath Iktinos's guard. The Axe of Mercaeno carved through one of Iktinos's knee guards, drawing blood, but the impact was not enough to discharge Sarpedon's psychic power through the blade. Iktinos rolled away and Sarpedon charged on, Iktinos slashing this way and that, Sarpedon too quick to be hit.

But the Axe of Mercaeno was too unwieldy to get through Iktinos's guard. The Soulspear's twin blades, each a vortex field caged by some technology long-lost in the days of the Great Crusade, would slice through the axe as surely as through flesh or bone. Disarmed, Sarpedon would be as good as dead. He feinted and struck, slashed and wheeled, but Iktinos was just beyond his blade's reach.

Iktinos had known this day would come. He knew how to fight with the Soulspear – he had gone over this fight Throne knew how many times in his head.

The two passed beneath the hull of the fighter craft. Sarpedon scuttled up the landing gear and clung to the craft's underside, trusting in the novel angle of attack to keep Iktinos off-guard. Iktinos paused in his counter-attacks, Soulspear wavering, waiting for a blow from Sarpedon to parry.

'Fate has a hold of you,' said Iktinos. His voice still betrayed little emotion, as if he were a machine controlled from far away. 'If you die, Daenyathos has planned for it. If you live, he has planned for that, too. If only you understood, Sarpedon, you would kneel down and accept a quick death for the blessing it is.'

'And if only you understood, Iktinos, what it means to be Adeptus Astartes.' Sarpedon hauled himself a couple of steps sideways, Iktinos mirroring his every movement. 'The Soul Drinkers are nobody's instrument. We are not here to be wielded and used as

Daenyathos or anyone else pleases. He chose the wrong puppets for his plan.'

'And yet,' replied Iktinos cooly, 'here you are, at the time and place of his choosing.'

'What I shall do to him is not something that he would choose.'

Iktinos darted forward and slashed at the landing gear. The Soulspear sliced cleanly through the steel and hydraulic lines and the craft shifted downwards, all its front-half weight suddenly unsupported. Iktinos dived out of the way and Sarpedon did the same in the opposite direction, yelling with frustration as he scrambled to avoid being crushed by the fighter's hull. The fighter thudded to the deck and rolled in Sarpedeon's direction, forcing him to back up further. Iktinos was out of sight.

'What does he want?' shouted Sarpedon. 'If his plan is already fated to succeed, then at least tell me that. For what purpose has he enslaved us?'

'For the galaxy's good,' came the reply from above. Iktinos stepped into view atop the fallen fighter craft, standing just above the cockpit. 'What is it that you have railed against for so long? The galaxy's cruelty? The Imperium's tyranny? Daenyathos saw it six thousand years before it ever occurred to you. He is not just going to batter his Chapter to pieces fighting against it. He is going to cure it.'

Sarpedon began to climb towards Iktinos, up the near-vertical curve of the fighter's hull. 'And how?' he demanded.

'What other cure is there for all mankind's ills?' said Iktinos. 'Blood and death. Pain and fear. Only through this can the path of the human race be made straight.'

Sarpedon was level with Iktinos now, the two Soul Drinkers facing one another on top of the fallen fighter craft. From here Sarpedon could see the dozens of such craft ranged along the deck, the cylindrical fuel tanks and racks of missiles standing between them. 'There is too much suffering,' said Sarpedon. 'There will be no more.'

'Not for you,' said Iktinos.

This time Sarpedon struck first, the Axe of Mercaeno flickering out too quickly for Iktinos to parry. A good blow from the Soulspear would slice the axe in two and make it useless, but Sarpedon was a fraction of a heartbeat too fast. The axe carved not into the ceramite of Iktinos's armour, but into the hull of the fighter beneath his feet. The hull's outer skin came apart under the axe's blade and Iktinos's foot was trapped. The Chaplain fell backwards, unable to arrest his fall. Sarpedon ripped the axe out of the hull and brought it down, but Iktinos forced his head out of the way just before Sarpedon bisected it. The axe was buried again in the hull, the whole head embedded in the metal.

Sarpedon pinned Iktinos's arm with one of his legs before the Chaplain could raise the Soulspear. He bent down and grabbed Iktinos by both shoulder guards, hauled him up into the air, and hurled him down off the fighter's hull with every scrap of strength he could gather.

Iktinos slammed down into the fuel tank standing beside the fighter. His impact half-flattened the cylinder of the tank and ruptured it. Thick reddish fuel spurted onto the deck.

Sudden pain flared in the leg with which Sarpedon had pinned Iktinos's arm. He looked down to see the stump of the leg, sliced so cleanly through, a scalpel could have left no neater a wound. The leg itself was sliding slowly down the curve of the fighter's hull. Iktinos had got off one last strike as he fell.

'Close, my brother,' called down Sarpedon. 'But I can live without that leg. I still have five, and that's more than I need.'

Sarpedon sprang down from the hull to the deck, just as Iktinos was extricating himself from the wreckage of the fuel tank. Fuel glistened all over him. 'Your fate is decided,' he said. 'What happens here means nothing. Nothing.'

'You betrayed us and you will die for it,' replied Sarpedon. 'That means enough for me.'

Sarpedon raised the Axe of Mercaeno and ran its blade along one of the stubby control surfaces of the fighter. The razor-sharp metal drew sparks, which fell white-hot into the rivulets of fuel creeping towards him from the ruptured fuel tank. The fuel caught light and flame rushed towards Iktinos.

The fuel tank bloomed in a tremendous billowing of blue-white flame. Sarpedon ducked behind the fighter to shield himself from the blast of heat. He caught a glimpse of Iktinos disappearing in the flame, the Chaplain's form seeming to dissolve in the heart of the fire.

The sound was a terrible roar, and the fighter shifted on the deck, pushing against Sarpedon as he crouched. The wave of heat hit and Sarpedon felt the chitin of his remaining legs blistering in it, the paint of his armour bubbling, the side of his unprotected face scalding.

The noise died down, replaced with the guttering of flame. Haphazard shadows were cast against the walls and ceiling of the hangar deck by the fire as it continued to burn. Sarpedon limped out from behind the fighter, his balance uncertain as he adjusted to moving with one fewer leg.

Iktinos, on fire from head to toe, dived out of the flaming wreckage. He crashed into Sarpedon who was unprepared, and fell to the deck under Iktinos's weight. Flames licked at his face as he stared for a moment into the skull-mask of the Chaplain's helm, like the face of one of the Imperial Creed's many damned, leering up from a lake of fire.

# CHAPTER TWELVE

THE DAEMONIC HORDE hit the Imperial Fists line in a tide of flesh.

It broke against barricades and makeshift bunkers, concentrated bolter fire chewing through the daemons as quickly as they could advance.

In other places it swept through in a flood, swamping Imperial Fists in a mass of limbs and bodies. Some defences were denuded by pink and azure flame, blasted from the orifices of misshapen creatures dragged along on the tide of Abraxes's own incandescent daemons. Others were outflanked by lightning-fast monsters with purplish skin and lashing tongues that swept around firepoints to strike from behind. A massive red-winged daemon, axe in one hand and lash in the other, strode at the head of its bloodletters and with vicious strike cleaved one of the tanks brought up from the *Phalanx's* hangars in two, spilling flaming promethium around its feet.

The Imperial Fists line bent under the weight of the assault, Space Marines vaulting their barriers to take up new positions closer to the Tactica before they were overrun. Bolter fire competed with the shrieking of daemons in the din of the battle. The whole deck seemed to bow and buckle under the weight of it, as the monastic cells and chapels of the Imperial Fists disappeared under the flood of Abraxes's assault.

At the heart of the line, Chapter Master Pugh stood with the Fangs of Dorn in his hands. One of the Librarium novices stood before him, holding up a huge tome normally bound closed by chains and psychic seals. It contained prayers of purity and strength of mind, of which a commander had to be mindful when facing the corruptive forces of Chaos. Ahead of him, Lysander marshalled the strongest defences, a handful of tanks and several squads of Imperial Fists along with Kolgo's Battle Sisters, holding position as the daemon army grew closer with every moment.

'What manner of foe is Chaos?' mused Pugh. Beside him stood Lord Inquisitor Kolgo, ready for battle with a power fist encasing one hand and a rotator cannon on the other, each weapon engraved with prayers and wards of destruction.

'Better men than I have gone mad seeking the answer to that question,' replied Kolgo. 'The question of Chaos cannot be answered.'

'And yet we must seek an answer,' said Pugh. 'For we must fight it. In ignorance, we fight as if in the dark.'

'Better that than be corrupted by what we see,' said

Kolgo. He flexed the mechanical fingers of his power fist, and they crackled as the power field sprung into life around them.

'I trust in the strength of my soul, Inquisitor,' said Pugh. Ahead, Imperial Fists were scrambling into cover beside the second line as the daemons galloped and shambled closer, multicoloured flames dancing over the battlefield. The pale, lithe shape of Abraxes himself was just visible in the rear ranks, watching and controlling his battle, using up the lesser daemons under his command to buy his victory one death at a time. 'I shall not become one with the enemy by understanding it. The more I learn of Chaos, the more I hate it, and the fiercer I fight.'

'Overestimating one's resolve is a more dangerous form of ignorance than fighting in the dark.' Kolgo span the barrels of his rotator cannon, jewel-encrusted hammers clicking down on gilded chambers.

'Then let us put our theories into practice,' said Pugh.

'I concur,' said Kolgo. Shall we?'

'Brothers!' yelled Pugh over the vox. 'To the fore, my brothers, with me! Through Hell and to victory, onwards!'

At Pugh's words, the Imperial Fists broke cover and charged. The reserve force holding the Tactica ran from behind its map tables and the shelter of its archways. The Space Marines crouched behind their defences, muttered their prayers and leapt over the defences, bolters blazing and chainblades whirring. Pugh led the counter-attack right into the face of the enemy.

The twin blades of the Fangs of Dorn were not made for an elegant battle. They were not weapons for duelling or weaving a dance of feint and deception. They were made for this brutal and ugly fight, the press of bodies and the triumph of strength and resolve over skill, where they could rise and fall with every stab piercing a belly or driving up into a throat.

Pugh slew a dozen daemons in those first few seconds, and Abraxes's horrors fell before him, opening up a gap in the daemonic lines. Imperial Fists charged in behind him and exploited the gap, forging in further.

Kolgo stood atop a rampart and hammered volley after volley from his rotator cannon into the host. The Battle Sisters formed up around him, Sister Aescarion directing their fire with a gesture of her power axe. A pair of Predator tanks rumbled up from either side of the Tactica, each roar of an autocannon echoed by an explosion of flame and torn daemonflesh deep within Abraxes's lines.

Without warning the horrors seemed to melt away, dissolving into the rear ranks at a mental command from Abraxes. In the few seconds of respite, the Imperial Fists saw ranks of bloodletters marching out to replace them. In their centre was a greater daemon of the Blood God, allied to Abraxes's cause by the raw slaughter that battle on the *Phalanx* promised. It stepped over the front rows of bloodletters and a massive cloven hoof slammed down among the Imperial Fists, crushing a battle-brother under its immense weight.

'Onwards! Onwards! The warp fears us so, to place

such horrors in our way!' Pugh's voice, even amplified over the vox, was barely audible over the foul,
shuddering gale of the greater daemon's roar. Pugh
hacked through the first couple of bloodletters to
reach him as he jumped up onto the half-fallen wall
of a chapel, tumbled and scorched in the first assault,
that brought him up above the level of the swirling
combat around him.

The greater daemon turned its shaggy, bestial head
towards Pugh. Imperial Fists were hacking their
way through the advancing bloodletters to form up
around their Chapter Master, but the greater daemon
could simply step over the melee, and in moments its
shadow passed over Pugh.

The Imperial Fist held the Fangs of Dorn out wide,
presenting himself as a target to the greater daemon,
taunting it with his refusal to flee from the monstrosity.

'You dare walk into my domain, and shed the blood
of my brothers?' yelled Pugh. 'Who do you think you
face here? What victory do you think you can win? All
the fury of the warp will falter against the soul of one
good Space Marine!'

The greater daemon bellowed and raised its axe,
already slick with Adeptus Astartes blood. The axe
arced down and Pugh jumped to the side, the blade
cleaving down through the ruined chapel. Pugh
stabbed both the Fangs of Dorn through the greater
daemon's wrist and ripped them out again, snapping
tendons and tearing muscle. The greater daemon
pulled its arm back and howled in anger, following
up its axe blow with a strike from its whip.

The whip moved too fast for even Pugh to avoid. Its barbs lashed around his leg and the daemon yanked him off his feet, into the air, and cast him down to the ground in the heart of the bloodletters.

THE SOULSPEAR WAS still in Iktinos's hand. Its glowing black blade was being forced up under Sarpedon's chin, towards his throat, to slice his head off. Sarpedon grabbed Iktinos's wrist and fought the Chaplain, but death had unlocked some new fortitude in Iktinos and in that moment the two were matched in strength.

Sarpedon could feel the skin on his face burning. Pain meant something different to a Space Marine compared to a normal man, but it was still pain and Sarpedon struggled as much to avoid blacking out as he did against Iktinos.

The Axe of Mercaeno was trapped under Iktinos. Sarpedon tried to wrench it free, but Iktinos would not relent. He tried to roll over so Iktinos would be trapped beneath, but the Chaplain would not budge, as if he was anchored to the deck.

'You obey,' hissed Sarpedon. 'Obedience only comes from one place.' He saw his own features reflected in the eyepieces of Iktinos's mask, the blistering wounds creeping up his face. 'It comes from fear.'

Sarpedon let go of the Axe and reached up to place his hand on the back of Iktinos's head. He found a grip and tore the Chaplain's helmet away.

Iktinos's face was charred and twisted by the heat. The bubbling skin was stretched tight over the skull, the eyes buried in scorched pits, the scalp coming apart. There was no dimming in the hate on Iktinos's features. The pain made it stronger. There was almost no resemblance to the face that Sarpedon knew, none of the Chaplain's calm and resolve, just the intensity of his hatred.

'I know what you fear,' said Sarpedon. His hand clamped to the back of Iktinos's burning skull, and he unleashed the full force of the Hell into the traitor's mind.

The pain helped. Normally Sarpedon unleashed the Hell out wide, capturing as many of the enemy as possible in its hallucinations. This time he focused it until it was a white-hot psychic spear, thrust into Iktinos's mind like a hypodermic needle loaded with everything the Chaplain feared.

He feared Daenyathos. Fear, in some deep and unrecognisable form, was the only thing that could force a Space Marine to obey with such unthinking, unquestioning ferocity. Everything that Sarpedon knew about the Philosopher-Soldier was forced into the point of fire and turned into something appalling.

Like a god of the warp itself, the form of Daenyathos loomed in front of Iktinos's mind's eye. Daenyathos appeared as he had in illuminated manuscripts of his Catechisms Martial, but vast in size and infinitely more terrible. Around his legs rushed a torrent of broken bodies, all the Soul Drinkers whose lives he had spent following his monstrous plan. His armour was inscribed with exhortations to death and torture, words of the Catechisms Martial twisted and devolved. Thousands of innocents were crucified against the armour of his greaves. His chest and shoulder guards were covered with the forms of the betrayed, sunk into the armour as if half-digested. The heroes of the old Chapter – Captain Caeon, Chapter Master Gorgoleon and the victims of the first Chapter war, manipulated into conflict to satisfy Daenyathos's desire for a Chapter at odds with the Imperium. The dead of Sarpedon's Chapter, from Givrillian to Scamander, Captain Kar-raidin, Sarpedon's dearest friend Techmarine Lygris and all the others who had fallen.

Around the collar of Daneyathos's armour were clustered his allies in treachery. The cruellest of inquisitors who had forced the Soul Drinkers into the extremes of exile. Aliens despatched by Sarpe-don and his brethren, as Daenyathos watched on, satisfied that they had played their part – the necron creature who had almost killed Sarpedon on Selaaca, the renegade eldar lord of Gravehnhold, the ork warlord of Nevermourn, all gathered in cel-ebration.

Alongside them were the very worst of his allies. The followers of the Dark Gods – Abraxes, Ve'Meth, a host of Traitor Marines and daemons. The mutant Teturact and his legion of the dead. And Daenyathos himself, his face lit by the fires of wrath itself, laugh-ing with the agents of betrayal of whose wickedness he had been the architect.

Daenyathos looked down at Iktinos, pinned squirming below him like something trapped in a microscope slide. The vastness of his displeasure, mixed with a terrible knowing mockery, hammered into Iktinos's mind as fiercely as any weapon that Sarpedon could have wielded.

Iktinos screamed. In his mind, the sound was lost among the laughter of Daenyathos, who revelled in seeing one of his most self-important pawns being forced to understand his own insignificance. In reality, the sound was so completely unlike anything a warrior of the Adeptus Astartes should ever utter that Iktinos ceased to be a Space Marine in that moment.

The Chaplain's grip relaxed. Sarpedon threw him off and rolled out of the flames. He stood over the prostrate Iktinos.

Iktinos's mind had utterly shattered. Sarpedon's psychic senses were not sharp, but even he could feel it, a growing void where once the Chaplain's soul had been, into which were tumbling the fragments of his broken personality.

'I own you now,' said Sarpedon. 'I am the one you obey. Tell me everything.'

THE FACES OF the daemons crowded round, twisted and jeering, the solid mass of their features broken by the black iron blades that cut down to finish off Chapter Master Pugh.

The Fangs of Dorn were just suited to fighting this close, where they parried and stabbed as if moving in Pugh's hand by some will of their own. Perhaps Dorn himself wielded them in those moments, reaching from the Emperor's side to lend his own skill to Pugh's struggle to survive.

It would not be enough. There were too many of them, every one eager to be the one who carried the skull of a Chapter Master back to the warp, to throw it at the foot of the Blood God's throne.

Pugh stabbed up into a daemon's ribcage even as he turned another blade away from his hearts, and prepared to die.

A streak of orange flame burned across his vision, swathing the contorted face in fire. He was aware of glossy black armour embellished in red, and the blade of a power axe shimmering as it cut in every direction. Hands grabbed him and dragged him out of the mass. Pugh looked up and saw the unfamiliar face of a woman above him, streaked with blood and grime, teeth gritted.

'Not while we live,' she hissed through her teeth, 'shall they take such a prize.'

She hauled Pugh to his feet. He recognised Sister Aescarion, the Superior of Lord Inqiusitor Kolgo's retinue. The jump pack she wore on her back smouldered, its exhaust vanes glowing a dull red, and the path she had carved through the daemons as she dived into the throng after Pugh was closing as the bloodletters fought to swamp him again.

'My thanks, Sister,' said Pugh as he found his footing.

'Through me, the Emperor works,' she replied.

The two stood back to back as the bloodletters closed. Now Pugh could let the Fangs of Dorn do their finest work, stabbing so rapidly up into the advancing daemon ranks that every moment another of them fell, ribcage split open or burning entrails spilling from a ruptured abdomen. Aescarion fought with her axe in one hand and a pistol in the other, quickly rattling off the pistol's magazine and then taking the axe in both hands.

A Sister of Battle could not match a Space Marine's sheer strength and skill. Few unaugmented humans could approach a veteran Superior's ability, but even so she was just that – human, without the extra organs and enhanced physiology of the Adeptus Astartes. But what she lacked in their physical superiority, she made up with in faith.

It was not a Space Marine's mental fortitude that Pugh witnessed in Aescarion. A Space Marine was a master of his fear, his mind so strong he could face even the daemons of the warp and remain sane. Aescarion was different. It was not conditioning and strength of duty, raw bloody-mindedness, that fuelled her. It was faith. She believed so completely in the Emperor's hand guiding her, in the place she had in His plan, that it was as plain to her as the enemy closing in around her. She did not fear them, because in her mind she was not a human being with human frailties. She was a hollow vessel that existed to be filled up with the will of the Emperor and used as He willed it. There could be no fear, when whatever end befell not her, but the Emperor.

Pugh led the way back towards the Imperial Fists lines, opening up a path as the Fangs of Dorn flashed as quickly and deadly as the teeth of a giant chainblade. He had to force his legs out of the sucking mire of gore and entrails around his feet. Aescarion's axe gave her reach and she swung it in great arcs as she followed, smashing falling blades aside and keeping a good sword's length between her and the bloodletters.

The mass parted and Aescarion's Battle Sisters crowded forwards, flanking Pugh and battering the daemons back with bolter fire. The Chapter Master could see Lysander atop a barricade, swatting aside one of the horrors with his shield and pointing with his hammer to direct the heavy weapons set up around the Tactica. Everywhere he looked, there was carnage. Here, the Imperial Fists launched forwards in a counter-attack; there, the line broke and leaping horrors or galloping fiends poured through the lines like air bursting from a hull breach.

Pugh made it over the altar of a shrine, used as the lynchpin of a barricade of chapel pews and statues. Inquisitor Kolgo was standing in the chapel, its columns fallen and its nave strewn with the bodies of daemons and Space Marines. With a moment to breathe at last, he turned to help drag the Battle Sisters following him over the altar into shelter. Aescarion leapt over the barricade on the exhausts of her jump pack, the gauntlets of her power armour smoking with daemon blood up to the elbow. Battle Sisters and Imperial Fists manned the barricade, pouring bolter fire into the bloodletters trying to follow.

'Did it work?' said Pugh, catching his breath. 'Is it fallen?'

By way of answer, Kolgo simply pointed towards the ruin where Pugh had made his stand against the greater daemon.

The winged daemon was slumped against the wall, its wings in bloody tatters and its armour torn. Another volley of heavy fire slammed into it, punching through its corded red muscles. One of its wings was sheared through and fell broken, tattered skin fluttering like the canvas of a ruined sail. Pugh had brought the daemon into the open, forced it to stand proud of the daemonic host while it fought him. He had bought his heavy weapons the time they needed to draw a bead on the target and spear it on a lance of concentrated fire.

The greater daemon was taking its time to die. Heavy bolter fire rippled up and down it. The daemon dropped its lash and tried to force itself back to its feet, leaning on the ruined wall for support. A lascannon blast caught it in the chest and bored right through it, revealing its gory ribs and pulsing organs. The daemon roared, blood spattering from its lips, and toppled over into the horde.

The Imperial Fists cheered as the daemon died. Lysander led them, raising his hammer high as if taunting the daemons to respond.

The sound was drowned out by the laughter that rumbled through the *Phalanx*. It was the laughter of Abraxes, observing the slaughter from the rear ranks. The object of his amusement lumbered into view on the Imperial Fists flank – a greater daemon of the Plague God, the enormous bloated horror that had killed Leucrontas and broken the force holding the Rynn's World memorial. The daemon's laughter joined Abraxes's own as it was herded forwards by its attendant daemons, and it clapped its flabby hands in glee at the prospect of new playthings.

'Can we kill another one, Chapter Master?' voxed Kolgo.

'It is not a question of whether we can or not,' replied Pugh. 'We will do so or we will be lost.'

'Behold this icon of sin!' shouted Aescarion to her Battle Sisters. 'Witness the corruption it wears! In the face of this evil, let our bullets be our prayers!'

The expression on the greater daemon's face changed. Its enormous mouth downturned and it frowned, its eyes widening in surprise, a caricature of dismay and shock. Tiny explosions studded the rubbery surface of its flesh, not from the direction of the Imperial Fists centre, but from behind it.

Pugh jumped onto a fallen pillar to get a better view. He glimpsed the flash of a power weapon – power claws, slashing through the plaguebearers, illuminating the edges of purple armour.

'It's the Soul Drinkers!' came a vox from the nearest Imperial Fists unit.

Pugh recognised Captain Luko now, followed by what remained of the Soul Drinkers Chapter. A bolt of lightning arced from the ceiling, earthing through the daemon, burning away masses of charred flesh – Tyrendian, the Soul Drinkers Librarian, marshalled the lightning like a conductor with an orchestra as the other Soul Drinkers ran into the fight around him.

Pugh paused for a second. The Soul Drinkers were the enemies of the Imperial Fists, rebels and traitors. But the daemons they both fought were a fouler enemy even than the renegade. The legions of the warp were the worst of the worst.

'All units of the 5th,' ordered Pugh. 'Join the Soul Drinkers and counter to our flank! 3rd and 9th, hold the centre!'

The Predator tanks emerged from the barracks they were using for shelter and rumbled towards the growing battle on the flank. Imperial Fists units broke from their positions and followed them. Pugh watched as the 5th Company and the Soul Drinkers caught the plague daemon's force from both sides.

'Dorn forgive me,' said Pugh to himself.

CAPTAIN LUKO LOOKED into the eyes of the daemon, and he saw there everything that mankind had learned to fear.

Something in those unholy eyes had tormented the sons of Earth ever since creatures first crawled out from beneath the mud. Humans had told tales of it, had seen it in their nightmares, before their species had finished evolving. It was the force that inspired the weak flesh to corrupt and rot away, the purest of fears, of death and pain and the unknown wrapped up into one faceless, malevolent will.

Since there had been intelligent minds to contemplate it, the Plague God had existed, turning vulnerable minds to corruption and evil through the fear of what it could do to their flesh. But now there were no vulnerable minds for it to exploit, no kernels of doubt that could grow into desperation and surrender. A Space Marine did not have that weakness. Now, this avatar of the Plague God had to fight.

The plaguebearers that attended the greater daemon were caught by surprise by the Soul Drinkers, who charged from the warren of the catacombs without warning. The daemons did not scatter or run as mundane troops might, but they did not have enough numbers in the right place and the Soul Drinkers had destroyed dozens of them in the first seconds. Luko had taken a worthy toll with his claws and bolter fire had done for the rest. Now Luko was face to face with the greater daemon, its burning and blood-covered form quivering with rage and pain, and everything they had earned in those moments would be lost if he faltered now.

'I have killed your kind before!' yelled Luko, knowing the daemon could hear him even through the battle's din. 'But you have never killed anything like me!'

The daemon snatched up one of the chains its followers had used to drag it. It raised the chain over its head and brought it down like a whip, the links of the chain slamming into the deck. Luko threw himself out of the way, the floor beneath him buckling under the impact.

Plaguebearers following the greater daemon shambled to its side. A dozen of them carried between them an enormous sword of oozing black steel, its pitted blade edged with bloody fangs that looked like they had just been torn from some huge beast's jaw. The greater daemon bent down and took up the sword in its other hand, and the pits in the metal formed mouths that screamed and howled. Luko saw the souls bound into the blade, pitiful souls who had pledged themselves to the daemon in ignorance or desperation.

The daemon raised the blade over its head, point down aimed at Luko. Luko got to his feet and slashed at the plaguebearers who tried to hem him in, the shadow of the blade falling over him as he realised he could not get out of its way.

A bolt of blue-white light hit the sword and the whole weapon lit up, power coursing through it. The daemon bellowed as the flesh of its hand burned off, falling in charred flakes. Its fingers, stripped to bloody bone, let go of the sword and it fell to the deck with a tremendous clang.

Behind Luko, Librarian Tyrendian leapt from the Soul Drinkers ranks. Lightning leapt from his fingers and played around Luko, burning away the plague-bearers who tried to close with him. A bolt struck the greater daemon, earthing in blue-white crackles of power through its skin and leaving crazed burn patterns across its bulk.

Luko leapt over the fallen sword and punched forwards with a claw, spearing through the back of the daemon's ruined hand. The daemon yanked the hand away and lashed at Luko with the chain again, as if it had been bitten by a troublesome insect and was trying to swat it before it could bite again. The chain whipped into Luko at chest height and threw him back into a pack of plaguebearers. Luko slashed in every direction, hoping that each wild strike would catch one of the diseased daemons closing on him.

'Brother!' yelled Tyrendian. 'Fall back! We cannot lose you!'

Luko flung the last plaguebearer off himself and rounded on the greater daemon again. Too late, he saw the daemon had loped a massive stride closer, the mass of its belly like a solid wall of flesh bearing down on him. Luko turned and tried to run but the daemon moved faster than its bulk should have allowed, hauling its weight off the floor on its stumpy back leg and stamping down next to Luko, bringing its weight down onto the Soul Drinker.

Luko crashed to the deck, his lower half pinned under the weight of the daemon. The foul, oozing mass of muscle and flab was crushing down on him with so much weight, Luko could feel the ceramite of his leg armour distorting under the pressure.

Luko twisted around as best he could, lightning claws held in front of him in the best guard he could manage. The greater daemon's face loomed past the curve of its belly, and it was smiling. Luko could feel the deep rumble of its laughter as it saw its prey trapped beneath it.

'Here!' yelled Tyrendian. 'Here! You want to eat?' Tyrendian put his hands together, as if in prayer, and thrust them forwards, a twisting bolt of electricity lancing into the greater daemon's shoulder. It bored through the flesh, charred layers flaking away to the bone.

Tyrendian was walking forwards, every step flinging lightning into the greater daemon. He passed into its shadow, his face edged in hard white and blue by the power playing around his hands.

'Tyrendian! No!' shouted Luko, but Tyrendian did not back off. As the daemon's gaze fell onto him he stood his ground, casting another lightning bolt up at the daemon's face.

The greater daemon dropped the chain, and reached a massive flabby hand over Tyrendian. Tyrendian did not move. Tyrendian had never picked up a scar in battle - never, it had always seemed, even been afflicted by the patina of grime and blood that covered every soldier. He always appeared perfect, less a soldier and more a sculpture, a painting, of what a Space Marine should be. Framed by the battling plaguebearers and borne down upon by the greater daemon, there could be no more powerful symbol of purity facing the very embodiment of corruption.

The daemon's hand closed on Tyrendian. Tyrendian gritted his teeth as the daemon lifted him off his feet, and the air thrummed with the power gathering around his hands. Crackles of it arced into the deck or into the daemon's hand, but it did not seem to feel them. It licked its lips and its mouth yawned wide, showing the multiple rows of teeth that led down to the churning acidic pit of its stomach.

'No!' yelled Luko, his words almost lost by the force with which he shouted them. 'Tyrendian, My brother. Do not do this, not for me. My brother, no!'

The greater daemon flung Tyrendian into the air, and the Soul Drinker disappeared into its mouth.

Luko screamed in anger, as if by doing so he could force the grief down and bury it.

The daemon laughed. So pleased was it by its kill, that it did not notice for a few seconds the blue glow growing in the centre of its belly.

Luko rolled back onto his front and covered himself with his lightning claws. He saw plaguebearers approaching to butcher him, or perhaps hack his legs off to free the rest of him so he could be fed to their lord. He had never seen anything so hateful as their one-eyed, horned faces split with rotten grins, gleeful at their master's kill and the prospect of feeding him another Soul Drinker.

The rising hum from inside the greater daemon told Luko he had only moments left. That was all the plaguebearers needed to get to him.

'Come closer,' he shouted at them. 'Let us become acquainted, my friends. Let me show you an Adeptus Astartes welcome.'

The hum turned to a whine. The greater daemon noticed it now. It groaned, and placed its hand to its belly, face turning sour and pained. It roared, and the terrible gale of it drowned out Luko's voice as he yelled obscenities at the plaguebearers.

The daemon's belly swelled suddenly, like a balloon inflating. The daemon's eyes widened in surprise. It was the last expression on its hateful face – surprise and dismay.

The daemon's belly exploded in the tremendous burst of blue-white power. Luko was slammed into the floor with the force of it. The plaguebearers were thrown backwards, battered by the wall of force that hit them. A great cloud of torn and burning entrails showered down, covering Soul Drinker and daemon alike. Lightning arced in every direction from the shattered body of the greater daemon, ripping into the plaguebearers surrounding it, lashing across the ceiling, boring through the floor.

In the old Chapter, some had speculated on just how much power Tyrendian could gather. If collat-eral damage and his own survival were no issue, it was guessed by the Librarium that their bioelectric weapon could detonate himself with massive force, as great a force of raw destruction as a whole artillery strike. They had never been sure, and never sought to find out, for Tyrendian was too valuable a weapon of war to risk him finding out how much power he could concentrate within himself.

Now, the question had been answered. Tyrendian could gather inside himself enough electric power to destroy a greater daemon of the warp. He had detonated inside the daemon's belly with such force that all that remained, tottering above Luko, was a thick and gristly spine on which was still mounted the ragged remnants of the greater daemon's skull. The shattered stumps of its ribs and a single shoulder blade, clinging by tattered tendons, alone suggested the bulk of its chest. Green-black brains spilled from the back of its ruptured skull, and across the front of it was stretched the daemon's face, still wearing that expression of surprise.

The daemon toppled backwards, the ruin of its upper body slapping to the deck. The weight on Luko relaxed and he dug a claw into the deck in front of him, dragging himself out from under the daemon. He looked back and saw that only the lower portion of its once-vast belly remained, its legs connected only by skin, the many layers of entrails and organs now just a charred crater.

The plaguebearers nearby had been blasted back off their feet. Many had been burst apart by the lightning unleashed by Tyrendian's detonation. The whole deck surrounding the daemon's corpse was buckled and burned. Luko's own armour was charred and bent out of shape, giving him only just enough free movement to walk away from the destruction towards the Soul Drinkers lines.

Luko's ears rang, and the sound of gunfire barely registered through the white noise filling his head. He looked around, dazed, trying to blink away the fog that seemed to smother his mind. There was no sign of Tyrendian. Quite probably he had been vaporised by the force of the power he had unleashed. There would be nothing to bury.

Sergeat Graevus ran forwards and grabbed Luko, dragging him away from the reforming plaguebearers and thrusting him behind a fallen pillar for cover.

Yellow-armoured figures came into view, approaching from the direction of the Imperial Fists centre. Without the greater daemon to anchor them, the plaguebearers wheeled in confusion, running in ones and twos into the bolter fire of the Imperial Fists, cut down and shredded into masses of stringy gore.

Graevus held his power axe high and yelled an order that Luko couldn't quite make out through the ringing. The Soul Drinkers vaulted from cover and advanced, bolters firing, even as the Imperial Fists did the same. Caught in a crossfire, leaderless, the plaguebearers seemed to dissolve under the weight of fire, as if in a downpour of acid.

Luko's senses returned to him as the whole flank of the daemon army collapsed, the servants of the Plague God ripped to shreds by the combined fire of the Soul Drinkers and the Imperial Fists.

The two Adeptus Astartes forces met as the last of the plaguebearers were being picked off by bolter fire. Luko found himself looking into the face of Captain Lysander.

'At last, we meet as brothers,' said Lysander.

'Thank the Emperor for mutual foes,' replied Luko without humour.

'Pugh has requested that we fight now as one. Will you take your place in the line?'

'We will, captain,' said Luko. 'There are but few of us, and one of our best was lost killing that beast. But whatever fight we can offer, the enemies of the warp will have it.'

Lysander shouldered his power hammer, and held out a hand. Luko slid his own hand out of his lightning claw gauntlet, and shook it.

'They're falling back,' came Pugh's voice over Lysander's vox. 'But in order. All units, withdraw to the centre and the Forge and hold positions.'

'Abraxes would not abandon the fight,' said Lysander, 'even with their flank collapsed.'

Luko watched as the last few plaguebearers fled through the ruins of barracks and shrines, as if responding to a mental command to give up the fight. They were cut down by bolter fire, sharpshooters snapping bolts into them as they ran. 'He has a plan,' said Luko. 'His kind always do.'

'WHAT ARE THEY doing?' asked Kolgo.

Sister Aescarion, crouched among the ruins of the front line's barricades, watched through her magnoculars a moment longer.

'They are building something,' she said.

The daemons had retreated a little under an hour

before, but not all the way back to the cargo holds. Instead they had formed their own lines a kilometre away, almost the whole width of the deck. They had cut power to as many of the local systems as they could, resulting in the overhead lights failing and casting darkness across the battlefield as if night had fallen. Fires twinkled among the daemons' positions, illuminating hulking shapes of iron with designs that could only be guessed at in the gloom.

'Building what?' said Kolgo.

Aescarion handed him the magnoculars. 'War machines,' said Aescarion. 'At a guess. It is impossible to tell.'

Kolgo focused the magnoculars for himself. Daemons danced around their fires and tattered banners stood, fluttering in the updrafts, casting flickering shadows on the engines they were building. 'Building them from what?'

'Perhaps they are bringing parts through from the warp,' said Aescarion.

The Imperial Fists had rebuilt what defences they could and were now holding their makeshift line again, watchmen posted at intervals to watch for any developments among the enemy. The Space Marine losses had been tallied, and they were heavy. Leucrontas's command had almost been wiped out; only a couple of dozen stragglers now joining the centre. Most other Imperial Fists units were little over half-strength. Borganor's Howling Griffons, in the Forge of Ages, had fended off skirmishing forces that tested their strength, and were mostly intact save for a few felled by shrieking, flying things that swooped down among them, decapitating and severing with their snapping jaws. The Imperial Fists now holding the line in front of the Tactica were crouched, much as Aescarion was, scanning the daemon lines for the first signs of an assault. The sound of metal on metal drifted across, along with strains of a grim atonal singing.

'Come,' said Kolgo. 'Pugh has called a council of war. We shall not have to settle for sitting and watching for much longer.'

Aescarion followed the inquisitor through the darkness. On every side were Space Marines who had suffered wounds in the battle but returned to the fray. Many were missing hands or limbs, or had segments of their armour removed to allow for a wound to be cast or splinted.

The most severely wounded were laid out in the Tactica itself, on or around the map tables. Apothecaries worked on chest and head wounds, with healthy brothers rotated in to serve as blood donors for transfusions. As Aescarion and Kolgo entered, another Imperial Fist was lifted off a map table by two of his battle-brothers and carried towards the archways leading to the building's rear, where the dead were being piled up. A lectern-servitor with a scratching autoquill was keeping a tally of the dead in a ledger.

Officers were gathered around one of the central tables, which represented the canyon walls and xenos settlement of some ancient battle. Pugh was there, along with Lysander, Borganor and Librarian Varnica of the Doom Eagles. With them stood Captain Luko and Sergeant Graevus of the Soul Drinkers.

Aescarion stood apart as Kolgo joined them.

'Lord inquisitor,' said Pugh. 'Now we are all present. I shall dispense with any formalities as time is not on our side. We must decide our next course of action, and do it now.'

'Attack,' said Borganor. 'I cannot say why Abraxes withdrew his army, for it is unlike the daemons' manner of war, but it is certain that we shall not get any such respite from them again. We must lead a counter-offensive as soon as we can, before they finish whatever infernal contraptions they are building. Therein lies the only chance of defeating them.'

'I agree, Chapter Master,' said Lysander. 'We have borne the brunt of their assault with greater fortitude than Abraxes expected. They regroup and perhaps reinforce as we speak. Attack them and destroy them. It is the only way.'

'They outnumber us,' countered Librarian Varnica. 'A full assault will result in defeat for us, every tactical calculation points towards it.'

'Then what would you have us do?' said Borganor. 'Wait for Dorn's own return? For Roboute Guilliman to appear amongst us?'

'Attacking would make the most of what advantages we have,' said Luko. 'We are at our best up close, charging into the face of the enemy.'

'So are daemons,' said Graevus.

'True,' said Luko. 'Very true.'

'There must be other ways,' said Varnica. 'We fall back to a smaller, more defensible part of the *Phalanx* and force them to attack on a narrow frontage. Lure them in and kill them piece by piece.'

'That would give them the run of the *Phalanx*,' said Pugh. 'Abraxes would do with this craft as he wished. His daemons could surround us and perhaps render the whole section uninhabitable by introducing hard vacuum or radiation. With Abraxes in charge they certainly would.'

'The question is,' said Varnica, 'does such a scenario promise our deaths with more or less certainty than walking across the barracks deck and into their arms?'

'So,' said Pugh. 'We give Abraxes my army or we give him my ship. Any other suggestions?'

'There is one,' said a newcomer's voice. The officers turned to see Apothecary Pallas. He was attending to one of the wounded nearby, using a cautery iron to sear shut the stump of an Imperial Fist's severed left arm.

'Pallas,' said Luko. 'I had not realised you yet lived. I did not think I would speak with you again.'

'Chapter Master,' said Pallas, continuing to work on the wounded warrior. 'What was to be our manner of execution?'

'We have not the time to waste listening to this renegade,' said Borganor.

'Execution by gunshot,' said Pugh, ignoring Borganor. 'Then incineration.'

'On the Path of the Lost?'

Pugh folded his arms and stepped back a pace, as if some revelation was growing in his mind. 'Yes,' he replied. 'You were to walk the Path.'

'It is traditional,' continued Pallas, 'that the condemned among the sons of Dorn be forced to walk the Path of the Lost. It runs from the Pardoner's Court, just a few hundred metres from this very building, and across the width of the *Phalanx* along the ventral hull. It emerges near the cargo holds, where our incinerated remains could be ejected from the ship. Is this not correct?'

'It is,' replied Pugh. 'You know much of this tradition.'

'I read of the ways in which we would die after I refused to join my brothers in their breakout,' said Pallas. 'It seemed appropriate for me to do so, that I might counsel my brothers when the time for execution came.'

'And what,' said Borganor, 'is your point?'

'My point is that Abraxes has at his command more than a mere army,' said Pallas. The cautery iron had finished its work in closing the wound and Pallas now wrapped the wound in gauze as he spoke. 'He brought his army onto the *Phalanx* somehow, and he brings components for his war machines and no doubt reinforcements for his troops. He has a warp gate, a way into the immaterium, and it is stable and open. Only this explains his capacity to attack the *Phalanx* at all.'

'And the Path of the Lost,' said Luko, 'leads from here to the region of the warp gate.'

'Among the dorsal cargo holds,' said Pallas. 'A sizeable force could not make it through the Path, certainly not without alerting Abraxes to divert his forces to defending the portal. The majority of the force must stay here to face his army and keep it fighting. A smaller force, a handful strong, takes the

Path of the Lost and strikes out for the warp gate's location. As long as Abraxes possesses a gate through the warp any attempt to defeat him here is futile, for he will just bring more legions through until we are exhausted.'

'Insanity,' said Borganor.

'Captain Borganor,' said Pugh. 'I have no doubt that your hatred for the Soul Drinkers is well deserved, for they have done your Chapter much wrong. But what Pallas says has merit. It does not matter if we shatter Abraxes's army, he still has a means to conjure a new one from the warp. Remove that, and we buy ourselves a thread that leads to victory.'

'You are not seriously considering this?' said Borganor.

'I will go,' said Luko. 'The Soul Drinkers have suffered at the hands of Abraxes before. If we are to die on the *Phalanx*, then let it be in seeking revenge against him.'

'And none but the Soul Drinkers have faced Abraxes before at all,' added Graevus.

'You will need a Librarian,' said Varnica. 'And since they are in such short supply, I had better go with you.'

'Varnica?' said Borganor. 'You were among the first to condemn the Soul Drinkers!'

'And if you are correct in your mistrust, I will be among the last to be betrayed by them,' said Varnica. 'But the Chapter Master is right. There is no other way. Thin as the thread is, unwholesome as the Soul Drinkers reputation might be, I must follow that thread for it is all we have.'

'And I,' said Sister Aescarion, stepping forwards. 'The Inquisition must have a presence. My Lord Inquisitor is most valuable here, leading the defence of the *Phalanx*. In his stead I offer myself to accompany the Apothecary's mission.'

'I shall appoint an Imperial Fists squad to accompany you,' said Pugh. 'I can spare no more. The rest of my warriors must remain to hold the line.'

'I wish Apothecary Pallas given leave to join us as well,' said Luko.

'You have it. Kolgo, Borganor, Lysander and myself shall continue to command the defence. These are the wishes of Chapter Master Pugh, and hence are the wishes of Rogal Dorn. Go now to fulfil your orders, brothers and sisters. Should I see you after the battle, then all shall be joyful. If not, I shall await you at the end of time, at the Emperor's side, when we shall have our revenge for everything the enemy has done to us.'

The officers departed to organise the defence of the Tactica and the Forge of Ages. Across the cavernous barracks deck, the war machines of the daemon army grew higher.

# CHAPTER THIRTEEN

IT WAS A dismal thing, killing Chaplain Iktinos.

Iktinos was, by then, a barely sensible wreck. The infliction of the Hell had broken his mind so thoroughly that there was nothing left of the Chaplain save for his physical shell. The man that had once been the paragon of the Chapter and the hidden traitor were gone.

Sarpedon had carried Iktinos to a cluster of saviour pods adjoining the fighter craft deck. In the event of the huge hangar doors failing or some disaster befalling the fighter deck, the crew could use the pods to escape the *Phalanx*. The entrances to the pods were circular shafts leading down from a slanting wall, like the open mouths of steel worms waiting to swallow the desperate crewmen as they fled. Oil stained the walls and ceiling, and the chill of the near-vacuum could not be completely kept out by the hull insulation. It was no place for a Space Marine to die, suited only to a shambolic, almost apologetic excuse for a death.

Should the saviour pods themselves be compromised, an emergency airlock was set into the outer skin of the hull beside the entrances to the pods. A crewman in a voidsuit who took that exit could conceivably survive an extra hour or two in space, and perhaps even be picked up by a rescue craft. Sarpedon placed Iktinos's limp form on the deck and turned the wheel-lock, opening the airlock's outer door.

'If you have anything you wish to add, Chaplain,' said Sarpedon, 'now is the time.'

Iktinos did not reply. Sarpedon looked down at him, at his burned face and scorched, dented armour, and regretted speaking. The Chaplain was barely drawing breath.

Sarpedon placed a hand against Iktinos's charred skull. Sarpedon had never possessed any great talent for diving into the mind of another. Some Librarians of the old Chapter had specialised in peeling apart another's consciousness, diving down and extracting secrets the subject himself did not know. Others read minds on a vast scale, divining troop movements from an opposing army as fast as their orders spread. Sarpedon had only been able to transmit, albeit at the tremendous telepathic volume that manifested as the Hell. Nevertheless he had sometimes caught echoes of the strongest emotions, an aspect of the sixth sense that all psykers possessed in some degree. He tried to read something from Iktinos then, to divine some final thought from the man he had once considered his closest ally in all the universe.

There was nothing. Complete deadness, as if Iktinos were an inert object with no mind at all.

Then Sarpedon caught something, faint and intermittent, like a signal from a dying transmitter light years away. It was the howling of a desolate wind, the sound of emptiness more profound than silence. It whistled through the ruined architecture of a mind as empty as a bombed-out city, as alone as a world where life had never evolved. It was as if there had never been a mind in there at all, scoured and scrubbed from the wind-blasted stones by a terrible extinction.

Sarpedon alone had not done this. The Hell was indiscriminate and crude, a force of destruction, certainly, but not accurate or thorough enough to erase the personality of another. Iktinos had done this to himself. The shattered fragments of his soul had gathered themselves into a whole coherent enough only to self-destruct. A logic bomb planted by Daenyathos's teachings, a way to destroy any compromising memories trapped in a fractured mind. An atrocity quite in keeping with the Philosopher-Soldier's conviction that everything he did, no matter how obscene, was for a good beyond the conception of lesser human beings.

Sarpedon knew now what Daenyathos planned. It was no less appalling than the betrayal of the Soul Drinkers had suggested. It was entirely appropriate that Abraxes, an icon of treachery and malice, should himself just be a cog in such a scheme. The annihilation of Iktinos's personality was similarly in keeping with Daenyathos's way of doing things.

Iktinos had not completed his mental suicide before the unconscious part of him, the one laid open by the Hell, had submitted to Sarpedon's request. Iktinos had, indeed, told Sarpedon everything.

Sarpedon hefted Iktinos's body into the airlock. He slammed the inner door shut and turned the wheel to lock it again. Through the thick portholes Sarpedon could see the multicoloured nebulae of the Veiled Region, unknowable and hungry. Sarpedon would give its ravenous young stars something to feed on.

He tried to think of something to say to Iktinos, some powerful parting statement that would both condemn the traitor and express regret that the Chaplain, his old friend, was gone. But there was no point. Iktinos could not have understood anything in his current state, even if the words did reach him through the heavy airlock door.

Sarpedon thumbed the control stud set into the wall beside the door. Pneumatic cables hissed as the airlock was depressurised. A warning light strobed, then the airlock's outer door opened and the remaining air whistled out. Silence followed and Iktinos's body, dislodged from its resting place by the final decompression, drifted out of the airlock and beyond the grasp of the *Phalanx*.

A craft the size of the *Phalanx* was typically surrounded by a halo of debris and thin gas out to a distance of several tens of metres. Sarpedon watched as Iktinos's body fell beyond the halo zone, into the pure void. At some point the Chaplain had finally died, but it hardly seemed much of a distinction with his mind already destroyed.

The outer door slid shut again, and Iktinos's body became lost through the condensation misting on the porthole as the airlock filled back up with air. Sarpedon turned away.

Iktinos was dead. Sarpedon had kept one of the promises he had made to himself. As tough as taking on Iktinos had been, the next promise would be harder to fulfil. Sarpedon knew where Daenyathos was and what he was trying to do, but the way he would stop the Philosopher-Soldier had yet to make itself clear.

It did not matter. The time for weighing up the risks and probabilities of battle had come and gone some time ago. Now, Sarpedon had something to fight for, and there was no deadlier weapon than that in a Space Marine's hands.

'THRONE BEHOLD US,' whispered Pallas as he set eyes on the Path of the Lost for the first time. 'Watch over us, my Emperor. Watch over us.'

The Path of the Lost, as recorded in the archives of the Imperial Fists, was a dark place. Its floors were covered with grates to allow the blood to drain out, and a thousand rusting torture devices were piled up as detritus in its shadowy corners as the fashions of punishment changed. An Imperial Fist might have the honour of being interrogated in the Atoning Halls or perhaps brought in chains before the Chapter Master – but those who were outsiders, prisoners of war or condemned heretics would be banished to the Path of the Lost. There would be doled out their tortures or executions away from the eyes of the Chapter down in the *Phalanx's* rusting, filthy underbelly.

That would have been bad enough.

The strike force advanced, fire teams covering one another, as they crossed the threshold and entered what the Path of the Lost had become. The horror of the warp's invasion had bled down inevitably into the Path, some unconscious malice dragging the warp's dark energies into the torture chambers and execution grounds.

Across the walls and floors shimmered the torn faces of the Path's dead. Delicate eldar features, each forced into a dying rictus, bulged from the warping metal. Like drowning swimmers struggling to the surface, humanoid shapes broke the surface to sink down again, an endless pulsating mass of bodies. The ghosts of mutant renegades, fouled with horns or sloughing skin, pushed against the fabric of reality, teeth gnashing.

'There must be a million dirty secrets down here,' said Luko, casting an eye across the constant parade of the executed and damned.

'Nothing of your concern,' said Sergeant Prexus. His squad had been charged with forming the bulk of the strike force, with nine more Imperial Fists under his command.

'I think it is, sergeant,' replied Luko. 'All those dark deeds the Imperial Fists thought hidden from the universe, they might well come back to bite us down here.'

'If you are finished,' said Sister Aescarion, walking between the Imperial Fist and the Soul Drinker, 'time is a factor.'

Prexus's squad advanced into the cluster of execution chambers that marked the entrance to the Path of the Lost. Pallas, Luko and Graevus followed the Imperial Fists in, Varnica and Sister Aescarion watching the angles behind them.

Several tiled rooms with drains built into the floor, walls crazed with old bullet holes, had seen hundreds of captives executed in the past decades and centuries. Now those walls bulged as if they held veins fed by a vast heart, faces and hands pressing against the surface. The floor quivered underfoot as grasping hands tried to snare the feet of the Imperial Fists.

'Steel your souls,' said Sergeant Prexus, his chainsword held ready as he took point. 'Recall the parables of Rogal Dorn. He walked into the hell of the *Vengeful Spirit*, and though assailed on every side, he did not fall. Though the Angel fell, the strength of our primarch's soul did not let him follow. Though the Emperor was laid low, Rogal Dorn did not know despair. Let his strength be your strength, my brothers. Let his strength be yours.'

'We are watched,' said Varnica. He slid a hand into his force claw gauntlet, and it snickered shut around his wrist.

A shape flashed through the execution chambers, half-glimpsed through the gaping doorways and holes in the collapsed walls. The Imperial Fists gathered into a battle formation, gathered around Prexus with bolters aimed out in all directions. Pallas was beside Prexus, his own bolter ready.

'They envy us,' said Varnica. 'No matter how grave our situation, it cannot compare to the unfinished business of the dead.'

More shimmering silver-grey forms rippled in and out of sight, flitting from electric chair to injection table to gallows. Quicker and closer they came, the howling of their voices growing, until they were like a tornado of torn souls with the strike force trapped in the storm's eye.

'Hold fast,' cried Prexus. 'The enemy shows its hand. Its foulness here is manifest.'

Reality bowed and flexed around Varnica's force claw as he channelled his psychic power into the Hammerhand. Aescarion dropped to one knee, power axe ready, and was taken aback to see Graevus take up the same posture beside her, his own power axe in his mutated hand.

One of the ghosts tore from the mass and arrowed towards them. Varnica leapt, drawing back his force claw. The spirit had the hollow face and alien eyes of the eldar, the inhuman geometry of its frame the very essence of the xenos. The ragged matter of its body echoed the curved shapes of its once-elegant armour, shredded into streamers of spirit-stuff by the ravages of its grim death.

Varnica's force claw closed on the spirit and sheared it in two. The wall of force generated by the eruption of his Hammerhand power ripped the xenos spirit apart, a sphere of energy bulging outwards from the impact.

Varnica skidded to the floor. With ear-splitting screams, more of the *Phalanx*'s dead were shrieking into the Imperial formation. Aescarion swatted at one, the blade of her power axe scything through a vaguely human mass of glowing energy. The discharging power field shredded the spirit into a cloud of falling sparks.

'Open fire!' yelled Prexus, and ten boltguns hammered in unison. Shapes rippled along the floor and grabbed at their feet, while ghostly hands reached from the floor. Prexus was snared by hands clutching at his ankles, and he cut them through at the wrist with a swipe of his chainblade. Apothecary Pallas speared an apparition through the throat with the needles of the narthecium he wore around one hand, the medical device doubling as a weapon up close.

From the maelstrom coiled a serpentine apparition, terminating in the gnashing face of some foul mutant, its features knotted into a mass of tentacles trailing behind it. Its long gnarled fingers were tipped with metal blades, and shards of bone stabbed from the echo of its form.

'The Vizier!' yelled Prexus.

The apparition grinned, its face almost splitting in two along a fissure lined with fangs. It dived, too fast for the Imperial Fist in its way to avoid it. The Vizier dived into the Space Marine, its whole length disappearing into the warrior's breastplate. The Imperial Fist was suffused with a blue-white glow bleeding from between the plates of his armour and shining through the eyepieces of his helmet, and he dropped his boltgun as he was wracked with sudden convulsions.

Varnica ripped one of the ghosts from the swirling mass, impaling it on his force claw, and slammed it into the ground where it dissipated. He turned to see the Imperial Fist in the throes of possession. Shards of bone were bursting from under the Space Marine's forearms and shoulder guards.

Prexus leaped onto his possessed battle-brother, wrestling him to the deck. Varnica pushed through the cordon of Imperial Fists to Prexus's side. He withdrew his hand from his force claw, attaching it back onto the holster at his side, and placed his hand against the possessed warrior's forehead.

Aescarion and Graevus joined the Imperial Fists cordon, slashing at the ghosts that swooped close. Luko was on his own, pivoting and slashing in every direction, his lightning claws perfectly suited to this fight where he was assailed from all sides. Scraps of spirit flesh floated down like shed leaves, faces breaking into ragged scraps of detritus as their distant screams died with them.

'In the name of the Emperor and His mighty soul that shields us all from the enemy,' yelled Varnica, 'I cast thee out. From this good brother's soul, where you shall find no purchase, I cast thee out!'

Power arced off the Imperial Fist's armour. The possessed form forced itself to its feet and threw off Prexus with strength beyond even a Space Marine. Prexus crashed into the tiled wall of an execution chamber, sliding down among the rubble and old bloodstains. Varnica kept hold of the possessed Space Marine, his hand still clamped against his forehead.

The faceplate of the Imperial Fist's helmet became

like liquid, rippling and shifting into a face that was an animal mass of tentacles. A forked tongue flickered from its lipless mouth.

'This spirit tastes good,' it hissed.

'Out, daemon,' shouted Varnica. 'The Emperor's light burns you. The iron of this warrior's soul cages you. Out, out, wither and die!'

'Do you know how much is left of him?' slavered the Vizier. 'He has barely a name. The rest of him I consume. I shall leave him a shell with the mind of an infant.'

'I said out!' yelled Varnica. The shape of the Vizier rippled around the Imperial Fist, stretching and deforming as if it were being pulled from the body by invisible hands. Finally, with a shriek, it came away and the Space Marine clattered to the floor, insensible.

Aescarion and Graevus leapt on the Vizier as it writhed, confused for a moment. Aescarion's axe bisected its face, the power field burning through the spectral matter. The Vizier threw her to the floor with a lash of its long tail, but Graevus's axe was already descending towards where its neck should be. The axe cut through it and its head was sheared from its body. The serpentine form dissolved into the air, and the head had shimmered away to motes of light before it hit the ground.

The ghosts dissolved away, slinking back into the shadows. The Imperial Fists tracked their bolters through the darkness as Luko watched the rag-like slivers of ghostly flesh erode away from his gauntlets.

Silence fell again, broken only by the plinking of

tiles falling from the bolter-scarred walls.

'What was it?' asked Pallas, cradling the fallen Imperial Fist's head and undoing the armour seals around his neck.

Prexus picked himself up from the deck. 'The Vizier,' he spat. 'A mutant warlord. A psyker. Centuries ago he was captured and brought to the *Phalanx*. He died down here. I do not recall the whole story.'

'I imagine it was far from unique,' said Luko.

Pallas removed the Imperial Fist's helmet. The faceplate was still twisted into a semblance of the Vizier's tentacled face. Underneath, the warrior's face was bloodied and battered, with growths of bloody bone poking through the cheekbones and scalp. He drew a shallow breath and winced.

'Brother Dolonis,' said Prexus, kneeling beside the wounded man. 'Can you fight?'

'No, my brother,' gasped Dolonis in reply. 'The pain… is everywhere. It has changed me. My body is not… not my own. I can still hear it laughing…'

Aescarion cast her eye over Dolonis's body. Shards of bone had penetrated through his armour all over. Knots of it were forcing his shoulder pads away from his body and knife-like growths jutted from his greaves. A pool of rapidly congealing blood was spreading beneath Dolonis.

'We must leave him,' said Aescarion.

'He is a battle-brother,' replied Prexus.

'He cannot fight and we cannot take him. And the enemy has been within his mind. He is a moral threat. If he lives, we will be back for him, but for now we must leave him.'

'I agree with the Sister,' said Varnica. 'You have not seen the ruin a possession can make of its victim. The possessor can plant a piece of itself that can continue even after the daemon is dead.'

Prexus stepped back from Dolonis. 'Brother. I cannot make this decision for you.'

'Leave me,' said Dolonis, the words causing him obvious pain. 'Just put my bolter in my hand.'

Prexus handed Dolonis his gun. Aescarion knelt beside him and took a loop of prayer beads from a pouch at her waist. She pressed them into Dolonis's free hand.

'Pray for us, brother,' she said. 'We will pray for you.'

Pallas gently lowered Dolonis to the deck.

'We need to move on,' said Luko, stepping over the rubble further into the tangle of execution chambers. The feeble light reached to the threshold of another warren, this time of cell blocks of tight winding tunnels lined with steel doors and stretches of manacle-hung walls. 'If Abraxes's influence has woken the old dead here, then he probably knows we have disturbed them. We must reach his portal before he sends his own forces down here.'

Prexus did not, or could not, say anything further. With a final glance at Dolonis, he led his squad out of formation towards the deeper regions of the Path.

'You fight well, Sister,' said Graevus as he and Aescarion took up their position in the middle of the marching order.

'You expected otherwise?' said Aescarion.

'I did not mean…'

'We are the daughters of the Emperor,' she said,

'just as you are his sons. I may not have two hearts or three lungs, but I have every bit the resolve of a Space Marine.'

'So I saw,' said Graevus. 'You were quick to leave Dolonis to his fate.'

'As I would with a sister of mine,' said Aescarion sharply. 'A sense of brotherhood has its benefits, but taken to extremes, I fear it can become a weakness as much as a strength. The history of the Imperium is a litany of failings caused by brotherhood misplaced.'

Graevus bit back any reply. The Path of the Lost closed around them, the cramped warrens of cells forcing the Space Marines to split up, and it felt for all the galaxy as if the *Phalanx* were swallowing them whole.

BY THE FIRES of the forges they had built, the daemons' war engines were taking shape. One of them was a huge horned thing, a battering ram with cylindrical cages for wheels in which some of the lumbering daemon-beasts would doubtless be herded to drive it forwards. Another was a catapult with a shield mantle reaching almost to the deck's high ceiling, piles of alien skulls being heaped up behind it as ammunition. A machine like a massive mechanical crab was being assembled with tanks of some caustic bilious substance on its back, hooked up to the cannon on its coiling tail. Impish daemon-wrights scrambled over the surfaces of the war machines, while legions of bloodletters stood guard and the shapeshifting horrors of Abraxes swarmed in an endless squirming dance. The remains of the greater plague daemon had been dragged behind the tumbledown fortifications and putrefied into a cauldron of bubbling rot, from which more plaguebearers were being birthed by the minute.

Lord Inquisitor Kolgo watched the flickering fires reflected off the pitted metal of the half-finished daemon engines. His Battle Sisters retinue shadowed him at a respectful distance as he leaned against a fallen wall behind which a couple of Imperial Fists had taken up their position in the line. 'We will have to attack before they are finished,' he said.

'I know,' replied Chapter Master Pugh. 'That is why Abraxes is building them. He wants us to emerge from safety and march towards them, to give them the defensive ground instead of us.'

'And we will attack,' said Kolgo. 'We cannot stand back and give them the *Phalanx*. It is written in the fate that Abraxes loves to weave so much.'

'It seems that you have divined the future, lord inquisitor,' said Pugh. Any bitterness in his voice was well hidden. 'Abraxes is not the only one reading the runes.'

'Fate has us all in its snares, Chapter Master. It is an Inquisitor's duty to perceive it.'

'And what does fate say will happen to us?'

'Truly? If you so wish, Chapter Master. Fate has decided that Abraxes shall bring his great cunning to bear and with it, defeat a force of brave but bull-headed Space Marines, bringing a great tragedy to pass.'

'That is fate?'

'That is fate.'

'Then, lord inquisitor, I shall fight fate.' Pugh pointed to a knot of rubble in the no-man's-land between the armies. It was the remains of a hero-chapel that had been toppled by the daemons' advance. 'There still stands the statue of Chaplain Pausanias,' he said. 'They could not topple him. See? He lacks an arm, and the rest of him has seen better days, but he stands.'

'Like us?' said Kolgo.

'You miss my point. Pausanias was a dark seed. He was brought onto the *Phalanx* as a novice, recruited like thousands of others. Unlike most of them, he was found worthy as an Imperial Fist. But there was a darkness in him. A pride. He sought the greatest glory in battle, and battle-brothers died for his failings.'

'A warrior's sin, rarely acknowledged,' said Kolgo.

Pugh ignored the inquisitor. 'We saw too late what he was,' he continued, 'and when his charge against a gunline, seeking to capture the standard of the enemy, cost the life of his squad's sergeant, he was banished to the Atoning Halls for his paucity of spirit. Fate had decided that Pausanias should be a lesson to us, lord inquisitor. He was destined to be a parable of warning to future novices, a disgrace as a Space Marine to be mourned and despised. But Pausanias was not resigned to accepting that fate. He scourged away his pride in the Atoning Halls. He returned lower than the novices, lower than our crew. He worked in the engines of the *Phalanx*, until the Chapter welcomed him back into its ranks. He died a Chaplain, a spiritual guardian of our battle-brothers, because he had fought that fate which had bound him so tightly and fought to live beyond it. He defeated his fate and is remembered here for it. I shall emulate him, if the Emperor wills it, and confound the designs of this daemon prince.'

'It sounds to me, Chapter Master, that an Imperial Fist does not know when to give in.'

'We do not know, lord inquisitor, what giving in even means.'

From the shadows cast by the daemons' fires, a Space Marine scout crept towards the Imperial Fist lines. The yellow of his armour was smeared with ash, as was his face, to break up his outline in the gloom.

'Scout Orfos,' said Pugh as the scout got closer, 'if these old eyes fail me not.'

'You shame me, Chapter Master,' said Orfos as he took his place in the line. 'I should aspire to get within a knife thrust of you before you notice me.'

'Friend and foe have tried, brother. That I still stand suggests no foe, at least, has succeeded yet. What news do you bring of the enemy?'

'Within two hours, they will finish building their war engines,' replied Orfos. 'They are preparing rituals to possess them with daemons. Heaps of skulls and entrails piled up, and sigils wrought in blood, I have seen. They have brought supplicants through, still human, though barely, and they writhe and chant to gain the attention of their gods. Such rites of the flesh I hesitate to describe, but the beasts they build will have a cunning born of their possession as well as their own raw strength.'

'Can we survive them, if they are sent against us?' said Pugh.

'I do not know if the *Phalanx* itself will survive them,' said Orfos. 'We counted six of them. The scorpion beast, the battering ram and the catapult are clearest to us from here. A burrowing worm of steel lies coiled and slumbering out of our view, with a contraption of brass and skulls that I suspect will house the spirit of a greater daemon and a beast of flesh knitted together, as if predators of the warp had been butchered and their carcasses divided to be formed into one single monstrosity. All look as if they are nearing completion.'

'You and your brother scouts have done well,' said Pugh.

Orfos saluted and headed back through the lines to join the other scouts arriving in ones and twos from their mission.

'Then within two hours,' said Kolgo, 'we attack.'

'That is one fate I will not seek to avoid. My Fangs of Dorn have not seen enough blood yet, not quite.'

'If Luko's mission does not succeed, this will be the last the *Phalanx* sees of any of us.'

'Are you afraid, lord inquisitor?'

Kolgo replied with a smirk and turned back towards the centre of the Imperial Fists position, where his Battle Sisters were waiting patiently for their master.

When Kolgo was out of earshot, Pugh looked again towards the daemon engines growing more complete by the moment. He took the Fangs of Dorn in his hands, their blades scarred with burning daemon blood and muttered to himself.

'Is it wrong that I have prayed for this?'

\* \* \*

By the time the strike force of Imperial Fists and Soul Drinkers reached the Panpsychicon, two more of Prexus's squad had been lost. In the warren of cells and tunnels, where the Space Marines were forced to move through each junction and bottleneck in knots of two or three, unseen foes had snatched at them from the darkness.

Befanged faces had loomed, gnashing and spitting bile. The walls had fallen in, or pits had opened in the floor. Cackling creatures had flitted past junctions ahead, too quick to see or shoot. One Imperial Fist had been dragged into a cell by hands of shattered, bloody bone; by the time his battle-brothers had reached him, there was nothing left in the cell but torn scraps of ceramite and the blood slathered across the walls and ceiling.

The second had been killed by invisible hands as his brothers watched. Even as they tried to haul him down from the ceiling where he had been carried, his head was wrenched around almost backwards and his spine snapped. The forces holding him had dissipated instantly, dropping the corpse to the deck and leaving only silence behind.

So the strike force warily emerged into the wide space ahead of them, leaving the labyrinth behind, only to wonder where the next threat would come from.

'What is this place?' said Luko, the first to step out of the cell block tunnel.

'The Panpsychicon,' said Prexus behind him. 'An experiment.'

'Was it successful?' asked Luko.

'It had lain down here unused for two hundred years,' replied Prexus. 'Is that answer enough?'

The circular expanse of the Panpsychicon was bounded by smooth walls inlaid with mosaics. The names of a hundred great battles from Imperial Fists history were depicted there in patterns of brightly coloured stone shards, surrounded by complex heraldries that spiralled into an unbroken pattern. Even the name Terra was picked out among the heraldry, commemorating the part the Imperial Fists had played in the battle for the Emperor's Palace ten thousand years before.

In the centre of the Panpsychicon was a device of steel and crystal that reached the ceiling, something like a set of interlocking spider's webs in which were suspended cut slabs and chunks of crystal-like giant gemstones. A rainbow of colours reflected from every surface, creating a maddening nest of shapes and light that refused attempts to view it as a normal object in three dimensions.

Luko's foot disturbed a manacle set into the floor. It was one of dozens set in concentric circles around the central device.

'Some enemies resist traditional interrogation techniques,' said Prexus. 'Psykers amongst them. The Panpsychicon was built to rid them of their mental barriers.'

'It is a machine,' said Sister Aescarion, 'for grinding down men's souls? The Inquisition makes use of such things, but with varying success. And never have I seen one on such a scale.'

'These are matters of the past,' said Prexus. 'We must

press on. We close on the cargo sections, but we must not allow ourselves to be slowed further.'

The whole room shuddered. Handfuls of dust spilled from cracks in the ceiling and the mosaiced walls shed their tesserae. The Panpsychicon's device shone and glimmered as its crystals shook and, with a grinding sound from beneath the floor, began to rotate.

'How many died down here?' asked Luko, crouching to keep his footing as the room shuddered with greater strength.

'That depends,' said Prexus, 'on what you mean by "die".'

Shapes of captives, manacled to the floor, flashed in the strange colours of light emitted by the spirit-grinder device. Crackles of light played across the walls.

'Go,' said Luko. 'Go, get through. Do not give it the chance to…'

Luko's sentence was cut off by the burst of energy that tore across the Panpsychicon. The Space Marines were picked off their feet and slammed into the wall, shattering the mosaics beneath them. Shackles of lightning held them there, struggling against the force. Graevus's mutated arm pushed free of his restraints but the rest of him was held fast.

Luko tried to shut his eyes, but the same force holding him in place was prising them open. He forced himself onto his side and pushed with an arm and a leg, feeling some give in his bonds.

'Resist!' he yelled over the growing sound, a rumble combined with a skull-shuddering whine, emitted by the spirit-grinder as it opened up into a mass of articulated arms dripping with shimmering crystals. 'Resist it. Fight back!'

Luko's bonds snapped. He slid to the floor, still pushed back by the wall of psychic power pulsing from the centre of the room. He could see Sister Aescarion screaming as her body, without the strengthening augmentations of a Space Marine, was battered against the wall like a plaything in the hand of a spiteful child.

Luko took a painful step towards the centre of the room. The apparitions manacled to the floor were writhing, contorted impossibly, as he stepped through them, forcing himself forwards.

*All I want is peace*, said a voice in the back of his head.

'No,' said Luko. 'No. Get out! Get out!' He pushed forwards another step.

He caught sight of his hands. The lightning claw gauntlets were gone. His hands were pitted and rotten, dead flesh peeling away from bone eroded by disease.

He forced himself to see the gauntlets and they crackled back into view, the illusion banished from his mind.

'Do not believe it!' he shouted, not knowing if anyone could hear him. 'We are Space Marines! We shall know no fear!'

The force was gone. Luko fell to the floor. But it was not the deck of a spaceship – it was mud, wet and deep. The hand he threw out to steady himself sunk into the mud up to his elbow and he felt it cold against his face.

Something whistled overhead. An artillery shell. Gunfire crackled from all directions.

Luko was surrounded by war. Mud and trenches, battalions charging to their deaths, armies locked face to face in dense jungles and shattered cities. Burning fighter craft fell like comets overhead. Battleships overturned, spilling thousands into an ocean covered with burning oil.

Luko had been in wars before. He had spent his life in them. But this was different. This was every war he had ever seen, every one he had ever heard of or imagined, all layered on top of one another in an awful mass of solid conflict and death.

He could see billions dying. He could see the face of every man and woman, no matter how distant or confused the slaughter, as they died. They struggled along the gore-filled trenches holding their guts in, laser burns all over their bodies, begging for the Emperor to deliver them death. A legion of them crawled on their bellies, blinded by clouds of corrosive gas, vomiting up a bloody torrent as their insides were eaten away. They screamed in silence, the sound robbed from their voices as they fought against the mudslides and building collapses that entombed them, their lungs crying out for breath they could not draw, limbs and organs crushed. They fell from the sky and were driven mad by the blind horror of a thousand battlefields hurtling up at them. They drowned. They burned alive.

The endless battlefield spread out as far as Luko could comprehend in every direction, and some monstrous trick of dimension told him that it went on forever. It was above him, where the embrace of the void snatched the breath and life from crewmen thrown from ruptured spacecraft. It was below him in the intense heat and pitch darkness where armies fought like rats, ignorant of friend or foe, reduced to terrified animals murdering one another with bare hands and teeth.

The weight of it, the certainty of its unending malice, slammed down on Luko and he could not get to his feet. He was in a filthy trench choked with bodies, a carnivorous jungle humming with disease and the bloating foulness of the dead, a ruined city where men died over a bullet-ridden room or a deathtrap crossroads, the hull of a dying spacecraft where all was darkness and fire. He was at the heart of every war that had ever been fought or ever would, and before him was played out every violent death that the galaxy would ever see.

His body was rotting away because he was dead, and yet he could not die. Death itself was not an escape. He would be here, witness this, forever.

It was not real. Luko knew it was an illusion. But it was not something projected into his mind – it came from inside him.

'Captain!' yelled someone very far away, with the unfamiliar cadence of a woman's voice. 'Captain, focus! Drive it out! Hear me!'

A hundred layers of war were piled up on top of one another. Luko forced himself to look at the bloodshed and the suffering, to go through every incarnation until he found one that didn't fit. A single circular room, haunted and tortured, on a spaceship. He saw himself lying on the floor, convulsing at the mercy of the Panpsychicon's spirit-grinder. He pushed himself to his knees, and so did the Luko he saw. He looked around and saw the face of Sister Aescarion ghosted over the trenchworks and burning fortresses.

Luko lunged drunkenly towards the spirit-grinder. His lightning claw sliced through the tangle of struts and wiring. Crystals rained down and shattered.

Sister Aescarion followed him in destruction. She buried her power axe deep in the machine's core, and grimaced as she tried to wrench it out. Luko was unable to judge distance or direction properly and slashed around him with abandon, scattering components of the psychic machine.

The thousand wars peeled away and fell apart. Fortresses turned to dust. The mud dried and blew away, leaving a desert devoid of battle. The Panpsychicon became the dominant reality, then the only one, and Luko was able to shake the confusion from his mind.

The Space Marines lay in various stages of consciousness. Varnica was on his feet, too. The Imperial Fists were scattered, groaning and shifting as their own realities returned to them.

One did not move. Pallas, holding his own head in pain, knelt beside the Imperial Fist and read his lifesigns off the fallen warrior's armour.

'He is gone,' said Pallas.

'What was his name?' asked Graevus, who forced the words out in between coughs as he knelt, bent double.

'Gorvan,' replied one of the other Imperial Fists.

'Prexus?' said Luko. 'Sergeant?'

Aescarion tapped Luko on the shoulder guard and pointed to the wall near the cell block warren. Prexus sat against the wall, his bolt pistol in his hand, his chainsword discarded on the floor. His head lolled, revealing the massive exit wound in the back of the skull. Prexus's brains were spread up the wall behind him, thrown across the mosaic in the characteristic pattern of a bolter wound.

No one said that Prexus had shot himself. They didn't need to.

'What must he have seen?' said Pallas.

'Think not on it,' said Varnica. 'Let us move. Sister, commend their souls.'

The strikeforce crossed the Panpsychicon, armoured feet crunching through the remains of the psychic machine. Aescarion, head bowed, followed the Space Marines towards the double doors at the far side of the room, murmuring a prayer for the departed.

SARPEDON BRACED HIS remaining talons against the floor and put all his strength into forcing the bridge doors open. The blast doors, automatically sealed in the event of boarders entering the *Phalanx*, creaked and gave way a little. Hydraulic lines split and the resistance lessened, and the doors slid open wide enough to admit the bulk of a Space Marine.

'Daenyathos!' shouted Sarpedon as he stepped onto the bridge of the *Phalanx*.

The bridge was a palace, built to glorify the captain who had once held court there – Rogal Dorn, primarch of the Imperial Fists Legion, the first master of the *Phalanx*. Under him, this ship had darkened the sky of Terra itself when Horus laid siege to the Emperor's Palace. A mighty throne, three storeys high, dominated the bridge, plated with gold. The flight of steps leading to the oversized pulpit-throne was flanked with displayed weapons captured from enemies or discovered during the Great Crusade.

The vast viewscreen facing the throne, taking up most of the curving wall of the bridge, showed a panorama of the Veiled Region, with the star Kravamesh glowing along one edge. Kravamesh had turned dark and smouldering, black swarms scudding across its burnt orange orb, as if the star were drained of power to fuel the gate across to the warp that had brought Abraxes into realspace. Below the screen were dozens of command helms, each controlling one of the *Phalanx*'s many vital systems, and even when stationary they should have been bustling with crewmen and Imperial Fist overseers. Now, only a few slumped dead crewmen remained, felled by bullet wounds where they had sat.

One body was piled on the floor beside his chair. In the chair, at the communications helm, sat a hunched elderly figure, bony fingers playing across the controls. The man turned at Sarpedon's voice, revealing an ancient, lined face broken by a smile.

'Lord Sarpedon,' said the old man. 'For so long I have waited for this. Of all the pieces of Master Daenyathos's future, you are the one that shines the brightest in his plan. I am Father Gyranar, honoured to lead my congregation.'

Sarpedon stalked warily through the bridge, casting his eyes over the monumental sculptures looming in the shadows around the edge of the bridge, the suits of ancient armour gleaming and polished around the foot of the throne-mount. 'Where is Daenyathos?' he said.

Gyranar stood up, his bent frame meaning he was barely taller than when he sat. A trembling finger pointed as the old man took a few steps towards Sarpedon. 'So blessed am I that I lived to see this. I dared not hope it might be during my lifetime that the threads would come together, that the one Daenyathos wrote of would lead his Chapter to the fulfilment of our dreams. But you stand before me, Lord Sarpedon. And we all stand at this confluence of fates.'

Sarpedon hefted the Axe of Mercaeno and scuttled within a lunge and a strike of Gyranar. 'I said, where is Daenyathos?'

'Threaten not those who are merely carried on the eddies of the fates we weave,' came an artificial voice, amplified from somewhere behind the throne-mount. 'Men like Father Gyranar are ignorant of their fate and impotent to change it. But you and I, Sarpedon, we are different. We are the authors of our fates. It takes men like you to forge the channels into which the future will flow. And men like me to decide what that future is.'

The shape of a Space Marine Dreadnought stomped from behind the throne-mount. The colours and heraldry of the Soul Drinkers were polished and gleaming now, as if it had just stepped from the forges of the old Chapter. A missile launcher and a power fist were mounted below its massive shoulders and purity seals fluttered from the blocky mass of the sarcophagus.

'Iktinos told me everything,' said Sarpedon. 'I know why you are here. You will take the *Phalanx* across the galaxy and disgorge Abraxes's armies everywhere you go.'

'That is true,' said Daenyathos. 'But did he tell you why?'

'He tried,' said Sarpedon. 'But I could not believe such a thing spoken from the lips of a Space Marine, even one as corrupted as Iktinos. So I would hear it from you first.'

'It is simple, Sarpedon,' said Daenyathos. The chassis pivoted so that the Dreadnought's head, shaped like an oversized Space Marine helm, looked up at the huge viewscreen and the stretch of void it showed. 'The galaxy is corrupt. Its people are damned and its rulers are cruel. This is the same conclusion as yours, is it not? The Imperium is a dark and savage place, a breeding ground for the desperation that gives the forces of the warp the chance to do their wickedness in our universe. It is through suffering that the Imperium will be remade. Great suffering, on a scale beyond the imaginings of lesser minds. Thanks to the plan crafted by me and executed by many, including you, Abraxes and the *Phalanx* will combine to spread such suffering that the Imperium will be remade stronger and more just.'

'And you will rule it?' said Sarpedon.

'Of course,' replied Daenyathos, the green-lensed eyes of the sarcophagus focusing on Sarpedon again. 'Who else could?'

'You understand,' said Sarpedon, 'that I must try to stop you. I may die, for no doubt you have included this very eventuality in your plan. Nevertheless, if there is the smallest chance that the people of the Imperium can be spared that fate, then I must take it.'

'Of course,' said Daenyathos. 'I would expect nothing less. You have been a loyal servant to me, Sarpedon, though you played your part unknowingly. It pains me not a little to have to kill you. But you will fight to the death to protect the same Imperium you profess to despise, and so I must ensure you hinder me no further.'

'It is the Imperium I hate. Not its people. Its people are innocent.'

'Innocence is a falsehood created by weak and fearful minds,' said Daenyathos.

'Well, then. I do not think there is anything more to say.'

'Indeed, Chapter Master Sarpedon. I would finish this without delay.'

'And I would oblige you.' Sarpedon crouched down on the five legs he had left, Axe of Mercano held low ready to charge.

Daenyathos's targeting auspex flickered as it registered Sarpedon, feeding information into the Dreadnought's internal cogitators.

Sarpedon yelled and sprang to one side as a volley of missiles shrieked from Daenyathos's launcher, and the bridge of the *Phalanx* was suddenly full of fury.

# CHAPTER FOURTEEN

THE SCOUTS BROUGHT back word that the daemons were loading their war engines with ammunition, heaps of smouldering skulls and ballista bolts of ensorcelled brass. The scorpion machine was being filled with boiling venom, biomechanical poison sacs swelling in billows of steam, daemons scrambling across its lacquered carapace.

Word reached the Imperial Fists lines. Chapter Master Pugh made his decision instantly, for there was, in truth, no decision to be made.

Lord Inquisitor Kolgo stood proud of the defences, his Battle Sisters gathered around him, the fires of the daemons' forges flickering against his polished Terminator armour. He watched the daemon masses swarming into formation in response.

'Lackeys of the warp!' yelled Kolgo. 'This is what you begged for. This is why you were spewed from the guts of the immaterium. To face us, the Emperor's own, the shield of Mankind! Well, now you have your wish. Rejoice as we cleave you apart. Give thanks as we shoot you down. This is what you wished for. Come, rush onto our blades!'

The daemons leapt over the barricades of wreckage, shrieking in response. The heralds of their gods bellowed and keened the songs of the warp, and darkness gathered around like the eclipse of a distant sun.

Into the darkness charged the Imperial Fists.

On the map tables of the Tactica Sigismundi were dozens of battlefields rendered in stone miniature, some of them depicting meticulous surgical strikes with every element of an Imperial Fists force working in harmony, perfectly coordinated, each squad shielding the next while catching foes in a lethal crossfire. Others were battles of attrition, the Imperial Fists relying on their enhanced bodies and wargear to keep them fighting when the enemy were breaking down. But some of them, the fewest, were headlong charges, frontal assaults into Hell which only a Space Marine could hope to survive. It was written in the Codex Astartes that a Space Marine should never be used in such a way, that his value to the Imperium was too great to be thrown away in a pell-mell slaughter in the teeth of an entrenched foe.

But the Codex Astartes could not cover every possible battle. It could not predict that one day the *Phalanx* itself would be invaded, and that between its survival and its destruction stood a last-ditch battle where the enemy could only be fought face to face in the open, with no strategy in the Chapter Master's arsenal to change it into anything other than a pitched battle, a duel to the death.

Pugh and Kolgo led the charge. The weapons already operating on the daemon engines opened up and flung burning comets into the midst of the Imperial Fists, throwing armoured bodies into the air. Daemons surged forwards, heedless of organisation or rank, overcome with a lust for the fight that spread like a fire.

This was the way it had to be. Pugh drew the Fangs of Dorn and dived into the mass of daemons. Kolgo followed him in, rotator cannon hammering, the barrels glowing hot.

The rest of the Imperial Fists crashed into the enemy. If they were to die, it would be in defence of their Chapter. Few of them gave any thought to the chance they might live.

SARPEDON SKIDDED ALONG the floor of the bridge as the missiles streaked over him, the sound of the air ripping behind him as scalding rocket exhaust billowed around him. The sound of the impacts behind him was so loud it wasn't even a sound, just a white wall of noise that blocked out all hearing except for the alien echo rippling around the *Phalanx's* bridge.

Sarpedon was ready for the shockwave. He took the worst of it on his shoulder and let the impact throw him into the foot of the throne pedestal, front legs collapsing beneath him to absorb the impact.

Father Gyranar disappeared in the mass of smoke and flame. Shattered components from consoles rained down, chunks of burning metal and cabling. Cracks ran up the viewscreen, marring the view of the Veiled Region with black jagged fingers.

Sarpedon dragged himself into the dubious cover of the nearest statue, an Imperial Fists Apothecary plated in gold.

'Did you think,' said Daenyathos's artificial voice from the throne, 'that I had not thought I would face you one day? You, or someone like you. Why do you believe I selected a Dreadnought as my vessel?'

Sarpedon hauled himself up the nest few steps, crouching down behind a statue of an Emperor's Champion from some campaign of distant legend. His nervous system seemed struck out of kilter by the missile impacts, his legs uncoordinated, his head ringing.

'If you know the future,' said Sarpedon, forcing his mind to keep up with his surroundings, 'then you know how this ends.'

The response was another burst of missiles, triple contrails spiralling towards Sarpedon. The Space Marine flung him across the steps leading up to the throne. The Emperor's Champion disappeared in a burst of golden shrapnel, and the other two missiles howled past to impact against the viewscreen. Sarpedon dug in with claws and fingers, clinging to the side of the throne pedestal. Bursts of pain against the side of his face registered, in a detached, soldierly way, as shards of shrapnel embedded in his skull. One eye suddenly shut down, his vision cut in half, depth gone, the scene in front of him becoming ever more otherworldly.

Massive shards of the viewscreen fell away like black glass daggers, shattering against the floor. Chunks of the Veiled Region seemed to have fallen away with it, the galaxy turning dark piece by piece, a broken mosaic of decay.

Sarpedon's nervous system caught up and the wrenching pain from his hips told him he had been hit worse than he realised. He looked down at the pulpy mess of fibrous muscle and broken exoskeleton. He had three legs left, and chunks of mutated limb lay straggling down the steps behind him. No wonder he had felt out of control. He was trying to push himself forwards on legs he didn't have.

Sarpedon scrambled forwards a little further, to the shadow of the throne. Daenyathos was in silhouette, the light from the viewscreen having died, and looming over Sarpedon he looked less like a Dreadnought and more like the vision that Sarpedon had forced into Iktinos's mind – vast, monstrous, toweringly powerful, invulnerable to the efforts of a mere man.

'It could have been anyone,' continued Daenyathos, the missile ports on his arm closing. 'Caeon could have led the Chapter astray. Gorgoleon. Iktinos. It could have happened centuries earlier or later. Whoever it was, I always knew I would have to face one of you. For you, this is the end. For me, this is just another footnote.'

The storm bolter on Daenyathos's power fist arm clicked its action and Sarpedon was suddenly looking down its barrel. Daenyathos couldn't fire any more missiles – Sarpedon was too close, the shrapnel too dangerous. Daenyathos could not risk damaging his Dreadnought chassis now.

Sarpedon tried to take cover again but Daenyathos's aim was too good. The first volley of bolter fire shredded the step in front of him, gold plate and granite dissolving under his hands. The second slammed two shots into his torso, the bolter shells penetrating the ceramite and bursting against Sarpedon's breastplate of fused ribs.

He felt the bone breaking. The sensation was clear among the shock that hammered through him. Twin craters were blown open in his chest and the air touched the mass of his lungs, the pulsing surface of his heart. Sarpedon fell onto the steps and rolled onto his back, gasping as his body recoiled.

He was a Space Marine. He would survive this. He could survive anything. Before, he had doubted. But now, so close to death, his certainty was complete. He would survive this. He was Sarpedon, Chapter Master of the Soul Drinkers, a man the galaxy had sought to kill, yet who had survived long enough to breathe the same air as the only enemy he had ever really had.

Sarpedon planted a hand on the step in front of him and turned himself over. His remaining legs fought to push him up onto his talons. He looked up, blood running down his face, thick gobbets of it pumping from the wounds in his chest. The Axe of Mercaeno was still in his hand.

'There is no future,' he said through blood-spittled lips. 'There will be others like us. They will break out of this cage of a galaxy, they will bypass everything you have engineered to stop you. Human beings cannot be kept caged by fate. Not all of them. Someone will remember us, and someone will follow.'

Daenyathos took careful aim and blasted another storm bolter volley into Sarpedon. This one hit the wrist and elbow of his right hand, the one in which he was carrying the Axe of Mercaeno. The bones of Sarpedon's forearm shattered and his arm fell useless, the Axe of Mercaeno clattering down the steps.

The pain did not come. Sarpedon did not let it. He forged forwards a few steps more, so the massive armoured legs of Daenyathos's Dreadnought were just a couple of metres from his face.

Daenyathos's power fist reached down and snatched Sarpedon up off the floor, the articulated fingers closing around his shoulders and waist. Sarpedon's head lolled like that of a rag doll, his legs dangling uselessly under him, as he was held immobile up in front of Daenyathos.

Sarpedon could see, through the eyepieces of Daenyathos's armoured helm, the eyes of the man inside. They were full of amusement, as if Sarpedon were an animal or a child playing at being a soldier, something to be pitied and taught its place, something to be mocked.

'Did you truly think something like you,' mocked Daenyathos, 'could kill me?'

'I didn't have to kill you,' replied Sarpedon. 'I just had to get you close.'

Sarpedon's one good hand reached into the ammo pouch at his waist. Daenyathos registered what Sarpedon was doing and the servos in his power fist whined.

The massive fingers of the fist closed. Sarpedon could feel the ceramite around his torso tensing and buckling, massive pressure crushing down. The seconds stretched out and he imagined, in precise detail, how his organs would look being forced out of his chest under the pressure, hearts bursting, tatters of lungs oozing out, entrails following, the awful wrongness of his distorted body filling him in the moments before death.

It seemed an age before his fingers closed around the haft of the Soulspear.

The artefact's twin blades speared outwards, caged vortex fields consisting of anti-space where no material substance could exist.

The pressure forced Sarpedon's right arm out of place. His shoulder blade split and the joint crumbled. Each segment of the destruction registered like stages in a scientific experiment, observed with calmness and detachment in those moments before the pain receptors fired and reached Sarpedon's brain.

Sarpedon whipped the Soulspear up, one blade swinging up through the sarcophagus that made up the armoured centre of the Dreadnought. Sarpedon's wrist flicked and the other blade arced up to complete the cut, two slashes of blackness that between them formed a plane separating the front of the sarcophagus from the body of the dreadnought.

The pressure relented. The power fist fell inactive, the energy no longer focused through its servos to crush Sarpedon's torso.

The energy finally went out of Sarpedon. The weight of the Soulspear, negligible as it was compared to a boltgun or the Axe of Mercaeno, was too much. The weapon fell from his fingers. The blades disappeared and the short metal length of its haft tumbled down the steps before the throne.

The front of Daenyathos's sarcophagus followed. It clanged as it fell end over end down the steps, the sound echoing off the walls of the bridge, the final sound as it hit the floor like the tolling of a bell.

Sarpedon's breaths were shallow. The ruination of his shoulder hit him and the pain was like a sun burning where his shoulder had once been, a ball of fire surrounding the mass of ripped muscle and cracked bone.

He forced the pain down. He had suffered before. It meant nothing. His eyes focused, and he was looking into the face of Daenyathos.

The whole front of the sarcophagus was gone, and the life support cradle was revealed in which Daenyathos had spent the last six thousand years. It was a biomechanical tangle of cabling and artificial organs, pipes and valves hissing cold vapour, blinking readouts mottled with the patina of centuries.

The Philosopher-Soldier hung among the cabling, restrains locking him into the life support systems. He was pale and withered, his limbs atrophied, the skin shrunken around his skull and ribcage. Red welts had swollen up where pipes and wires pierced his skin, carrying the mental signals that moved the Dreadnought body around him. His eyes were squinting in the sudden light, pupils shrunk to nothing.

Sarpedon had never seen such a pathetic example of a Space Marine. The musculature was gone, the skin stretched around a body starved of movement for six millennia. Daenyathos gasped in shock, the feeling of outside air alien to him now.

The grip of the power fist relaxed. Sarpedon clattered

onto the steps of the throne mount. Daenyathos was
in shock, unable to function, and for a few seconds
he would be unable to know where – or even what –
Sarpedon was.

Sarpedon, one arm hanging limp and useless at
his side, clambered up the front of the Dreadnought
until he was level with Daenyathos. He tore out handfuls of cabling, wires slithering out of Daenyathos's
stick-thin limbs. Dribbles of watery blood spattered
onto the gilded steps. Sarpedon grasped Daenyathos around the neck – his hand easily encircling the
scrawny throat – and pulled Daenyathos out of the
sarcophagus.

The Philosopher-Soldier's body came away easily,
Daenyathos unable to put up a fight. Sarpedon carried him down the steps to the deck of the bridge,
his remaining talons kicking aside chunks of smouldering debris. The Dreadnought chassis remained
standing before the bridge captain's throne, gutted of
its occupant, silent and unmoving.

'Wait,' gasped Daenyathos in a voice that could
barely struggle above a whisper. 'You are a part of
this. You can be something great. Imagine the role
you could play in a galaxy remade by me. Imagine it.'

'I have a better imagination than you realise,' said
Sarpedon, grimacing as he dragged himself towards
the blast doors at the back of the bridge. 'I have seen
it, and it is no place for me.'

'Where are you taking me?' hissed Daenyathos, a
desperation in his voice that had never been there
before.

Sarpedon did not answer. Daenyathos's protests

were lost in the sound of the flames licking up from the ruined bridge.

'FORGE ON,' CRIED Luko as he forced himself another pace through the sucking mire of gore. 'Just a few paces more. Onwards, there he stands, our prey. Onwards!'

The daemonic cyst had responded to the strike force like an organ threatened by infection. It had filled back up with blood, its fleshy walls erupting in tentacles to snare the intruders and drag them down into the gore. Attendant daemons had uncoiled from the filth and leapt to attack.

Abraxes stood up from his throne of twisted corpses, the spectral image of the battle on the barracks deck fading around him as the newcomers grabbed his attention.

'You are beneath my notice, and yet I must stoop to kill you,' he said, his voice like a bass choir. 'Your presence offends me.'

The remnants of Squad Prexus crashed into the horrors forging through the lake of blood. The Imperial Fists wrestled with things that grew new limbs and fanged mouths at will. One Space Marine was dragged down into the blood and half a dozen horrors leapt on top of him. Spiny hands ripped him apart. An armoured leg was thrown between them, a trophy of the hunt, and the warrior's head was pitched against the fleshy wall.

Sister Aescarion and Graevus fought like one individual, the axe of one parrying while the other struck. The two whirled in a dance that took them through

the assaulting daemons, cutting mutating bodies
open and shattering horned skulls. Luko followed
in their wake, stabbing the surviving daemons with
both lightning claws, lifting them proud of the blood
and thrashing them into shreds.

Behind Abraxes burned the portal. It was a shimmering circle, edged in blue fire. Beyond it could
be glimpsed something that resembled the void of
space only in its darkness. The masses of power, like
mountains of seething energy, loomed in that darkness, and carried with them a sense of appalling
intelligence. They were watching, these powers of the
warp, eager for the last obstacles to be removed so
they could force the whole potential of their chaotic
hatred through into realspace.

The sight of them could drive men mad. The Space
Marines had to force their eyes away, for they could
become lost in contemplation of that towering evil.
Even this slight glimpse of the warp could corrode
the mind. On the shore in front of the portal were
still engraved, on the rotten remains of the cargo bay
deck, the sigils that had called the portal into beings,
and they burned blood-red with anticipation.

Abraxes strode into the gore. A blade appeared in
his hand, a sword of frozen malice, and he cleaved it
down into the battle around his feet.

Luko felt his gut tighten as he saw Apothecary Pallas in the blade's path. Pallas tried to yell something
in defiance, but Abraxes was pitiless and did not grant
him the chance. The blade carved down through Pallas's shoulder and came out through his abdomen
on the other side, slicing him in two across the torso.

The two halves of the Apothecary's corpse flopped into the blood. Daemons pounced on them to tear the remains apart.

Luko realised he was yelling, a cry of horror and anguish. Pallas was his friend, in a galaxy where friends were rare.

Aescarion reached the shore where Abraxes's throne stood. Graevus was still waist-deep in the blood, fending off the daemons that sought to drag them both down.

'What means your strength?' shouted Aescarion over the cackling of daemons and the thrumming of the gate. 'That your arm can lay low a Space Marine? What does this mean laid against the might of the God-Emperor's children?'

Abraxes turned to look down at the Battle Sister. 'It means that you die, whelpling girl,' he replied, shaking Pallas's blood from his sword.

'Destroy my body if you will,' shouted back Aescarion. 'But you cannot break my spirit. A prince of daemons might claim the heads of every enemy he faces, but he will never count the soul of a Battle Sister as a trophy!'

Abraxes raised a hand, and purple-black fire flickered between his talons. 'You do not challenge the warp, child,' he sneered. 'I shall keep your mind as a pet, and you will worship me.'

Fire lashed down at Aescarion. The Sister of Battle was driven back by the force that hammered into her, and a halo of flame played around her head as Abraxes's magic tried to force open her mind.

The Battle Sister screamed, but she did not fall.

Luko realised what Sister Aescarion was trying to do. He threw aside the body of the daemon he had killed, and pushed on through the gore.

LIBRARIAN VARNICA REACHED the metallic shore. The portal howled above him, the winds of the warp tearing at him as he tried to keep his footing. He clambered out of the blood, kicking free of the sucking limbs that tried to ensnare his ankles.

He had to force himself not to stare up through the portal. He could feel the vast intelligences beyond probing at his mind, pushing against the mental shield that every Librarian built up over years of psychic training. They were whispering to him, promising him power and lifetimes of pleasure, or threatening him with such horrors a human mind could not comprehend.

Varnica snapped himself free of their influence. He could not let them trick him, not now, not when he was so close, when the means for closing the portal were right in front of him.

He broke the fascination with the portal just in time to register the power hammer arcing towards him.

Varnica brought up his force claw to turn the hammer aside. The hammer's head slammed into the ground, throwing shards of metal everywhere. Varnica rolled back, shrapnel pinging off his armour.

Reinez stood over him. The Crimson Fist was a hideous sight – scorched and battered, his helmetless skull little more that burns and new scars. The deep blue and crimson of his armour was almost lost under the grime of battle. Reinez pointed his hammer at Varnica.

'You,' he said. 'You spoke against them. Now you fight alongside them. You fight to take the gate for yourselves! You are one with them in perdition!'

'Damn you, Reinez!' retorted Varnica. 'Have you become so blind? The warp has played us all; you, me, the Soul Drinkers, all of us, and we have to put it right!'

'Lies!' yelled Reinez.

Anger made him careless. The hammer blow was a haymaker and Varnica dodged back from it easily, raising his claw ready to snap it forwards. But Reinez had strength on his side, born of a desperate hatred. If Varnica was caught, he would die.

Varnica's muscles tensed for the strike. But it felt like he had hit a wall, as if something invisible was holding him fast.

His enemy was a Space Marine. Varnica had never raised arms against a brother of the Adeptus Astartes before. The wrongness of it stayed his hand. He could not shed a brother's blood. Even now, with all Hell erupting around him, he could not do it.

Reinez jinked forwards and drove the butt of the hammer into Varnica's midriff. Varnica stumbled back, almost pitching into the blood. Varnica kicked out at Reinez's legs and the Crimson Fist was caught, stumbling a half-pace onto one knee. Varnica rolled out of his way and used the second he had bought to jump back to his feet.

'Think, Reinez!' said Varnica. 'The warp has used your anger. It has turned you against your brothers! Join us and help end all this!'

Reinez's reply was a wild swing that almost took Varnica's head off. Varnica forced his eyes away from the hellish vastness of the portal overhead, channelled a torrent of psychic power into his claw, and prepared to take a Space Marine's life for the first time.

SISTER AESCARION FELT her mind pried from her head and crushed in Abraxes's claw.

She fell to her knees. The screaming agony in her head blocked out everything save the shadowy image of Abraxes, edged in black fire, and the wicked bone-white slash of his grin.

She felt a million vicious hands reaching through her soul and clawing at the inside of her head. She heard a million voices cackling about what they would do to her when she was broken. Place her in the body of a monster, rampaging through the warp's enemies, fuelled by her pain. Rend her into a thousand pieces, each one imprisoned in some maze of torment. Send her shrieking through the immaterium, a formless ghost driven mad by the warp's malice. Turn her into one of them. Use her as their slave and visit a million indignities upon her.

The tiny sliver of Aescarion that remained scrabbled at the walls of her skull, trying to find some purchase to keep herself from falling into nothingness. Then, she found it.

A golden figure, his armour burning with the fire of faith, in his hand a blade that was justice. He was crowned with dominion over Mankind. The Emperor, the protector of the human race. Though

Aescarion might have nothing left save that which was in Abraxes's hand, she still had her faith. That was something the daemon prince could never have. That was what she had taunted him with – that core of her, the armoured and inviolate place that all the powers of the warp could never hope to breach.

Abraxes roared. He wanted it. He wanted to shatter that faith. But he could not. She denied him, and in his rage he forgot everything else unfolding around him.

LUKO SCRAMBLED UP the pinnacle on which Daenyathos had stood to watch the opening of the portal. The spire of corroded metal still stood proud of the gore, its pitted surface affording enough hand and footholds for Luko to reach the top. From here he could see the whole cyst, and the sheer futility his strike force faced.

Three Imperial Fists remained. Graevus fought off the daemons trying to rush Sister Aescarion. Aescarion was on her knees, screaming, linked to Abraxes by a torrent of black flame pouring from the daemon prince's hand. Varnica was wrestling at the threshold of the warp portal with Reinez, the Crimson Fist kneeling on Varnica's chest and pounding down at the Librarian with gauntleted fists.

Each Space Marine was an island in a sea of daemons. More of the things were emerging from the gore with every moment, and it would take seconds for them to overwhelm the warriors.

One part of Luko told him that they had done well to get this far, that to die facing Abraxes toe-to-toe was as good a death as any of them could have hoped to drag back from fate.

But the rest of him, the greater part, was driven only by rage. The Soul Drinkers had destroyed Abraxes once already, and lost many of their battle-brothers in doing so. Now he had returned as if he had a right to walk in the same universe as the Soul Drinkers, as if the lives lost to banish him had meant nothing.

Sarpedon had impaled Abraxes on the Soulspear, an image still burned into Luko's mind. It had been the moment that the warriors of the Chapter realised what they must truly be – slave to neither the Imperium nor the warp. Abraxes's return had undone that moment. That he had dared, that he had sought to make the Soul Drinkers very existence meaningless, sent anger pouring through Luko that he couldn't have stemmed if he had wanted to.

And he didn't want to. It felt good. This was what warriors spoke of when they talked of the glory, the rush, of battle. This was what Luko had never truly felt; now it was impossible to resist.

He crouched and drew back both claws, an animal ready to pounce. Abraxes's attention was focused on Sister Aescarion and the daemon prince had no idea Luko was even there.

It would be a difficult leap. There was nothing easy about what he would have to do if he made the jump. But the anger in him swallowed up those useless facts and bade him dive from the pinnacle towards the twisted grin on Abraxes's face.

\* \* \*

AESCARION SAW THROUGH her haze of pain as Luko dived towards Abraxes. The Soul Drinker thrust his twin lightning claws into the daemon's face.

The claws punched through Abraxes's skin around his left eye, sinking up to the knuckle. Luko braced his feet against the daemon's upper chest and yelled as he pulled, muscles of his neck standing out as sharp cords as he put all his considerable strength into it.

Abraxes had not seen it coming. He had been savouring peeling apart Aescarion's mind, and the shock of Luko's assault stunned him for a moment. That was all the time Luko need to wrench Abraxes's eye out of its socket, a flourish of his claws throwing the orb down to the bloody shore like a comet with a tail of ragged flesh.

Abraxes screamed. Wrapped up in his howl was a strangely human sound, a note of pain and shock. It was the first sign of weakness Abraxes had shown, an echo of some frailty that a human could recognise. He took a step backwards, scattering bodies from the foot of his throne as he stumbled towards the portal.

Luko hit the ground hard beside Aescarion. She still knelt, one hand on the floor, hair clinging to the sweat on her face. She was pale and blood ran from her nose and ears.

Luko looked away from her. The momentum he had bought would not last for long. Aescarion would have to fend for herself.

Luko ran forwards, rolled past Abraxes's cloven foot and slashed at the back of his ankle. His claws bit through daemonic flesh and severed tendons whipped from the gash. Abraxes fell back another half-pace, his screams turning to anger.

Graevus leapt from the gore to join Luko. His axe hacked down into Abraxes's knee and the leg buckled, Abraxes putting a hand down to steady himself.

Abraxes, falling back, had passed halfway through the warp portal behind him. His hand pushed down against a silvery island of power that gathered in the warp, the dark intelligences of the immaterium buoying him up. They would force him forwards again, expel him from the haven of the warp to finish the job of killing the Space Marine standing between the Dark Gods and an eternity of slaughter.

Graevus leapt up onto Abraxes's chest.

'We killed you once,' he snarled, swinging his axe up high. 'And this time, we've had practice.'

Graevus drove the axe down into the daemon prince's chest. The blade carved down through muscle and bone. From the cavernous wound burst a fountain of light, raw power unleashed like blood from an artery. It caught Graevus square in the chest and threw the Soul Drinker to the ground, armour smoking.

Abraxes got onto one knee and held his sword up, point first. Glowing blood poured from his ruined eye as he measured the blow and stabbed the sword down into Graevus's right hip, impaling the Space Marine through the meat of his leg and pinning him to the ground.

'Killed me?' hissed the daemon prince. 'Soul Drinker, you did nothing that day but bring your own death a moment closer!' Abraxes twisted the blade and Graevus's leg came apart, a welter of blood mixing with the gore spattered across the metallic ground in front of the portal. Graevus screamed and his axe fell from his mutant hand.

Luko charged at Abraxes, knocking the blade aside with a swipe of both claws. Abraxes's remaining eye narrowed as it focused on Luko.

REINEZ KNEED VARNICA in the midriff hard enough to dent his armour. The Librarian fell to the ground and Reinez straddled his chest, bringing his hammer over Varnica's skull head-down, ready to piston it into the Doom Eagle's face.

Reinez's gaze fell on the lump of seething putrescence that a few moments a go had been Abraxes's eye. It lay in a whiteish mass, dissolving its way through the cargo bay floor, its pupil breaking up in its corrupt substance.

Beyond the eye, Luko was battling the daemon prince, fending off a swipe of the daemon's claws with his own gauntlets.

'We're trying to kill it,' said Varnica, following Reinez's gaze. 'It's the only real enemy here. No matter what you think of us, Reinez, killing Abraxes goes beyond it.'

Reinez said nothing. Varnica rolled out from under him, struggling to one knee. He was battered and broken, bones fractured all over his body, bruised organs bleeding inside. Reinez was a better warrior than Varnica. If he made the decision, the Crimson Fist would kill him.

Varnica saw, as Reinez did, that Abraxes was halfway through the portal, straddling the gap between reality and the warp.

'We have to close it,' said Varnica. He pointed to the sigils on the floor beneath the feet of the two warriors. 'The blood of Dorn opened it. The same blood will close it.'

'You spoke against them,' said Reinez, breath heavy. 'You… you wanted them dead.'

'No one is leaving this place alive, Reinez,' said Varnica. 'The Soul Drinkers will die. You have your wish. Now kill this blasphemy. Guilliman's blood runs in my veins, and Throne only knows what runs in the Soul Drinkers. Only Dorn's blood will seal the gate. Only yours.'

Varnica couldn't be sure if Reinez understood. He certainly couldn't be certain that the Crimson Fist, as he stepped back and dropped his guard, was inviting him to strike. Perhaps Reinez left himself undefended as he absorbed the realisation that Abraxes was the true force for destruction, that the Soul Drinkers, the *Phalanx*, the carnage around him were all parts of what the Daenyathos and the daemon prince had orchestrated. Or perhaps he really did understand that his blood alone would seal the gate, just like N'Kalo's had opened it.

Varnica did not wait for clarification.

He forced every drop of pain in him into the pit of his mind, and channelled it, ice-cold, into the psychic circuits built into his force claw. He lunged and punched the claw into Reinez's chest.

The Crimson Fist's mouth opened and a breath escaped him, the shock to his body too much for him to form words.

Varnica yelled and the psychic power discharged

like a massive electrical surge through the claw, the Hammerhand snapping the blades open and tearing Reinez's chest almost in two. Organs glinted for a moment in red light bathing the cyst.

Reinez fell back and the wellspring of blood inside him burst up through his ruined chest. The blood of a Crimson Fist, spiced with the gene-seed taken from the genetic print of Rogal Dorn, washed over the glowing symbols on the floor.

Varnica placed a palm on the floor, Reinez's blood lapping around it. He had unleashed a great deal of his psychic reserves in killing Reinez – Reinez, as hard to kill as he was, had needed a massive burst of psychic power to ensure his death. Varnica would have to use everything he had left, drain himself past the limit of safety – and sanity.

Varnica wrapped his mind around the unreality of the portal above him, drawing on the power that surged through the sigils on the floor, and began to crush the warp portal closed with the force of his will.

LUKO LEAPED OVER the stricken Graevus and slammed into Abraxes. He speared both claws into the sides of the daemon's jaw and headbutted Abraxes in the nose. Gristle split and blood sprayed. Abraxes shook his head and threw Luko off.

Luko skidded along the blood-slick ground. Graevus was trying to get to his feet nearby, one leg buckling under him, his thigh a bloody ruin of pulpy flesh and shattered bone.

'What matters this effort?' said Abraxes. 'Why must you fill what remains of your lives with such toil?'

'Think on what remains of your life, daemon,' spat Luko. 'My toil will go on. Yours ends here.'

'Pitiful,' sneered Abraxes. 'Which one of you can face me that will not pay for it with his life? What mere man stands my equal, to fence words with me?'

'I seem to remember,' said Luko, 'that it was a mere man who speared you through the chest and threw you back to the warp to begin with. It was men who brought you back. *You* should be kneeling to *us*.'

Abraxes bellowed in rage. He snatched up his fallen blade and charged. Luko met the charge with his own, shoulder down, sprinting at the daemon prince. Luko dropped to the ground and rolled, just as Abraxes's sword sliced towards him at chest height. The blade passed over him and Luko sprang up, driving both claws through Abraxes's foot.

Abraxes bellowed and wrenched his foot off the ground, Luko's claws sliding from the flesh. The daemon prince took another step back, and blinded for the moment by his anger, he did not see that once more his back foot passed beyond the boundary of the warp gate.

The circumference of the gate shrunk. Varnica was closing it, metre by metre. Luko ran forwards and speared down through Abraxes's other foot, pinning it to the ground. The power field discharged in a staccato of noise and light, energy arcing to the floor.

The warp gate's uppermost edge closed down on Abraxes, like a slow-motion guillotine. Abraxes saw, perhaps a second or two too late, what Luko was trying to do.

A single Space Marine could not kill Abraxes.

Sarpedon had managed it, but he was a mutant beyond a human's strength and speed, and he had wielded the Soulspear. Luko couldn't do it on his own. But he didn't have to.

The edge of the shrinking gate bit down into Abraxes's shoulder. It sliced through tendons and bone, and daemonic blood dribbled glowing from the wound. Abraxes's face creased in agony and shock.

He tried to force himself out from the gate, but Luko kept him pinned in place. The gate bit down further into Abraxes's upper chest, and blood sprayed now from sundered arteries.

From beyond the portal, from the endless masses of hatred that boiled there, a terrible wave of scorn burst out. The warp's evils saw their servant trapped and dying, and saw all that he had promised withering away. The strands of fate he had woven, which would take him across the galaxy disgorging the warp's malice in the form of torrents of daemons, were snapping. The future galaxy where the *Phalanx* travelled the stars bringing Chaos everywhere it went, that dark tapestry Abraxes had concocted with the human Daenyathos, was unravelling.

They were disappointed. Whatever they truly were, whatever passed for emotions in their godlike souls, the powers of the warp were most disappointed in Abraxes's failure.

The daemon screamed, but the sound did not last long. His lungs and windpipe were severed. His body reformed around the damage, echoing the mutability of the horrors he commanded, but it was not enough. Tentacles slithered from his wounds and bony growths burst in every direction, but the force was too great.

Luko pulled his claws out and stumbled backwards. The portal was closing, and it was cutting the daemon prince in two. Abraxes was wedged in, the sides of the portal slicing into him – he didn't need Luko keeping him in place now.

Luko knelt beside Graevus. 'Come, brother,' he said.

'Where?' said Graevus, watching the portal slicing down through Abraxes's sternum into his abdomen. 'There is nowhere left for us.'

'There is one place,' said Luko. 'Let's go.'

CAPTAIN BORGANOR'S HOWLING Griffons smashed into the daemonic host, joining the Imperial Fists in the wild melee seething around the daemon engines.

But the daemons were legion. Tens of thousands had gathered, and every one now dived into the slaughter. The scorpion-like daemon engine rumbled and raised its segmented body up on eight armoured legs, the tail coiling over its back.

On columns of fire, the Angels Sanguine leapt through the air onto the daemon engine. The engine shuddered and its tail swept them off its back. Commander Gethsemar was thrown to the ground and the engine's insectoid head loomed over him, bronze mandibles dribbling liquid metal.

'Not yet, brother!' shouted a voice, and Siege-Captain Daviks plunged out of the daemon throng to grab the Angel Sanguine by the gorget. He dragged Gethsemar out of the way of the engine, even as it vomited molten metal from its fanged mouth.

A hundred similar stories were playing out amid the butchery. Men were dying for their brothers, or killing all around them in revenge for seeing their friends fall. But there would be no one to remember them.

The daemonic army was too big. The war engines were being completed even as daemon blood swamped the deck, ankle-deep. The Imperial Fists and the Howling Griffons, and all the souls who had come to the *Phalanx* for the trial of the Soul Drinkers, were going to die there.

A terrible scream erupted from every direction at once. It was a strong as a gale, and it shuddered the fabric of the *Phalanx*. Space Marines stumbled, stunned by the force of the noise. But daemon hands and blades did not take advantage of the distraction to cut the Space Marines down.

The daemons were howling, but not with rage – they were struck with a terrible anguish, dropping to their knees or just standing and screaming. Iron swords fell from bloodletters' hands. Horrors turned in on themselves, liquid flesh imploding constantly as if trying to escape to some place inside.

Pugh shook the bedlam from his head. It was a sound of abandonment and death, the dying cry of something tremendously powerful, something that had not believed it could die.

'Abraxes has fallen!' yelled Pugh, barely even to hear himself over the echo in his ears. 'The head of the beast has been struck off! Brothers, sisters, sons and daughters of the Emperor! Call down death on what remains!'

The Fangs of Dorn seemed to flash of their own accord in his hands, stabbing through the crush of daemons around him. Gethsemar and Daviks got to their feet, pushing back the horrors that had closed in over them, and fought side by side as the warriors of their Chapters carved through the mass to reach them.

Lord Inquisitor Kolgo shouldered his way into the shadow of the daemon engine. His rotator cannon hammered volley after volley into the bronze skull of the engine, and the machine reeled as if in shock, the daemons possessing it unable to strike back. The Battle Sisters accompanying the Inquisitor lent their own fire, and heavy weapons from Imperial Fists at the back of the battlefield sheared its legs off and bored bleeding holes in its carapace. A burst of las-cannon fire severed its tail and the weapon toppled to the ground without firing a shot. Stricken, the daemon engine let out a metallic groan as it sunk to the ground, accompanied by the shrieks of the daemon spirits inhabiting it.

Lysander led the way. His thunder hammer was a beacon that the other Imperial Fists followed. It rose and fell, leaving mountains of torn bodies and lakes of daemon blood in its wake. The Imperial Fists rampaged over the barricades and stormed through the daemon forges, clambering over the unfinished war engines to batter back the warp spawn that tried to regroup to face them.

The daemons fought with no coordination or intelligence. Many collapsed, flesh discorporating as the warp-magic that sustained them in realspace failed.

The Imperial Fists gathered in firing lines to shred their enemies with bolter fire, or launched massed assaults with chainblades and glaives. Siege-Captain Daviks and the surviving Silver Skulls directed the heavy weapons towards the largest daemons, the warp-heralds, before they could organise a resistance.

It was grim, bloody work. There was no joy in this victory. It was a crude and brutal business, wading through the remains of the enemy, as the Imperial Fists passed through the forges and pushed on towards the cargo bays where the heart of the infestation had been planted.

Varnica picked up the semi-conscious Sister Aescarion and carried her clear of the collapsing portal. Abraxes was dead, his physical form split almost in two by the shrinking portal, and his spirit ripped out and thrown back into the cauldron of the warp to be punished. Luko and Graevus knelt by the portal and Varnica followed their gaze as they looked across the cyst to where the first of the Imperial Fists were entering.

Lysander was the first to wade towards the collapsing portal, through the blood which was choked with the bodies of daemons and the strike force's Imperial Fists. The captain cast an eye over the carnage, over the unnatural warping of the ship around him, at the sorry remains of Apothecary Pallas, Reinez, and the last of Prexus's squad.

'Brother Varnica,' said Lysander. 'Is it done?'

'It is done,' said Varnica. 'I and this Battle Sister, and these two Soul Drinkers, are the only survivors. But it is done.'

Lysander stepped up onto the ground that broke the blood surface around Abraxes's throne. The throne of corpses was withering and flaking into dust, as if years of decay were piling on them at once. 'Captain Luko. And Brother Graevus, if I am not mistaken.' He held out a hand. 'There is nothing left for you to fight for. I am sure that many will argue for leniency, but you are still in the custody of the Imperial Fists. Come with me.'

Luko stood up, and hauled Graevus unsteadily onto his feet. Beside him, the portal had shrunk to just over head height, and Abraxes's body was cut all the way down through his abdomen, leaving the half outside the portal completely severed.

'Captain Lysander,' said Luko, 'there is no place in this galaxy for the Soul Drinkers. Not in the cells of the *Phalanx*, or in the grip of whatever punishment is decided for us. Not even in freedom. The whole galaxy has been against us for so long that there is nowhere we could go and nothing we could do. So no, we will not hand ourselves over to your custody.'

'I'm ready,' said Graevus.

'As am I, brother,' said Luko. He looked back towards Lysander, and the other Imperial Fists making their way into the cyst. 'Wish us luck. You are our brothers, in spite of everything. I have one thing to ask of you. The Inquisition tried to delete us from history. Please, make sure that we are not forgotten.'

Luko helped Graevus limp towards the portal. Lysander watched them go, and with a wave of his hand stayed the guns of his Imperial Fists.

Luko and Graevus walked through the portal, into

the warp, into whatever waited for them there.

The portal closed completely, cutting off the madness of the warp from realspace, and the cyst fell dark.

IT WAS SOME time later, as the Imperial Fists and Howling Griffons were killing off the last of the daemons running loose around the cyst, that a blade of black energy sliced through the fleshy growths on the walls. Behind the growth was a doorway from one of the other cargo holds, in the direction of the *Phalanx's* bridge. The blade was that of the Soulspear, and it was in the hand of Sarpedon.

The Chapter Master of the Soul Drinkers was near death. Torn stumps of legs dripped ichor. Half his face and one eye were a torn mess, shredded by shrapnel still poking from the pulpy flesh. Open bullet wounds, plugged by congealed blood, were livid against his chest, and one arm hung shattered from a twisted shoulder joint. Sarpedon seemed barely able to walk on the three legs that remained – but the Imperial Fists did not see a defeated man. Wounded, near death, but not defeated.

Sarpedon placed the Soulspear's haft back in an ammo pouch and picked up a pale, tangled shape at his feet – a body, atrophied with age, which had once been that of a Space Marine.

The Imperial Fists gathered without an order, their bolters levelled at Sarpedon. Chapter Master Pugh stood to their front, both Fangs of Dorn in hand.

Sarpedon limped to where half of Abraxes's corpse still lay, his blood drying on the sigils scorched into the floor. They were all that remained of the portal

that had opened there. The Imperial Fists saw the
wounds on Sarpedon, the torn stumps of severed
legs, the twisted shoulder and dented armour. Sarpedon looked like he had gone through enough to kill
any other warrior of the Adeptus Astartes twice over.

Sarpedon held up the body in his hand, carrying it
by the scruff of the neck. It was alive, and it looked
across the assembled Imperial Fists with fear on its
face.

'This is Daenyathos,' said Sarpedon, 'This is the
man who brought Abraxes forth from the warp. This
is the man who manipulated my Chapter and yours,
because he believed that mankind had to suffer to
make it stronger.'

Imperial Fists took aim along their bolter sights at
the mutant.

'Hold your fire, brothers,' said Pugh.

'But he was wrong.' Sarpedon dropped his arm
and let Daenyathos hang down, dragging along the
floor. 'He thought mankind did not suffer enough.
But it suffers too much. Men like Daenyathos, like
the powers of the warp themselves, are symptoms of
humanity's misery. But we can put it right.'

'Just as you did, Sarpedon?' said Pugh. 'You are the
only one of your Chapter remaining. Even if your
path could redeem the Imperium, how can it be
walked when you yourself could not walk it?'

'Because I was a fool,' replied Sarpedon. 'I did not
see that Daenyathos was pulling the strings. I walked
into the role he had prepared for me, and I almost
played it to the end. But you have seen my failings.
You know the pitfalls. And when you fail, those who

follow you will learn from you, too. And we are the only ones who can begin it. We, the Space Marines, we have the closest thing this Imperium has to freedom.'

Lysander stepped forwards. 'And what is to say that one of us will take up this torch, Sarpedon?' he said.

'Nothing,' replied Sarpedon. 'If you can ignore your conscience. If you can see the Imperium in the new light the Soul Drinkers have shone on it, and yet still do nothing to stem its suffering, then I suppose there is nothing to say that. If you are content to continue witnessing the death throes of the human race, that is. If you can think your work complete when the Imperium devours itself day by day. If you can do all that, then the light will die out here, with me. But if the conscience of a single battle-brother here, or of any who even hear of us, is inflamed as ours was, then it will burn on.'

'You have said your piece, Sarpedon, 'said Pugh. 'We must take you back in. Your case will be decided anew. Daenyathos must be punished. Cast down the Soulspear and let Lysander place you back in custody. It's over, all of it.'

Sarpedon looked down at the sigils branded on the floor around his feet.

'I understand,' he said, 'that only the blood of Rogal Dorn could open the Eye of Kravamesh. And whatever flows through me, it is not Dorn's blood. Correct?'

The floor beneath Sarpedon glowed and smouldered. The thrum of caged power reverberated through the cyst.

'Sarpedon,' croaked Daenyathos. 'What are you doing?'

Light gathered and crackled, sending haphazard shadows across the cyst.

'Stop!' shouted Pugh. 'We will open fire!'

'The blood of Dorn,' shouted Sarpedon over the growing sound, 'flows through those who fight his fight. When he marched in the Great Crusade, it was to save humanity in unity, not to unite it only to cast it back into the dark. This was the Emperor's goal. Though His road has not been travelled for ten thousand years, you can put the human race back on it. If you choose to. If you dare.'

Light crackled, flaring across the cyst like a tongue of flame from a star. A crack in reality re-opened, the impossible colours of the warp seething beyond.

'Sarpedon!' screamed Daenyathos. 'No! You do not know what lies beyond!'

'But you do,' replied Sarpedon. 'And I see how you fear it. Perhaps I should fear it too. But I can fight it, and you cannot.'

Daenyathos's last words devolved into a scream as Sarpedon carried him through the portal, dragging the Philosopher-Soldier over the threshold and out of reality.

The portal slammed shut behind them, its fires darkening again, leaving only an echo of its power.

SISTER AESCARION BLINKED in the light, her eyes struggling to kill the glare. She had been asleep for a long time, and her head still pounded.

The last thing she remembered was Abraxes

standing over her, his grin turning to a scowl of frustration just as Luko dived into him, ripping out the daemon's eye. Everything after that had been a blur of noise and fury.

She sat up and swung her legs over the edge of the bed in which she had awoken. She was in the apothecarion of the *Phalanx*. Dozens of Imperial Fists lay comatose in the beds around her, their armour piled up beside them, lifesign monitors blinking and beeping. A spindly medical servitor trundled between them, reading off vitals and administering doses.

Aescarion was a little unsteady on her feet. She was wearing the shapeless under-robes that Battle Sisters wore when not in armour. Her wargear was piled up beside her bed, and from the scars on her armour and the blade of her power axe she wondered that she could walk now at all.

She wandered through the apothecarion. All was cool and quiet, the wounded tended by servitors or lying in suspended animation induced by their catalepsean nodes. Aescarion felt the cold metal of the deck on her bare feet as she walked out of the apothecarion and into the great lofty passageway, one of many running most of the length of the *Phalanx*.

Scaffolding stood against the walls, servitors and crew members working at the dark stone that clad the passageway. Statues and inscriptions lined the passage and a great panel of plain stone could be seen between the scaffolds. The servitors and masons were working at one of the lower corners with chisels and granite saws, a drift of stone dust building up at the base of the wall.

Chapter Master Pugh approached. His armour was clean and repaired, but he still had the minor scars of the recent battles on his face. The crew saluted and bowed their heads as he approached.

'Sister!' he said. 'It is good that you are again among us. Varnica explained to me your actions at the portal.'

'They are not something I wish to revisit,' replied Aescarion. 'I shall meditate on them myself. Such things should be considered in private.'

'An Imperial Fist would be lauded as a hero,' said Pugh.

'I am not an Imperial Fist. A daughter of the Emperor cannot be prideful.'

'Perhaps the same can be said of a Space Marine,' said Pugh. 'Though even a Chapter Master must be careful to whom he says it. Our next journey is to the Segmentum Solar, Sister. Lord Inquisitor Kolgo suggested that we take the *Phalanx* to Saturn, where his colleagues from the Ordo Malleus can assist in cleansing the daemonic stench from this ship. It will take time, and no little negotiation with the daemon-hunters, but the *Phalanx* will fly as holy ground again.'

'That we stand here now tells me that Abraxes was defeated,' said Aescarion. 'But what of our own? How many were lost?'

'More than half those who fought,' replied Pugh. 'A terrible blow. But we will recover. We have done so before.'

'And the Soul Drinkers?'

'None remain,' said Pugh.

'Then it is over.'

'In a manner of speaking,' said Pugh. He turned to continue up the corridor in the direction of the bridge. Aescarion watched him go, not sure what to make of his parting words.

She turned back to the wall, where the masons were starting to work again. She walked between them, running a hand over the surface, the still-rough letters awaiting detailing and polishing.

TYRENDIAN, read the letters that passed under her fingers.

LUKO.

GRAEVUS.

The next column bore the names of Imperial Fists – Sergeant Prexus, who had died in the Panpsychicon, Castellan Leucrontas, all the Imperial Fists who had died. And alongside them, listed as brothers in death, were the Soul Drinkers.

SARPEDON, read the last name to be inscribed.

In a manner of speaking, it was over. The Soul Drinkers were gone. Abraxes was destroyed. But the idea of them remained. Their names were listed among the fallen, and in the Tactica Sigismunda the battle in the cyst would be recreated. Generations to come would live in a galaxy where the idea of the Soul Drinkers existed, an idea that had so nearly died in the execution chambers of the *Phalanx* and the book furnaces of the Inquisition.

It would live on among the Sisters of Battle, too. It was not Aescarion's place to judge the right or wrong of what Sarpedon had stood for – but it would not die when she could keep it alive. Even if only as a warning, the cautionary tale of Daenyathos who pulled puppet strings that almost threw the Imperium into a new age of darkness, she would remember.

She turned away from the inscriptions and walked back towards the apothecarion, still unsteady. At Saturn, in the Inquisitorial dockyards of Iapetus, she could try to put her thoughts in order and decide how the story of Soul Drinkers should be passed on so it would remain intact among the currents of the future. But there were wounds that needed to heal first. She would decide that another day.

The masons continued their inscribing as Aescarion walked away, carving the story of the Soul Drinkers into the stone among the lists of the dead.

## ABOUT THE AUTHOR

Author of the Soul Drinkers and Grey
Knights series, freelance writer **Ben
Counter** is one of Black Library's most
popular SF authors, and has written
RPG supplements and comics books as
well as novels. He is a fanatical painter
of miniatures, a pursuit which has
won him his most prized possession: a
prestigious Golden Demon award. He
lives in Portsmouth, England, where he
can sometimes be seen indulging his
enthusiasm for amateur dramatics on the
local stage

HAMMER AND BOLTER

ISSUE 1

WARHAMMER
WARHAMMER 40,000

JOSH REYNOLDS
ANDY SMILLIE
GAV THORPE
TOM FOSTER
GRAHAM McNEILL
BRADEN CAMPBELL

ISSUE 13

WARHAMMER
WARHAMMER 40,000

NIK VINCENT
DAN ABNETT
NICK KYME
CHRIS DOWS
DAVID GUYMER

HAMMER AND BOLTER

ISSUE 14

# Hammer and Bolter

Featuring

Dan Abnett  Gav Thorpe
Nick Kyme  Ben Counter
Anthony Reynolds
and a host of others

*Hammer and Bolter* is Black Library's download only monthly fiction magazine. Each issue is packed with short stories, serialised novels, interviews, previews and more.

## Download your monthly fix of action at www.blacklibrary.com